THE HARDER THEY FALL

THE HARDER
THEY FALL

A NOVEL

By BUDD SCHULBERG

With a New Foreword by the Author

> "I sorrow'd at his captive state,
>   but minded
> Not to be absent at that
>   spectacle."
> JOHN MILTON: Samson Agonistes

ELEPHANT PAPERBACKS
Ivan R. Dee, Publisher, Chicago

First ELEPHANT PAPERBACK edition published 1996
by Ivan R. Dee, Inc., 1332 North Halsted Street, Chicago
60622. Manufactured in the United States of America
and printed on acid-free paper.

The words of the songs that appear in this book are
reprinted by permission of the copyright owners: pages
101, 104, King Jazz, Inc., as recorded by Coot Grant and
Sox Wilson; page 140, from "I Cried for You," copyright
1923 by Miller Music Corp., used by special permission;
page 140, from "Fine and Mellow," copyright by Edward
B. Marks Music Corp., used by permission.

Library of Congress Cataloging-in-Publication Data:
Schulberg, Budd.
     The harder they fall : a novel / Budd Schulberg :
with a new foreword by the author.
     p.   cm.
     "Elephant paperbacks."

     ISBN: 978-1-5663-107-5

     1. Boxing—Corrupt practices—United States—
Fiction. 2. Boxers (Sports)—United States—Fiction.
I. Title.
PS3537.C7114H3   1996
813'.52—dc20   95-26632

For Vicki, Ad, Ben,
for Saxe and Bernice,
and for Jimmy, Paul and Fidel,
who helped

Foreword

This novel was written in the bad old days of the fight game (in the late 1940s) when Frankie Carbo—the Mob's ambassador to the world of the Sweet Science and Boxing Commissioner Without Portfolio—called the shots. He seemed to have a corner on the middleweights, and there was a time when Mr. Carbo and Co. could decide who should wear the crown and who should be denied, no matter how deserving. In the year this book appeared, Jake La Motta, the celebrated "Raging Bull," was technically and most suspiciously knocked out by Billy Fox, in the fourth round of a contest boxing writers had great difficulty describing with a straight face. Fox was enjoying a season of happiness as an undefeated, coming champion, and anybody who questioned his string of victories was apt to find a gun gently nuzzling his temple. The stakes were high and "the boys" played rough. Jake was second only to Sugar Ray Robinson as the middleweight of his day but apparently he owed the boys a favor, and the tough banger from the Bronx went out with a whimper when the word came down that it wasn't his night.

In the early fifties, when TV was taking over the fight game, the young white college kid from Michigan, Chuck Davey, was just what the money-boys needed to bring in a new class of fight fans for the new age of national television. For the bobby-soxers, Chuck Davey was Frank Sinatra in boxing trunks. Middle-class mothers took him to their hearts. He enjoyed four years without a defeat, his hair rarely mussed as the former national collegiate amateur champion danced nimbly around and won decisions over a series of name pugs who were rendered strangely unpugnacious when they faced clean, neat, well-spoken, and oh-so-white Chuck Davey. Finally, in a bout with Kid Gavilan, "with the handcuffs off," as they say in the cynical fight game, the flashy but thoroughly professional "Keed" from Camaguey exposed Davey as the unsuspecting fraud he really was.

One could recite a litany of fixed fights arranged by the Frankie Carbos who have made their odiferous contribution to the game legendary boxing writer Jimmy Cannon called "the slum of the sports world." One of my favorites was the Gavilan–Johnny Saxton fight for the welterweight title in Philadelphia with Mr. Blinky Palermo, another Commissioner Without Portfolio, nurturing his champion, Mr. Saxton. Anyone who sees boxing as a brutal sport would have been reassured that evening, when the usually aggressive Gavilan was rendered totally passive and the two fighters performed what I described as "a hitless mazurka," with the decision in Saxton's favor so bizarre that my report began: "Johnny Saxton may be an orphan, but no one can say he lacks for cousins in Philadelphia. . . ."

The piece was titled "Boxing's Dirty Business Must Be Cleaned Up Now," and when *Sports Illustrated* took out a full page in the *New York Herald Tribune*, running it verbatim, my reward for telling hard truths was to be banned from the Mecca of Boxing, Madison Square Garden.

Four decades later, the fight game is as desperately in need of reform—make that a thorough housecleaning—as it was in the Carbo-Palermo days. Don King—the promotional genius who studied Shakespeare and Machiavelli in the slammer after the fatal stomping of a Detroit numbers runner who made the mistake of welshing on a transaction—controls the heavyweight championship as totally and cynically as Frankie C. once ruled the middleweights. His controlee is Iron Mike Tyson, sprung earlier this year from three years in the pen in Indiana on charges of raping a black beauty contestant. Although inactive for four years, Mike won instant recognition from the World Boxing Association and the World Boxing

Council as their No. 1 Contender. For his "Welcome Home" comeback debut, Mike was fed an Irish hulk from Boston whose record of 36 and 1 was impressive until you checked out the opposition, a sorry lineup of professional losers. Don King quickly added a catchy nickname, "Hurricane," to Peter McNeeley, and rushed the unskilled kid into prime time, with a record pay-per-view charge of fifty dollars. Seven seconds into this travesty, the wind was gone from the Hurricane as he fell from a glancing blow to his inviting Celtic chin. A minute later, McNeeley's manager, said to be not unacquainted with Boston wiseguys, jumped into the ring to save his hapless entry.

"Toro Molinos" come in all colors and nationalities. There is Frans Botha, the "White Buffalo" from South Africa, who was ranked No. 2 by the WBA and No. 1 by still another entry in the ever-thickening alphabet soup, the International Boxing Federation, with the German Axel Schulz as No. 2. And who is Frans Botha? A softly padded gentleman from the white suburbs of the Transvaal who went into the recent Schulz fight undefeated, 35 and 0. Thirty-five wins over nameless and shameless "opponents." His fight, or slow dance on the shilling ground, with Schulz in Germany for the "vacant heavyweight championship of the world" left an aroma that reminded me of the Primo Carnera days of the thirties when poor Primo, the 270-pound circus giant from Italy, was building his undefeated record over an impressive list of roundheels and overnight pacifists, winning the championship from a suspiciously tamed Jack Sharkey.

Watching Botha lumber through his lackluster twelve rounds with Herr Schulz, gasping for breath after six rounds, and losing the last six to the more agile and slightly more accomplished Schulz, staggering through the final round as if he had trained in a German beer hall, only to have his hand outrageously raised in "victory," I found myself thinking again of my victim/champion Toro Molino. The only injuries inflicted in this alleged combat took place after the decision when three ladies were struck by the flying beer and champagne bottles that filled the air as the frustrated German fans staged a full-scale riot.

Caught up in this drama on television, I couldn't help wondering if the judges had been threatened, or bribed, or just considered it better wisdom to go along with Don the King, who had just left behind him in New York a hung jury, unable to decide that King had bilked Lloyds of London by claiming $350,000 in training expenses to Julio Cesar Chavez after a training injury canceled a Chavez title fight. Chavez swore in court that he never saw that tidy six-figure sum, and King's former accountant, a Mr. Maffia, testified that he had been ordered to pad the Chavez expenses that Sr. Chavez never received. In that case both the prosecutors and the boxing press thought that the law had finally caught up with the Teflon Don. But there he was in the German ring, heroically dodging bottles and embracing his exhausted White Buffalo, who when queried on his future plans said, "I want to thank Mr. King. Mr. King give me my big chance. Whatever Mr. King says, I do."

Tim Witherspoon, Mr. King's champion in the eighties, could warn him that Mr. King bilked him of at least a million dollars, and dropped him like a counterfeit C-note when his services were no longer needed. As the bottles littered the ring where the once-respected "heavyweight championship" had been trashed again, I could see the King scenario unfolding, a nineties reflection of the scenario in the novel that follows. Today there are at least three "heavyweight champions"—Frank Bruno, WBC; Bruce Seldon, WBA; now Frans Botha, IBF. The three together don't add up to one deserving title-holder. Mike Tyson could make $25 million for fighting each one of these "Toro Molino champs," and the big winner once again will be Don King, who stands to make even more millions than Tyson if things go according to plan, as they have a habit of doing for this Machiavelli of the Mass Media. Years ago I had described the fight game as "show business with blood"; but I hadn't forseen a business so inflated that if a

Tyson fight could gross $70 million for an eighty-nine-second farce, a $100 million worldwide gross for even a bogus title fight awaits him in '96.

When this novel was first published, it was considered the strongest indictment of the fight game ever written. Strange, coming from a writer who has loved and followed it all his life. It still cries out for the reforms I called for when the book appeared. "Boxing's Dirty Business Must Be Cleaned Up. . . ." I'm no longer so sure about that "Now." So I keep waiting, and hoping, and meanwhile I'm on my way down to see Mike Tyson in a rollover against Buster Mathis, Jr. I saw Buster Mathis, Sr., who couldn't punch either, so I know what to expect. Well, gentle readers, as we used to call you, read on and weep. Read on and hope. And maybe one of these days we'll rescue a fascinating sport, full of brave warriors and honest practitioners, from the gutter which it still finds so congenial and profitable.

Brookside, New York
December 1995

THE HARDER THEY FALL

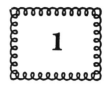

1

W<small>HEN</small> I came into the story I was having a quiet conversation over a bottle of Old Taylor with my friend Charles the bartender at Mickey Walker's, the place Mickey hasn't got any more at 50th and Eighth Avenue, right across the street from the Garden. I like Charles because he always serves up a respectable two-ounce whisky and because of the talks we have about oldtime fighters. Charles must know as much about the old days as Granny Rice. He must be sixty or seventy years of age, with baby-pink skin and hardly a wrinkle in his face. The only give-away to his age is his spare white hair that he insists, for some reason, on dyeing a corny yellow. He's seen a lot of the fighters who are just names to me —legendary names like Ketchell and Gans and Mexican Joe Rivers. One of the last things he did before he left London (a faint cockney echo lingers in his speech) was to see the famous Peter Jackson-Frank Slavin fight at the National Sporting Club. This afternoon, as on so many other afternoons, we were back in the crucial twentieth round, and Charles, with his hands raised in the classical nineteenth-century boxing stance, was impersonating the dark-skinned, quiet-spoken, wonderfully poised Jackson.

"Fix the picture in your mind, sir," Charles was always saying. "Here's Jackson, a fine figure of a man, the first of the heavies to get up on his toes, faster than Louis and every bit the puncher. And here in front of him is solid Frank, a great rock of a man who's taken everything the black man had to offer and had him on the

3

verge of a kayo in the early rounds. They're locked for a moment in a furious clinch. Jackson, who's made a remarkable recovery, a miraculous recovery, sir, breaks away and nails old Frank with a right that travels just this far—" Charles demonstrated, reaching over the bar and rapping me sharply on the side of the jaw—"just that far."

At this point in the battle Charles switched sides. He had been in vaudeville once, and during the early days of the depression he had picked up a couple of bucks playing butlers on Broadway. He should be paying regular dues to Actors Equity because he's acting all the time. Now he was the staggering, glassy-eyed Slavin, reeling back from Jackson's short punishing blow. "Fix the picture in your mind, sir," he repeated. His chin was resting on his chest and his body had gone limp. "His hands are at his side, he can't raise his head or lift his feet, but he won't go down. Peter Jackson hits him again, and Frank is helpless to defend himself, but he won't go down. He just stands there with his arms at his side, waiting to be hit again. He's made quite a boast of it before the fight, you see, sir, that there's no nigger in the world good enough to make Frank Slavin quit to him. I never use the word 'nigger' myself, you understand, sir, I'm just trying to give you the picture as it was. In my business, you see, sir, I judge a man by the color of his deeds, not the color of his skin. This Peter Jackson, for instance. A finer sportsman never climbed through the ropes than this dark gentleman from Australia."

Now Charles was Jackson again, magnificently proud and erect as the crowd waited for him to finish off his battered opponent. "But at this moment, a memorable thing happened, sir. Instead of rushing in and clubbing the helpless Slavin to the canvas, Jackson stood back, risking the chance that Slavin with his bull-strength might recover, and turned to the referee. You could hear his calm, deep voice all the way back to where I was

4

sitting, sir. Sounded more like a preacher than a fighter, he did. 'Must I finish him off, Mr. Angle?' he said. 'Box on,' said Mr. Angle. Black Peter turned back to his man again. In spite of all those taunts about the color of his skin, you could see he had no stomach for the job. He tapped Frank on the chin once, twice, three times—little stiff punches that would put him away without breaking his jaw—and finally on the fourth, down went old Frank, cold as the proverbial mackerel, for all his boasts. And all the gentlemen who had come to the Sporting Club to see the white man get the better of the black couldn't help rising to their feet and giving Jackson one of the longest rounds of applause that had ever been heard in the Sporting Club."

"Give me another shot," I said. "Charles, you're wonderful. Did you really see the Jackson-Slavin fight?"

"Would I lie to you, Mr. Lewis?"

"Yes," I said. "You told me you were one of Joe Choynski's handlers the time he fought Corbett on that barge off San Francisco. Well, over on Third Avenue I found an old picture of Choynski and Corbett with their handlers just before the fight. You don't seem to be in it."

Charles uncorked the Old Taylor again and poured me another one. "You see, a man of my word," he said. "Every time you catch me in an inaccuracy, Mr. Lewis, I buy you a drink."

"An inaccuracy is an accidental mistake," I said. "What I caught you in, Charles, was a good old-fashioned lie."

"Please, Mr. Lewis," said Charles, deeply offended. "Don't use that word. I may on occasion, for dramatic emphasis, fib. But I never lie. A lie is a thief, sir, and will steal from anybody. A fib just borrows a little from people who can afford it and forgets to pay them back."

"But you actually saw this Jackson-Slavin fight?"

5

"Say 'bout,' sir, the Jackson-Slavin bout. You'd never hear a gentleman calling a boxing contest a fight."

"Here on Eighth Avenue," I said, "a gentleman is a fellow who calls a woman a broad instead of something else."

"It is unfortunately true," Charles agreed. "The gentlemen in the pugilism business are conspicuous by their abstinence."

"That includes me in," I said. "What do I owe you for this week, Charles?"

"I'll tell you before you leave," Charles said. He never liked to talk about money. He would always scribble the amount on the back of a tab and then slip it under my glass like a secret message.

A sharply dressed, nervous-looking little man stuck his head in the door. "Hey, Charley—you seen the Mumbler?"

"Not today, Mr. Miniff."

"Jeez, I gotta find him," the little man said.

"If he shows up I'll tell him you're looking for him," Charles told him.

"T'anks," said Miniff. "You're m' boy." He disappeared.

Charles shook his head. "It's a sad day, Mr. Lewis, a sad day."

I looked at the big oval clock over the door. A little after three. Time for Charles' over-the-bar address on the decline and fall of the manly art. "The people who come into this place," Charles began. "Grifters, chiselers, two-bit gamblers, big-time operators with small-time minds, managers who'd rather see their boys get killed than make an honest living and boxers who've taken so many dives they've got hinges on their knees. In the old days, sir, it was a rough game but it had some . . . some character to it, some dignity. Take Choynski and Corbett fighting on that barge. Skin gloves on Choynski, two-ouncers on Corbett, to a finish. No fancy percentages, no non-title

6

business, just winner take all, may the best man win. A man squared off for his own pride in those days. He was an athlete. If he made a little money at it, fine and dandy. But what have we got today? Champions with mobsters for managers who stall for years fighting over-weight bouts because they know the first time they climb into the ring with a good man it's good-bye, championship."

Charles turned around to see if the boss was watching and had one himself. The only time I ever saw him take one was when we were alone and he got going on this decline-and-fall thing.

He washed his glass and wiped it clean, to destroy the evidence, and looked at me steadily. "Mr. Lewis, what is it that turned a fine sport into a dirty business?"

"Money," I said.

"It's money," he went on, as if he hadn't heard me. "Money. Too much money for the promoters, too much money for the managers, too much money for the fighters."

"Too much money for everybody except the press agents," I said. I was feeling sorrier for myself at the moment than I was for the game. That's what the bottle always did to me.

"I tell you, Mr. Lewis, it's money," Charles was saying. "An athletic sport in an atmosphere of money is like a girl from a good family in a house of ill fame."

I pulled out the gold-banded fountain pen Beth had given me for my birthday, and made a couple of notes on what Charles was saying. He was made to order for that play I was going to write, the play on the fight game I had been talking about so long, the one Beth seemed to be so sure I was never going to finish. "Don't spill it all out in talk," she was always saying. Damn Beth and her bright sayings. If I had had any sense I would have found myself a nice dumb broad. But if I could only set the play down the way I felt it sometimes, in all its sweaty violence—not a nine-dollar bill like *Golden Boy*—no

7

violinists with brittle hands, no undigested poetry subtle as a train wreck, but the kids from the street as they really were, mean and money-hungry, and the greed of the mobsters who had the game rigged; that was the guts of it and I was the boy to write it.

One solid job could justify all the lousy years I had frittered away as a press agent for champions, deserved and otherwise, contenders and bums, plenty of the latter. You see, that play would tell Beth, I haven't really fallen so low as you thought. All the time it seemed as if I were prostituting myself by making with the adjectives for Honest Jimmy Quinn and Nick (The Eye) Latka, the well-known fistic entrepreneurs, I was actually soaking up material for my masterpiece. Just as O'Neill spent all those years as a common sailor and Jack London was on the bum.

Like O'Neill and London. It always made me feel better to make those notes. My pockets were full of notes. There were notes in every drawer of my desk at the hotel. The notes were kind of an escape valve for all the time I wasted getting loaded, cutting up touches with Charles, sitting around with the boys, going up to Shirley's, and ladling out the old craperoo about how old Joe Round-heels, who couldn't lick my grandfather and who had just been put away in two over at the Trenton Arena, was primed (I would be starving to death without that word *primed*) to give Jack Contender the fight of his life.

"What are you doing there, Mr. Lewis?" Charles said. "Not writing down something I say."

A good bartender, Charles never pried into his customers' affairs. But he was beginning to break down with me because he liked the idea of getting into my play. I wish Beth had as much faith in me as Charles. "You know what you ought to do, you ought to quit leaning on your elbows and get to work," she was always saying. But Charles was different. He'd tell me something and then he'd say, "You ought to put *that* in your play." We talked about it so long that my work of art came to have a real identity. "If you're going to put me in your show," Charles would say, "please call me Charles. I like to be called Charles. My mother always called me Charles. Charley sounds like—a puppet, or a fat man."

The door swung open and Miniff popped his head in again. "Hey, Charley, still no signa the Mumbler?"

Charles shook his head gravely. "No signa the Mumbler whatsoever, Mr. Miniff." Charles was a snob. It gave him pleasure to exercise his talent for mimicry at the expense of his ungrammatical clientele. Miniff came in and climbed up on the stool next to mine. His small feet didn't reach the foot-rest at the base of the stool. He pushed his brown felt hat back on his head desperately. He ran his hands over his face and shook his head a few times, his fingers covering his eyes. He was tired. New York is hot when you run around all day.

"Have one with me, Miniff," I said. He waved me off with a small, hairy hand.

"Just the juice of the cow," he said. "Gotta keep my ulcer quiet." From his breast pocket he took a couple of short, stubby cigars, shoved one into his mouth and offered the other one around.

"No, thanks," I said. "If I smoked those six-for-a-quarters I'd have ulcers too. If I'm going to have them, I want expensive ulcers, bottled in bond."

"Listen," Miniff said, "it ain't the hemp. It's the headaches I got. Nervous digestion." He drank his milk carefully, letting it trickle slowly down his throat for maximum therapeutic effect.

"Jeez, I gotta find the Mumbler," he said. The Mumbler was Solly Hyman, the matchmaker for St. Nick's. "I looked everywhere already, Lindy's, both of them, Sam's. Up at Stillman's I hear Furrone can't go Tuesday. Gotta bad toot'. Jeez, I gotta guy to take his place. My bum'll look good in there."

"Who you got, Mr. Miniff?" Charles said, still mimicking.

"Cowboy Coombs."

"Oh, my God," I said.

"He can still go," said Miniff. "I tell ya he c'n stay three-four rounds with the shine, maybe go the limit."

"Cowboy Coombs," I said. "The grandfather of all the bums."

"So he ain't no Tooney," Miniff said.

"Fifteen years ago, he wasn't Tunney," I said.

Miniff pushed his hat back an inch or two on his forehead. His forehead was shiny with perspiration. This Cowboy Coombs thing was no joke. It was a chance to hustle a fast fifty. The way Miniff works he picks up some down-and-outer or some new kid from the amateurs and he angles a spot or two for him, if he can. It's strictly quick turn-over. If the bum goes down, Miniff can't do anything more for him anyway. If the kid is good, smarter managers with better "ins" always steal him away. So for Miniff it's mostly a substitution business, running in a bum or a novice at the last minute, so the box office doesn't have to buy the tickets back, or picking up a quiet C by arranging for one of his dive-artists to do an el foldo.

"Listen, Eddie," Miniff said to me, working all the time, "Coombs has got a wife and five kids and they gotta eat. All he's been doin' is spar work the last year or two. The bum needs a break. You could maybe write up something in one of the rags about him. How he got canned for settin' the Champ down in a workout. . . ."

"That's not the way I heard he got canned," I said.

"All right, all right, so it happened a little different, maybe the Champ slipped. I suppose you never write stuff it ain't a hunert percent kosher!"

"Mr. Miniff, you impugn my integrity," I said. The stuff a guy will write to pay his rent and keep himself in whisky! The things a guy will do for 100 bucks a week in

10

America! Eddie Lewis, who spent almost two years at Princeton, got A's in English, had a by-line in the Trib and has twenty-three pages of a play that is being systematically devoured by a little book club of hungry moths who can't tell a piece of literature from a square meal.

"Go on, Eddie, for a pal," Miniff pleaded. "Just one little lineroo about how the Cowboy is back in great shape. You could work it into almost any colyum. They go for your crap."

"Don't give me that Cowboy Coombs," I said. "Coombs was ready for the laughing academy when you had to talk through a little hole in the door to get a drink. The best thing that could happen to Mrs. Coombs and those five kids is for you to climb down off Mr. Coombs' back and let him go to work for a change."

"Aaaah," said Miniff, and the sound was so bitter it could have been his ulcer talking. "Don't sell that Coombs short. He c'n still lick half the heavyweights in the business right now. Whadcha thinka that?"

"I think half the heavyweights in the business should also climb back on their trucks," I said.

"Aaaaaah," Miniff said. He finished the milk, wiped his lips with his sleeve, pulled some of the wet, loose leaves from the end of his cigar-butt, stuck it back between his teeth again, pulled down the brim of his old brown hat, said, "Take it easy, Eddie, see ya, Charley," and got out in a hurry.

I drank slowly, letting the good warm feeling fan out gradually from my belly. The Harry Miniffs of the world! No, that was taking in too much territory. America. Harry Miniff was American. He had an Italian name or an Irish name or a Jewish name or an English name, but you would never find an Italian in Italy, a Jew in Palestine, an Irishman in Ireland or an Englishman in England with the nervous system and social behavior of the American Harry Miniff. You could find Miniffs everywhere, not just the fight game but show-business, radio, movies, the rackets, wholesale houses, building trades, blackjack unions, advertising, politics, real estate, insurance—a disease of the American heart—successful Harry Miniffs, pushing their way to the top of steel institutes, oil combines, film studios, fight monopolies; and unsuccessful Harry Miniffs, born with the will but not the knack to catch up with the high dollar that keeps tempting them on like a mechanical rabbit which the whippet can't catch unless the machine breaks down, and can't eat if it does.

"The last one in the bottle, Mr. Lewis," Charles said. "On the house."

"Thanks," I said. "You're an oasis, Charles. An Eighth Avenue oasis."

Someone in a booth had dropped a nickel in the juke slot. It was the only good record in the box, the Bechet version of "Summertime." The haunting tone of Sidney's clarinet took over the place. I looked around to see if it was Shirley. She was always playing it. She was sitting in a booth by herself, listening to the music.

"Hi, Shirley, didn't hear you come in."

"I saw you was talking with Miniff," she said. "Didn't want to interrupt a big important conversation like that."

She had been around for ten or twelve years, but there was still a little Oklahoma left in her speech. She came to town with her husband, Sailor Beaumont—remember Billy Beaumont?—when he was on the up swing, after he had licked everything in the West and was coming to New York for a shot at the bigtime. He was the boy who crossed the wise money by going in on the short end of 10-1 to win the welterweight title. He and Shirley rode pretty high for a while. The Sailor was an unreconstructed reform-school graduate from West Liberty who threw most of his dough into such routine channels as the fleshpots, the ponies and the night spots. All the rest went for motorcycles. He had a white streamlined motorcycle with a sidecar on which, if you were good at reading

12

print cutting through downtown traffic at sixty miles an hour, you could make out the words "Sailor Beaumont, the Pride of West Liberty." That's the kind of a fellow he was. Lots of times, especially in the beginning when they were still getting along together, I remember Shirley riding in that sidecar, with her dark red hair flying out behind her. She was something to look at in those days, before the beers and the troubles caught up with her. You could still see some of it left, even with the crow's-feet around the eyes and the tell-tale washed-out look that comes from doing too many things too many times. She still had something from the neck down too, even if her pinup days were ten years behind. She was beginning to spread, just this much, in the rump, the belly and the bust, but there was something about the way she held herself—sometimes I thought it was more in her attitude toward men than anything physical—that made us still turn around.

"Have one with me, Shirley?" I called over.

"Save it, Eddie," she said.

"Not even two fingers, to be sociable?"

"Oh, I don't know, maybe a beer," Shirley said.

I gave Charles the order and went over to the booth. "Waiting for anyone?"

"For you, darling," she said, sarcastic. She didn't bother to look at me.

"What's the matter? Hung?"

"Aah, not really, just, oh, the hell with it . . ."

Shirley was in a mood. She got that way every now and then. Most of the time she was feeling good, a lot of laughs—"What the hell, I'm not getting any richer and I'm not getting any younger, but I'm having fun." But once in a while, especially when you caught her alone in the daytime, she was this way. After it got dark and she had had a few, it would be better. But I've seen her sit there in a booth for hours, having solitary beers and dropping nickels in the slot, playing "Summertime" or

13

"Melancholy Baby" or another of her favorites, "Embraceable You." I suppose those songs had something to do with the Sailor, though it always struck me as profane to associate the tender sentiments of those excellent lyrics with a screwball slugger like Beaumont. He'd lay anything that stood still for thirty seconds. If Shirley ever asked for an explanation she got it—on the jaw. He was one of the few professionals I ever knew who indulged in spontaneous extra-curricular bouts in various joints, a practice which did not endear him to Jacobs' Beach and brought him frequently and forcibly to the attention of the local gendarmerie. When he finally had a blowout on that hotcha motorcycle of his and left in a bloody mess on the curb at Sixth Avenue near 52nd Street what few brains he had salvaged from ninety-three wide-open fights, the people who took it hard could be counted on one finger of one hand, and that was Shirley.

She reached into her large red-leather purse, took out a little white bag of fine cut tobacco, carefully tapped it out onto a small rectangle of thin brown paper with a practiced hand. She was the only woman I had ever seen roll her own cigarettes. It was one of the habits she brought with her from the hungry years in West Liberty. While she twirled the flat wrapper into an amazingly symmetrical cylinder, she stared absently through the glass that looked out on Eighth Avenue. The street was full of people moving restlessly back and forth in two streams like ants, but with less purpose. "Summertime," she sang under her breath lackadaisically, a snatch here and a snatch there.

The beer seemed to do something for her. "You can draw me another one, Charles," she said, coming up out of her mood a little, "with a rye chaser."

After all these years, that was still one of the pub's favorite jokes. Shirley looked at me and smiled as if she were seeing me for the first time.

"Where you been keeping yourself, Eddie? Over in Bleeck's with my rival again?"

14

This had been going on for years. It had been going on so long there probably was something in it. Shirley was all right. I liked the way she was about men. She never really let you forget that there were anatomical differences between you, and yet she didn't make a conflict of it. I liked the way she had been about Sailor Beaumont, even if he was a wrongo. There were so many American wives who gave most of their energy to trying to make their husbands vice-presidents or head buyers or something. Twice a week they did him a big favor. That was called being a good wife. Shirley, if she hadn't fallen in love with an irresponsible, physically precocious kid who came in wide-open but had a knockout punch in his right hand, would have made somebody in West Liberty an exceptional wife instead of making Eighth Avenue an exceptional madame.

"Favor us with your presence this week, Eddie," she said. "Come in early and I'll have Lucille fry us some chicken and we'll play a little gin."

"Maybe Friday night, before the Glenn-Lesnevich fight," I said.

"That kid Glenn! A jerk thing Nick did, bringing him along so fast," Shirley said. "Those overgrown boys who get up in the heavy dough because they can sock and can take it—thinking they're King of the May because they got their names in lights outside the Garden, when all they got is a one-way ticket to Queer Street. Glenn draws four good gates to the Garden because the customers know he's going to try, gets himself slapped around by men he's got no business in the same ring with, goes back to LA to be a lousy runner for a bookie or something, and the manager gets himself another boy. That's what he did with Billy. Nick Latka, that crumb!"

"Nick isn't so bad," I said. "Pays me every Friday, doesn't look over my shoulder too much, kind of an interesting feller, too."

"So is a cockroach interesting if it's got Nick's money in the bank," Shirley said. "Nick is marked lousy in my book because he don't look out for his boys. When he has a good one, he's got the dough and the connections to get him to the top, but down under that left breast pocket, he's got nothing there for the boys. Not like George Blake, Pop Foster. Their old boys were always coming back for a touch, a little advice. Nick; when you're winning nothing's too good for you. You're out to that estate over in Jersey every week-end. But when you're out of gas, that's all, brother. You got about as much chance of getting into that office as into a pay toilet without a nickel. I know. I was all through that already, with Billy. And how many has he had since Billy? And now Glenn. And next week maybe some skinny-legged speed-ball from the Golden Gloves. They're so pretty when they start, Eddie. I hate to see 'em run down."

Now that Billy was gone, I think Shirley was in love with all fighters. She loved them when they were full of bounce and beans, with their hard trim bodies moving gracefully in their first tailor-made full-cut double-breasteds with peg-top trousers narrowing at the ankles in a modified zoot. And she loved them when the shape of their noses was gone, their ears cauliflowered, scar-tissue drawing back their eyes, when they laughed too easily and their speech faltered and they talked about the comeback that Harry Miniff or one of his thousand-and-one cousins was lining up for them. Lots of ladies have loved winning fighters, the Grebs, the Baers, the Golden Boys, but it was the battered ones, the humiliated, the washed-ups, the TKO victims with the stitches in their lips and through their eyelids that Shirley took to her bosom. Maybe it was her way of getting Billy back, the Sailor Beaumont of his last year, when the younger, stronger, faster boys who did their training on Eighth Avenue instead of on 52nd Street were making him look slow and foolish and sad.

"Well, first one today," Shirley said, and tossed it off, exaggerating the shudder for a laugh.

She reached into her purse again and took out a very small Brownie snapshot, slightly over-exposed, of a well-set-up kid grinning under a ten-gallon hat.

"New picture of my kid the folks just sent me."

While I took a dutiful hinge at it she said, "He's the image of Billy. Isn't he a doll?"

He did look like Beaumont—the same overdevelopment from the waist up, with the legs tapering down nicely. On his face was a look of cheerful viciousness.

"He'll be nine next month," Shirley said. "He's with his grandparents on a ranch near home. He wants to be a veterinary. I don't care what he does, as long as he stays out of the ring. He can be a card player or a drummer or a pimp if he wants to. But, by God, if I ever hear that he's turning out to be a fighter like his old man, I'll go home and kick his little annyfay for him."

2

W<small>HEN</small> I am in a pub and the phone is for me I am never too happy about it. It means the natural rhythm of my day is about to be interrupted by the unexpected. Shirley had gone back to the place, "to make a new girl feel at home," as she put it, and Beth had dropped in to pick me up. She was annoyed because I was slightly swizzled when she came in. Beth wasn't WCTU or anything, but she liked me to do my drinking with her. She thought I wasted too much time shooting the breeze with Charles and Shirley and the other characters. If my job didn't take up all my time, she said, I should plant myself in the room at the hotel and try to finish that play.

The big mistake I made with Beth was that once when I had her up to my room—in the days when I still had to impress her—I showed her that unfinished first act. Beth didn't have too much to say about it, except for wanting me to get it done. That was the trouble with Beth: she always wanted me to finish things. I proposed to her once in a drunken moment and I think secretly she always held it against me for not mentioning the proposal again when I sobered up. I guess she just wanted me to finish whatever I started.

When I first met her, Beth was fresh out of Smith College, where her Phi Bete key had been good for a $25-a-week job with *Life*, in their training squad for researchers. Everything she knew came out of books. Her old man taught Economics at Amherst and her old lady was the daughter of a Dartmouth dean. So when I first began to tell her about the boxing business, she thought it was fascinating. That's the word she used for this business—fascinating. This fight talk was a new kind of talk for Beth, and all the time she was professing to despise it, I could tell it was getting to her. Even if only as a novelty, it was getting to her and I was the ideal interpreter of this new world that repelled and attracted her. That's how I got to Beth myself. I was just enough of a citizen of this strange new world to excite her and yet—since Beth could never completely recover from her snobberies, intellectual and otherwise—there was just enough Ivy still clinging to me, just enough Cottage Club, just enough ability to relate the phenomenon of prize fighting to her academic vocabulary to make me acceptable.

I think my talking about trying to write a play on boxing gave her a justification for being interested in me, just as it seemed to justify my staying in the game.

But this is taking us back a year and a half. It's almost another story. In the story I am telling here, Beth is miffed again—her impatience with me had been increasing lately—and somebody wants me on the telephone.

It was Killer Meneghemi. Killer was a combined bodyguard, companion, masseur and private secretary to Nick. I don't really think the Killer had ever been responsible for anybody's funeral, but the legend had sprung up that the Killer would have been a featherweight champ if he hadn't killed a man in the ring his third time out. I had looked it up, but no Meneghemi, and the *Ring Record Book* almost always gives the boys' right names in parentheses under their professional names. Nat Fleischer, that eminent historian, had never heard of him either. So you could take heavy odds that the Killer's alleged mayhem had no resemblance to any character living or dead, as they always say.

"Hey, Eddie, d' boss wants ya."

"Now, goddamit, Killer," I said. "I'm with a lady. Can't a man settle down to a little companionate drinking without Nick putting his hounds on me?"

"The boss wants ya to get your ass up here," Killer

answered. Take away those three- and four-letter essential Anglo-Saxon words and Mr. Menegheni would have to talk with his fingers.

"But this lady and I have plans for the evening," I said. "I don't have to come running every time Nick lifts a finger. Who does he think he is?"

"He thinks he's Nick Latka," said the Killer. "And I never seen d' day he wasn't right."

For the Killer, that was considerable repartee. "Say, you're pretty sharp today," I said.

"Why not?" the Killer said. "I scored with that red-head from the Chez Paris last night. Just seventeen years old. Beauteeful."

The Killer, only five-six in his built-up shoes, was always flashing us the latest news of his daily conquests.

"You would make a good leg-man for Krafft-Ebing," I said.

"I ain't changing places with nobody. I do all right with Nick."

"Well, I'm glad you're happy," I said. "Pleasant week-end, Killer."

"Hey-hey-hey, wait a minnut," the Killer said quickly. "This deal what the boss wants to see you about. It must be very hot. I'll tellum yer on yer way up."

"Listen," I said, "you can tell him for me"—O Lord, the fear that eats into a man for a hundred bucks a week—"I'll be up in fifteen minutes."

I started back to the booth to break it to Beth. She was always turning down good things to keep Saturday night for me. Saturday nights we'd usually hit our favorite spots together, Bleeck's and Tim's and when we wanted music, Nick's for Spanier and Russell and Brunis, and Downtown Café Society, when Red Allen was there, and J. C. Higginbotham. Sunday morning we'd wake up around ten, send down for coffee and lie around with the papers until it was time to go out for lunch. Beth would kick about the *News*, the *Mirror* and the *Journal*

20

because she was a pretty hot liberal as well as a snob, but some of my best plants were picked up by the tabs and I liked to read the *Journal* for Graham, one of the town's oldest and hardest-working sports writers.

I don't know if it was love with me or not, but I'll put it this way: I never slept with anybody I was so glad to see in the morning as Beth Reynolds. I've known other girls who were more beautiful, more passionate or more experimental, but who turned out to be a drag in the morning. With Beth, having a drink, seeing a fight, listening to Spanier, going to bed, nursing each other's hangovers, arguing about Wolfe and getting sore at some new stupidity of some old senator's—it was all one, all good, all close, and when you are pushing into your middle-thirties and beginning to need a slow count to get up in the morning, that outweighs the dime-a-dozen ecstasies.

Not that Beth wasn't exciting enough, in her own way. She met you with a small, intense passion that seemed surprisingly wanton for a girl with a pretty-plain school-teacher face, who couldn't see very well without her glasses. I hadn't been her "first man" (Beth's words, naturally, not mine), for that honor had been reserved for an Amherst boy from a distinguished Boston family who had been madly and incompetently in love with her. He had made such a mess of things, apparently, that she had shied away from further intimacies until I came along. I don't quite know yet how I got her to try again. She just decided it for herself one evening. It was the night we had gone back to her apartment after I had taken her to see her first fight. I think she always distrusted me a little for helping make it so successful. That academic, puritanical background didn't stop her from enjoying herself. It just prevented her from respecting herself for what she had allowed herself to do. That's why, when she took off her glasses and the other encumbrances, she was wanton. For only the true Puritan can know that delicious sense of falling from grace that we call wantonness.

More than once, in my cups, I had proposed that we make an honorable girl of Beth. She didn't approve of the way we were living, but she always preferred to wait and see if a similar offer would be forthcoming under the influence of sobriety. But somehow I could never quite muster up enough marital determination to make a legitimate proposal without the nudge of friendly spirits. The closest I could ever come was to say, with what was meant for levity, "Beth, if I ever marry anyone, it's got to be you."

"If you insist on prefacing all your proposals with the conditional conjunctive," she had answered, "you will end up a lecherous old bachelor and I will end up married to Herbert Ageton."

Herbert Ageton was a playwright who had written militant proletarian dramas for the Theater Union back in the early thirties, when he was just out of college and hardly knew how to keep his pipe lit. Much to his horror and indignation, MGM had bought one of his radical plays, and brought him out to adapt it. When he got up to two thousand dollars a week he was analyzed at one hundred dollars an hour by a highly successful female practitioner who made him realize that his proletarian protest against capitalism was only a substitute for his hatred of his father. Somehow the signals got crossed and he came out still hating his father but feeling somewhat more kindly toward capitalism. Since that time he had only been on Broadway twice, with symbolic plays about sex relations which all the critics had panned and all the studios had scrambled for. They turned out to make very good pictures for Lana Turner. Or maybe I was just jealous. Herbert used to call Beth from Hollywood all the time. And every time he came to town he took her to "21" and the Stork and the other meeting places of good-time counter-revolutionists and their opposite numbers.

"Baby," I said, when I got back to the booth, "this is lousy, but I've got to go up and see Nick a minute."

"A minute. Nick and his minutes! You will probably end up out in Jersey at his country place."

That had happened once and Beth would never let me forget it. I had left a message for her at Walker's, but by the time it got through she had taken an angry powder.

"No," I said, "this is strictly business. If I'm not back in one hour . . ."

"Don't make it too drastic," she said. "If you're back in one hour it will be the first time. You know I could have gone out with Herbert tonight."

"Oh, Jesus, that again."

"How many times have I told you not to say 'Jesus'? It offends people."

"Oh Je— I don't mean Jesus Christ. I just mean Jesus Ageton."

"He's an interesting guy. He wanted me to have dinner at '21' and then come back to his hotel and hear his new play."

"What hotel? Don't tell me. The Waldorf?"

"Hampshire House."

"The poor kid. Have you ever slept with anybody in the Hampshire House?"

"Edwin, when I get you home tonight, I'm going to wash your mouth out with soap."

"Okay, okay, be evasive. Sit tight, honey. I'll go up and see what the Big Brain has on his larcenous mind."

* * *

The office of Nick Latka wasn't the tawdry fight manager's office you may have seen on the stage or that can actually be found along 49th Street. It was the office of a highly successful business man who happened to have an interest in the boxing business, but who might have been identified with show business, shirts, insurance or the F.B.I. The walls of brown cork were covered with pictures of famous fighters, ball players, golfers, jockeys and motion-picture stars inscribed "to my pal Nick," "to a great guy," "to the best pal I had in Miami." On the desk was a box of cigars, Nick's brand, Belindas, and pictures in gold-plated frames of his wife when she was a lovely brunette in a Broadway chorus, and their two children, a handsome, conceited-looking boy of twelve in a military-school uniform, who took after his mother, and a dark-complexioned girl of ten who bore an unfortunate resemblance to her father. Nick would give those kids anything he had. The boy was away at New York Military Academy. The girl went to Miss Brindley's, one of the most expensive schools in the city.

No matter how he talked in the gym, Nick never used a vulgar word in the presence of those kids. Nick had come up from the streets, rising in ordinary succession from the kid gangs to the adolescent gangs that jimmied the gum and candy machines to the real thing. But his kids were being brought up in a nice clean money-insulated world.

"I don't want for Junior to be a mug like me," Nick would say. "I had to quit school in the third grade and go out and hustle papers to help my old man. I want Junior to go to West Point and be an Air Corps officer or maybe Yale and make a connection with high-class people."

Class! That was the highest praise in Nick's vocabulary. In the mouth of a forty-year-old East-Side hood, who had been raised in a cold-water flat and wore patched hand-me-downs of his older brother, class became an appraisal of inverted snobbery, indicating a quality of excellence the East Side could neither afford nor understand. A fighter could run up a string of six knockouts and still

24

Nick's judgment might be, "He wins, but he's got no class." A girl we'd see in a restaurant might not be pretty enough to get into the row at the Copacabana, but Nick would nudge me and say, "There's a tomato with class." Nick's suits, tailored by Bernard Weatherill, had class. The office had class. And I remember, of all the Christmas cards I received, picking out one that was light brown with the name tastefully engraved in the lower right-hand corner in conservative ten-point. That was Nick's. I don't know how he happened to choose it or who designed it for him, but it obviously had class.

If Nick thought you had it, he could be a very respectful fellow. I remember once he was chairman of a benefit fight card for the infantile-paralysis fund and had himself photographed turning over the take to Mrs. Roosevelt. This picture, autographed by Eleanor, hung in a position of honor over his head, right next to Count Fleet. The boys used to get a laugh out of that. You can imagine the gags, especially if you are a Republican and/or have a nasty mind. But Nick wouldn't have any of it. Anybody throwing them low and inside at Mrs. R. was sure to get the back of his hand. And it wasn't just because Nick's partner was Honest Jimmy Quinn who had the Tammany connections. Mrs. Roosevelt and Count Fleet belonged up there together, the way Nick saw it, because they both had class.

Nick had made a good living prying open the coin boxes of nickel machines when most of us were home reading the Bobbsey Twins and he had already escaped from the Boys Correction Farm when you and I were still struggling with first-year Latin. By dint of conscientious avoidance of physical work, a nose for easy money and constant application of the principle Do Unto Others As You Would Not Have Them Do Unto You he had worked himself up to the top of a syndicate that dealt anonymously but profitably with artichokes, horses, games of chance, women, meat, fighters and hotels, a series of commodities which in our free-for-all enterprise system could be parlayed into tidy fortunes for Nick and Quinn, with large enough chunks for the boys to keep everybody happy. But he was still a sucker for class, whether it was a horse, a human being or a Weatherill sports suit.

The reason he kept me on the payroll, I think, was because he thought I had it too. He had the self-made man's confusion of respect and contempt toward any-body who had read a couple of books and knew when to use *me* and when to say *I*. But whenever he was with me I noticed he cut the profanity down to those words he just didn't have any respectable synonym for. Even Quinn, who had worked himself up through a logical sequence from ward boss to high-level rackets, didn't always get the velvet-glove treatment. And when Nick was dealing with what he considered his inferiors, fighters, other managers, bookies, collectors, trainers, honest but intimidated mer-chants, the only way to describe his talk would be to compare it with the vicious way Fritzie Zivic used to fight, especially when he was sore, as in the return match with poor Bummy Davis after Bummy had got himself dis-qualified for conduct even less becoming a gentleman than Zivic's.

Probably the biggest mistake that Nick had ever made in picking class was very close to home. It was his wife Ruby. When Nick was in the liquor business back in Prohibition he had sat in the same seat for George White's *Scandals* twenty-seven times because Ruby was in it. Where Ruby had it over the rest of the line was she was beautiful in an unusually quiet way, like a young matron who would look more at home in a Junior League musical than in a Broadway leg-show. On stage, so the boys tell me, even in the scantiest, she carried herself with an air of aloof respectability which had the actual effect of an intense aphrodisiac. The other girls could dance half naked in front of you and, if you thought about anything, you'd wonder how much it would cost. But seeing Ruby with her black lace stockings forming a sleek and silken path to her crotch was like opening the wrong bedroom door by mistake and catching your best friend's sister.

That's the effect Ruby had on Nick. And the physiological accident that gave Ruby Latka an austere beauty was accompanied by a personality adjustment that developed a quiet, superior manner to go along with the face. The combination drove all other women out of Nick's life. Until then he had been giving the Killer competition, but from the first time he had Ruby he lined up with that small, select group who believe in monogamy and that even more select group who practice it. In fact, the first three years of his marriage Nick had it so bad he hardly ever bothered to look at another woman's legs. Even now, in an environment which, to put it euphemistically, smiled on adultery, Nick never cheated on Ruby unless it was something very special and he was a long way from home. But the ordinary stuff that was always there, the showgirls and the wives who float around the bars when their husbands are out of town, Nick never bothered with. The ones who simply wouldn't have minded never got a play, and the ones who had already made up their minds almost always got the brush. Most of it was the way he felt about Ruby. But what made it easier was the way he worked. He was all the time working, in the clinches, between rounds, always moving in, throwing punches, heeling, butting, elbowing, like Harry Miniff, only it was done on the top floor of a great office building and it wasn't for nickels but for very fancy folding money.

There was a glutton's hunger for money in him. Maybe it was the pinched childhood, the gutter struggle, the fearful itch of insecurity that drove Nick on to his first hundred thousand and his second. And now, without even letting him sit down to catch his breath and enjoy himself a minute, he was pushing toward his third. If it hadn't been for Ruby, Nick would never have had that place in Jersey with the riding horses and the swimming pool and the terraced barbecue pit. Ruby, who had been a working girl all her life, found no trouble at all in double-clutching into a life of leisurely hedonism. Nick would enjoy a swim when Ruby nagged him into it. He liked to get some of the boys out for the week-end and sit up until Sunday morning, playing pinochle. But it's hard to relax when you're possessed by a lean, sharp-faced kid from Henry Street who's always got an eye out to pry the back off another coin machine.

The Killer was on the phone in the outer office when I got there, laying his plans for the evening or vice versa. He had a way of addressing his women in terms of exaggerated endearment that suggested a deeply rooted contempt. "Okay, honey chile . . . Check, sugar . . . You name it, beauteeful . . ." A psychiatrist, observing the Killer's hopped-up promiscuity and his chronic inability to settle down to any female, probably would have described him as a latent homosexual. But the Killer himself wasn't at all reticent about pressing his claim not only to the virility championship of Eighth Avenue, but also to the possession of physiological attributes of heroic proportions. He wore the pants of his snugly fitting suit almost skin tight, so you couldn't help noticing. He had short stocky legs and a four-inch chest expansion which he often showed off, even during normal conversation, by suddenly inhaling deeply and holding his breath. If you have ever seen a bantam rooster penned up with a flock of hens you would have a nice sharp picture of Killer Menegheni.

"Hang on a sec, beauteeful," he said into the phone when he saw me come in. "Cheez, Eddie, hodja come, by way of Flatbush?"

"I always ignore rhetorical questions."

"Cheez, listen to them words," said the Killer.

This had been going on between us ever since we met. The Killer seemed to take my two years in Princeton as a personal affront.

"Better get your ass in there," Killer waved me in. "D' boss is bitin' his nails."

When I went in, Nick was in his private bathroom, shaving. He had a heavy beard that he always shaved twice a day, leaving a smooth blue patina on his face. He always came to his office in the morning from an hour in George Kochan's barbershop. He was kind of a nut on barbershops. His nails were always trimmed and polished, his black kinky hair was singed and greased and the constant sun-lamp treatments had given his skin a tanned and healthy look. He wasn't a handsome man, but the facials, the oil shampoos and the meticulous grooming gave him a smooth, lacquered appearance.

"Hello, Eddie," he said, with his back toward me, wiping the last of the cream from his face as I came up behind him. "Sorry to louse up your evening this way, but I got no choice." He still pronounced it as *cherce*, but he no longer contracted his *th*'s to hard *d*'s the way the Killer did.

"Oh, that's all right, Nick," I said. "The evening isn't dead yet."

"But it will be," Nick said. "Got a big job for you, kid. Think you're gonna go for it."

He took a handsome leather-encased bottle from the cabinet and turned around to face me as he applied the toilet water to his face and neck. "Great stuff," he said, holding the bottle to my nose. "Smell."

Like most things Nick said, it sounded more like a command than a friendly suggestion. I smelled.

"Hmmmmmm," I nodded.

"Whatta you use?" Nick said.

"Oh, anything. Mem's, sometimes Knize Ten," I said.

"Hmm," said Nick. He turned back to the medicine cabinet again. "Here," he said. "The best. Old Leather. It's yours."

He handed me a sealed bottle of it. If he liked you, he was always giving away stuff like that. "Aw thanks, Nick," I said, "but it's your stuff, you like it. . . ."

29

"Don't be a sucker," Nick said, and he shoved the bottle into my belly with a gesture so emphatic that it ended the argument. Nick was accustomed to leaning his weight on you, even when he was doing you a kindness. "I've been able to do a couple of little favors for the chairman of the board of the outfit that puts this stuff out—so he sent me a case of it the other day."

Nick was always getting or doing little favors he never elucidated, little favors that meant a quick turn-over for some favored party in four, five, maybe six figures. I never knew what they were, and although I had the natural curiosity of anybody working in an atmosphere of big, quick, hushed money, I didn't let myself get too anxious to nose into subterranean affairs of the syndicate. It was a long time ago but I still remembered what happened to Jake Lingle in Chicago. First you get curious, then you try to find out, then you know too much, then you get paid off, then you get knocked off. It happens. So I just assumed that Nick let this toilet-water king in on a horse that was coming in at Bay Meadows, or maybe it was that waltz in the Garden last Friday night when the gamblers cashed in on the short end or maybe it was girl trouble the big shot wanted Nick to get Honest Jimmy to fix up with an assistant district attorney who was a buddy-buddy of his. It could be any one of a dozen things because Nick lived in a mysterious world of secret tips and special favors, a two-way street of silk-monogram intrigue that could lead from the cruddiest gin mill to the smartest house in Sutton Place.

Nick led me back into the office, picked up the dark mahogany box full of slender Belindas, offered me one, snipped the end off his with a silver cigar-cutter, and got down to business.

"I guess you know, Eddie," he said, "I've had the feeling a hell of a long time that your—" he reached for it— "capabilities—hasn't really been extended by our organization. It's like we got a good fast boy—champeenship material—he's fighting four-round curtain raisers all the time. A guy like you, he's got something up here, he can write, he's got whatcha call it, imagination, he needs something he can get your teeth into. Well, Eddie, the dry spell is over. You're out of the desert. I got a little project for you that will really get your gun off."

"What are you handing me, Nick, the Latka Fellowship for Creative Writing or something?"

"Don't worry. Nick never steered you wrong, did he? You're my guy, ain't you? I'm handing you a new deal, Eddie. Forget all about Harry Glenn and Felix Montoya and Willie Faralla and the rest of the bums we got in the stable. Don't even bother with old man Lennert."

That was Gus Lennert, the ex-heavyweight champ who, for want of anything better, was still rated No. 2 in the heavyweight division. Gus wasn't really a fighter any more. He was just a business man who went to work occasionally in bathrobe and boxing gloves when the price was right. After dropping his crown seven years ago to a rough aggressive boy he could have put away any time he wanted to in his fighting days, Gus had hung up his gloves. He was pretty well fixed with a couple of trust funds and a popular little bar and grill in his home town, Trenton, N. J. called "Gus's Corner." But when we got down to the bottom of the barrel and Mike Jacobs was drawing big gates with heavyweight main events between alleged title contenders who had been spar-boys or washed-up a year or so before, Gus couldn't resist the temptation to come back for a little of the easy scratch. Under Nick's guidance, Gus had easily outboxed three or four bums who were masquerading as headliners in the Garden. With me beating the drums about how the great Gus Lennert had come back to realize his dream of being the first heavyweight champion to regain his title we were on our way into working poor old Gus into a shot at it.

"Forget Lennert," Nick said. "Get Lennert out of your mind. I got something better. I got Toro Molina."

"I never heard of Toro Molina."

"Nobody ever heard of Toro Molina," Nick said. "That's where you come in. You are going to make everybody hear of Toro Molina. You are going to make Toro Molina the biggest thing to hit the fight racket since Firpo came up from the Argen*tine*, or *teen* or however the hell you say it, and dropped Dempsey into the ringside seats."

"But where'd you get this Molina, who sold him to you?"

"Vince Vanneman."

"Vince Vanneman, for Christ sake!"

As Kid Vincent, Vanneman had been a pretty fair middleweight back in the Twenties until he crawled into the wrong bed one night and crawled out again with a full set of *spirochaete pallida*, known to the world as syphilis and to the trade as cupid's measles. The docs didn't know how to clean it up in five and a half seconds, more or less, the way they do today. As a result Vince's case was developing into what the medics called the tertiary stage, when it begins to get to your brain. Pardon me, Vince's brain. But a little thing like a decaying brain cell or two didn't seem to have anything like a deleterious effect on Vince's ability to turn a dishonest dollar. So I was a little surprised that Nick, whose larceny was on such a high level that it approached the respectability of finance capitalism, would get himself involved with a minor-league thief.

"Vince Vanneman," I said again. "A *momser* from way back. You know what the boys call him—The Honest Brakeman. He never stole a boxcar. When Vince Vanneman goes to sleep he only closes one eye so he can watch himself with the other."

When Nick was impatient he had the habit of snapping alternately the thumb and second finger of each hand in nervous staccato rhythm. I've seen him do that when he wanted his man to start carrying the fight to his opponent and the boy couldn't seem to get going. "Listen," he said, "don't tell me about Vanneman. The day I can't handle Vanneman I turn over the business to the Killer. I made a nice deal with Vince. We only give him five G's for Molina and he rides with us for five percent of the profits. The South American jerk, who brought the boy up here, Vince gives him twenty-five hundred and we also cut him in for five percent."

"But if this—what's-his-name, Molina?—is such a find, what's Vince doing selling out so fast?" I asked. "Vince may be suffering from paresis, but he's not so dumb he doesn't know a meal ticket when he sees one."

Nick looked at me as if I were a high-grade moron, which, in this business, I was. "I had a little talk with Vince," Nick said.

I could picture that little talk—Nick cool, immaculate, quietly implicit; Vince with his tie loosened so he could open his shirt and let his fat neck breathe, the sweat coming out of his fleshy face as he tried to wriggle off Nick's hook—just a talk between two business men concerning lump sums, down payments and percentages, just a quiet little talk and yet the atmosphere tense with unheard sounds, the blackjack's thud, the scream torn from the violated groin, the spew of blood and broken teeth.

"Anything I want to do is a hundred percent okay with Vince," Nick said.

"But I don't get it," I said. "Why all this trouble about Molina? Who'd he ever lick? What's so special about Molina?"

"What is so special about Molina is he is the biggest son-of-a-bitch who ever climbed into a ring. Six feet seven and three-quarters inches tall. Two hundred and eighty-five pounds."

"You all right, Nick?" I said. "Not on the stuff or anything?"

"Two hundred and eighty-five pounds," Nick said. "And no belly on him."

"But he could be a bum," I said. "Two hundred and eighty-five pounds of bum."

"Listen for Chri'-sakes," Nick said. "The Statue of Liberty, does she have to do an adagio to draw crowds every day?"

"Come one, come all, see the human skyscraper," I said. "Captured alive in the jungles of Argentina—Gargantua the Great."

"You laugh," Nick said. "Maybe I never went to college, but I sure in hell can add better 'n you. Not two 'n two neither. Two hundred G's and two hundred G's. Tell you what I'm gonna do with you, wise-guy. You'll get your straight C every week and on top of that I'll cut you in for 5 percent of our end. If we do two hundred thousand the first year, you'll make a little money."

"Two hundred thousand!" One hundred thousand was a good year's take for a name who packs the Garden. Anything over that was big-name heavyweights in outdoor shows. "Pass that opium pipe around and let's all take off."

"Listen, Eddie," Nick said, and his voice had the self-satisfied tone it always took on when he took himself seriously, like a self-made Kiwanian explaining his success to his fraternal brothers. "I learned one thing when I was a kid—to do big you got to think big. When we used to jimmy those penny machines, for instance, you know, peanuts, chewing gum, hell, we was always getting caught. Then I got the idea of mugging the collector who went from one machine to another every Friday, emptying out the coin boxes. It was safer to get him on his way back to the office at night, and hit the jackpot, than it was to work those machines over in broad daylight and pick up a few pennies. That's what I mean. If you got to think, think big. What the hell, it don't cost you nothing to think. So why think fifty grand when you can think a hundred and fifty grand? Now tomorrow I got this Molina and his spic manager, Acosta, coming out to the country.

34

You better come too. Bring the broad along if you want. Take Acosta aside and get the story—you know, how the big guy was discovered and all that crap. Then we'll sit down together and work out the angles. Wednesday morning I wanna hit the papers. The suckers open their papers and right away like this" (he snapped his fingers) "there's a new contender for the championship."

Nick stood up and put his hand on my arm. He was excited. He was thinking big. "Eddie," he said, "you gotta work like a son-of-a-bitch on this. You make with the words, I work the angles and if that big Argentine bastard gives us anything at all, we'll all make a pisspot full of dough."

If I ever got five thousand dollars ahead, I was always thinking, I'd throw up my job, get a little cabin in the mountains somewhere, take a year off and write. Sometimes I was going to write a bright, crisp, wisecracking comedy, the George Abbott type, and make a hatful of dough. And sometimes I was going to pour out everything I had seen and learned and felt about myself and America, a great gushing river of a play that would get me a Pulitzer prize. After the play opened, Beth and I would take a honeymoon cruise around the world, while I outlined my next. . . .

"How about a shot?" Nick said. He rose, pressed a button in the wall near his desk and a panel rolled back, revealing a small, well-fitted bar, and brought out a bottle of Ballantine's, the twenty-year old.

"To Señor Molina," I said.

"And to us," Nick said.

He filled the two pony glasses again. "That girl you got, she's a writer too, ain't she?" he said. The only serious reading Nick ever did was the *Morning Telegraph* and the *Racing Form* but he always got an earnest, respectful note in his voice when he spoke about writers. "A smart girl like that, she must make out pretty good," he said. "What does she make on *Life*, eighty, ninety a week?"

"You're high," I said. "Took her three years to get up to fifty."

"Fifty," Nick said. "Jesus, a preliminary boy in the Garden gets a hunerd'n fifty."

"Beth figures she'll last longer," I said.

"You oughta marry a dame like that," Nick said. Whenever Nick hit a mellow stretch he liked to concern himself with matrimony and legitimate genesis. "No kidding, you should get yourself hitched. Hell, I was in the saddle with a different tomato every night until I got hitched. You oughta settle down and start having some kids, Eddie. Them kids, that's what makes you want to work like a bastard."

From his inside pocket, Nick drew a handsome leather wallet, initialed in gold, N.L., Jr. "Here's what I'm giving Junior for his graduation—he finishes the lower form up at N.Y.M.A. next week."

I took the wallet and turned it over in my hand. It was from Mark Cross, the best. Inside was a brand-new hundred-dollar bill. "He's a smart kid," Nick said. "Been skipped twice. He's the company commander's orderly or adjutant or whatever the hell it is. Pretty good athlete too. Plays on the tennis team."

You couldn't help liking Nick sometimes, the way he said things. That tennis, for instance. The awe and the wonder of it. Nick, who played punchball on Henry Street against tenement walls decorated in chalk with a childish scrawl of grown-up obscenities, the ball bouncing back into the crowded streets, over pushcarts, under trucks honk-honking drivers' hot disgusted shouting *Git outa there you little sonofabitch*; and Junior white as the saints in his flannels and sportshirt with the school crest over his heart, the warm silence broken only by the sharp crack of racket and ball and the gentlemanly intrusion of the judge on his high cool seat, *Game, to Mr. Latka. He leads, first set, five games to two.* Old Nick and Young Nick, Henry Street and Green Acres, the military school on the Hudson and PS 1 on the corner of Henry and Catherine Streets battleground of Wops and Yids invading Polacks and crusading Micks energetic young Christians brandishing rock-filled stockings crashing down upon the heads of unbaptized children falsely accused of murder committed nineteen hundred years ago. *Your serve. Sorry, take another. Please take two.*

"Killer," Nick called into the outer office, "hang up on that broad and get Ruby on the phone. Tell her to hold that steak for me, I'll be out ina nour."

He tapped me lightly on the side of the jaw with his knuckles. It was one of his favorite signs of affection.

"See ya mañana, Shakespeare."

After Nick left I sat down at his desk to call Beth. There was a small telephone pad near the phone, with Nick's name printed in the upper left-hand corner. There was something in Nick that desired constant re-establishment of his identity. Shirts, cuff-links, cigarette lighters, wallets, hat-bands were all smartly initialed. The matchbooks he handed you said "Compliments of Nick Latka."

Nick had been doodling. The top page of the pad was full of large and small ovals representing punching bags: the long sand-filled heavy bags and the smaller, inflated light bags. All the bags were covered with little pencil flecks that looked like miniature s's. I looked at them more carefully and saw that two thin vertical lines ran through them. All the punching bags had broken out in a hive of dollar signs.

As I left, the Killer was just putting on his coat, a form-fitting herringbone with exaggerated shoulders. "Jeez, have I got something lined up for myself tonight," he was saying. "The new cigarette girl at the Horseshoe. Knockers like this. And loves it like a rabbit."

"Killer," I said, "have you ever thought of writing your memoirs?"

Hacking down Eighth Avenue, past the quick lunches,

the little tailor shops, the second-hand stores, HONEST PRICES FOR GOLD, past the four-bit barbershops, the two-bit hotels, the Chinese laundries, the ten-cent movies, I thought of Nick, and of Charles and his Jackson-Slavin fight, the magnificent ebony figure of Peter Jackson with his great classical head, his innate dignity, poised and magnanimous in his moment of triumph. Jackson, black athlete from Australia, a pugilist in the great tradition, worthy descendant of the ancient Sumerians, whose boxing contests are depicted in frescoes that have come down to us through six thousand years; and of Theagenes of Thaos, Olympic Champion, who defended his honor and his life in fourteen hundred contests with steel-pronged fists four hundred and fifty years before Christ; of the great British bare-knuckled forefathers who developed the manly art of self-defense; John Broughton, first to give the ring a written code, who, egged on by his impatient backer, the Duke of Cumberland, while being beaten to blindness by a powerful challenger, said, "Tell me where my man is and I will strike him, sir"; Mendoza the Jew, Champion of England, undersized giant-killer who fought the biggest and best his island could boast, bringing a new technique of movement to the slow, savage game; the mighty Cribb and the indomitable champion, Tom Molineaux, the liberated slave who stood up to Cribb for forty bruising rounds and would have won but for a desperate ruse; Englishmen, Negroes, the Irish, Jews, and in our time Americans with Italian names, Canzoneri, La Barba, Genaro; Filipinos, Sarmiento, Garcia; Mexicans, Ortiz, Arizmendi—all sprung from fighting stock, practicing an ancient sport already old in Roman times, a cruel and punishing enterprise rooted deep in the heart of man that began with the first great prehistoric struggles and has come down through the Iron Age, the Bronze Age, the dawn of the Christian Era, medieval times, the eighteenth and nineteenth century renaissance of pugilism, until at last New York, heir to Athens,

38

Rome and London, has made the game its own, entrusting it to one of its more successful sons, Uncle Mike Jacobs, unchallenged King of Jacobs' Beach, perhaps the only unlimited monarch still in business, who, by crossing the boxing racket with ticket speculation has produced a hundred-million-dollars-a-year industry that Daniel Mendoza, poor old Peter Jackson or the blustering John L. would never recognize as their brave old game of winner take all.

3

BETH drove down with me to Nick's place over near Red Bank, about forty-five minutes from New York, not very far from Mike Jacobs' own little Versailles. In fact, if I remember right, he heard of Green Acres through Mike when he was down there for a week-end five or six years ago. It had belonged to a millionaire Wall Street broker whose marriage went on the rocks and who decided to unload it in a hurry. Nick had got it for around fifty thousand. But there must have been an easy hundred thousand sunk in it, with the twenty-three-room house, hundred and twenty acres, swimming pool, tennis court, hot-house, screened-in barbecue, four-car garage and twenty-horse stable.

It was hard to understand what the broker was thinking about when he built the house. It was neo-Gothic, if you could call it anything, an architectural Texas-leaguer that fell somewhere between medieval and modern design, a formal, urban dwelling that looked out of place in the country and yet would have looked equally incongruous in town. It was beautifully landscaped, with smartly trimmed hedges bordering the well-kept lawns dressed up with circular flower beds. We drove around the house to the garage, where Nick's chauffeur was washing the big black Cadillac four-door convertible. He was bare from the waist up, and although there was a bicycle tire of fat around his middle, the chest, back, shoulders and over-developed biceps were impressive. He looked up when he saw me and his frank, flattened face opened in a gummy smile.

"Whaddya say, Mr. Lewis?"

"Hello, Jock. How's everything?"

"Ain't so bad. You know the wife's home with the new kid."

"Yeah? Swell. How many's that make it?"

"Eight. Five boys and three goils."

"Take it easy now, Jock," I said. "You never did know your own strength."

The chauffeur grinned proudly until his eyes, puffy with scar-tissue, pressed together in the grimace of a cheerful gargoyle.

"The boss around?"

"He's out horse-back ridin' with Whitey."

Whitey Williams was the little ex-jockey who won a nice chunk of change for Nick at Tropical Park one season when he booted home forty-five winners. Now he took care of Nick's horses for him and taught him how to ride. They were out on the bridle path together almost every Sunday.

"How about the Duchess?"

That was Ruby. Anybody who had been around the place very long knew whom you meant.

"I just took her over to ten-o'clock mass. She'n this big fella from the Argentine."

"Oh, he went, too? What does he look like?"

"Well, if anyone tags him he's got a long way to fall."

"See you later, Jock."

"You bet, Mr. Lewis."

"That's Jock Mahoney," I told Beth as we walked up toward the large lawn that stretched between the main house and the garage, over which Jock, the missus and the seven kids lived in five small rooms. "A good second-rate light-heavyweight in the days when Delaney, Slattery, Berlenbach, Loughran and Greb were first rate. Very tough. Could take a hell of a punch."

"He doesn't talk as if he has a brain full of scrambled eggs," Beth said.

41

"They don't all come out of it talking to themselves," I said. "Take McLarnin, fought the toughest—Barney Ross, Petrolle, Canzoneri—and his head's as clear as mine."

"This morning probably clearer," Beth said.

I was still thinking about Mahoney. Old fighters will always get me. There is nothing duller than an old ball player or an old tennis star, but an old fighter who's been punched around, spilled his blood freely for the fans' amusement only to wind up broke, battered and forgotten has got the stuff of tragedy for me.

"The only thing soft about Mahoney is the way he laughs," I said. "All you have to do is look at him and he laughs. That's usually a sign you're a little punchy. The time Berlenbach tagged him with the first punch he threw in the third round, Jock was out so completely he went over to Berlenbach's corner and flopped down. But the way he was grinning and laughing, you'd've thought he was home in an easy chair reading the funny papers."

"That's what I don't like about it," Beth said. "The way they laugh."

"When they laugh, Beth, it usually means they're hurt," I said. "They just want to show the other guy that they aren't hurt, that everything's okay."

"I read something about laughter once," Beth said. "The idea was that laughter is just a display of superiority. Laughing when somebody slips on a banana peel, for instance, or gets a face full of pie. Or take the whole line of Scotch-Jewish-Darky jokes. The thing about them that makes people laugh is the warm feeling that they aren't as tight as the Scotchman, as beaten down as the Negroes and so on."

"But if we follow that theory," I said, "shouldn't the fellow who does the laughing be the one who throws the punch, not the one who catches it?"

"It's not that simple," Beth insisted. "Maybe the guy who gets hurt laughs to hang on to his superiority—or is that what you said in the first place?"

"That's the trouble with you psychologists," I said. "You can take either side and sound just as scientific."

We had reached the lawn nearest the house, where a row of round metal tables had been set out with brightly colored beach umbrellas rising through the centers. Lying on the grass in the shade of one of these umbrellas was a slight, middle-aged man with gray hair and a sickly white face, eyes closed in the heavy stupefaction of alcoholic sleep. A folded *Racing Form* he had used as an eye-shade had slipped off his forehead. He was snoring strenuously through a badly broken nose, the only punished feature in an otherwise unmarked face.

"There's Danny McKeogh," I said. Around Stillman's they call it "McCuff."

"Is he alive?" Beth asked.

"Slightly," I said.

"He's got a sad face," Beth said.

"He's one of the right guys in this business," I said. "He'd give you his shirt if you needed it, even if he didn't have a shirt and had to go borrow one off somebody else. Which has happened."

"A generous member of this profession? I didn't know there was such an animal."

As we walked along the volcanic career of Danny McKeogh registered its peaks and valleys in my mind.

He never took a drink until the night he fought Leonard. Danny was a beautiful gymnasium fighter, a real cutie from way back. He never made a wrong move in a gym. He wasn't a cocky kid ordinarily, but he was sure he could take Leonard. Nobody had done it yet, not even Lew Tendler, but Danny felt sure. He studied Leonard in all his fights and even went to see movies of him. Kind of a nut on the subject, like Tunney with Dempsey, only with a different ending. After all the build-up, Leonard knocked him cold in one minute and twenty-three seconds of the first round. Got his nose busted in the bargain. That was curtains for Danny as a fighter. Almost curtains in other ways too. For the next couple of years he gave a

43

convincing imitation of a man who was trying to drink up all the liquor there was in New York.

Then, one day, hanging around the gym with a bad breath and a three-day growth—it was up on 59th Street at the time—he happened to see a skinny little East Side Jewish boy working out with another kid. Right away Danny decided to get a shave and sober up. It was love at first sight. The boy was Izzy Greenberg, just a punk skinny sixteen-year-old kid then, training for a newsboy tournament. Danny must have seen himself all over again in that kid. Anyway he stayed on the wagon. He worked with Izzy every day for a year or more, boxing with him, showing him, very patient, showing him again—and there's no better teacher in the world than Danny when he's sober. Even drunk he still makes more sense than almost anybody around.

Danny brought Izzy right to the top. He looked like another Leonard, one of those classy Jewish lightweights that keep coming up out of the East Side. Three years of consistent wins and they've got the championship. They travel around the world, picking up easy dough, meeting the Australian champion, the Champion of England, the Champion of Europe, which is not as much trouble for Izzy as slicing Matzoth balls with a hot knife. Then they come back to the big town, and Izzy defends his title in the old Garden against Art Hudson, a slugger from out West. Danny, who always backed his fighters heavily—old-fashioned that way—had his friends cover all the Hudson money they could find. They only found ten thousand dollars. Sixty thousand if Danny lost. But Danny liked the bet, called it easy money.

The first round looked like curtains for Hudson. Izzy left-handed him to death, and that jab of his wasn't just scoring points; it could carve you up like a steak knife. Thirty seconds before the end of the round Hudson went down. Izzy danced back to his corner, winking at Danny, nodding to friends around the ring, waving a glove at the large Jewish following that was letting itself go. He's all ready to go in and get dressed. And Danny's already thinking of how to parlay the ten grand. But somehow or other Hudson was on his feet at nine and rushing across the ring. He was really a throw-back to Ketchell and Papke. All he knew about boxing was to keep getting up and keep banging away. Izzy turned toward him coolly, did a little fancy footwork and snapped out that fast left to keep Hudson away. But Hudson just brushed it aside and banged a wild left to the body and a hard roundhouse right to the jaw.

Izzy was out for twenty minutes. His jaw had been broken in two places. A reporter who was there in the dressing room told me Danny was crying like a baby. He rode with Izzy up to the hospital and then he went out and had a drink. That time he stayed drunk for almost three years.

Then one day at the Main Street gym out in L.A., where Danny looks like any other flea-bitten bum, he spots another little kid, Speedy Sencio. Same thing all over again. On the wagon. Fills the little Filipino full of everything he knows. Cops the bantamweight crown and everything's copasetic until Speedy goes over the hump and starts going downhill. Danny goes back on the flit again.

By this time Danny has made a couple of hundred thousand, gone mostly to the horses. He is also a great little check-grabber and highly vulnerable to the touch, especially when it comes from one of the fighters who used to win for him. Like Izzy Greenberg. Danny put fifteen thousand in a haberdashery business Izzy was starting, and six months later the business went the way of all Greenberg enterprises. He is not nearly the flash in business he was in the ring. But Danny gave him ten thousand more and he went into ladies' wear on Fourteenth Street.

The crash put the finisher on Danny's chips. The only chance he saw of getting it back fast was the horses, and the only way of getting enough for the horses was finding a friend to put it on the cuff. Nick Latka turned out to be the friend, and he seemed to be all cuff where Danny was concerned. Danny didn't know there was a catch to it until he was into Nick for around twenty G's. "Who's worried about it?" Nick had said every time Danny mentioned something about hoping to clean up enough soon to pay some of 'it back. Then one day Nick sends for Danny and all of a sudden wants his dough. Danny is just back from Belmont, where his tips have been worse than his hunches. So Nick says, "Tell you what I'll do with you, baby. You come to work for me for two fifty a week, building up a stable and handling the boys. You keep a C for yourself and one and a half cuts back to me until we're even. And just to show you how I feel about you, I'll put you down for a bonus of ten percent on everything we make over fifty G's a year."

So that's where Danny's been ever since. Even if he developed another Greenberg or a Sencio it wouldn't be his any more. So the incentive to say no to the bottle is practically nil. Now it's reflex action for him to reach for one in the morning, and he tosses them off in quick nervous motions until somebody puts him to bed. He has never been known to come in loaded on fight night when he is working a corner. But when he is sober everybody wishes he would take one to relax. He's so sober he gets the shakes. It's really a heroic and terrible effort for Danny to be sober, but he does it, because, for all the disappointments, he's still got his heart in the game. There's nobody hops into a ring at the end of a round faster than Danny and there is something wonderful about the loving way he leans over his fighters, rhythmically rubbing the neck, the small of the back, with his thin, nervous lips close to his boy's ear, keeping up a quiet running patter as he improvises new tactics for the boy's defense and spots holes in the opponent's.

A great manager, Danny McKeogh, in the big tradition of great managers. Johnston, Kearns, Mead. Or at least he was a great manager before Nick Latka brought him into bondage.

As I stood there looking down at him, thinking about him, a fly lit on his nose, was brushed away, only to return to his forehead. Danny shook his head, let a crack of light into his eyes and saw me standing there. He sat up slowly, rubbing his eyes.

"Hello, laddie."

Everybody he liked he called laddie. For people he didn't like, it was mister.

"Hello, Danny. How's the boy?"

Danny shook his head. "Pretty tough," he said, "pretty tough."

"By the way, Miss Reynolds, Mr. McKeogh."

Danny began to tuck one foot under him as if he were going to rise. Beth put her hand out to stop him. "You look much too comfortable," she said. "I'm not used to such gallantry."

That kind of courtesy was part of Danny, drunk or sober. He had that big Irish thing about women, reverent when he mentioned his mother, sore at guys who profaned in the presence of ladies, which was the entire opposite sex in Danny's book, regardless of rep or appearance. But Danny didn't have that other Irish thing, the three-drink belligerence. When he drank himself into a stupor he did so quietly and gradually like the death of Galsworthy's patriarch in *The Indian Summer of a Forsyte*. No fuss and never any fights, even when goaded by a champion like Vince Vanneman. He was one of the few men I've ever known who could pass out and not lose either his cookies or his dignity.

"Seen your new heavyweight yet?" I said.

"No," he said. "I been pounding my ear. You see him?"

I shook my head. "He's gone to mass with the Duchess."

"Well, we'll take a look at him in the gym tomorrow."

"Nick's all excited," I said.

"Yeah," Danny said.

A loud yawn escaped him. "Scuse me, ma'm."

"Who's the biggest guy you ever handled before, Danny?"

Danny thought a moment. "Big Boy Lemson, I guess. Scaled around two-thirty. Looked tough, but he was muscle-bound, had a glass jaw. I tell ya, Eddie, I don't get excited about these jumbo heavyweights. Hundred 'n eighty, eighty-five, that's all you need to knock out anything, if you know how to punch. Dempsey was only one-ninety at Toledo. Corbett's best weight was around one-eighty."

"Nick sees a sensational draw in this Molina," I said.

"Yeah," Danny said.

That's about the most combative Danny ever got, that "yeah." It would be harder to find two guys further apart in the boxing business than Danny and Nick. Nick was all business. For him the fix was second nature. To Danny it wasn't a sport any more either. It was a trade. He happened to be an honest craftsman. His way was to start from scratch, pitting his brain and his kid's natural talent and ability against all comers. That was too haphazard for Nick. Whether it was horses or fighters, he liked to play sure things.

"You could use a little more shut-eye, Danny," I said. "We'll catch you later."

"Right, laddie," Danny said. There was still the echo of a brogue. He stretched out on the grass again. Beth took my arm and we walked on.

Under the next umbrella sat a couple of gamblers. It sounds like easy generalization to look at a couple of guys you have never seen before and flip your mind down to G like a card-file, right away, "Gamblers." But I would have laid five-to-one that's what they were, if I hadn't learned my lesson a long time ago never to stake my judgment against the professional players'. One of the gamblers had done too well for a long time and it was all in his face and his belly. The other had started out with

48

a very good physique and still kept a little pride in it. Once in a while, when he got into a bathing suit, he probably felt a twinge of self-consciousness about the surplus fat on him and subjected it to the hard mechanical hands of the steam-bath rubber. They were both dressed in easy, comfortable clothes that added up to the kind of country ensemble that looks expensively cheap. The fatter one was wearing a yellow flannel sports-shirt that must have cost sixteen bucks at Abercrombie & Fitch. But there was nothing Abercrombie & Fitch about the short hairy arms, the fat neck and the sweat staining the shirt-front even in the shade. You would think the Scotch or the British or whoever knitted his socks would have known better than to waste pure wool on such corny patterns.

"Gin," the leaner one said, pushing back an expensive Panama hat from a low forehead tanned from bending over racing programs in the sun near the railing.

The fat man threw his cards down in disgust. "Gin," he said, nodding his head in weary resignation and turning to us as if we had been there all the time, appealing to us as sympathetic onlookers witnessing a catastrophe. "Gin. Every five minutes gin. All the way up from Miami it's all I hear—gin, gin, gin! Three hundred and two dollars he's into me before we hit Balteemore. The cards he gives me, I shoulda got off at Jacksonville."

"You're breaking my heart," the man with the Panama said. "How many you got?"

"Twenty-eight," the fat man complained, and began to turn the cards over sorrowfully.

"Wait a minute, wait a minute, let *me* count," the other man said. His eyes did a quick recap of the fat man's cards. "Twenty-*nine*," he announced triumphantly, "twenty-*nine*, jerk."

"So twenty-nine," the fat man shrugged. "He's cutting my throat by inches and he's worried about a little pinch in the behind."

This fat one, Barney Winch, made gambling his business; but it was also his recreation. His success was due to the fact that he never allowed the business and the recreation to overlap. Strictly speaking, Barney was in the gambling business the way a saloon keeper is in the drinking business, although he never has one himself until the chairs are on the tables and the door is bolted for the night. If Barney were betting on a football game, he would figure out a way to bet on both teams so there was no chance of losing and yet a better-than-even chance of winning on both. That is how he was supposed to have cleaned up on a Southern Cal-Notre Dame game a few years back. First he had laid two and a half to four on the Irish, to win. Then he had turned around and taken Southern Cal and seven points. Notre Dame won by a single point, and Barney collected on both bets. Barney hedged his fight bets the same way, and he never faded in a crap game unless the percentage was with him. If you ever caught Barney betting only one side of a fight or putting a big wad down on the nose of a horse, you would be safe in assuming that these contests had lost their element of chance.

What Barney did for recreation was another story. His hands felt empty when they weren't holding cards. But he wasn't a particularly expert poker player nor invincible at gin. He never cheated at cards because cards was something he did with his friends, and a man like Barney Winch would never give the business to a friend. If *the business* was slang, it was highly literal slang, for it meant to Barney exactly what it had to Webster, that which busies or engages one's time, attention or labor, as a principal serious employment. When something went wrong with Barney's "principal serious employment" there was never so much as a sigh out of him. There was the time Barney had dropped forty thousand because a certain middleweight of Nick's who was supposed to fall down for a price double-crossed his managers and the smart money by staying on his feet and winning the decision. Barney took it philosophically. He shrugged and paid off. The double-cross was one of the risks of the business, like unseasonable rain for the farmer. Only as a little ethical reminder to the disobedient pugilist, a couple of goons were waiting for him outside his Washington Heights apartment when he got home after the fight, anxious to convince him of his mistake. They left him lying unconscious in the hallway with a convincing two-inch blackjack wound in his head.

If it was business, Barney never bellyached. The day he won enough to shoot up into the highest income brackets (if such profits were declared), he could be weeping because he was a sixty-one-dollar loser in a rummy game.

Barney rearranged his new hand, looked it over and shook his head with the clucking sound of self-pity. "Jacksonville," he said, "I shoulda got off at Jacksonville."

Just a hot, quiet Sunday morning at Green Acres, Nick off on the bridle path, Ruby at church and none of the usual Sunday-dinner crowd out of bed this early. We walked out toward the tennis court, where Junior Latka, slender and full of grace and conceit in his white ducks and white jersey with the school crest over the heart, was in the middle of a long and well-played rally with another young man almost his equal. Junior hit a hard deep forehand drive which his opponent had to return as a lob that Junior put away with an overhead smash. The other boy ran back and made a futile pass at it as it bounced high over his head.

Behind the tennis court was a carefully cultivated flower garden where a weather-beaten, runty old man was working quietly on his knees. He looked up when we passed and waited for us to admire his flowers. He had the face of a kid, with big ears and small, grinning eyes.

"The flowers look good this year, Petey," I said.

"T'anks, Mr. Lewis," he said. "I started dem earlier

dis year. Dese white bride roses is comin' out better'n I expected."

He went back to his weeding as we walked on. "How old do you think he is?" I said.

"Oh, forty-eight, fifty," Beth guessed.

"He stayed twenty rounds with Terry McGovern before we were born," I said. "He must be crowding seventy. Petey Odell, a great old-time featherweight."

"I suppose he wound up better than most of them," Beth said. "At least he's here in Nick's old fighters' home."

"They come up to Nick's all the time to put the bite on him. I guess it makes Nick feel good to take care of some of them. And of course it pays off. Nick's charities always pay off. They're grateful slobs, these old fighters. Good-hearted, loyal as hell and work like fools. Especially if you show an interest in what they're doing. That Jock Mahoney. I think he loves that Caddy more than he does his wife. All you have to do to make him happy is ask him how he manages to get such a high polish on those fenders. Old Petey's the same way about his garden. If he saw us go by and we didn't say anything about that garden he'd sulk all day. Just a little punchy."

"What a business!" Beth said. The more she saw of it, the less "fascinating" it seemed.

"Mahoney or Hayes, they aren't so bad. They know what day it is. Give them a definite job to do and they'll throw themselves into it. But just the same when you talk to them about anything but the job or maybe their families, you hit something fuzzy, as if they've got a layer of cotton around their brains."

"It's a filthy business," Beth said suddenly. "In your heart you know it's a filthy business."

"Last Friday night you were yelling your head off," I reminded her.

"That's true," she admitted. "I was rooting for the colored boy. He looked so thin and weak compared to the other one. When he started to rally, when he actually had that big Italian boy groggy, well"—she had to smile —"I guess I got excited."

"It's been exciting people a hell of a long time. Look at Greek mythology—full of boxers. Wasn't it Hercules who fought that very tough boy who grew stronger each time he was knocked down because the earth was his mother? What was his name?"

"Antaeus," Beth said.

"That's why it pays to court a *Life* researcher," I said. "Antaeus. Homer wrote a hell of a piece about that fight. And Virgil covered one of the first great comebacks of a retired champ. Remember how the old champ doesn't want to accept the challenge of the young contender from Troy because he complains he is way out of condition and all washed up, a sort of ancient Greek Tony Galento? But when he's finally goaded into fighting he puts up a hell of a battle, has his man on the verge of a kayo when the King steps between them like Arthur Donovan and gives it to the old champ on a TKO. Of course, Virgil made it sound a little more poetic, but that was the guts of it."

Beth smiled. "You shouldn't be a tub-thumper for a stable of fighters. You should write essays for *The Yale Review*."

"Nick pays me for the tub-thumping," I said. "This kind of talk I have to do for free."

We had almost reached the house. Nick and Whitey Williams were just coming up the driveway, at a slow trot. In contrast to Whitey, who sat his horse as if it were an overstuffed easy chair, and looked as much at home, Nick's seat was very erect, a little ill at ease, and when he posted you felt he was conscious of doing so with perfect form, which always results in something less than perfect in sport technique.

He swung off his horse, a big, deep-chested bay, and handed the reins to Whitey, who led both horses back to the stable. Nick was wearing Irish boots, chamois breeches and a brown polo shirt.

"How long you two been here?" he said pleasantly.

"About half an hour, Nick," I said. "Wonderful day."

"It must be a sweat-box in town," Nick said, gloatingly. "We useta knock the head off the fire plug an' take a shower bath in the street." He gave a little laugh, thinking how far he had come. "Eddie been showing you around the joint?"

"It's perfectly beautiful," Beth said.

"Didja show her the vegetable garden?" Nick said. "We got a thousand tomato plants. Raise all our own stuff. You like corn, miss? I'll betcha never tasted corn like this. Corn like this, you'll never get it in the stores. When you go home take some with you, all you want."

"Thanks very much," Beth said.

"Aah, it's nothing," Nick waved it aside. "This place is lousy with stuff. If you don't take it, my bums will eat me out of it anyway. That Jock Mahoney, he sits down to corn, he doesn't get up till he's finished thirteen-fourteen ears. He'd rather eat 'n . . ." He look at Beth and stopped. "Even when he was supposed to be trainin', he ate like a pig."

We were back on the terrace. Danny McKeogh was still sleeping, his legs spread apart and his arms outstretched, like a man who had been run over. The gamblers were still hunched over their cards.

"How's it going, Barney?" Nick said.

The fat man's body rose and fell in an exaggerated sigh. "Don't ask. He's murdering me. There oughta be a law against what he's doing to me."

Nick laughed. "No wonder Runyon called him the Town Crier," he said. "Even when he wins, he cries, because it wasn't bigger."

He dropped his hand on my shoulder. "This fella Acosta is inside on the screen porch. This oughta be a good time to talk. Come on in." Then he remembered Beth. "Sorry to grab the boy-friend away," he said with what was for Nick a very courtly gesture. "Ruby oughta be back in a couple of minutes. There's plenty of papers on the terrace if you feel like readin'. And if you wanna drink, just call the butler, the guy with the little black bow-tie."

"Who is he, Gene Tunney?" Beth asked.

"Tooney," Nick said, "Tooney gives me a pain in the . . . excuse me, miss, but I'd throw Tooney the hell off the place."

He maneuvered me toward the door. "Just do anything you feel like, take anything you want like it was your own home."

"You boys go ahead," Beth said. "I'll amuse myself."

I watched her for a moment as she started back across the terrace. She was wearing a yellow-brown linen skirt, only a shade darker than her tanned legs and arms. Even in the city, where the only exercise most people get is running for a bus or hailing a cab, she always got down to the courts at Park and Thirty-ninth at least twice a week when the weather was right. She looked very sharp from where we stood, not the dream figure, a little too athletic maybe, a little too thin in the legs and not quite enough in front. But there was something attractively capable about the way she walked. I made a mental note to mention this to her later.

She puzzled me. She was the kind of girl to whom I was always going to say something nice a little later. What kept me back, perhaps, was that she would only half believe what I told her, always holding something in reserve. Maybe it was her upbringing, the kind that demands a strict balance all the time. Maybe it was the old Puritan strain in her. Maybe it was a bad inheritance of fierce convictions. Whatever it was, a nice girl like Beth, good respectable family, good schooling, good brain, was still a question mark to me. Passion and restraint, in equal portions, end up in a no-decision fight.

"She's all right," Nick said. "You got yourself something there. Plenty of class."

4

We walked through the spacious living room, an over-decorated hall of mirrors that looked unlived-in, to the sun-porch. When he saw us, the little Argentinian rose quickly to his feet, stiffly formal, his teeth showing in a rehearsed smile. He was a short dumpy man with a large nose, a swarthy complexion and a half dozen strands of hair angled back from his forehead in a strategic but unsuccessful effort to hide his baldness. He wore spats, a white-checkered vest and the kind of four-button sports suit belted in the back we haven't seen around here in quite a while. On the fourth finger of his short stubby hand was what might have been a ruby.

"Eddie," Nick said, not bothering to introduce me, "this is Acosta. You guys got some work to do, so I'll leave you alone."

Acosta began a little bow and started to say something like "Charmed . . ." or "Very pleased . . ." but Nick caught him in the middle of it. The courtesies were all right with Nick, if they didn't get in the way of business. "I dialed out on you," he said to Acosta, "because I don't hafta hear all that crap about the village and the wine barrels. I'm a business man. I take one hinge at the boy and I see he's got something. I can sell him. But," Nick squeezed my shoulder affectionately, "I want you to give my boy here the full treatment."

"Yes, yes, I understan'," Acosta said, bowing slightly toward Nick again, as if what he had just said had been graciously friendly.

"Don't forget now, the full treatment," Nick said, using the same tone on Acosta he used on the bums around

56

the office. "Including dessert and the finger bowls."

"Meester Latka, he has a very smart head for business," Acosta said to me when Nick left us alone. "Very strong mind, very intelligent. When El Toro and I come to North America I never even have the dream to be the partner of such a big man as Meester Latka."

"Yes," I said.

He reached into his inside pocket and brought forth a silver case from which, with an elaborate gesture, he offered me a cigarette. "Perhaps you do not mind smoking an Argentinian cigarette," he said. "Very mild, very nice smoke. If you will pardon me for saying, I like better than your Chesterfield and Lucky Strike." Again he smiled with his teeth to show that this was not an issue of nationalist rivalry but merely a little joke, and fitted his cigarette nicely into a slender tortoise-shell holder. He spoke better English than the Killer or Vanneman, but with a strong affinity for the present tense and a tendency to louse up his present and past perfects.

"Meester Lewis," Acosta began, "for me to meet you is a very great pleasure. Meester Latka, he has tell me about you the many good things. You are a very great writer, yes? You will make very famous my great discovery El Toro Molina and his little manager Luis?"

This was said with a little laugh, as if to show we both understood that Luis was not nearly so aggressive and self-seeking as he made himself sound. Luis had shrewd little eyes that appraised you too carefully all the time he was smiling at you. For all the Argentine schmalz, it wasn't too difficult to see him promoting up and down Jacobs' Beach with the best of them, spats and all.

Well, the overture is over and the curtain's going up, I thought.

"Tell you what you do, Mr. Acosta," I said. "Give me the whole thing. From the beginning. Where the guy comes from, how you found him, when he started fighting, the works."

"Please?" Acosta said.

"You know, the whole story, complete in this issue."

"Oh, yes, yes I understan'," Acosta said. "It is very very interesting the story of El Toro and I. Very romantic. Very dramatic. But first if you please I will warn you of something. El Toro Molina, he is a very young boy. He does not have yet twenty-one years. He comes from a very little village in the Andes, above Mendoza. All the people there, they are of very simple minds. Not loco you understan', just of simple minds. All their life they work in the vineyards of the great *estancia* de Santos. Of the world outside, they know nothing, not even of the capital of their state, Mendoza. Buenos Aires, it is not as real as heaven to them, and North America it is as far away as the stars."

Acosta smiled for Toro's innocence.

"So it is of this matter that I will warn you, if you please, Meester Lewis. I cannot make El Toro come to North America without I promise to take care of him with very great *fidelidad,* er . . ."

"Faithfulness," I said.

"Ah, ¿habla usted español?"

"Un poco," I said *"Muy poco. Seis meses en Méjico."*

"Good, very good," he said warmly. *"Su acento de usted es perfecto."*

"Mi acento es stinko," I said.

"Ah, you have the sense of humor," Acosta said. "In my Argentina we have the saying: A man who cannot laugh is a man who cannot cry."

"On Eighth Avenue life is not so simple," I said.

"Around the Madison Square Garden it is very impressive, yes?" Acosta said. "That is where they make the big business, the ringside ticket for maybe thirty dollars. In my country a hundred pesos. ¡*Fantástico*! My ambition it is to see the name of El Toro Molina in the lights of the Garden *marquesina,* this peasant clay that I have carve into work of art. It is my big dream, my big promise to El Toro."

He wasn't kidding. You could see from the intense way his eyes worked that he wasn't kidding. He was a little man, both in stature and achievement and he came from an under-populated, second-rate country. This was his way of dreaming greatness. The way he lived it, Toro Molina was David to his Michelangelo.

"But you must think I am a man of very much wind," Acosta said. "I have talk all this time and I have not tell you this matter of the warning. El Toro, I love him like my son, but he has no head for the business. Only me he trusts to take care of his money. For this he comes with me, to take back the big money to his family in the village. So I cannot tell him of the business of Meester Latka. He will not understan' how I have sell fifty percent to Meester Vanneman and how Meester Vanneman has turn around and sell forty percent to Meester Latka and how Meester Latka has also buy from me another forty percent. This business El Toro will not know how to understan'. It will make him very frighten', I think. So it is better for El Toro if he think the agreement we come to New York with is not change. It is better if he think Meester Latka is only my very good friend, a very big North American sportsman. So when he sees Meester Latka around very many times he has no sospecha, sos . . ."

"Suspicion," I said.

"*Exactamente*," Acosta said, "suspicion."

"In other words, when I see the boy, you want me to dummy up about how he is being sliced up like corned-beef in a delicatessen," I said.

"Please?" Acosta said.

"Dummy up," I said. "Keep quiet about your little deal with Vanneman and Latka."

"Ah, your slang, they are so colorful," Acosta said. "I would like before I go back to the Argentine to learn them all."

"Before you go back to the Argentine," I said, "you will learn a great deal."

"Thank you very much," Acosta said.

"Now let's get back to this work-of-art of yours," I said. "You really believe you've got a fighter, huh?"

That look came into his eyes again. "Argentina, it is a land of great fighters," he began. "Luis Angel Firpo would have won the knockout over Dempsey if the sporting writers had not lift him back into the ring. Alberto Lovell wins the amateur championship of the world in the Olympic. But El Toro Molina—he is our greatest, the greatest of all. In Argentina the mountains are very high, the pampas are very wide, it is a big country, big cattle, big men, but El Toro—his mother calls him El Toro because when he is born he weighs twelve pounds ten ounces—he is *gigantesco*, with the neck and the shoulders of a fighting bull and muscles in his arms as big as melons and legs as strong as the great *quebracho* trees of the Andes."

"Tell me," I said. "Just where did you find this mythological conglomerate of fighting bull, mountains, melons and *quebracho* trees?"

"Ah, you mean where have I make my great discovery?"

"*Sí, dígame*," I said. Nick should dig my *dígame*, I thought. I should get a couple of extra sawbucks for doing the Spanish version.

"Two years ago I have a little traveling circus in Mendoza," Acosta began. "There is Miguelito, the clown; there is the bareback riders Señor and Señora Mendez and their horse; there is Juanito Lopez with his dancing bear; there is Antonio the Magician which is me (one day I will make a card trick for you); and there is Alfredo el Fuerte, Alfredo the Strong-one. At the end of his act Alfredo always makes the challenge to lift up anything that three men in the audience can carry up on the stage together.

"When we come to the little village of Santa Maria in

the beautiful wine country of the Andes, we are ask to present our performance in the great patio for the amusement of the de Santos family who have the great *casa de campo* on the highest peak overlooking thousands and thousands of hectares of their beautiful grapes. It is the name day of the head of the de Santos family, and while they watch from the balcony, all the villagers crowd around our little portable stage in the courtyard. Things are passing very excellently. Yes, everything goes very excellently until my last act, Alfredo the Strong-one. Alfredo is a very accomplish strong-man, only he has one weakness, which is a very great thirst for champagne brandy. The evening before our performance Alfredo has make a rendezvous with the youngest daughter of the butler of the de Santos *casa*. The next morning when I smell the breath of Alfredo, it is even stronger than he is. I find it out that the little *muchacha* has stolen for him a bottle of champagne brandy from the cellar of the great house with the keys of her father. So when Alfredo makes his challenge to pick up anything three men can carry up on the stage he is already puffing like a big fish in the net. . . ."

"This is all very interesting," I said, "but I'm not doing the life story of your circus. All I need is the stuff on Molina."

"Please," Acosta said, as if I were a heckler climbing up on the stage in the middle of his act, "they are all threads in the same rug, how I have come to make the great discovery of El Toro Molina." He fitted another cigarette into his holder and gave me his cold social smile. "When I see in what weaken condition is Alfredo the Strong-one I am praying to Saint Anthony of my devotion that nothing heavy will come up on the stage. But Saint Anthony does not hear me. Because three of the biggest men I have ever see are carrying up on the stage the biggest barrel of wine I ever see. One of the men is old, of very little more height than I have, but

61

he is almost as wide as he is tall. The other two are young *gigantes* who have over six feet in height and weigh more than Luis Firpo.

" 'Who are these big fellows?' I ask. 'They are the Molinas,' I am told. 'Very famous of this village. The short one is Mario Molina, the barrel-maker, and those are two of his sons, Rafael and Ramon. At all our feast-days when it comes to the wrestling, old Mario was always the champion. And now his sons can throw him on his back as easy as you can swallow a grape.'

"That's good," I said. "That's in the script. I can use that."

"Please," Acosta said. "I will give you what Meester Latka call 'the whole treatment.' Now the big wine barrel is on the stage and if Alfredo cannot lift it I have promise to pay each of the men who have come up on the stage one peso. And if, God forbid, anyone in the audience can come up and equal Alfredo's feat, I have promise to pay five pesos. Poor Alfredo he puts his arms around the barrel and the sweat is running down both sides of his nose in two steady streams and I swear on the faithfulness of my mother to my father I can smell the champagne brandy. Yes, there is much sweat and much noise but no lifting of the barrel. All the villagers have begin to shout rude remarks and Alfredo has much anger in himself and sucks in his breath until the ribs begin to show through the fat. But still there is no lifting of the barrel. The villagers are throwing vegetables at Alfredo. Then some one calls out, 'El Toro, we want El Toro' and soon everyone is shouting 'El Toro, El Toro'!

"Out of the crowd a giant rises up and he seems to get bigger and bigger as he comes. When he climb up on the stage he move very slow but very *poderoso*. . . ."

"Powerful," I said.

"Thank you," Acosta said. "Very powerful, like an elephant. He seem very embarrass. 'I do not wish to come up, señor,' he say to me, 'but it is the wish of my friends

62

who I cannot insult.' Then, I swear by my sainted mother, El Toro reach down and lifts the barrel high in the air. The crowd laughs and shouts *Mucho, mucho, viva* El Toro Molina. 'Who is this fellow?' I ask. 'He is the youngest son of Mario Molina,' they say to me, 'the strongest man in Argentina.'

"When I pay this young giant the five pesos he has win I say to him, 'Perhaps you will like to come along with me and take the place of my Strong-one. You will have much money in your pocket and see many fine cities and everywhere you go beautiful señoritas will marvel at your strength and be yours for the taking.'

"But El Toro says, 'I wish to stay with my people. I am content here.'

" 'How much are you pay by the *estanciero?*' I say.

" 'Two pesos a day.'

" 'Two pesos! That is but the droppings of the sparrow. From Luis Acosta you will receive five pesos and when we are performing in Mendoza and the crowds do not keep their hands in their pockets you will make ten, maybe fifteen, pesos a day. You will come back to Santa Maria and take the most beautiful girl in the village for your wife.'

" 'You mean Carmelita Perez?' El Toro says.

"At last I have found the soft spot. 'Of course I mean Carmelita,' I say. 'Who else but Carmelita? You will come back with money enough to build a house for yourself. For you and Carmelita. And from Mendoza you will bring her a beautiful silk dress as fine as anything worn by the daughters of de Santos.'

"El Toro looks at me a long time and I can see that my words are working in his head. 'I will ask permission of my father,' he says to me. The father talks it over with Mama Molina who has never travel more than fifty kilometers beyond Santa Maria. She is very much frighten for what will happen to her *infante muy grande*, when he goes down into the great cities. But the brothers

Ramon and Rafael they urge the father very much to give El Toro the permission. The brothers have convince Mario to give El Toro the permission. Then there is much embracing and weeping and *Vaya con Dios*, and El Toro lifts his giant body onto my truck and waves good-bye to his family with his enormous hands. I drive down the mountainside with as much speed as I can because I am afraid if El Toro will change his mind."

"Giant son of peasant barrel-maker leaves village in Andes to be strong-man in traveling circus," I scribbled. It was one of those stories you could push beyond the sports page. The *Post* or *Collier's* might go for it. There might even be a little extra dough in a piece that gives a name and a personality to the human desire for size and strength. I could start with a mention of the Jews of Palestine and give them Samson. It would sound learned to show how the Greeks worshipped Atlas, Hercules and Titan. How Rabelais dreamed up Gargantua. And now, Toro Molina. For modern times we'd dish up a giant of our own, worthy to stand shoulder to shoulder with great and ancient company. What mighty feats would our giant perform, equaling those of Samson who came down from the hills to champion his subjugated people, Atlas who supported the world on his muscled back, and Hercules who fought his way up onto Mount Olympus! To keep the classical flavor, we could even ring in the *deus ex machina* in the person of Nick Latka, post-graduate hoodlum, soft-shoe racketeer and country gentleman as the means by which a giant peasant from the highest mountains in the New World follows the old pattern from man of the people to hero to demigod and finally joins the deities of contemporary mythology.

"Everywhere I go I have a very big success with El Toro," Acosta was saying while I played with the idea of becoming a god-maker. "The people have never see such bigness, such magnificence of muscles. Because I love El Toro so much I do not give him ten percent of

64

the collection; I let him keep twenty-five percent, for I have promise that when he go back to the village, he will have more money than all the peasants together. But El Toro goes to the great marketplace in Mendoza and like a child he spends every last centavo. For his mama he buys the bandana and for Carmelita a fine black lace gown and for himself a top-hat which he brings back wearing on his head. Such a child is El Toro and so little he knows of the world.

"Across the promenade from my circus at the great fair in Mendoza is my good friend Lupe Morales who is the old sparring partner of Luis Angel Firpo. Lupe makes the challenge to anyone in the audience to stay in the ring with him for three minutes. I see the collection of Lupe Morales and I watch that of El Toro Molina and I am surprise to see that Lupe who is all wash up in the boxing brings more money than El Toro. Why am I wasting my time picking up little coins in a side-show when I have in my hands a gold mine?

"So I make a deal with my friend Lupe that he will teach El Toro the science of the prize fight in return for five percent of all the money El Toro will make in the ring. When I tell El Toro what I have arrange, he says he does not like. 'Why should Lupe hit me and I hit Lupe back when we are not angry with each other?' he says. Poor El Toro, he has a body like a mountain but a brain like a pea. 'To be angry is not necessary, El Toro,' I say to him. 'The boxing is a business.' But El Toro is not convince.

"I have much worry because all my life I think, Luis, you are too clever to die in the province with your little traveling circus. Some day you will find something equal to your brain and showmanship. And now it is in my hand. But I am not thinking only of Luis Acosta. I think of El Toro also, who is become like a son to me. I have see his house in the village and I know how poor he lives even with their four pairs of arms of such strength.

"So I say to El Toro, 'I offer you the opportunity to make more money than you ever dream was in the world. Just to climb into the ring and box half of one hour you will make five hundred, maybe one thousand, pesos. Come with me to Buenos Aires and I will make so much money for you that you will be able to go back to Santa Maria and pay off the debt on your father's house and hire a maid for Carmelita. You can lie in bed after the sun is up and cuddle your wife and go to cockfights and sit at the café and sip your wine. How can you say you are in love if you are not willing to do this little for the happiness of Carmelita?'

"And so at last I have convince El Toro because in my own language I am very *elocuente*, although perhaps you cannot tell it from my English which suffers from a shortness of vocabulary."

"Don't worry about your English," I said. "Compared to the gentlemen who hang around Stillman's, you have the vocabulary of a Tunney. And he had to sweat for his too."

"You are very kind," Acosta said. "So now I am ready to make my peasant giant into a champion. Lupe does not know the science of *el box* like your Tunney or the little heavyweight Loughran who keeps his left glove in the face of Arturo Godoy in the big fight in Buenos Aires. But he knows to show El Toro how to put his left foot forward and hold his left hand out, with the right hand under the chin to protect the great jaw. He knows to show him how to balance on the balls of the feet, so he is ready to move forward or backward, and he knows to teach him how to lead with his left hand and cross with his right and snap back once more into position. What you call the fundamentals of self-defense, yes? He shows him how to throw the uppercut when he is in close and how to hold his arms in to his body in the clinch, so his opponent cannot hit him in the kidney and the rib. And that is all Lupe can teach, because there is even more to the science than Lupe knows.

68

"Little by little El Toro learns, for he is always serious in his work and tries to please me very much. In the sparring with Lupe he is very strong because he has the wind of a bull and in the clinch he can toss Lupe around like a feather, and when he has train nearly two months Lupe says now he is ready for the fight in Buenos Aires.

"So at last we are in Buenos Aires, where Lupe Morales has arrange for Luis Angel Firpo himself to box an exhibition with El Toro. When it is finish Firpo tell the newspapers that El Toro is stronger than Dempsey when Dempsey knock him down six times in the first round of their million-dollar fight in the state of New Jersey. So now El Toro Molina already has much fame in Buenos Aires and he is match to fight Kid Salado, the champion of La Pampa. Outside the arena the poster in very large letters has the name El Toro Gigantesco de Mendoza, the Giant Bull of Mendoza. And under this in little letters, 'Under the Exclusive Management of Señor Luis Acosta.' Every time I see this poster, it make me feel very good. How Luis and his giant have come up in the world! We are making everyone sit up and notice. Two days before the fight there are no more tickets to sell. Out of this great piece of peasant clay I find in the mountain I have make the biggest drawing card in South America."

"Okay, okay, but what happened with Salado? This suspense is killing me," I said.

"In the fight with Salado it is ten rounds to a draw, which is all right for El Toro in his first time. You must remember that Salado is a boxer of much experience who knows many tricks and has three times knock out Lupe Morales. For this fight they pay me one thousand pesos, from which I give Toro five hundred, in spite I am taking all the risk by giving up my circus business and putting all my eggs on El Toro Gigantesco. With the five hundred pesos El Toro is very happy, especially when I take him down to the great shopping center on the Roque Saens Pena. I take him to a tailor who makes especially

67

for him a fine brown suit with red and blue stripes which make El Toro laugh with happiness because he has never own a suit of clothes before. 'You see,' I say to him. 'You trust Luis who takes the place of your father, and everything will happen good for you as I have promise.'

"This is all fine," I cut in, "full of stuff I can use, but we're getting close to chow and we're still down in B.A. Bring me up to date, how you happened to come to town."

"For many many years," Acosta began, "I myself have the dream to come to North America. I cannot bring my little circus. I do not have money enough to go for pleasure. But now that I have El Toro I know it is my opportunity. The people of North America, I have hear, spend much money on the sports. And also they make themselves into big crowds to see something new. My El Toro Gigantesco, I think, if he makes one thousand pesos in one night in Buenos Aires, he can make ten thousand dollars for one fight in North America. The people of North America are—you will excuse me—a little loco when it comes to the number of them who will pay big money to see a heavyweight fight. Lupe remembers from 1923, when he is with Luis Angel Firpo, the night eighty thousand people pay to see our Wild Bull of the Pampas fight Jess Willard when Willard has forty years of age. So I have great confidence that El Toro will make an even bigger success in North America than Firpo who has make in two years here nearly one million dollar.

"When I tell El Toro we will take a boat to North America, he is very frighten. He remembers that the old man of the village says the people of North America do not like the dark skins. The parents of El Toro are of Spanish blood, but there is from the grandfather a little of the *Negro*, perhaps a drop or two. The skin of El Toro is yellow-brown, from standing so many years in the Andean sun. El Toro has heard that in your country they burn the dark ones. He has not the intelligence to understan' that this is not an occurrence of every day.

"So I say to El Toro, 'You know the great house of the de Santos that rises from the highest hilltop overlooking your village and the Rio Rojas. When you come back with me from North America, you will have money enough to build a house of such elegant proportions on the other side of the valley. The people of your village will lift their eyes to the *casa de Molina* and say "Look, it is even greater than the *casa de Santos.*" ' To El Toro this sounds like the biggest of all dreams, but he has learn to have faith in his Luis and to follow him like an obedient son. So at last we are here in North America, four thousand miles from the village of Santa Maria. When you put it in the papers, please write how proud is Luis Acosta to introduce to your great country the first authentic giant to climb through the rope and seek the championship of the world."

"Is that all you have to say for publication this morning?" I said.

"One more little thing," Acosta said. "When you spell my first name please be so kind as not to put an *o* in the middle—just the four letters, please: L-u-i-s, pronounce Looeeess."

"I'll remember," I said.

"Thank you very much," Acosta said. He was an intense, self-centered little man who obviously loved to hear himself tell this story over and over again. His personality was compounded of romanticism and materialism, benevolence, acquisitiveness and too many years of unsatisfied vanity, all resolved now in his paternal and profitable creation.

"And now there is just one little personal matter of which I will ask your advice," Acosta said. "It is the matter of the percentage. When I come to New York I have very much difficulty arranging a match for El Toro. To get a good match, you need to have very often your name in the papers. You must have much money for the build-up. And to fight in the Garden, it is necessary to know Mr. Jacobs."

"How long you been around here now, Acosta?" I said.

"We are now in your country nine weeks."

"You're doing all right," I said.

"Twenty-five years in the circus business," Acosta said. "I learn to fool the people and not myself. I see very quick the American boxing business is closed tight for Luis. It is entirely necessary to have partner who has what you call the 'in.' I meet Meester Vanneman in the gymnasium. From the way he talk he is a manager of very big importance. So I sell him fifty percent of El Toro for twenty-five hundred dollars. But a week later I am astonish to hear that Meester Vanneman has sell forty percent of his share to Meester Latka for thirty-five hundred dollar. Then Meester Latka sends for me. Meester Vanneman cannot get El Toro into the Garden, Mr. Latka say to me. He is the only one who has the connection to do that, he say. So he makes me the offer to buy forty percent of my share for thirty-five hundred dollars also. Only, if you will excuse me for saying, it is not exactly an offer. If I do not give him this forty, Meester Latka says to me, I might as well take my El Toro back to Argentina. It seems he has the power to keep me out of the Garden and any other place. So you see, Meester Lewis, for me the position is very difficult. For all my work I am left with only ten percent. And from this I have promise to pay half to Lupe Morales. I did not come for money only, but to me this is a very great disappointment."

I ran through the stockholders in my mind, eighty percent of the manager's end to Latka, which meant 40-40 for him and Quinn, ten for McKeogh, ten for Vanneman ten for me, five for Acosta, five for Morales, added up to 120 percent. A little complicated. Not as complicated as some of Nick's deals, but well beyond simple arithmetic. Not the kind of equation to figure in your head, unless

70

you had Nick's head, in which case you didn't worry about such mathematical problems as how to cut a pie into five quarters. Either Nick's head or Nick's book-keeper, Leo Hintz. Leo was a neat, serious, middle-aged man who looked like a small-city bank-teller. In fact that's what he had been, in Schenectady, until his thirty bucks a week made him feel that a change was necessary. Unfortunately for Leo the change he decided to make was a slight alteration in some of his entries, a little matter of a digit here and there that added up to an extra zero on the end of Leo's $1560 a year. Not long afterwards, however, Leo's income was suddenly cut to fifty cents a day, which is what the State of New York pays the inhabitants of Sing Sing prison. Leo was a sort of mathematical genius with a natural talent for quiet larceny, the modern highwayman who has swapped his black mask for a green eye-shade.

"Meester Lewis," Acosta continued, showing his small, white teeth in an anxious, mirthless smile, "since you are so *simpático* I will take the liberty to ask a very big favor. Meester Latka likes you very much, so I am thinking perhaps if you will be so kind to ask him please to make a little bigger my share of the . . ."

"Look, *amigo*," I said. "Don't give me that *simpático* crap. In Mexico every time somebody told me I was *simpático* I got taken. Nick likes me because he needs me. But he doesn't need me that much. You've got your deal. If you want my opinion, you were lucky to come out with ten percent. Maybe that's his idea of the Good-Neighbor Policy."

Acosta crossed one short leg over the other, drawing up his pants carefully to protect the creases. He must have been a sharp little business man in Mendoza. Here he was just another peddler. "But ten percent, which I must share with Lupe Morales, is like the droppings of a fly. Especially when it *is* my idea, the big idea of putting boxing gloves on a giant, a conception that will make much money for Meester Latka. He will be grateful, yes?"

"He will be grateful, no," I said. "Now *useful* he understands, but grateful, that's too abstract."

Acosta shook his head in uneasy bewilderment. "You North Americans, you are so direct. You not only say what you mean but you say it immediately. In my country"—he indicated a large circle in the air with his cigarette holder—"we say things like this, instead of"—he bisected his imaginary circle with a sharp downward stroke—"like *that*." He closed his eyes, massaging the right lid with his thumb, the left with his forefinger, as if his head ached. Here he was, four thousand miles from Santa Maria, with only five percent of a dream.

5

WHEN you saw Toro Molina for the first time he was so big you had to focus on him in sections, the way a still camera photographs a skyscraper. The first shot took in no features at all, just an impression of tremendous bulk, like the view a man has of a mountain when he's standing close to its base. Then, as Nick led him into the sun-room, where Acosta and I had been waiting for them, I made an effort to look up at the face which rose a full foot above mine. I felt like a kid in a sideshow peering up at the Tallest Man in the World.

When I stared at Toro that first time the word *giant* that Acosta had been beating me over the head with didn't occur to me at all. It was *monster* that was in my mind. His hands were monstrous, the size of his feet was monstrous and his oversized head instantly became my conception of the Neanderthal Man who roamed this world some forty thousand years ago. To see him move, slowly, with an awkward loping gait, into the sun-room, bending almost double to come through the doorway, was as disconcerting as seeing one of the restored fossils of primitive man in the Museum of Natural History suddenly move toward you and offer a bony hand in greeting. But if anyone were making book on who was the most disconcerted, he would have had to string along with Toro.

Toro acted like a large field animal, a bull or a horse, that has suddenly been lassoed and led into a house. But when he saw Acosta he looked relieved. Acosta said, quickly in Spanish, "El Toro, come over here, I want

you to meet a new friend of ours," and Toro came obedi-
ently, placing himself a little behind Acosta, as if seeking
protection from the pudgy little man who would have
to stand on his tip-toes to tap him on the shoulder. That
brown suit with the red and blue stripes that Acosta had
bought for him in Buenos Aires was pinched in the
shoulders; the pants were tight and the sleeves fell short
several inches above the wrist. Looking at him more
closely as the first shock was wearing off, I remember
having the impression of seeing a trained monkey of
nightmare proportions dressed up like a man mechanically going through his act under the watchful eye of the
organ-grinder. Only in this case Luis Acosta didn't need
an instrument strapped over his shoulder. He played his
own music and wrote his own words and apparently could
grind them out tirelessly.

"El Toro," Acosta said (and even the way he snapped
the name out and paused a moment reminded me of the
way an animal trainer fixes the attention of his beast
before giving the command), "shake hands with Meester
Lewis."

Toro hesitated a moment, just the way you've seen
them do it hundreds of times in the animal act, and then
obeyed. I was afraid it was going to be like putting my
hand in a meat-grinder, but he didn't grasp it very hard,
wasn't sure enough of himself, I guess. Instead it felt like
the end of an elephant's trunk pushing into your hand
when you're feeding it peanuts, heavy and calloused, unnatural, and with a strange massive gentleness.

"*Con mucho gusto,*" I said, throwing six months of
Mexico into the breach.

Toro just nodded perfunctorily. After we shook hands
he stepped back behind Acosta again, looking down at
him inquisitively, as if waiting for the next command.

"Whadya think of him, Eddie?" Nick said. "Think we
oughta start renting him out by floors like the Empire
State?"

74

That was the first of the Toro Molina jokes. This time I laughed, but, oh, how weary I was to become of those jokes about Molina's size!

When Nick made jokes he was feeling good. "Well, did you get everything you want?" he asked me. "Did the little guy talk?"

"To fill a book," I said.

"Hey, that ain't such a bad idea, a book," Nick said. "Maybe one of those comic books. Like this Superman. Know what Superman sells? Eight, ten million copies. At a dime a throw, not bad."

Some day, when they put out a new edition of old Gustavus Meyer's *History of the Great American Fortunes* you may be reading how Nicholas Latka ("illustrious great-great-grandfather of Nicholas Latka III") got his. It may be right in there with the Vanderbilts and the Goulds and the rest of the fancy who knew when to break a law and when to make one.

"Come on out," Nick said. "I wanna show him around to the boys." He nodded toward Toro with a laugh. "Follow me, half-pint."

Acosta leaned over and said under his breath, "Follow him." Toro nodded, in the obedient peasant way he had, carrying out Acosta's imperative literally and walking directly in Nick's footsteps with that slow awkward lope. Suddenly Nick stopped and said, half-kidding, "Tell 'im, for Christ sake, to stop walkin' behind me. Makes me feel like I'm being tracked down by a neliphant."

Acosta translated and Toro must have taken it for censure, for he hurried to catch up with Nick. In his haste, one of his ponderous feet tripped over a lamp wire and he lurched forward, almost losing his balance. He flailed the air clumsily to right himself. He was definitely no Nijinsky. But you couldn't always tell by that. I've seen quite a few flat-footed, awkward fellows look pretty shifty and smart inside the ropes.

"What was that, Eddie," Nick said, "a clean knock-down or just a slip?"

He turned to me with a wink and tapped me playfully on the jaw.

Beth was sitting on the terrace, alone and a little bewildered, for Beth.

"Sorry to be so long," I said. "Everything okay?"

"I'm glad I came," she said ambiguously. "But next time I think I'll let you go alone."

Maybe it had been a mistake to throw Beth in with Nick's crowd. She was a girl who had made an easy adjustment from Amherst to New York, but you didn't have to be a clairvoyant to see that this was a world she never knew and didn't want to know. And yet, in spite of herself, she found herself curiously attracted to all this, as to a sideshow of freaks. She telegraphed me a quick smile with a suggestion of panic in it.

"What are the amenities about the hostess in this party?" she asked.

"Oh, Ruby can take her guests or leave them. I kind of like Ruby."

"She makes me nervous. I haven't been able to talk with her. I tried my best, and it wasn't good enough to take her away from the book she was reading."

I took Beth by the arm and led her over to Ruby, who was stretched out on a lawn couch on wheels. When she looked up at us, I said, "What book you reading?"

She held it up for us to see. "It's the Number One Best-seller," Ruby said. It was one of those eight-hundred-page packages with the cover featuring a seventeenth-century Hedy Lamarr bursting her bodice. *The Countess Misbehaved*, this one was called.

Ruby spent most her time in the country reading novels like this Countess business. I know Nick was rather proud of her intellectual pursuits, the way she went through these books week after week. "We've got a hell of a library out there," Nick had told me. "I'll bet Ruby knocks off three books a week. Remembers what she reads too." So Ruby, who had never exposed her lovely, unlined face to the pressure of literature until she got out in the country and didn't know what to do with herself, had developed an intimate relationship with European history. She could talk with as much authority about the back-stair affairs of the hot-blooded ladies-in-waiting at the court of Charles the First as she could about the marital difficulties of Ethel her cook.

When Ruby wasn't consuming her marshmallow history, she was either driving to church in her station wagon or drinking Manhattans. Her life in the country seemed to break up into those three phases. She was sentimental about her religion and retained a schoolgirl's admiration and sense of responsibility to her devotions. The only thing that would get her out of bed before noon was church services, if her hangover wasn't too bad. The nipping usually started around three. I stayed out there through a week once to get some work done, and Ruby would come down for cocktails every evening with a good three-hour start. An outsider might not have been able to tell the difference. She handled it well enough, but her eyes became very set and moist and, depending on what mood she was in when she started drinking, she usually brought the conversation around to religion or sex, working her way up to the latter by way of Metternich's mistress or Napoleon's sister or some other full-bosomed footnote to history. When this happened she had a way of leaning toward you, talking feverishly with her face closer and closer to yours, which made you feel it could happen if you really tried.

This may be an injustice. Nothing ever happened between us and I wouldn't have been too surprised if Ruby had turned out to be as virtuous as she felt on her way home from church on Sunday morning. I wouldn't have been too surprised if she had turned out to be any or all of the things the gossips had her figured for. Her manner was always composed and ladylike, but there was something about her eyes, black and unusually dilated, which left you with the uneasy impression of a deep, controlled instability.

It was this undefined but vivid impression, I think, rather than anything one could be sure of, that started rumors about Ruby. Felix Montoya, the Puerto Rican lightweight, one of Nick's boys, had told me a tall one about something he claimed had happened while he was out training at the place. Nick has his own gym out there with a ring and nice equipment. Felix was there for three weeks when he was getting ready for his title bout with Angott. What Felix told me is that he had Ruby every night except the week-ends when Nick came down. What Felix also told me is the part I keep thinking about. Felix paid her the highest compliment he knew when he said that her response compared very favorably with the best Puerto Rico had to offer. But it made him very nervous, he said, when, as they lay in her great double bed, she would reach her arm out to the phone on the bed-table and call Nick in New York. Then, while holding Felix to her with one arm but giving him the sign to be as quiet as possible, she would hold a typical wifely conversation with Nick. "Hello, honey. How's everything in the city? . . . What time will you be out Friday? . . . Anything special you want me to get you for dinner? . . . Sure, I miss you, silly. . . . Be a good boy now. . . . Bye-bye, honey."

Of course that's Felix's story, and Felix sleeps with every woman he meets, if you listen to Felix. If he hadn't left his fighting strength in somebody's bed, I didn't know how else to account for the farce he made with Angott. On the basis of Felix's waltz, I was half inclined to buy his story. But that telephone business was too wild to be credible. Yet, I'd slug toe-to-toe with myself in this one-man debate; it was so bizarre that it didn't seem

78

probable that Felix would have the imagination to dream up such a fantasy.

At any rate, no matter where the needle really pointed, Nick was satisfied. If he were to hear these stories from anyone it would have been the Killer, and Ruby was the only woman in the world about whom the Killer observed strict discretion. So Nick still felt as he had when he married Ruby, that this was the smartest thing he ever did. Those were the words he often used to describe it, as if Ruby were a prize member of Nick's stable. And Ruby was a good wife to Nick, always there when he wanted her, warm and gracious as a hostess, well-spoken, beautifully groomed, with plenty of class in her choice of clothes and her way of wearing them, a good girl who went to church every Sunday and read books.

From where we sat we watched the crowd that had gathered on the terrace and the lawn beyond. Nick's partner, Jimmy Quinn, and his wife and Mrs. Lennert, the wife of the old heavyweight champion, were chatting together. Quinn's face and figure, his baldness, his clothes and the way he had of laughing from his belly, are what we have come to expect from too many Irish politicians. In his youth it must have been a strong, aggressive face, but years òf ease and self-indulgence had softened the hard lines with fat and a hearty red complexion, which was really high-blood pressure but gave him the cheery, benevolent look of a beardless Santa Claus. He was ostentatiously good-humored and, faithful to the conviction that all Irishmen are great wits, he was addicted to puns and hoary dialect stories. Quinn's concession to country life had been to remove the coat of his single-breasted, three-button suit, and now he was sitting with his collar open, in white suspenders and white arm-garters that hiked up his sleeves, high-laced black shoes and a snap-brim straw hat. Quinn had just said something intended for humor, for he threw his head back and belly-laughed while the women smiled obligingly. When he caught me looking over he waved affably and said, "How ya, young fella?" with his big vote-getting grin. There was nothing mechanical about the cordiality of Honest Jimmy Quinn. He slapped your back, shook your hand and made you chuckle as if he really enjoyed it. He was one sweet guy, Jimmy Quinn, that's what everybody said, one sweet guy. There was nothing in the world Honest Jimmy wouldn't do for you if you asked him, unless you happened to have the misfortune of being a yid, a jigaboo, a Republican or unable to return a favor.

Mrs. Quinn was a formidable, bosomy lady. She always referred to her husband as "the Judge" because he had had the boys put him up for the municipal bench in the early days when he couldn't afford to carry the Party work without being on somebody's payroll.

By contrast, Mrs. Lennert was a plain, quiet woman who looked more like the wife of a truck-driver or a coal-miner than of a famous pugilist. She didn't drink. She sat patiently with an attitude of polite boredom, only breaking her silence with an occasional, "Gus, a little quieter," or "Paul, not so much noise," as she kept a motherly eye on her three sons, aged fourteen, twelve and eight, who were out on the lawn throwing a softball around with their old man.

Big Gus was a good all-around athlete who had done a little pitching for Newark before he broke into the fight game. Boxing was just bread-and-butter. His real love was baseball. I don't think the Yanks have played a double-header at home for years without Gus and the three kids being up there in their usual seats, behind first base. Gus wasn't the most popular fellow in the sports world because word had gotten around that he would back up from a waiter's check as if it threatened to bite his hand. Gus was a business man. He knew he had just so many fights left in him, so many purses, and he wanted to make sure he had a little more than enough when he settled down to the restaurant business again.

On the lawn Nick was introducing Acosta and Toro to Danny McKeogh, who appraised them sourly, and to the Killer and the little pekinese-faced hat-check girl from the Diamond Horseshoe who had just arrived in the Killer's yellow Chrysler roadster. Acosta kissed the doll's hand and bowed easily to the others. Toro stood uncomfortably at his side. The Killer stepped into a fighting pose and feinted with his left as if he were going to lay one on Toro. Everybody laughed except Toro, who just stood there waiting for Acosta to tell him what to do.

When we sat down to lunch in the formal dining room, with its marble statue of Diana with her bow, I took a quick census that totaled twenty-three of us—a typical Latka Sunday dinner. Nick sat at one end of the table, still in riding clothes, Ruby at the other. Next to Nick were the Quinns who flanked a gentleman who maintained a strict anonymity. Then came Vince Vanneman, Barney Winch and his lieutenant. Farther down were the Lennerts, the Killer, the pekinese, Junior and his tennis partner, Danny McKeogh, then Toro and Acosta, with Beth and me on either side of Ruby. The men had not bothered to put on their coats, and Nick tilted back in his chair as he always did in the office, but if the butler, elegant in tuxedo, felt any contempt for this motley assembly, he hid his feelings behind a carefully cultivated deadpan and served each diner, regardless of posture or grammar, with the impersonal solicitude and excessive formality that mark his trade.

The anonymous gentleman had a thick, shrewd face, with dark, heavy jowls set in a permanent expression of inscrutability. Nick did not trouble to introduce him to the company and he sat silently rolling breadcrumbs. When Vanneman spoke to him it was with an awed deference and without any expectation of response. My first guess, later confirmed, that he was topman in a mob that had muscled in on Nick's racket was based on no more than a hunch. I did learn, subsequently, a little about him. He was wanted for questioning in connection with a murder one of his boys was supposed to have pulled off on the Upper East Side. At one time he had just about cornered the market on first-rate middle-weights and he was still a good man to have on your side if you wanted to get the breaks in the Garden. Just what he was to Nick or Nick to him, it would be healthier not to ask.

"Everything you're gonna eat came right off this place," Nick shouted down the table. "It's all our own stuff, even the meat."

"Your own steer, huh?" Quinn said. He turned to Barney and the other gambler, beginning to laugh already. "Hey, fellers, you don't think Nick would give us a bum steer?" He roared with laughter, looking around at everyone to see that they were with him, then repeated himself and was off again. Toro ate his fruit salad hungrily, keeping his head down like a child who has been told not to intrude on adult conversation.

Nick looked down at Toro and nodded. "You're lucky you don't understand English, kid. The rest of us have to laugh at Jimmy's lousy jokes."

The Killer began the laughter like a claque. Everyone looked at Toro, nodding and snickering. Toro stopped and stared around questioningly. From where he sat, it must have seemed as if they were laughing at him. He pressed his thick lips together and his eyes sought Acosta with confusion. Acosta said a few hurried words in Spanish and Toro nodded and went on eating. I watched his big face work as he chewed. It wasn't the face of Colossus, noble and magnificent. It was essentially a peasant face with soft brown eyes, heavy-lidded, a bulbous nose, a big, sensuous mouth with dark hollows pressing in on either side of it, suggesting some unhealthiness, glandular per-haps, and an elongated jaw. It was a head for El Greco to have painted in his dark, moody yellows, with the model already magnified and distorted by the artist's

82

astigmatism. If he looked up at all, I noticed, he stole quick, furtive glances at Ruby. This was understandable, for Ruby had magnetism in her white diaphanous silk, with back-swept hair and jade earrings swaying as she talked animatedly, half Park Avenue, half Tenth.

"Isn't that a swell book?" Ruby was saying. "I can hardly wait to see the movie. Who do you think oughta play Desirée? I read in Danton Walker where it says Olivia de Havilland. Can you see her as Desirée? Paulette Goddard, all the time I was reading I could see Paulette Goddard."

Beth caught my eye for a second but she didn't say anything. I mean she didn't say any of the obvious things you could have said to Ruby. There was something touching about Ruby's discovery of literature, and Nick's pride in this, that made the easy wisecrack catch in your throat. It was like the Dead End Kid who glides up and down in the gutter crying out in wonder *Look at me, I'm dancin'! I'm dancin'!* For Ruby it was *Readin'! I'm readin'!*

"I'm just nuts about history," Ruby said. "It's so much more interesting than what's going on today. I try to get Nick to read sometimes, but he's hopeless."

"Hey, baby," Nick yelled down from the other end of the table, gesticulating with a big cob of yellow corn in his hand. "Everything under control on your end, baby?"

Ruby gave him an indulgent smile and looked at us apologetically. You had a pretty good idea of what there was between them in that smile and that look. Nick was a wonderful husband, a good provider and still nuts about Ruby. She wished he would begin to get over these crudities. All these books, the decorum of social life, the polished manners of the cavaliers had given her a point of view from which to criticize Nick and his loudmouth friends.

"Look at Ruby," Nick laughed. "She thinks I'm making a bum out of myself in front of Albert." Albert was passing the roast beef around again. Not a muscle in his face betrayed his having heard his name brought into this. As he lowered the big silver platter to Nick's place, Nick said, "Just because I eat with my fingers and don't put my coat on, you don't think I'm a bum, do you, Albert?"

"No, sir," Albert said, and moved on to serve Quinn, who took three more pieces of roast beef and two large potatoes.

"There, whaddya think of that, Ruby?" Nick shouted down the table. "The best-dressed guy in the joint and he takes my side."

Nick knew better than this, a little better than this, but he liked to put the mug act on sometimes to show off for his friends and annoy Ruby. It didn't exactly fit with the clothes, the "class" he always wanted or his attitude toward Ruby. I used to wonder at this at first, but I finally decided why Nick seemed to delight in publicly degrading himself sometimes. It provided measurement by which to judge his progress. For he timed these gaucheries to the moment of his most lordly circumstance, such a moment as this when he sat at the head of a twenty-three-place table, presiding over a lavish feast that would have satisfied the greediest tyrant. "Look," his actions seemed to say, "don't forget that the master of this mansion with the marble statue, the formal butler, his own beef hanging in his own cold-storage plant, is still Nick Latka the hustler from Henry Street."

When we finally managed to get up from the table after an hour of over-eating, Nick came over and put his hand on my shoulder. "Want to talk to you," he said. "Let's go out to the sun-house."

The sun-house was just behind the swimming pool, a circular stucco job with no roof. Inside were sun-mats and rubbing tables. Nick took off his clothes and stretched out on his back on one of the mats. He inhaled deeply, seeming to take sun and air in at the same time. His body had a dark even tan and was in wonderful condition for a man in his early forties. It looked lean and energetic everywhere except at the belly, where there was the beginning of a paunch.

"Tell the Killer I want him," Nick said.

I went out and shouted up to the Killer. He came right away. "Wot's on yer mind, boss?" he said.

"That sun oil," Nick said, "that new stuff I got. What's it called?"

"Apple erl," the Killer said.

"Yeah, rub some on me. And bring an extra bottle for Eddie," he called when the Killer had reached the medicine chest.

The Killer handed me a bottle and began to anoint Nick's chest and shoulders. I looked at the label. "Apolloil" it was called. "This not only gives you a tan but it puts vitamins into yer skin," Nick said. "Works right into yer pores. Real high-class stuff. Put out by the same outfit that makes that toilet water I gave yer." He took another deep, healthful breath. "Now lower, Killer. Pour some down there." He looked at me and winked. "It's supposed to be good for that too," he said.

While the Killer rubbed the oil into Nick's thighs, Nick said, "Well, let's get down to business. Acosta give you any ideas?"

"Well, the way he found him is colorful enough," I said.

"I don't want this long-winded crap," Nick said. "You know the fight business as good as I do. It's show business with blood. The boys who fill the house aren't always the best fighters. They're the biggest characters. Of course nothing helps your character like a finishing punch. But the fans like a name they can latch on to. Like Dempsey the Manassa Mauler. Greb the Pittsburgh Windmill. Firpo the Wild Bull of the Pampas. Something to hit the fans over the head with. A gimmick."

85

"Well," I said, half-kidding, "I suppose we could call Molina the Giant of the Andes."

Nick sat up and looked at me. "Not bad. The Giant of the Andes." He repeated it. "It's got something. We're making money already. Keep thinking."

"You mean this kind of stuff," I said. I ad-libbed: "Up from the Argentine charged the Wild Bull of the Pampas to knock Dempsey through the ropes and come within a single second of bringing the world's championship home with him. Now comes his protégé, the Giant of the Andes, to avenge Luis Angel Firpo, his boyhood idol."

"Keep talking, baby," Nick said. "Keep talking. You're talking us into a pisspot full of dough."

I thought this would be as good a time as any, so I said, "By the way, Nick, Acosta doesn't seem too happy about the split."

"There's a law says he has to be happy?" Nick said.

"No," I said, "but the little guy did put a hell of a lot into this. He really discovered Molina, gambled on him, and . . ."

"You feel so sorry for him maybe you want to give him your ten percent."

Life was much less complicated when you agreed with Nick.

"No," I said, "but . . ."

"How do you like that little grease-ball!" said Nick, a great non-listener when you weren't speaking for his benefit. "He hasn't enough connections to get Molina into a pay-toilet in the Garden. Any more crap out of him and we take him down to the boat and kiss him off."

He rolled over and let the Killer massage his back. "Keep your mind on your racket," he said. "I'll take care of mine."

When we came out, everybody had moved down to the pool. The gamblers were at it again, at a table under the awning. Barney Winch, the fatter one, was finally winning. "Only two," he was protesting to the world. "When I gin, he's got only two. What've I done to anybody I deserve such punishment?" Gus Lennert and the three boys were back on the lawn tossing the ball around. "Alla way, Pop," the youngest one was shouting. Quinn was sleeping in a deck chair with his straw hat pulled down over his face. Junior and his guest had apparently gone back to the court. Beth was in the water, swimming a relaxed crawl. The Killer's little pekinese blonde was lying on the edge of the pool working on her tan. She wore black, modern-shaped sun-glasses and she had untied the bra of her dainty two-piece bathing suit so as to expose to the sun as much of her provocative little body as possible. Danny McKeogh was talking to Acosta. He looked a little more alive since he had eaten, but from where I stood his watery light-blue irises hardly stood out at all from the white of his eyes, giving his face a deathly quality. He was back on his favorite subject, training. He really knew how to train fighters and liked to work them hard.

"When I was a kid the boys were in much better shape," he was saying. "Imagine any of these punks today going thirty, forty tough rounds like Gans, Wolgast or Nelson? They'd drop dead. They don't like to work as hard as we used to, and they haven't got the legs. Too much riding around, taxis, subways . . ."

Ruby was lying in the hammock reading *The Countess Misbehaved*. Who would play Desirée? On the opposite side of the pool a portable radio was blaring loudly, but nobody seemed to be listening to the comic whose formula jokes were punctuated by the feverish applause of an enthralled studio audience.

I wondered where Toro was. I looked around for him, but I didn't see him right away because he was standing so quietly, staring into the lattice archway of the grape arbor beyond the pool. His enormous head almost reached the top of the arch, and with his back to the sun his extraordinary size cast a mountainous image that overshadowed the entire arbor. I wondered what was in his mind. Did these dark ripe grapes evoke the sight and smell of home, of friendly Santa Maria, of his mother and father, of Carmelita, of the cheers that rose from the throats of fellow-villagers when he lifted his wine barrels, of the warmth and security of being born into, working and dying in an isolated, intimate community? Or was Toro's mind computing the conspicuous riches of the Latka estate and dreaming of the day he would return to Santa Maria in triumph to build the castle that would rival the very de Santos villa which the barefooted peasants of his village had always looked up to as the ultimate in luxurious shelter, at least in this life and perhaps in the next?

6

Americans are still an independent and rebellious people—at least in their reaction to signs. Stillman's gym, up the street from the Garden, offers no exception to our national habit of shrugging off small prohibitions. Hung prominently on the gray, nondescript walls facing the two training rings a poster reads: "No rubbish or spitting on the floor, under penalty of the law." If you want to see how the boys handle this one, stick around until everybody has left the joint and see what's left for the janitor to do. The floor is strewn with cigarettes smoked down to their stained ends, cigar butts chewed to soggy pulp, dried spittle, empty match cases, thumbed and trampled copies of the *News, Mirror* and *Journal*, open to the latest crime of passion or the race results, wadded gum, stubs of last night's fight at St. Nick's (managers comps), a torn-off cover of an Eighth Avenue restaurant menu with the name of a new matchmaker in Cleveland scrawled next to a girl's phone number. Here on the dirty gray floor of Stillman's is the tell-tale debris of a world as sufficient unto itself as a walled city of the Middle Ages.

You enter this walled city by means of a dark, grimy stairway that carries you straight up off Eighth Avenue into a large, stuffy, smoke-filled, hopeful, cynical, glistening-bodied world. The smells of this world are sour and pungent, a stale gamey odor blended of sweat and liniment, worn fight gear, cheap cigars and too many bodies, clothed and unclothed, packed into a room with no noticeable means of ventilation. The sounds of this world are multiple and varied, but the longer you listen, the more definitely they work themselves into a pattern, a rhythm that begins to play in your head like a musical score: The trap-drum beating of the light bag, counter-pointing other light bags; the slow thud of punches into heavy bags, the tap-dance tempo of the rope-skippers; the three-minute bell; the footwork of the boys working in the ring, slow, open-gloved, taking it easy; the muffled sound of the flat, high-laced shoes on the canvas as the big name in next week's show at the Garden takes a sign from his manager and goes to work, crowding his sparring partner into a corner and shaking him up with body punches; the hard-breathing of the boxers, the rush of air through the fighter's fractured nose, in a staccato timed to his movements; the confidential tones the managers use on the matchmakers from the smaller clubs spotting new talent, *Irving, let me assure you my boy loves to fight. He wants none of them easy ones. Sure he looked lousy Thursday night. It's a question of styles. You know that Ferrara's style was all wrong for him. Put 'em in with a boy who likes to mix it an' see the difference;* the deals, the arguments, the angles, the appraisals, the muted Greek chorus, muttering out of the corner of its mouth with a nervous cigar between its teeth; the noise from the telephones; the booths "For Out-going Calls Only," *Listen, Joe, I just been talking to Sam and he says okay for two hundred for the semi-final at . . .* the endless ringing of the "Incoming Calls Only"; a guy in dirty slacks and a cheap yellow sports-shirt, cupping his hairy hands together and lifting his voice above the incessant sounds of the place: *Whitey Bimstein, call for Whitey Bimstein, anybody seen Whitey . . .";* the garbage-disposal voice of Stillman himself, a big, authoritative, angry-looking man, growling out the names of the next pair of fighters to enter the ring, loudly but always unrecogniz-ably, like a fierce, adult babytalk; then the bell again, the footwork sounds, the thudding of gloves against hard bodies, the routine fury.

The atmosphere of this world is intense, determined, dedicated. The place swarms with athletes, young men with hard, lithe, quick bodies under white, yellow, brown and blackish skins and serious, concentrated faces, for this is serious business, not just for blood, but for money.

I was sitting in the third row of the spectators' seats, waiting for Toro to come out. Danny McKeogh was going to have him work a couple of rounds with George Blount, the old Harlem trial-horse. George spent most of his career in the ring as one of those fellows who's good enough to be worth beating, but just not good enough to be up with the contenders. Tough but not too tough, soft but not too soft—that's a trial horse. Old George wasn't a trial-horse any more, just a sparring partner, putting his big, shiny-black porpoise body and his battered, good-natured face up there to be battered some more for five dollars a round. There were sparring partners you could get for less, but George was what Danny called an honest workman; he could take a good stiff belt without quitting. To the best of his ringwise but limited ability he obliged the managers with whatever style of fighting they asked for. He went in; he lay back; he boxed from an orthodox stand-up stance, keeping his man at distance with his left; he fought from out of a crouch and shuffled into a clinch, tying his man up with his club-like arms and giving him a busy time with the in-fighting. Good Old George, with the gold teeth, the easy smile and the old-time politeness, calling everybody mister, black and white alike, humming his slow blues as he climbed through the ropes, letting himself get beaten to his knees, climbing out through the ropes again and picking up the song right where he had left it on the apron of the ring. That was George, a kind of Old Man River of the ring, a John Henry with scar tissue, a human punching bag, who accepted his role with philosophical detachment.

In front of me, sparring in the rings and behind the rings, limbering up, were the fighters, and behind me, the non-belligerent echelons, the managers, trainers, matchmakers, gamblers, minor mobsters, kibitzers, with here and there a sports writer or a shameless tub-thumper like myself. Some of us fall into the trap of generalizing about races: the Jews are this, the Negroes are that, the Irish something else again. But in this place the only true division seemed to be between the flat-bellied, slender-waisted, lively-muscled young men and the men with the paunches, bad postures, fleshy faces and knavish dispositions who fed on the young men, promoted them, matched them, bought and sold them, used them and discarded them. The boxers were of all races, all nationalities, all faiths, though predominantly Negro, Italian, Jewish, Latin-American, Irish. So were the managers. Only those with a bigot's astigmatism would claim that it was typical for the Irish to fight and Jews to run the business, or vice versa, for each fighting group had its parasitic counterpart. Boxers and managers, those are the two predominant races of Stillman's world.

I have an old-fashioned theory about fighters. I think they should get paid enough to hang up their gloves before they begin talking to themselves. I wouldn't even give the managers the 33⅓ percent allowed by the New York Boxing Commission. A fighter only has about six good years and one career. A manager, in terms of the boys he can handle in a lifetime, has several hundred careers. Very few fighters get the consideration of race horses which are put out to pasture when they haven't got it any more, to grow old in dignity and comfort like Man o' War. Managers, in the words of my favorite sports writer, "have been known to cheat blinded fighters at cards, robbing them out of the money they lost their eyesight to get."

I still remember what a jolt it was to walk into a foul-smelling men's room in a crummy little late spot back in Los Angeles and slowly recognize the blind attendant who handed me the towel as Speedy Sencio, the little

Filipino who fought his way to the top of the bantam-weights in the late twenties. Speedy Sencio, with the beautiful footwork who went fifteen rounds without slowing down, an artist who could make a fight look like a ballet, dancing in and out, side to side, weaving, feinting, drawing opponents out of position and shooting short, fast, punches that never looked hard, but suddenly stretched them on the canvas, surprised and pale and beyond power to rise. Little Speedy in those beautiful double-breasted suits and the cocky, jaunty but dignified way he skipped from one corner to the other to shake hands with the participants in a fight to decide his next victim.

Speedy had Danny McKeogh in his corner in those days. Danny looked after his boys. He knew when Speedy's timing was beginning to falter, when he began running out of gas around the eighth, and when the legs began to go, especially the legs. He was almost thirty, time to go home for a fighting man. One night the best he could get was a draw with a tough young slugger who had no business in the ring with him when Speedy was right. Speedy got back to his corner, just, and oozed down on his stool. Danny had to give him smelling salts to get him out of the ring. Speedy was the only real money-maker in Danny's stable, but Danny said no to all offers. As far as he was concerned, Speedy had had it. Speedy was on Danny all the time, pressing for a fight. Speedy even promised to give up the white girl he was so proud of if Danny would take him back. With Danny it was strike three, you're out, no arguments. Danny really loved Speedy. As a term of endearment, he called him "that little yellow son-of-a-bitch." Danny had an old fighter's respect for a good boy, and, although it would make him a little nauseous to use a word like dignity, I think that is what he had on his mind when he told Speedy to quit. There are not many things as undignified as seeing an old master chased around the ring, easy to hit, caught flat-footed, old wounds opened, finally belted out. The terrible plunge from dignity is what happened to Speedy Sencio when Danny McKeogh tore up the contract and the jackals and hyenas nosed in to feed on the still-warm corpse.

Strangely enough, it was Vince Vanneman who managed Speedy out of the top ten into the men's can. Vince had him fighting three and four times a month around the small clubs from San Diego to Bangor, any place where "former bantamweight champion" still sold tickets. Vince chased a dollar with implacable single-mindedness. I caught up with him and Speedy one night several years ago in Newark, when Speedy was fighting a fast little southpaw who knew how to use both hands. He had Speedy's left eye by the third round and an egg over his right that opened in the fifth. The southpaw was a sharpshooter and he went for those eyes. He knocked Speedy's mouthpiece out in the seventh and cut the inside of his mouth with a hard right before he could get it back in place. When the bell ended the round Speedy was going down and Vince and a second had to drag him back to his corner. I was sitting near Speedy's corner, and though I knew what to expect from Vince I felt I had to make a pitch in the right direction. So I leaned over and said, "For Christ sake, Vince, what do you want to have, a murder? Throw in the towel and stop the slaughter, for Christ's sweet sake."

Vince looked down from the ring where he was trying to help the trainer close the cuts over the eyes. "Siddown and min' your own friggin' business," he said while working frantically over Speedy to get him ready to answer the bell.

In the next round Speedy couldn't see because of the blood and he caught an over-hand right on the temple and went down and rolled over, reaching desperately for the lowest strand of the rope. Slowly he pulled himself up at eight, standing with his feet wide apart and shaking

94

his head to clear the blood out of his eyes and his brain. All the southpaw had to do was measure him and he was down again, flat on his back, but making a convulsive struggle to rise to his feet. That's when Vince cupped his beefy hands to his big mouth and shouted through the ropes, "Get up. Get up, you son-of-a-bitch." And he didn't mean it like Danny McKeogh. For some reason known only to men with hearts like Speedy Sencio's, he did get up. He got up and clinched and held on and drew on every memory of defense and trickery he had learned in more than 300 fights. Somehow, four knockdowns and six interminable minutes later, he was still on his feet at the final bell, making a grotesque effort to smile through his broken mouth as he slumped into the arms of his victorious opponent in the traditional embrace.

Half an hour later I was having a hamburger across the street, when Vince came in and squeezed his broad buttocks into the opposite booth. He ordered a steak sandwich and a bottle of beer. He was with another guy, and they were both feeling all right. From what Vince said I gathered he had put up five hundred to win two-fifty that Speedy would stay the limit.

When I paid my check I turned to Vince's booth because I felt I had to protest against the violation of the dignity of Speedy Sencio. I said, "Vince, in my book you are a chintzy, turd-eating butcher!"

That's a terrible way to talk and I apologize to anybody who might have been in that short-order house and overheard me. The only thing I can say in my defense is that if you are talking to an Eskimo it is no good to speak Arabic. But what I said didn't even make Vince lose a beat in the rhythmical chewing of his steak.

"Aaah, don't be an old lady," Vince said. "Speedy's never been kayoed, so why should I spoil his record?"

"Sure," I said, "don't spoil his record. Just spoil his face, spoil his head, spoil his life for good."

"Go away," Vince said, laughing. "You'll break my frigging heart."

*   *   *

The bell brought me back from Newark, from Speedy Sencio with his lousy job in that crapper and, I thought, from Vince Vanneman. Then I saw Vince himself coming in. I realized this must have been one of those times when the mind seems to sense someone before the image strikes the eye so that it appears a coincidence when the very man you're thinking about comes in the door. He was wearing a yellow linen sports-shirt, open at the neck, worn outside his pants. He came up behind Solly Prinz, the matchmaker, and gave him the finger. Solly seemed to rise up off the ground and let out an excited, girlish scream. Everybody knew Solly was very goosey. It got a good laugh from the circle Solly was standing with. With the rest of his fingers bent toward his palm. Vince held the assaultive middle finger lewdly. "See that, girls?" he said. "That's what a Chicago fag means when he says he'll put the finger on you." That got a laugh too. Vince was a funny guy, a great guy for laughs, just a big fun-loving kid who never grew up.

Vince came over and ran his hand over my hair.

"Hello, lover," he said.

"Balls," I said.

"Aw, Edsie," Vince pouted, "don't be that way. You've got it for me, baby." He threw his head back in an effeminate gesture, flouncing his fat body with grotesque coyness.

It was another Vanneman routine, always good for laughs. Humor was intended to lie in the margin of contrast between the fag act and Vince's obvious virility. I used to wonder about it.

"Seen him box yet?" Vince said.

"He'll be out in a minute," I said. "Danny's having Doc look him over."

"When you gonna break somethin' in the papers about him?"

"When Nick and I figure it's time," I said.

"Get him, get him!" Vince said. "What are ya, a goddam primmer-donner? Damon Runyon or something? I got a right to ask. I'm a partner, ain't I?"

Edwin Dexter Lewis, I mused, born in Harrisburg, Pa., of respectable churchgoing Episcopalians, nearly two years in the Halls of Nassau with First Group in English and a flunk in Greek, the occasional companion, intellectual and otherwise, of a Smith graduate and *Life* Magazine researcher, an imminent playwright, clearly a man of breeding and distinction—if not of honor. At what point in what I smilingly refer to as my career was it decided that I was to become a business associate of Vincent Vanneman, two hundred and fifteen pounds of Eighth Avenue flotsam, graduate of Blackwell's Island, egger-onner of beaten fighters, contemporary humorist and practical joker.

"This isn't a partnership," I said. "It's a stock company. Just because we both have a couple of shares of the same stock doesn't make us brothers."

"What'sa matter, Eddie, can't you take a rib any more?" Vince grinned, wanting to be friends. "I just thought maybe when you put something in the paper you c'n drop in a line about me, you know, how it was me discovered the big guy."

"You mean how you muscled in on Acosta?"

"I don't like them words," Vince said.

"Forgive me," I said. "I didn't know you were so sensitive."

"What the hell you got on me?" Vince wanted to know. "Why you always try to give me the business?"

"Take it easy, Vince," I said. "I'll give you a nice big write-up some day. All you've got to do is drop dead."

Vince looked at me, spat on the floor, leaned back on his fat rump and opened his *Mirror* to the double-page

97

spread on the Latin thrush who beat up the band-leader's wife when she surprised them in a West-Side hotel.

Behind me a familiar voice was saying, "I wouldn't kid ya, Paul, I've got a bum what'll give yer customers plenty of action. Never made a bad fight in his life."

I looked around to see Harry Miniff talking to Paul Frank, matchmaker for the Coney Island Club. Harry's hat was pushed back on his head as usual and a dead cigar hung between his lips as he talked.

"You don't mean that dog Cowboy Coombs, for Chrisake?" Paul said.

Miniff wiped the perspiration from his lip in a nervous gesture. "Whaddya mean, dog? I'll bet ya fifty right now Coombs c'n lick that Patsy Kline who's supposed to be such a draw out at Coney."

"I need somebody for Kline a week from Monday," Paul admitted. "But Patsy figures to murder an old man like Coombs."

"Whaddya mean, old?" Miniff demanded. "Thirty-two! You call that old? That ain't old. Fer a heavyweight that ain't old."

"For Coombs it's old," Paul said. "When you been punched around fifteen years, it's old."

"I tell ya, Coombs is in shape, Paul," Miniff insisted, but the desperate way he said it made it sound more like a plea than a statement of fact. "And win or lose, he's a crowd-pleaser. Ya know that, Paul. Kline'll know he's been in a fight."

"What about that last one up in Worcester?" Frank said.

"T'row that one out," Miniff dismissed it, reaching quickly into his coat pocket and coming up with a handful of worn newspaper clippings. "Sure, sure, in the record book it's a TKO for La Grange. But read what they said about us in the Worcester papers. Coombs woulda gone for a win if he hadn'a busted his hand on the other bum's head. Here you c'n read about it right here!"

He held the clippings up in front of Paul's face, but the matchmaker waved them away.

"How's the hand now?" Paul said.

"Good's new, good's new," Miniff assured him. "You don't think I'd send one of my boys in with a bum duke, do ya?"

"Yes," Paul said.

Miniff wasn't hurt. There was too much at stake to be hurt: five hundred dollars if he talked Paul Frank into using the Cowboy with Patsy Kline. One sixty-six for Miniff's end. And he could improve that a little if he held out a few bucks on Coombs' share of the purse. Miniff could use that kind of money. The Forrest Hotel, on 49th Street, had put up with Miniff's explanations for six or seven months.

"I'll tell you what I'll do with you, Paul," Miniff said. "If you want to be absolutely sure that your customers get their money's worth before Kline puts the crusher on Coombs . . ." He paused and looked around with a conspirator's discretion. "Come on out'n the sidewalk," he said, "where we can talk private."

"Awright," Paul agreed, unenthusiastically. "But cut it off short."

Relaxed and poker-faced, Paul moved toward the wide doorway with the undersized, over-anxious director of the destiny of Cowboy Coombs hanging onto his arm and talking up into his face, sweating to make a buck.

Toro had to duck his head to fit through the doorway from the locker room. Usually the boys were so absorbed in their own work-outs that they hardly looked up. I've seen the biggest draws in the business working shoulder to shoulder with some fifty-buck preliminary boy and nobody seeming to know the difference. But when Toro came in, everything seemed to stop for a second. He was dressed in black—long black tights and a black gym shirt which would have reached the ankles of the average Stillman boxer. In his clothes, which had been at best haphazardly fit, he had loomed to elephantine proportions. One felt overawed by a shapeless mass. But stripped down to gym clothes, the mass became molded into an immense but well-proportioned form. The shoulders, growing out of the long, muscular neck, were a yard wide but tapered sharply to a lean, firm waist. The legs were massive, with tremendously developed calves, and biceps the size of cantaloupes stood out in his arms. The short-legged Acosta, Danny, and Doc Zigman, the hunchbacked trainer, coming out of the locker room with Toro, looked like stubby tugs escorting a giant steamer. Danny, the tallest of the three, a man of average height, only reached his shoulder.

Toro moved into the big room slowly, shyly, and again I had the impression of a great beast of burden moving along with an obedient eye on its master. Acosta looked up and said something to Toro, and he began to go through warming-up calisthenics. He bent at the waist and touched his toes. He sat on the floor and raised his enormous torso until his head was between his legs. He was limber and, for a man of his size, surprisingly agile, though he didn't perform his exercises with the authority, the zip, of the boxers around him. Again I had the image of an elephant that performs its feats in the circus ring. Slowly, mechanically and with a sullen acquiescence, it executes every command its trainer gives it.

When Danny thought he had warmed up enough, Acosta and Doc prepared him for the ring. They fastened around his neck the heavy leather headgear that protected the fighter's ears and the vulnerable areas of the brain. They fitted over his teeth the hard, red rubberized mouth-piece. With the big sixteen-ounce training gloves on his hands he climbed up to the ring; the bulky headgear and the way the mouth-piece exaggerated the already abnormal size of his mouth gave him the frightening appearance of an ogre from some childhood fairy tale. On the apron, just before climbing through the ropes, he paused a moment and looked over the hundred-odd spectators staring up at him with casual curiosity. He would never face a more critical audience. Some of them were Eighth Avenue *aficionados* who paid four bits to Curley at the door for the privilege of seeing some favorite scrapper knock his sparring partners silly. But most of Toro's audience were professional appraisers who chewed their cigars with cold disdain and sized up the newcomers with shrewd eyes.

"Moliner," Stillman said matter-of-factly, his gravel voice lost in the general hubbub, and Toro climbed into the ring. Toward the ring at a shuffling pace came big, easy-natured George, muttering one of his favorite songs:

"Give me a big fat woman with the meat shakin' on her bones . . .
Give me a big fat woman with the meat shakin' on her bones . . .
And every time she shakes it some skinny woman loses her home."

Danny put his hand on George Blount's heavy black forearm to give him last-minute instructions on how he wanted him to fight Toro, the different points of Toro's style he wanted George to test. I saw the Negro nod with his warm, good-humored smile. "You get it like you want it, Mr. McCuff," George said, climbing up into the ring with the businesslike air of a laborer punching in for a hard day's work.

The bell rang and George shuffled toward Toro amiably. He was a big man himself, six foot two and around two fifteen, but he fought from a crouch, hunching his head down into his thick shoulders to present a difficult, weaving target. He could be a troublesome fighter, though men who knew what they were doing straightened him up with right-hand uppercuts, reached through his short, club-like arms to score with stiff jabs and stopped him with a hard right-hand over the heart

101

every time he flat-footed in for his round-house, haphazard attack. Toro held his long left hand out as Acosta had undoubtedly schooled him and pushed his glove toward George's face in what was supposed to be a jab. But there was no snap to it. George waded in, telegraphing a looping left, and Toro moved as if to avoid it, but his timing was off and he caught it on the ribs. George walked around Toro, giving him openings and feeling him out, and Toro turned with him awkwardly, holding out that left hand, but not knowing what to do with it. George brushed it aside and threw another left hook. It caught Toro in the pit of the stomach, and he grunted as they went into a clinch.

Acosta was leaning against the ropes just below them, tensed as if this was for the championship of the world and not just the warm-up round of a training workout. He shouted something up to Toro in shrill Spanish. Toro charged in, moving his body with awkward desperation, and hit George with a conventional one-two, a left to the jaw and a right to the body. George just shook them off and smiled. Despite the size of the body from which they came, there was no steam to Toro's punches. His fists shot out clumsily without the force of his body behind them. George moved around him again, ducking and weaving in the oldtime Langford style, and Toro tried his one-two again, but George easily slipped his head out of reach of the left, caught the slow right on his glove and drew Toro into a clinch again, tying him up with his left hand and his right elbow, but managing to keep his right glove free to work into Toro's stomach.

The bell rang and Toro walked back to his corner, shaking his head. Acosta jumped into the ring, talking and gesticulating excitedly, jabbing, uppercutting, knocking George down in pantomime. Toro looked at him gravely, nodding slowly and occasionally looking around in bewilderment, as if wondering where he was and what was happening.

The second round was no better for Toro than the

first. George was moving around him with more confidence now, cuffing him almost at will with open-gloved lefts and rights. Acosta cupped his hands to his mouth and shouted, *"Vente, El Toro, vente!"* Toro lunged forward with all his might, swinging so wildly with his huge right arm that he missed George completely and plunged heavily into the ropes. Some of the spectators laughed. It made them feel better.

Just before the round ended, Danny caught George's eye and nodded. George closed his gloves and crowded Toro into a corner, where he feinted with his left, brought Toro's guard down and cracked a hard right to the point of Toro's jaw. Toro's mouth fell open and his knees sagged. George was going to hit him again when the bell rang. Like a man who drops his hammer at the first sound of the whistle, George automatically lowered his hands, ambled back to his corner, took some water from the bottle, rolled it around in his mouth, spat it out, and, with the same easygoing smile with which he had entered the ring, climbed out again.

Toro leaned back against the ropes and shook his head in a gesture of confusion. For two rounds his giant's body had floundered as if it had lost all connection with the motor impulses in his brain.

Acosta was at Toro's side quickly, wiping the sweat from his large, solemn face while Doc Zigman kneaded the long thick neck with his capable fingers. Then, while Acosta held the ropes apart for him, Toro climbed ponderously out of the ring.

"Didja see that big bastard?" a regular behind me said. "Couldn't lick a postage stamp."

"From one of them chile-bowl countries," said his companion. "El Stinkola, if you understan' Spanish."

I turned to Vince, who was quiet for a change. "You sure know how to pick them," I said.

"Don't jump me," he said. "Nick's the brain and he thinks he can build 'im."

"If we could only get them to decide the championship

103

on form like a beauty contest, Toro would walk away with it. But how can a guy who looks so invincible when he's standing still turn into such a bum when he starts moving?"

"Danny can teach him plenty," Vince said.

"Danny's the best," I agreed. "But if Danny knows how to make a silk purse out of a sow's ear, he's been holding out on us."

"Why don't you try talkin' like everybody else?" Vince said. "All them five-dollar expressions, nobody knows what the futz you're talkin' about."

"In other words, you become nobody by self-appointment," I said. "You got something there, Vince."

George was leaning against the wall near the ring, waiting to go another round with a new Irish heavyweight from Newark, just up from the amateurs. I could recognize a couple of lines of the song that seemed to play continually in his head.

> *"Gimme a fat woman for a pillow where I can rest*
> *my head . . .*
> *Gimme a fat woman for a pillow where I can rest*
> *my head . . .*
> *A fat woman knows how to rock me till my face is*
> *cherry red."*

"How do *you* do, Mr. Lewis?" George said when I came up. He always asked it as if it were really a question.

"How do you feel, George?"

"Ready to go," George said. I had never known him to give any other answer. The night Gus Lennert banged him out in one round, when Gus still had something, and George hadn't come to until he was back in his dressing room, that had still been his answer to "How do you feel?"—"Ready to go."

"What do you think of Molina, George?"

"Big man," George said.

George never put the knock on anyone. Anger seemed

unknown to him and the common expressions of derision and contempt in which nearly all of us indulge were never his way. I've often wondered if George hadn't fought all the meanness and bad temper out of his system, if it hadn't all been blotted up in the canvas along with his sweat and his blood.

"Think he'll ever make a fighter, George?"

His black face creased in a wise smile. "Well, I'll tell you, Mr. Lewis. I'd like to have the job of working out with him all the time. I'd like that fine."

As I went into the dressing rooms, George was squaring off with the Irish heavyweight. The big Irish kid fought with a set sneer on his face and neither knew how to nor wanted to pull his punches. He tore into George at the bell and whacked him a terrible punch under the right eye. I saw George smile and work his way into a clinch as the door swung closed behind me.

Inside, Toro was stretched out on one of the rubbing tables and Sam, a bald-headed, muscular fat man was working him over. Toro was so oversized for the ordinary rubbing table that his knees reached the end and his legs dangled down over the side. Danny, Doc, Vince and Acosta were standing around. Acosta turned to me and began a long-winded, excitable explanation. "El Toro, today you do not see him on his best. It is perhaps the excitement of his first appearance before such important people. Since the climate is very different from when he fight in Buenos Aires, I think . . ."

"I theenk," said Vince, exaggerating Acosta's accent, "he's a bum. But don't worry, chumo. We've made a dollar with bums before."

"All right. Out of here! I want everybody out of here," Danny said. The only way you could tell he had been at the bottle was that his voice was pitched a little louder than usual. But it wasn't only the bottle talking. It was Vince, to whom he had given the silent treatment ever since that Sencio affair. It was Acosta, who was getting on Danny's edgy nerves. It was Toro, this Gargantuan excuse for a fighter.

Nobody moved. Danny became petulant. "You think I'm talking for my health? I want everybody the hell out of here!"

Acosta drew himself up to his full five-feet-five. "Luis Acosta is not accustom to such insult," he said. "El Toro Molina is my discovery. Wherever El Toro is, I must be also."

"Nick Latka owns the biggest piece of this boy," Danny said flatly. "I work for Nick. A boy can only have one manager telling him what to do. I don't want to hurt no feelings, but I'll see you outside."

Acosta puffed up as if he were going to do something, but he only bowed his head stiffly and went out.

"That's puttin' the little spic in his place," Vince said.

"I said I want everybody out," Danny snapped.

"Listen, I'm one-a the partners, ain't I?" Vince demanded.

Danny never addressed him directly. "I'm responsible to Nick for his fighters' condition. I don't want to have to tell him people are getting in my way."

The word *Nick* dropped on Vince like a sand bag. "Okay, okay, the bum is yours," he said and sauntered out.

"I think I better go take a look at Grazelli's hand," Doc Zigman said. He and Danny were old friends. He knew the order hadn't been for him. "See you later, Danny."

I started to follow him out, but Danny said, "Stick around, laddie. You handle this boy's lingo, don't you?"

I went over to the table and looked down at Toro. "*¿Puede usted entenderme en español?*" I said.

Toro looked up at me. He had large, liquid, dark-brown eyes. "*Sí, señor,*" he said respectfully.

"Good," Danny said. "I've got a few things I want to

tell him about that workout before I forget. But we'll wait till Sam gets through. A boy's got to be relaxing completely when he's being rubbed down. That's why I ran those guys out of here."

After Sam finished up, Toro raised himself to a sitting position and looked around. "Where is Luis?" he said in Spanish.

"He is outside," I said. "You will see him soon."

"But why is he not here?" Toro said.

I nodded toward Danny. "He is your manager now," I said. "Danny will take very good care of you."

Toro shook his head and, with wide, thick lips in a child's pout, he said, "I want Luis."

"Luis will continue to stay on with you," I managed to say. "Luis is not going to leave you. But to be a success here you must have an American manager."

Toro shook his head sullenly. "I want Luis," he said. "Luis is my *jefe*."

It's time he heard, I thought. Time for this great hulk of an adopted son to learn the pugilistic facts of life. Better to hear them from me with all the cushion I could give them in my limited Spanish than to pick them up from the gutter-talk of Vince and his brothers, as he was sure to do.

"Luis no longer owns you," I said, wishing I had more words with which to make the subtle shadings. "Your contract is divided up among a group of North Americans, of whom Mr. Latka has the largest share. You must do everything he says, just as if he were Luis. He knows much more about boxing than Luis or your Lupe Morales, and can teach you many things."

But Toro just shook his head again. "Luis tells me to fight," he said. "Luis takes me to this country. When we have enough money to build my big house in Santa Maria, Luis will take me home again."

I looked at Danny. "Maybe we better get Acosta back in here to straighten him out," I said.

"Okay," he said. "Call him in. What I got to tell the boy will still be good tomorrow."

I found Luis pacing up and down on the spectators' side of the rings. From the way he looked at me I could see his insides were tied into knots. "Your boy is all mixed up," I said. "He doesn't know what's happening to him. You better go in and get him straightened out."

"You are all jealous of me," Acosta said as we walked back toward the dressing rooms. "You are all jealous because it is Luis who has discover El Toro and so you want to separate us. You do not understand that I am the only one who can make El Toro fight."

"Look, Luis," I said, "you're a nice little guy, but you might as well get straightened out yourself. You can't make Toro fight. There's nobody in the world who can make Toro fight. If anybody comes close, it's Danny, because there isn't a better teacher in the business than Danny McKeogh."

"But Luis Firpo himself has tol' me how magnificent is my El Toro," Acosta said.

"Luis," I said, "on Sunday I listened to all this crap, because I was trying to be polite. And because I hadn't seen this overgrown peasant of yours yet. But now you might as well have it between the eyes. Even your Luis Firpo was a bum. All he had was a Sunday punch. He didn't know enough boxing to get out of his own way."

Acosta looked at me as if I had insulted his mother. "If you will pardon me," he said, "how do I know that is not just your North American arrogance? Actually Firpo has knock out the great Dempsey that day, but the judges did not want to let the title go to the Argentine."

"If you will pardon me," I said, "that is just pure Argentine horse manure."

Acosta sighed. "For me this is very sad," he said. "Always I dream of New York. And from the first moment I see El Toro . . ."

"I know, I know," I cut in impatiently. "We've had all

that." And then I thought of that epic figure of a man and that big trusting puss being cuffed around by an old pro like George Blount and I was seized by the indignity of it and I said, "Goddamit, Luis, you've pulled him out by his roots. You should've left him there in Santa Maria, where he belongs."

Acosta shrugged. "But it was for his own good that . . ."

"Oh, if you will pardon me," I said, "balls! All your life you were a little frog in a little pool. A little frog with big dreams. And all of a sudden you saw a chance, saddled yourself on Toro's back, to make a big splash in a big pool."

"In my country," Acosta said pompously, "such a remark can lead to a duel."

"Don't take me too seriously, Luis," I said. "In your country I hear you like to shoot off guns. Here we just like to shoot off our mouths."

We had reached the door to the rubbing room. "Now go in there and explain to Toro how Danny is the boss," I said. You could almost hear the air rushing from his deflated ego as he went in. He barely nodded to Danny, who joined me in the hall.

"Luis, ¿qué pasa? What happens? Explain to me. I do not understand," I could hear Toro saying as the door closed.

7

I wanted to walk down to Walker's, which felt like the home-team dug-out, but Danny couldn't wait five blocks for the first-one-today. So we ducked into the nearest of the gloomy little saloons that tunnel off Eighth Avenue. Danny was one of those fellows who could want a drink so badly that it was an effort for him to make polite conversation until he had the first couple under his belt. When the bartender set it up for him—Jamieson's Irish was his drink—he tossed it off with a quick, nervous motion of his wrist. After the second, he exhaled slowly in a gesture of relaxation. Danny was a thin, taut man who acted as if his nerve-ends were on top of his skin. Everything he did, the way he drank, the way he smoked his cigarettes, the tic-like way he had of suddenly brushing his cheek with the back of his hand, the way he talked, had this nervousness in it.

The bartender left the bottle in front of Danny and went on about his business. Every few minutes Danny would pour us another one as we talked.

"Well," Danny said, "don't we have a dilly? Isn't he a beaut?" Danny talked a kind of slang that sounds archaic nowadays. He still said things like "dilly," and he was inclined to refer to beautiful babes as "stunners."

Danny studied the bottle reflectively. "If he just didn't know anything, laddie, that wouldn't be so bad. I've started from scratch before. Bud Traynor was green as grass when I first got hold of him, but at least there was plenty of fight in Bud. Even when he was a dub he was always dangerous. But this ox—" he threw off another one—"he's nothing. Just a big clown. Doesn't even have the moxie for it."

He held up his jigger ceremoniously. Danny liked to drink fast, but with a certain amount of formality. "Happy days," he said.

There was some color in Danny's face now. His eyes were brighter. He wiped his mouth with his hand, and said, "You know, laddie, maybe I caught one too many myself, but I still love this damn game. Even with all the things wrong with it, I love this lousy game. Especially when I have a boxer. Give me a new clever kid and let me bring him along nice and slow like I did Greenberg and Sencio and I'm up in heaven. Happy days," he said.

He seemed to be reading the label on the bottle carefully. "Yes, laddie, maybe I let them reach me once too often, but there's nothing I like better in this world than working a corner when I've got a nice smart boy who can do all the things I ask him. That's the way Izzy Greenberg was, up to the Hudson fight. The Hudson fight took something out of Izzy that's hard to describe, but you're just no good without. I was like that myself after Leonard. You look good as ever in the gym and it's not that you've got any geezer in you when you climb through the ropes. It's just that your confidence is shot. Your chemistry, I guess you'd call it. Your chemistry is changed. That's when I quit. I'd probably be singing nursery rhymes to myself right now if I hadn't called it a day. That's why I never regretted that dough I loaned Izzy to set him up in business. I'd rather lose the spondoolicks than see him get his brains knocked loose. Well, happy days."

From the bar radio we had been ignoring came the call of the starter's signal at the track. Danny brushed his hand against his face in that nervous gesture of his and said, "Wait a minute. I've got something good in the first race."

"In the first at Jamaica," the cold, mechanical voice of the announcer said, "they were off at two-thirty-seven.

111

The winner, Carburetor. Place, Shasta Lad. Show, Labyrinth. The Gob ran fourth. Track, clear and fast. Time one minute, twelve and four-fifths seconds. The winner paid seven-eighty, four-ninety and four-ten."

Danny took a tab out of his pocket and tore it in two.

"Who were you on, Danny?"

"The Gob," he said. "He figured to win that one. Dropping down in class. Only carrying a hundred and fourteen pounds. And the distance was right." He reached for the bottle again. "Well, happy days."

"No, thanks, Danny," I said.

"Go ahead, laddie, keep me company."

"I've got to go up and see Nick after a while."

"Hell with Nick," Danny said. "That's the trouble with this lousy game. Too many Nicks in this lousy game."

"Well, make mine a short one," I said.

"Gotta keep me company," he said. "We're in this together, laddie. Hell with Nick. It's Nick that's driving us to drink, with his lousy freaks he wants us to handle. Happy days."

"It's not just Nick," I said. "I gotta meet my girl later too."

"Now that's a different story, laddie. Never let it be said that Danny McKeogh came between a swain and his lady-love. Here, just let me pour you a drop or two, so I don't have to feel I'm drinking by myself."

He held his jigger up in front of him and stared into it. "It's pitiful," he said, "watching a freak like that. That's what it is, pitiful." He reached for the bottle again. "If there's anything I hate to watch, it's a fighter with no ability. It rubs me the wrong way. If they really want to punish me for my sins, they should find a gym for me in Purgatory and lock me up with nothing but bad fighters." He grinned. He had a nice, boyish grin that made you want to smile with him. He was feeling better. The liquor was good for him. If only he could quit now, he would be all right. Nice and easy and relaxed inside, what they mean by that old definition of happiness: the absence of pain.

Doc Zigman came in and took the empty stool next to Danny.

"Draw a beer for my friend, John," Danny called down to the bartender.

Doc never drank anything stronger than beer. He was dark-complexioned, with a high intellectual forehead and a sharp, sensitive face that looked damp all the time. Tuberculosis had made his spine rise to a peak between his shoulders and bent him over as if he were under an unbearably heavy weight. It gave him more the appearance of a scientist or a scholar than a member of the boxing fraternity. Maybe that was merely because he was what I always pictured when I thought of Steinmetz. As a matter of fact, Doc just missed being a legitimate M.D.

The orthopedists tried their best with their rack-like contraptions when he was a kid, and got nowhere. They only succeeded in keeping him out of school long enough to smother his dream of becoming a physician. But what may have hurt more than the "cures" was the progress of his younger brother, now one of the top surgeons in New York. There are hints that Doc is not very welcome in his brother's home, and I suppose it would be easy for a psychoanalyst to trace the feud back to an early trauma. What's obvious is that it's not very easy to subordinate all your ambitions to a kid brother, especially if he is favored with a straight back.

I can't quite remember how he drifted into the boxing racket, but I think it was through a kid from his block— on the Upper East Side—who was fighting main events at St. Nick's. Doc worked like a doctor, more efficiently than a lot of these stuffed-shirts with enough political pull to get themselves appointed medical examiners for the boxing commissions. I've never seen anybody stop a cut like Doc. In those short sixty seconds between rounds his long thin fingers worked medical magic. And it's not only external medicine he knows. He's made a kind of informal study of punch-drunkenness, with a lot of stuff on concussion and cerebral hemorrhages. The strange thing is that, coming up out of a tough block and being around mugs so much of the time, he doesn't sound exactly like Doctor Christian and yet I've heard him talk to doctors about "Parkinsonian syndromes" and "post-traumatic encephalitis," and from the way they listened, he must know what he's talking about.

"Well, what do you think of our Superman, Doc?" I said. "How do you figure him physically?"

"I'll tell you, Eddie, if you want me to level," Doc said. "For one thing, he's got the wrong kind of muscles. Big square muscles. He's done a lot of lifting. There's no give, no speed to muscles like that. He's over-developed in the biceps. Works like he's a little muscle-bound. That's sure to slow him up pretty bad."

"Happy days," Danny said.

"How about his size?" I said. "What makes a guy that big? Can that be natural? Or is that something glandular?"

"Well, I wouldn't like to say without knowing more about his history," Doc said, just the way doctors always sound. "But just from looking at him I'd say he's what the Medical Center boys call 'acromegalic.' "

"Is that bad?" I said.

"Oh, it's not serious," Doc said, "but overactivity of the pituitary gland isn't the healthiest condition."

"Well, what are the symptoms?" I said. "Or the syndromes, or whatever you geniuses call it."

"A hyper-pituitary," Doc said, "well, I'll tell you, a hyper-pituitary usually has a misleading appearance. He is abnormally large, and his nervous system sort of hasn't had a chance to keep up with him. So he's apt to act kind of sluggish, kind of dopey, even though his brain may be perfectly okay. It's like the wires between the brain and the body aren't hooked up very good. The chances are he can't take punishment like the shorter, stockier guys. He'll probably go into shock faster. His resistance isn't too good."

"That's great," I said. "That's just great. I can see myself selling that one to the sport desks. 'See Man Mountain Molina, the Hyper-Pituitary, Argentine's gift to medical science.' "

"Happy days," Danny said.

We had struck bottom on that bottle. Danny held the empty up to prove his plight to the bartender. "John," he said.

The bartender turned to bring up another fifth, and set it in front of Danny. Danny reached into his pocket, brought out a wad of bills and handed it over the bar. "Here, John," he said. "When you close take out what I owe you, keep a fin for yourself, stick the rest in my inside pocket and put me in a cab."

"Yes, sir, Mr. McKeogh," John said respectfully. With an air of solid dependability he ripped a strip off a newspaper, scribbled Danny's initials on it, fixed it to the wad with a rubber band and rang up No Sale to deposit it in the cash register.

The starter's call came over the radio again. Danny leaned forward just a little. "The second race at Jamaica. Off at three-ten and one-half. The winner, Judicious. Place, Uncle Roy, Show, Bonnie Boy. El Diablo ran fourth. The time . . ."

While the announcer gave the rest of the details, Danny reached into his breast pocket and tore up another tab.

"Who'd you have that time?" I said.

"Uncle Roy, on the nose," Danny said. He tilted the fresh bottle. "Gentlemen, happy days."

From the other end of the bar a guy in a shabby suit came toward us with the jerky, telltale gait of the punchdrunk. His pug-nose, ageless face bore the marks of his former profession: the eyes drawn back to oriental slits, a puffy ear, the nose spread over his face and a mouth full of store teeth. He threw his arms around Danny's neck and rocked him back and forth with muscular affection. "Hul-la-la-lalo, Danny, old b-b-boy-oh-b-b-boy-oh-boy," he said. As the words came up out of his throat they seemed to stick on the roof of his mouth and he'd twist his head to the side in a spastic motion to dislodge them.

"Hello, Joe," Danny said. "How you feeling, Joe?"

"Oh s-s-s-s-swell, Danny, oh-boy-oh-boy-b-boy," Joe said.

When he talked you tried not to watch the muscles in his neck that tightened in the effort of human speech.

"Hey, John," Danny called the bartender, "set up a glass for Joe Jackson."

The way Danny said that name you could tell he still liked the sound of it. He had won plenty of fights with Joe Jackson.

Danny lifted his jigger and tapped it nicely against his old fighter's. "Happy days," he said. "God bless you, Joe."

We had to pretend not to notice how Joe spilled a little off the top as his shaky hand brought the jigger to his lips. He set it down with a laugh. "Boy-oh-boy-oh-boy, that sure h-h-h-h, that sure h-h-h-h-, that sure h-its the spot," he said. He started to laugh again, and then he stopped himself with his mouth suddenly twitching to one side—Doc's "Parkinsonian syndrome"—and he started to say, "Hey, Danny, c-c-c-c-c, c-c-c-c-c—" but this one really stuck to the roof of his mouth, caught up there by some shapeless inhibition that stirred in his punished brain.

"Sure," Danny said. "How's a double saw-buck? You c'n owe it to me."

"I'll p-p-p, I'll p-p-p, I'll let you h-have it back Monday," Joe said.

Joe threw his arms around Danny again. "Thanks a m-million, Danny, oh-boy-oh-boy-oh-boy," he said and he lurched back to his place farther down the bar.

116

"He's getting worse," Doc said.

"Looks like he's got a one-way ticket to the laughing academy," I said.

"Were you in the house the night he fought Callahan?" Danny said. "Oh, was he a sweetheart the night he fought Callahan! He was right up there with the gods that night, laddie."

"This must get kind of expensive," I said.

Danny shrugged. "What's the diff? It's only money."

* * *

When I got up to Nick's office, his secretary, Mrs. Kane, said would I please sit down and wait, Mr. Latka was in conference at the moment. Mrs. Kane always managed to make Nick's conferences sound at the very least like a meeting with the mayor to decide the city's budget. Her voice always dipped in a respectful little curtsey when she mentoned Nick's name. She was a plump, happy-faced, handsome woman, who, on Nick's insistence, corseted her body into smartly tailored suits. Nick had kept her with him for years, not only for her personal loyalty but because she was Gus Lennert's sister and the wife of Al Kane, who fought as a heavyweight before Nick put him on the payroll as a collector in Prohibition days. Nick figured that with that kind of a family, Emily Kane would have less trouble beating off the wolves. Nick didn't like that kind of stuff around the office. If he overlooked it in the Killer, it was because the Killer, in addition to his numerous other duties, had the leeway of a court-jester.

While I was waiting, I wandered down to the little office between the reception room and Nick's sanctum, which said "Executive Secretary" on the door. That's where the Killer hung out. The Executive Secretary was lying on the couch combing back his black shiny hair with a comb he always carried in his breast pocket.

117

The Killer was a vain little man, giving to running a comb through his hair so often that it became a kind of nervous habit.

"Hello, Killer," I said, "who's in there with the boss?"

"Copper O'Shea."

"Oh, hell, and she calls that a conference. That isn't even a meeting."

Copper was just one of Nick's legmen. He got that name from the time he put in on the Police Force before one of those seasonal reform shake-ups exposed his connections with the mob. After they took the shield off him, he made it official by going to work for Nick, or rather continuing to work for Nick.

I started into Nick's office, but the Killer waved me back. "Better hold it up. The Boss is pinnin' Copper's ears back. He don't like nobody to go in when he's runnin' off at the mouth like that. I guess he likes everybody to think he's a sweet, lovable character."

"What's the matter with Copper?"

"Aw, the Copper's just dumb," the Killer said. "He don' know howta adjust. That's what the boss says. The Copper's out sellin' the music, see? Well, some of them hash joints, they don' want the music. So Copper hangs one on the guy. He can't get useta the new way a doin' business, see? This burns the boss. The boss just won't buy the rough stuff no more."

The door opened and Copper O'Shea came out. Like so many of his former buddies on the Force, he was a big man with a hard, beefy face and a belly that hung over his belt. "I gotcha now, boss," he was saying. "I gotcha. I gotcha."

Nick looked mean and aroused. "I only say things once. I don't want you to hit nobody. One more time and you're off my list. You know that, don't you?"

Copper knew it. One thing about Nick, he always kept his word. Whether it was a promise to do you a

118

favor, or to fix your little red wagon, Nick always came through.

Nick just turned away from Copper as if he weren't there any more and put his arm around me. "Come on inside, Eddie," he said with a friendly wink, as he led me into his office. "Sorry to make so much noise about that. Those stupid bastards. All they know about psychology is to pull a guy's coat off his shoulders to tie up his arms and then kick him in the nuts. They'd rather make four bits and crack somebody's skull than make a legitimate buck." He took a Belinda from his silver-edged mahogany humidor, and offered me one. "But I got my lesson learned. Why waste all that time and dough messing around with the cops and the courts, putting in the fix here, paying off a guy there, when I can get richer playing strictly legitimate? Just the juke boxes and the gambling, a couple of concessions and some big money fighters—that's all I need to get along. I don't want to hurt nobody and I don't want to wind up with a nice little room on the third tier. I had that already."

A long time ago Nick had done a ten-month stretch on some kind of technical charge, one of those delicious legal fictions our Justice Department dreams up. Except for the temporary inconvenience, his business had been so well organized that he was able to conduct it smoothly right from his cell by means of visiting-day meetings with his lieutenants.

"Nick," I said, "I've got no ambition to share that tier with you. That's why I'm worried. If you stay with your idea of building this Molina into a big-time heavyweight, I think we've all got a good chance of being held as accessories to a murder."

"You mean Molina's liable to kill somebody?" Nick grinned.

"I mean Molina's liable to catch pneumonia and die from the draft he creates missing all those punches. Seriously, Nick, this guy is a joke. I watched him work

119

this afternoon. He hasn't got a thing. All those big beautiful muscles and he doesn't hit hard enough to break an egg."

"Look, Eddie," Nick said, "I want you to go out and sell Toro Molina. Let me worry about how he lives up to his publicity."

"But you don't seem to understand, Nick. I'm telling you this guy can't lick a lollipop. Why, any professional fighter who knows his trade—even old Gus Lennert—is liable to murder Molina. And I mean the coroner stuff, not the kind you read about in *Variety*."

"Molina will get along all right," Nick said.

"I don't see how you figure that."

"You don't have to see how I figure it." Nick was drawing in the slack of affability now. "Just take my word for it. You go out and plug Molina like you never plugged anything in your life. Man-Mountain Molina. The Giant of the Andes. That crap. And leave the rest to me."

"I can get him space," I said. "I can get him all the space you want, as long as he gives us something. I can alibi a loss here and there, but it's only with consistent wins that we really get snowballing."

"We'll have consistent wins," Nick said. And there was something about the flat, quiet way he said it that made me realize for the first time that Toro Molina, the Giant of the Andes, was going to have consistent wins.

It had been done before. Not every fight, but enough to fatten up the record and put them in the money. Young Stribling had knocked out his chauffeur (known variously as Joe White, Joe King, Joe Sacko, Joe Doktor, Joe Clancy, Joe Etcetera) in practically every town in America.

"But even making them look good is a big order for this barrel-lifter. No kidding, Nick, our god not only has feet of clay, the feet are size sixteens and probably flat at that."

"That gives me an idea," Nick said. "Take him down to Gustav Peterson and get him measured for half a dozen pair of special built shoes. Get 'em made up even a couple of inches longer'n he needs. Get the newspaper cameras down to shoot him trying 'em on. Now that's the side of the street I want you to work. Leave the guy's ring work to Danny. He's a master, even if he hates my guts. Leave the opponent's performances to Vince. You and I both know him for a grifter but that's why he's right for the job. The little guy—" He meant Acosta. "Keep him along for the ride. Someone for the big guy to talk to. But lemme know if he makes any trouble."

"He's all right. He means well."

"The hell with that," Nick said. "That don't sell any tickets. The first time he gets in the way we put him on the boat."

He looked at his watch. "Jesus, I gotta go down and try on a suit." He went to the door and called, "Hey, Killer, tell Jock to pick me up in front of the door right away."

"Okle-dokle," the Killer said. "Where we goin'?"

"Down to Weatherill's. For that fitting you was supposed to remind me of."

"Jeez, boss," the Killer said. "I always remember them things. But I don' know, today I got a lot on my mind."

Nick put on his Chesterfield and winked at me. "Hear what he calls it, Eddie, his mind." He made a fake pass as if to let him have one where he lived.

In the rear seat of the Caddy, Nick leaned back against the seat and blew smoke against the roof. From the fitting he would go to the Luxor for a rub and a steambath and then he was meeting Barney and Jimmy for ribs at Dinty's before going up to see the ball game.

On our way to Walker's, where Nick was dropping me off, he said, "You got the pitch now. Anything else on your mind?"

"We haven't even started," I said. "How do you think

I'm going to be able to sell this guy if everybody gets a line on him at Stillman's? All you have to do is take a quick gander and you can see he is from Dixie in B flat with the emphasis on flat."

"Where you want to take him?" Nick asked.

"As far from the wise boys as possible, where the sharpshooters like Parker or Runyon don't knock us off before we get started."

"Ojai," Nick said.

"Where the hell is that?"

"A couple hours out of L.A. We had Lennert up there for the Ramage fight once. Nice quiet joint. Nobody t' bother you. And now that I think of it, the West Coast is the place to interduce the Man Mountain. They don't get too many good fights out there anyway. They probably won't know the difference. They'll go for stuff like this. They matched Jack Doyle, that Emerald Thrush, and Enzo Fiermonte, one of Madeline Force Astor Dick's husbands. Anybody who paid to see that one will do anything."

"L.A. is all right," I said. "I've always wanted to get a look at L.A."

"I've got a couple addresses I'll give you out there," the Killer said. "Stock girls." He gave the wolf call.

"Leave Eddie alone," Nick said. "He's got to work out there." He put his hands on my leg just above the knee and squeezed the tendons until I jumped. It was a sign of affection. "You've got to really sock it to them out there, kid. Take a nice big cut at the ball. Spend dough. Make them sport editors so goddam sick of your Man Mountain Molina that they'll spread him over a page to get rid of you. Make out like you can't get an opponent for him the first month or so because nobody around there's got the guts to get in the ring with him. You know the routine. Then bring somebody out from the East, a nice soft touch that's never been west of the Rockies before, so nobody knows what a dog he is. Then give him the big build-up about how he's come out to California because he's so tough none of the name-fighters in the Garden want to have anything to do with him. Let Vince find you a bum."

I thought of Harry Miniff. This would be a nice way to make a couple of bucks for Harry. "I know a good bum," I said. "Cowboy Coombs."

"Jesus, he still alive?" Nick said.

"Harry was up at the gym trying to sell him this afternoon. He'd be very grateful to make a buck, Harry would."

"How does that Coombs look these days? Will the fans take him serious?"

"The Cowboy has the most menacing scowl of any heavyweight in the business today," I said.

"Okay, I'll tell Vince to get Coombs for us," Nick said. "Come up tomorrow afternoon and pick up the tickets."

"What tickets?" I said.

"The railroad tickets," Nick said. "I'll get you out on the Limited tomorrow night."

"That's kind of on the quick side, isn't it?"

"Why not the quick side?" Nick said. "You tell me the smart boys will begin to catch if we let him hang around here. Then let's make our move fast. I'll have them tickets at four o'clock. So any last-minute business, last-minute humping or anything else you got on your mind, you better get it done tonight."

The shiny black Cadillac dropped me in front of Walker's and cut through law-abiding traffic to shoot out into the clear. Nick carried an honorary badge from the Police Department, so the boys in blue wouldn't give him any trouble.

Things were still pretty quiet along the bar. Just the bums and the strays. The guys who dropped in for the quick ones on their way home from work and the boys who came to spend the evening would be along after a while. Now it was just me and a guy down the bar who looked as if he were studying to be his own worst enemy. The cat that occasionally walked along the bar brushed against him and he patted it absently while staring over the bar with his eyes turned inward in a lonely trance. A couple of ladies of the evening were resting their feet in one of the booths.

Charles set me up with the usual and then slowly wiped the bar in front of me, which was his way of coming around to conversation.

"Well, how are you today, Mr. Lewis?"

"Great, great," I said. "One more and I'll be walking around on my knees."

"I've never seen you take one you don't need," Charles said, which was always the way he put it when a customer anesthetized himself beyond reason.

"Celebrating," I said. "Going to California tomorrow."

"California," Charles said. "I was out there a good many years ago. Worked as helper to a bartender at the old California Athletic Club. That was before you were born."

He drew a couple of beers for two newcomers and came back to his story. "Yes, sir, the California A.C. The greatest heavyweight scrap in the history of the ring was fought at the old CAC. I'll never forget it, sir, if I live to be a hundred. Corbett and Jackson. The greatest white champion and the greatest black champion that ever drew on a glove. Fix the picture in your mind, sir. Black Prince Peter and Gentleman Jim. Marvels of science, both of them. As fast as lightweights they were, and for sixty-one three-minute rounds they went at it that night, four hours and three minutes, enough to kill off a dozen ordinary men. When the referee finally stopped it for fear one of the men would drop dead of exhaustion before he'd holler quit, there was hardly a mark on Peter and Jim for ducking, slipping and catching each other's punches. Like pieces of quicksilver they were, and neither one of them slowed down until they had fought thirty of the fastest and most evenly matched rounds anyone will ever see."

Charles wiped the bar shiny where my glass had left its damp imprint. "And all this before five hundred people for a purse of ten thousand dollars, winner take all." He looked at me significantly. "Today the same fight would draw two million dollars into the ball park. But they weren't fighting for money in those days. All the loser got was his carfare home. It was a sport when I was a lad, Mr. Lewis, a rough sport, but a sport nevertheless. None of these ring-around-the-rosie, you-hit-me-and-I'll-hit-you affairs like these heavyweights are often having in the Garden."

"Just a minute, Charles," I said, "I just thought of something. Wasn't that Corbett-Jackson fight a year or so before the Slavin fight you were telling me about?"

Charles looked off vaguely. "I'd better see what that gentleman wants," he said, leaving me to ponder the problem of how Charles could have been in California a year before he left England.

"Charles," I said, when I finally got him to answer my finger, "how can you lie like that? You never saw the Corbett-Jackson fight."

"It's not a lie, sir," Charles insisted.

"Well, what would you call it?"

"A mere stretching of the truth, Mr. Lewis. I did work at the CAC, in Oughty-ought. And some of the old members were still talking about that fight, arguing who'd've won if they had let it go the distance. One day Mr. Corbett stood right up at the bar himself, when he was champion of the world, and gave me his own first-hand description. 'Charles,' Mr. Corbett says to me, and he's standing there just as close to me as you are, 'Jackson had everything. He could beat any heavyweight I ever saw. Try to box him and he'd out-box you. Start slugging and he'd slug you right back. He was the Master, that black wizard, the genuine Nonpareil.' "

125

"Charles," I said, "you are the truth-stretchingest man I ever met. You stretch it out so far I forget where it started from."

"Dramatic license," Charles shrugged.

I told Charles to put the bottle away because it was beginning to catch up with me and I didn't want to louse up my last night with Beth. I walked back to the Edison thinking about this Molina deal. My mind was already working ahead to the angles. As soon as we hit L.A. I'd get all the sports writers together and toss a party and fill them full of flit. Deaden their powers of integrity and self-criticism. Then slip them a little something to make their readers feel they were getting their nickel's worth. It didn't have to be true.

8

Beth said she would probably be a little late getting away from the office. So I stretched out on the bed with my copy of *War and Peace*. I have been reading *War and Peace* since I was a high-school senior and have now succeeded in getting almost half way through it. It's not that I haven't found it interesting. But it was written on a large *dacha* in Russia before the age of electricity, motor cars or radios, and sometimes I think I will have to approximate those conditions in order to finish it. I read a couple of chapters and then can't find time to go on. When I'm ready to dip into it again, I have forgotten who Marya Dmitrevna is and have to thumb back two or three hundred pages to pick up the thread. If *War and Peace* has given me trouble, it's nothing I blame on the Count or myself. It's more the fault of the Hotel Edison and my room which overlooks Strand's bar and the horse players who usually assemble on the curb under my window. This is far more conducive to reading *Racing Form* and *Ring Magazine* than Russian literature.

I was lying on my bed with my shoes and socks and shirt off and a glass on the floor where I could reach it when Beth came in.

"Hello, honey," I said.

The sweet name only brought a sour expression to her face. She never liked it.

She looked around for a cigarette and I tossed her one from the bed. She came over and reached down to me to light her cigarette from mine. I put my arm around the back of her legs the way I often did.

I could tell from the way she held herself against my arm that something was wrong. That's the way Beth was. Her passion had its irregular tides. One evening she would come into my arms with a wanton hunger the moment the door was shut and the next evening she had to be as carefully seduced as if it had never happened between us before.

"Darling," I said, "don't be like that. I'm leaving for California tomorrow."

"Oh!" Beth hesitated. "Maybe it's a good idea."

My hand came away from her as if it had a mind of its own. "Well, that's a nice loving send-off."

She sat down on the edge of my bed and deliberately snuffed out her cigarette. Beth could hold a pause longer than was comfortable. I knew I was in for it when she began slowly, "Now, Eddie, don't get sore."

She looked at me seriously and seemed to be debating with herself whether she should say any more. I tried to feint her into a new lead.

"Lots of writers go to California."

"To write?" she asked, and didn't wait for an answer. "Let's get things straight, Eddie. I think it's just about time one of us went out to California."

"You mean for good?"

"I don't know yet. I haven't thought that far. All I know is that we're getting nowhere in New York, because, I guess, you won't let yourself think about where you want to go. The trouble seems to be, I'm the only one who has any idea where you're going. You're always stopping somewhere, to have a drink, to make some soft money, to put off what you ought to do. Just starting, never finishing. This fight business . . . You know, when you first told me about it, I was fascinated. It seemed to have something, a force, a vitality that's missing in so many other things. But you were in your early thirties then. Now it's the middle thirties, thirty-five, thirty-six, come November. That's a dangerous age, especially in your job, Eddie. A fighter's press agent at thirty-one is kind of an interesting fella. You can see it on book jackets—newsboy, copyboy, reporter, merchant seaman, fighters' press agent, advertising writer. You know how they always sound. But a fighters' press agent at forty, that's a little sad. At fifty, it's very sad. And at sixty you're a bum hanging around those Eighth Avenue saloons boring everybody with the names of great fighters you used to know."

"You've really got my life laid out for me," I said. "Doesn't sound so bad."

"You can't laugh it off, darling. The midtown bars are full of guys like you. They come to town because they have something on the ball. Look at yourself, you've got some talent for writing, but you're too lazy or too frightened or too tied up to develop it."

"Boy," I said, "it's a good thing I'm pulling out of here tomorrow."

"What'll you be doing in California?"

I told her a little about the set-up we expected to have on the Coast, about the plans for making Molina, the Giant of the Andes, a household word.

Beth shook her head. "That's exactly what I mean. What kind of a job is that for a guy who . . ."

"Who what? Who doesn't have to go begging for assignments from the slicks? Who doesn't want to hang around the fringe and starve a little? Who wants an easy buck—and lots of them—on the chance of salting away enough to sit down and see what he can write some day?"

"Some day! Some day! Eddie, do you want those two words for your epitaph?"

"Well, what the hell's the difference?" I said. "So I sell Molina. Another guy works for J. Walter Thompson and sells soap. Or he writes perfume ads, telling the girls how his particular poppy juice will make every guy they meet want to lay them. Only he uses ten-dollar words like 'enticing mystery' and 'bewitchment of the night.'

129

He probably went to Princeton too. Or Yale or maybe even Harvard. But if you peek under those beautifully starched white cuffs with the delicate monogram, just above the wrist you will definitely see the shackles. Or take that friend of mine Dave Stempel who published that little book of poems when he was still in school, *The Locomotive Dream*—remember, we read it together? —well, he's out in Hollywood writing stinking Class B melodramas. Where's the difference between that and my job with Nick?"

"But I'm not talking about the ad writer with the starched cuffs. Or Dave Stempel. I'm thinking about you. I mean I guess I'm really thinking about me. I'm a big girl now. I'm twenty-seven. It's time I knew the man I was sleeping with. I never know whether I'm going to bed with one of Nick's boys or someone who can think for himself."

I looked down into the loud and garish night of 46th Street. I could see across the street where old Tommy the bartender was leaning on his elbows talking to Mickey Fabian, a gimpy little gnome who gambled his entire disability pension from World War I every month on his judgment of the relative speed of our four-legged friends. Later on, I'd probably wander over and lift a glass with Mickey and hear how they ran for him at Saratoga. They were my guys. Crumbs, some of them, touch artists and no-goods, but still my guys. Maybe that's what Beth meant. It's part of my racket to sit around the various joints enjoying a friendly powder with the boys. The talk is whether Joltin' Joe has got it any more, and was the Commish justified in tying up both those bums' purses after the waltz last Friday night. A fellow gets to like that kind of life. It's no way to live, but he gets to thinking it is and he can't do without it. I wanted Beth and still I wanted to be free to sit around with the boys, if that's the way I felt. That must have been why I never got around to that proposal unless I had had a few, and after I had them and they worked their quick depressive magic, that was when she knew me better than I knew myself.

"I guess I'm one of Nick's boys," I said. "Oh, sure I like to read a book once in a while and I'm not so dumb I can't see how the profit system takes the manly art out behind the bushes and gives it the business. But I'm strictly a saloon man. Every once in a while I like to pick up the checks all around the table and I like to have enough in my kick to pay my tabs. Nick's dough may look a little soiled but they still exchange it for nice crisp new bills at any window."

"What happens after California?" Beth said.

"Don't know yet. We'll have to see how things break. Probably work our way east knocking over the usual clowns."

"So what you'll really be is a barker for a . . . circus freak."

"For Christ's sakes, what do you want me to do, sell my poems on the corner of Washington Square and starve with the rest of the screwballs? For a hundred a week and a slice of the pie—I bark."

Beth rose from the edge of the bed and said with an air of finality, "Okay, Eddie. But I think you sell yourself awful short. I guess you know what you want. I just wish you wanted a little more."

Then she relaxed into her own self a little and put her arms around me and kissed me quickly. "Take care of yourself."

"You too, kid."

"You're sore," she said. "I hoped you weren't going to be sore."

"I'm not sore," I said. "I'm just . . ."

"Write me once in a while."

"Sure, we'll keep in touch."

"Hope everything goes the way you want it."

"I'll be okay."

We looked at each other, probably just a second or two, but it seemed longer. There is always that moment when you seem to be able to see in each other's eyes a flash of the things that might have happened if your cards had been a little better or you had played them differently.

"Maybe this breather is just what we needed," I said. "Maybe we can get married when I get back."

"Maybe," Beth said. "Let's see what happens."

"Swell. Be good, coach."

"Good-bye, Eddie."

"See you, Beth."

I stood at the window and watched her go out onto the street. I saw how the boys instinctively turned for a hinge of the gams as she went past. That trim figure of hers never quite looked as if it should belong with her bright and agreeable but untheatrical face. I stayed at the window until her rapid stride was lost in the crosscurrents of human traffic sweeping over the corner.

I bought myself another drink, but it backed up on me. I lay down on the bed again and tried to get back into *War and Peace*, but the scene and the characters had lost contact with me and the words ran into each other meaninglessly. I went over to the dresser and looked at the other books. A Fleischer's *All-Time Ring Record Book*, a two-bit copy of *Pal Joey*, Cain's *Three-in-One*, the *Runyon Omnibus* and an old marked-up edition of *The Great Gatsby*. I picked up the *Gatsby* and turned to one of the passages I had marked. It was that terrible scene where Daisy, Tom and Gatsby finally bring it out into the open. One of the best damn scenes in American fiction, but I couldn't keep my mind on it.

God Almighty, maybe Beth was right. Who was I? Who *had* she been sleeping with? The reader who marked and studied those lines of Fitzgerald? Or the guy who dished out the hyperbolic swill about Joe Roundheels and Man Mountain Molina? What were they to each other, the reader and the raver? Just two fellows who lived under the same skin, strangers sharing a common roof.

I threw the book down impatiently and started dressing for the street. Toro and Acosta were at the Columbia Hotel around the corner. For need of something to do I thought I'd check on whether everything was set with them for the trip tomorrow night.

The Columbia was one of those innumerable hotels in the Times Square area with the same nondescript street-front, the same lonely people drinking the same cut stuff from the same chromium bars, the same harassed-looking clientele of unlucky horse players, theatrical agents without clients, stage actors without parts and managers of derelict prize fighters like Harry Miniff. The lobby of the Columbia seemed to be full of small, shabby groups addressing themselves in sly undertones to the petty conspiracies devoted to the cause of running down a buck without physical effort.

Toro and Acosta had what the Columbia calls a suite, which was a sitting room not much larger than a phone-booth leading into a small double bedroom.

"Ah, my dear Mr. Lewis," Acosta said when he came to the door and did his little bow. He looked very dapper in his bow-tie and black smoking jacket, with his long-handled cigarette holder and a book under his arm.

"Disturbing you?"

"Please? Oh, no—no, I am just passing the time study-ing English." He held the grammar out to show me.

"This is one language I'm glad I learned early," I said.

"Yes, the verbs—the verbs are very difficult," Acosta agreed. "But you have a fine language. Not so musical as Spanish perhaps, but very virile, very strong."

"That's us all right," I said.

He led me to the most comfortable chair and bowed me into it with the automatic deference of a headwaiter. "Please," he said. From the bottom drawer of the desk he brought forth a half-empty bottle which he placed on the coffee table with a nice little flourish.

"Please, you will have a little brandy?" He touched the bottle fondly. "I bring this all the way from Mendoza."

"Thanks," I said. "I think I'd better pass. I've been on whisky all day, and this is the only stomach I've got."

Acosta laughed the way men do when they don't understand.

"Well, how do you feel about California?" I said.

"Oh, I am very excite—excited," Acosta said. "All my life I have hear—heard of Los Angeles. Some say it is even more beautiful than our own Mar del Plata. And I think for El Toro it will be very good too. He will have a climate more like he is use to. Here it is so *humedo*. Perhaps that is why he has look so sluggish in the ring."

I had said everything there was to say on the subject of Toro's ability that afternoon, so I didn't grab at this one as it went by.

"Where is Toro, by the way?"

Acosta pointed to the bedroom. "Already in the bed asleep. Poor El Toro. Tonight he feel very bad. He feel he has make this afternoon a very poor showing and he has the wish to go home to Santa Maria. I try to explain to him that now with the interest of Mr. Latka and Mr. McKeogh he will make more money than Luis Firpo. But you know how boys are. Now and then they get the homesickness."

"He doesn't really like to fight? He hasn't really got his heart in it, has he, Luis?"

Acosta had a disarming smile. "The killing instinct, he does not have, perhaps no. But with a man of his strength, when Mr. McKeogh has teach him how to punch . . ."

"Does he get this thing very often, the homesickness?"

"Oh, it is nothing," Acosta assured me. "In the morning after a good sleep he will be hokay. I have the same trouble with him back in Mendoza. When we have first come

134

down the mountain from Santa Maria sometimes he just sits in the truck all day long and I know he has the homesickness very bad. I feel very sorry for him, so one day I go to the daughter of a gypsy fortune teller who has a tent down the way and I say to her, 'In my truck is a young man who is very unhappy. Here is ten pesos for you if you will go into the truck and make him happy.' After that I find the two best ways to keep El Toro from this homesickness is to feed him very much—maybe five times a day—for he can eat like a lion, and to give him the frequent opportunity of girls, for *tiene muchos huevos* and his appetite for the *muchachas* is truly magnificent. It is fortunate for me I find this out, for without the girls I think perhaps it is possible that El Toro goes back to his village and closes the door on his big opportunity."

Acosta's shrewd little eyes glowed with self-importance. Oh, it was not so easy as you think to bring this giant so far up the ladder, they seemed to say. I have had tremendous difficulties to overcome. I have had to use my head.

"Since you have the charge of the public relations," Acosta went on, "there is something I will tell you of El Toro which is of course not for the publications. He comes from such a very little village where the people know nothing of the world. So El Toro in the hands of women of experience is like *arcilla* . . ."

"Clay," I said.

"Thank you. My English has improve a little, yes? To explain how little El Toro knows of the world, one day in Mendoza, when we are still with the circus, Señor Mendez is away having new shoes put upon the feet of the bareback horse. That evening just before the performance El Toro comes to me and says he must see the priest right away, to confess the sin of adultery. In all his life he has never commit the sin of adultery. And now he has very much fear that he will never go to heaven. Like all the people of his village, he believes everything of the Church

135

and would rather go to heaven when he dies than lie down with Carmelita in this present life.

" 'With whom do you commit the adultery?' I say to El Toro.

" 'With Señora Mendez,' he says.

" 'Señora Mendez!' I say. 'But why do you bother with such an old one when the fair-grounds are full of willing *muchachas*?'

" 'I did not even want Señora Mendez,' El Toro says to me. 'But she comes into the truck when I am lying down. She smiles at me and comes over and sits on the edge of my cot. She talks to me and strokes my head and before I realize what has happen, I have commit the adultery.'

" 'Do not look so sorry, El Toro,' I say. 'With Señora Mendez you cannot be blame for committing the adultery. Every time Señor Mendez goes into the city for the day, Señora Mendez commits the adultery. Señora Mendez has now almost forty years, and she has been committing the adultery twice a month since she is sixteen. So if it is a sin to be a *contribuidor* to a lady's five hundred and seventy-fifth adultery, it is surely nothing more than the very little tiniest sliver of a sin.' "

"If he pulls anything like that up here," I said, "the public is off him like a shot. We like our heroes to eat wheaties, be good to their mothers and true to their childhood sweethearts."

"You understan'," Acosta said, "I only tell you this now because we are become like one big family."

Just one big unhappy family, I thought.

"I hope I have not make El Toro sound like a bad boy," Acosta continued. "He is only a powerful *joven*—youth with healthy appetites. But I tell you this, since you will have occasion to be with him much in public and perhaps can help to guard him against certain women he will meet who will have interest in him like Señora Mendez."

Siamese twins pulling in opposite directions struggled for possession of my spine. The student of modern Ameri-

136

can writing, of Fitzgerald and O'Hara, had hired out as male nursemaid to an overgrown adolescent pituitary case who allows himself to be seduced by middle-aged bareback riders.

The heat of the night was heavy in the airless room and the walls were too close to each other. Suddenly I had had enough of Acosta with his ungrammatical long-windedness, his charm, which was largely a matter of teeth, and his protestations of benevolence toward El Toro. If Toro had been the victim of seduction, it was a far more radical seduction than the dallying attention of Señora Mendez.

But maybe this time Toro would make it pay. He had the size. Honest Jimmy had the connections. Nick had the money. I had the tricks. And the American people, God bless them, had the credulity. You couldn't blame them entirely. They were a little punchy too. They had taken an awful pasting from all sides: radio, the press, billboards, throwaways, even airplanes left white streamers in the sky telling them what to buy and what to need. They could really absorb punishment, this nation of radio listeners and shop-happy consumers, this great spectator nation. Only like the game fighter who smiles when he gets hit and keeps boring in for more, they were a little more vulnerable for every encounter. Now perhaps, if the winds are favorable (and if they aren't it may be possible to move wind machines up into the wings), they will be swept on to El Toro Molina, the Giant of the Andes, come down from the mountain heights to challenge the Philistines, like Samson, and avenge a countryman's defeat.

"Well, we'll pick you up tomorrow about an hour before train time," I said.

"Hokey-doke," Acosta said. "We will be very please."

From the bedroom came a loud somnolent groan and the sound of a heavy churning of bed-clothes. Acosta went to the bedroom door and looked in. I stood behind him, having a clear view over his shoulder. Toro had kicked off his covers and was lying naked on the bed. The bed was not long enough to accommodate him and a chair had been placed at the end of it to support his feet. This gave an unnatural appearance to the scene. It was as if a tremendous marionette, bigger than life, had been put away between performances. In sleep his face had the set, oversized features of a dummy's head exaggerated for comedic effect.

And I thought, here we are planning his career, patterning his life, taking him to California, matching him with Coombs, surrounding him with managers, trainers, fixers, press agents, and yet he has never been consulted. I could induce the people of America to love him, hate him, respect him, fear him, laugh at him or glorify him, and yet I had never really spoken to him. What were his preferences, his feelings, his ambitions, his most intimate hungers? Who knew? Who cared? As soon ask Charlie McCarthy whether he would object to doing two extra Saturday performances. Toro had been put away for the night. When Jimmy and Nick and Danny and Doc and Vince and I were ready to pull our particular strings in a co-ordinated effort, the Giant of the Andes would be made to bend his massive torso through the ropes; another tug and his hands would go up in the stance traditional to pugilists for five thousand years; and then he would be guided through the motions calculated to please the cash customers who put their money down to see what is technically supposed to be an exhibition of the manly art of self-defense.

Restlessly Toro rolled over on his side and muttered something in Spanish that sounded like *Sí, sí, Papá, ahora, ahorita*—yes, yes, Father, now, right away. How many thousand miles was Toro from the Columbia Hotel? What little task had his father given him, so trivial and everyday and yet so deeply cut into the section of the brain that never sleeps, that keeps working on like an automatic furnace in a dark, sleep-ridden house?

138

Perhaps Papa Molina had told Toro to carry the completed barrels out and set them in front of the shop. Toro might have been sitting down to midday *comida* with his brothers and was wolfing his third helping of *pollo con arroz*, while his father, wiping the hot sauce from his mouth with his sleeve and patting his belly indulgently, was saying, "All right, my boys, a good meal for a good day's work. Now back to the shop."

Outside, the street was full of people for whom midnight is noon. Broadway was charged with their insomniac energy. Just as in a protracted visit to a hospital one often begins to feel symptoms of illnesss, so on Broadway in the early A.M., caught up in the restless over-stimulated going-and-coming, you suddenly find your second-wind and your eyes snap open in exaggerated wakefulness. So I turned west off Broadway, heading for the row of shabby brownstone houses between Eighth and Ninth Avenues where Shirley's place was.

Shirley lived on the top floor, in one of those flats which turn out to be surprisingly comfortable after you've climbed the dark narrow stairs that look as if they should lead to a tenement. She had the whole floor, two bedrooms (with coy little boy-and-girl dolls perched at the head of each bed) a living room, a small barroom and a dinky kitchen. It wasn't set up as a place where men came to have women. It was really a kind of informal call house, with the girls going out to work. Only once in a while, if he were someone Shirley had known a long time, a fellow could use the extra bedroom. The other part of Shirley's business moved over the bar that usually kept busy until after the good people had punched in for their morning work. The shades were always drawn in that little room and the lighting was so discreetly low that I still remember the oppressive sense of decadence that came over me one morning when I thought I was leaving there around four and came out to face the blinding, accusing daylight and the sober, righteous inhabitants of an eight-A.M. workaday world.

I was admitted by Lucille, the dignified colored maid. From the barroom I could hear Shirley's Capehart, her prize possession, playing one of her records: Billie Holiday, with Teddy Wilson on piano behind her, singing, "I Cried For You." It was so dark in the little room that at first all I could see was the glow of customers' cigarettes and Shirley behind the bar, with a drink in her hand, smoking one of her roll-your-owns. She was wearing something long, cut low in front and zipping all the way up the side that was either an evening gown that looked like a fancy housecoat or the other way around. She was singing along with Billie:

> "... I found two eyes just a little bit bluer,
> I found a heart just a little bit truer."

When she saw me she said "Hello, stranger," and gave me the big squeeze. She was feeling good tonight.

The record changer had dropped on another Holiday, the slow and easy "Fine and Mellow," and Billie's voice, lowdown and legato, belonged in the room.

> "Love is like a faucet . . .
> It turns on and off . . .
> Love is like a faucet . . .
> It turns off and on . . ."

In the loveseat by the window a statuesque blonde with a face that would have been beautiful if it had been less frozen was trying to fit into the arms of a runty Broadway comic. Sitting on the floor with his back against a chair was a big, fine-looking Negro. In the chair, running her hands through his hair, but not getting much of a play from him, was a white woman in her late or middle thirties who looked like one of those lushes who come from very good families with plenty of lettuce. As she reached down to embrace the Negro, she brushed her drink off the arm of the chair.

Like any fastidious hostess, Shirley glared. "In about

140

three seconds," she said to me in an undertone the woman should have been able to hear if the flit hadn't stopped up her ears, "I'm going to give that lush the brush."

Leaning over the radio was a slender Latin girl with an unexpectedly beautiful face. "She's my new girl," Shirley said when she saw where I was looking. "Seems like a nice kid."

We had had a talk about Latin girls once and she knew I thought they were the only ones who went into this business without losing their basic love for men or their enthusiasm for the act of love. Anglo-Saxon professionals, as a group, are a sullen, miserable lot who dispatch you with business-like efficiency or cold-blooded bitterness.

"Come here, Juanita," Shirley said. "I want you to meet an old friend of mine.

"Isn't she something?" she said, as we shook hands. Juanita looked down in embarrassment. She patted the girl's hand fondly. "Have a drink, dear?"

"Coca-cola," the girl said, making it sound Spanish.

While Juanita's eyes were hidden in the glass, Shirley nodded toward her and then raised her eyebrows in a quick questioning gesture. I shook my head. Juanita was obviously an admirable girl, but she wasn't what I had come for.

"How about a little gin? I'm leaving for the Coast tomorrow and I want to try and get even. This is strictly a business call."

"Come into my parlor," Shirley laughed. "You're just in time to pay my bills for the month."

I pulled the oil-cloth off the kitchen table while Shirley got some cold chicken from the icebox.

I dealt. Shirley picked up her cards and said, "Oh, you stinker."

"Sorry dear," I said. "I feel mighty tough tonight."

"Want some beer with the chicken?"

"Mmmm." My mouth was full of chicken. "Damn good chicken."

"I fried it myself. No one else ever gets it crisp enough for me."

Shirley played her hand skillfully and caught me with nine.

We laughed. I was beginning to feel better. I always picked up around Shirley. She generated an atmosphere of health and—yes, security. It was strange after all these years in New York that a gin game in Shirley's kitchen with cold chicken on the table and a beer at my elbow was the closest thing to home I had found in Manhattan.

Half way through the next game, Shirley said quietly, "What gives with you and my rival your last night in town?"

"Oh, hell, I don't know. I'm loused up over there."

"Feel like talking about it?"

Shirley seemed to be paying more attention to her cards than to my troubles, but she always had a knack of listening in a kind of detached, almost disinterested way that made it easier to go into things like these.

"I guess this Molina thing is kind of the pay-off," I said. "She wants me to quit the business. Hell, I know it stinks. Just between us, I know Nick's deal doesn't smell like a rose. But at thirty-five you don't start over so easy. I like to see the ready coming in every week."

"How is three?" Shirley said.

"I'm dead," I said. "Twenty-nine. That puts you over, doesn't it?"

"A blitzeroo," Shirley said. "Well, that's the phone bill. Now I have to go after the rent."

I thought she wasn't even listening, but after she made her first discard, she went back to where I had left it, as if there had been no interruption.

"I'll tell you one thing, Eddie, love can't take any kind of a punch at all. If this chick of yours don't like the fight business and you think the business is for you—well, maybe the girl is smart to knock it on the head right there."

"You wouldn't do that," I said.

"Don't be too sure. This fight crowd can lead a lady a hell of a chase. Too much of this sitting around with the boys. The wives and the girl friends don't get much of a shake. I'd never tell nobody else but you, Eddie, but this town damn near loused up Billy and me. If I hadn't been with that sonofabitch—God rest his soul—since I was fifteen I sure in hell would have hit out for Oklahoma."

Like everyone else, I had heard something of the highs and lows in Shirley's relationship with the Sailor, but she had never brought it up before and I had never pressed her. But my leveling on Beth seemed to have loosened something that had been fastened tight inside her.

"You know Billy was a wild kid. He drank a lot before he started boxing serious. I guess we both did back in West Liberty. We were a couple of crazy punks. Every time I read of some kid and his babe robbing some guy who picked 'em up on the road, I think that could've been Billy and me. Billy wanted things awful bad. And I was so stuck on him I would've done anything he said. If he hadn't turned out to be able to get things with his fists, God knows what would have happened to us.

"But one thing I'll say for Billy in those days, he never played around. It wasn't till he hit this town and got to be a name at the Garden and fell in with those creeps who have connections with the clubs. I felt like jumping out the window the first time it happened. It was the night of the Coslow fight that everybody said was going to be such a tough hurdle. Billy won it without even getting his hair mussed. I never went to his fights because I didn't want to see anything happen to him, but I listened on the radio, which was almost as bad. Well, after I hear 'em counting Coslow out I get myself all fixed up because I think maybe Billy wants to celebrate. It turns out he's got his own ideas about celebrating. He doesn't come in till around six in the morning. He stinks of whisky and the smell of another woman is still sticking to him. Next evening when he wakes up it's, Baby forgive me, I'll never do it again. Six weeks later he takes the championship from Thompson in five, and I get the same shoving business all over again. After a while, I got to dreading Billy's winning another fight. Finally he's signed with Hyams and he won't listen to anybody about training—tells Danny McKeogh to duck himself—thinks he can mix fighting with funning around. I guess you remember the Hyams fight. Hyams busted his nose and cut him bad under both eyes. If the referee hadn't stopped it, he probably would've killed Billy. Billy was almost crazy, he had so much guts. Well, that night Billy comes home right after the fight. I keep him in bed for a week and he won't let anybody else come near him but me, not even Danny. And he's just as sweet and loving as a little baby.

"After that I swear to Jesus I used to actually pray that Billy would get licked. Because every time he got licked it was the same thing. He'd come home just as meek as a lamb and I'd have my Billy-baby all to myself again. I'd put cold compresses on his swellings and I'd wash the cuts and read the funnies out loud to him. I know it sounds screwy, but I swear I'd hate to see him get up out of bed."

As she talked, something Willie Faralla told me fell into place. Willie had taken an awful shellacking from Jerry Hyams in the Garden and Willie's state of mind was even worse than the way he looked. So he decided to drop up to Shirley's place and have a little fun. As soon as Shirley saw him with that bad eye and his lip split down the middle, she put him right to bed. She doctored him all evening, and at last, when everybody had gone home, she had climbed into bed with Willie and let him sleep with his head on her breast. Willie stayed there for almost a week, he said. "And the funny part about it was, it was all for free."

Willie was a good-looking kid, and he figured that

Shirley just went for him in a big way. Well, a couple of weeks later Maxie Slott gets flattened in a semi at the Garden and he has heard about this Shirley deal from Willie. So he decides to try it. Now Maxie is short and chunky and has a face he could rent out to haunt houses, but Shirley takes him right to her bosom just like Willie, waits on him hand and foot and practically lives in bed with him for a week. And this, to Maxie's amazement, is also for free. After that, any battered, beat-up pugilist who could even crawl up the three flights checks in at Shirley's. No matter how busy she is, she always has time to bathe an ear or bring down a swollen eye. And though there isn't a day goes by that she doesn't get invited by the best, the only men Shirley ever goes to bed with for love are beaten prizefighters.

Not only for free, as Willie had put it, but really for love, for love of a mean little sonofabitch from West Liberty, Oklahoma, who only belonged to her when he was too bloodied and too ashamed to be seen in public. And Shirley would love him as long as she lived, though sometimes he appeared in the form of the tall, lean Faralla and sometimes in the form of the short, squat Maxie Slott.

"Hey, look at the time," I said. "I've got a big day tomorrow. I mean today."

"You can't take any more, huh?"

"I know when I'm licked, chum. I'm throwing in the towel."

"Okay, take another beer out of the icebox. I'll see what this little visit cost you."

It came to forty-two dollars. "I wish you weren't going to California," Shirley said. "My favorite pigeon."

She walked me to the door. "This Molina you're working with, he's not exactly sensational, is he?"

"How do you know? Someone up from Stillman's tell you?"

"No, nobody told me—not even you. That's what

made me wonder. Usually you sell your boys like you thought I was Uncle Mike."

"Well, you've got to promise to keep this under your hat or down your neck or wherever you hide your secrets, but this Molina might give a third-rate lightweight a hell of a battle. But don't say anything. Because I'm going to have him breathing down the champion's neck."

"All I know is what I read in the *Mirror*," Shirley said.

"Thanks, Shirley, be a good girl."

"Not too good or I'll starve to death." She kissed me on the cheek. "And stay away from those movie stars."

I slapped her fondly. "I'll say one thing for us, we have the sexiest platonic relationship in town."

Usually when you get off a train in L.A., you expect that gag about how hard it is raining in sunny California. But this time it was only a light summer drizzle. I would have been glad to get off in a hail storm. Four days and three nights cooped up with this team could seem like a long time. I shared a compartment with Danny; Vince and Doc had another; and Toro and Acosta a third. George Blount, politely Jim Crowed, had an upper out there with the common people. Danny never gave Vince any time at all, and Vince certainly wasn't a fellow I'd pick to be marooned with, either. Luis studied English and told any strangers who would listen long enough about his great discovery of El Toro Molina. Danny and I stayed in our compartment, nipping most of the time, sleeping as late as we could in the morning to shorten the ride. Among the things we settled was who had the best claim to be called the greatest all-time heavyweight, an honor we arrived at by a complicated rating system that included points for hitting power, boxing skill, ability to take punishment, fighting spirit and all-around savvy. That is the kind of thing that begins to happen to you on a train. We came out with Jim Corbett on top and Peter Jackson right behind him. The quietest man in the party was Toro, who sat at the window day after day, looking out at the country phlegmatically, never saying anything. Once, as we roared through the great grazing lands of Kansas, I dropped into the seat beside him and said, "Well, what do you think of it?"

"Big," Toro said. "Like the pampas."

The day before we got in, when the setting sun was coloring the surrealist southwestern landscape spectacularly, I noticed Toro sitting with a pad propped up on his knees, with his head bent intently toward something he was drawing. I dropped into the seat beside him to see what he was doing. He didn't even look up. His mind was focused down to the point of his pencil, all the way down to Santa Maria. For the paper was full of rough, half-doodled sketches of village scenes, the bell in the church tower, an uneven row of peasant houses perched on a hillside below a great castle-like mansion that dominated everything below it. And on another hill, on the opposite side of the village, Toro was drawing another great house, even larger. I knew this must be the house Luis had promised him, the dream-castle in Santa Maria. The surprising thing about the drawings was that, although they were the most casual kind of pencil sketches, they were not the childish scribbling I would have suspected. They were three-dimensional and revealed a definite sense of form. I watched his heavy-featured face as he added little finishing touches to the sketch. Like everyone else, I had assumed that Toro was just an overgrown, retarded moron. But the drawings made me wonder.

When we pulled into the station I looked around for the cameras, for I had wired ahead to alert the local press on the arrival of the Giant of the Andes. L.A. isn't much of a newspaper town, for all its sprawling size, with only two morning papers, the *Times* and *Examiner*. The *Times'* sports editor was an old elbow-bending partner of mine, Arch Macail, with whom I had covered lots of fights before that non-understanding M.E. caught up with me. So I figured Arch would give us a break. Both papers had their men on the platform all right, but we had a little competition from another athlete, with whom we had to share the spotlight, an All-Mid-West high-school quarterback who was coming out to play for Southern

Cal, from whom, he had boyishly confided to me on the observation platform one afternoon, he had received the best offer, including a four-year scholarship for his girl.

The photographers got their picture of Toro holding Acosta up on one arm and waving the other hand, with a silly grin on his puss. Then the boys wanted one of Toro carrying Acosta and Danny, but Danny wouldn't play. "Leave me out of this malarkey, laddie," Danny protested. Danny didn't buy this high-pressure stuff.

But Acosta looked into those lenses as if they were the eyes of a long-lost love. It was a big moment for little Luis, his first public recognition. Vince wasn't exactly camera shy either. He made sure he got his fat face in there, with his arm around Toro's waist, grinning up at him, the first time I had seen him throw the boy a friendly glance. Toro seemed neither pleased nor surprised by the reception. He just played it unself-consciously and deadpan, as if being greeted by newspaper photographers happened every day. You had to like the big guy. A man his size behaving as shyly and reticently as a child in a strange house isn't easy to hate.

"What's the pitch on this big joker?" a young, pudgy-faced reporter asked.

"He just won the South American heavyweight title," I improvised. "He's ready to meet anybody in the world, including the champion."

"Who's he gonna fight here?"

I figured we'd save the Cowboy Coombs announcement and blow that up to another story. So I said, "Anybody the local promoters can get to fight him. We bar nobody."

"What're the immediate plans?"

"To get some of your California sunshine and fresh air. That's the reason we came here, because Doc Zigman, the trainer, says it's the healthiest climate in the world."

That wasn't Eddie Lewis with his lightest touch, but it couldn't do us any harm. L.A. papers always have a little space for visitors loving up their climate.

"Will he be training in town or . . ."

"Ojai," I said. "But we don't want the fans to come up there for a while. We know there must be thousands anxious to see him, but I wish you'd tell them we'll let them know when we're open to the public. Toro's just been through a grueling South American campaign, and, with all this traveling, he needs a good rest."

I figured this would keep the sightseers off our necks till Danny had a chance to smarten him up a little.

"Any chance of Molina's fighting Buddy Stein out here?"

Stein was the best heavyweight developed on the West Coast since Jeffries. The boys who know had told me he had the hardest left-hook since Dempsey. Nobody in California had been able to stay with him more than five rounds. If there was a heavyweight alive we didn't want for Toro, it was Buddy Stein.

"We will fight Stein anywhere, any time," I said. "In fact, we're so sure we can take Stein, we'll fight him winner take all."

Stein was pistol-hot, so I thought we might as well cut ourselves in on some of his publicity. It wasn't quite as rash as it sounded because I had it straight from the Garden office that Kewpie Harris, Stein's manager, didn't want any part of any more West Coast fights. Stein was ready for New York, where the money is, and Kewpie wanted either a shot at the championship or an outdoor fight with Lennert and a fat guarantee.

The young reporter scribbled our challenge down on the back of an envelope with a weary, skeptical obedience. Suddenly he turned to Toro.

"You think you can lick Stein?"

"¿Qué?" Toro said.

Acosta talked to him quickly. "The man asks you if you are sure you like California," he said in rapid Spanish.

"Sí, sí, estoy seguro," Toro said.

150

"Did you get that?" I said. "Yes, yes, I am sure."

Toro was beginning to draw a crowd. "Hey, lookit, there's Superman," a little kid said.

"Let's get out of here," Danny said. "I want to get up to the hotel and take a bath."

"Drop up around six, boys," I told the reporters. "We're having a little tea party."

On our way down the platform we passed the All-Mid-West quarterback. "Well, it's a funny thing how I happened to choose Southern Cal," he was telling reporters. "Y'see, I want to be an architect, and one of my coaches— I mean my teachers—told me the best school of architecture in the country is out here at Southern Cal."

When we reached the Biltmore, Vince told George to take the cab down to the Lincoln, on Central Avenue, in L.A.'s Harlem. I think George was getting the best of it, at that.

"Sorry we've got to break up this way, George," I said.

"Don't worry about this boy, Mr. Lewis," George said. His eyes looked as if they were laughing and his whole body shook with a chuckling that came up out of his belly. But I had the uncomfortable feeling that his laugh was on us.

The cocktail party is America's favorite form of seduction, arranged by press agents, full of gin and bourbon, paying off in news-space. The plot is always the same. Come up to my room and have a drink. And whether the object is physical passion or getting your client's name into the headlines, the method is standard: to weaken their resistance with let-me-pour-you-another-one, until they open their arms or their columns to you in an alcoholic daze. Of course there will always be some ladies, and members of the working press, who bounce back regularly after each seduction, holding out their empty glasses, eager to sacrifice themselves again. Often the girls are nice girls and the representatives of the press are good men who had some talent and some standards once upon a time.

The little tea party we threw in our suite at the Biltmore to introduce Toro to the local sports fraternity followed all the rules. Columnists who arrived as skeptics were ready to take my word for it after an hour of the amber. There was only one who gave me any trouble, a lank, dyspeptic-looking fellow from the *News*, the afternoon tabloid, Al Leavitt, who ran a column called "Leveling with Leavitt." He took his work seriously. "I'll wait and see this guy before I buy him," he told me. "I've never seen an oversized heavyweight yet who could get out of his own way. Back in the Seventies there was a guy called Freeman, seven feet tall and three hundred pounds, and he couldn't punch his way out of a paper bag."

A historian yet! In every town you hit, there's always one jerk like that, the natural enemy of a press agent, the guy with integrity.

"Write anything you want, Al," I said, pouring him a drink, because in this business you've got to like everybody. "But remember the farther out on a limb you get the sillier you'll look when Toro comes through the way I know he's going to."

Leavitt gave me a slow, knowing smile. But the rest of the boys were willing to play. I latched Acosta onto Joe O'Sullivan, who ran the *Examiner's* fight column. Luis gave him the full treatment, the whole 7000 miles from Santa Maria to L.A., at three words a mile, and Joe bought it for a Sunday feature. Charlie King, who ran a little weekly magazine for the fight fans called *Kayo*, sold at the arenas on fight nights, promised us a front-page picture and a full-column plug. Lavish Lew Miller, who covered fights for the *Times*, passed out, and I had Toro pick him up like a baby and put him to bed. Everything worked out fine. It was a good party. We were off to a good start.

In the morning we hired a car for the drive up to Ojai, all except Vince who was staying in town to work out details of the match with Nate Starr, the matchmaker for the Hollywood Club.

Ojai turned out to be a long valley, full of fruit trees and lots of other kinds of trees I never learned the names of. Mountains rose steeply on both ends of the valley, like the head-and-foot-boards of a giant bed. If you were a country lover, Ojai had it. Its air was the kind you breathe in deeply and hold in your chest, feeling yourself growing healthier every second. We had a couple of cottages at a rich-man's health camp which catered chiefly to business executives who took it into their heads to work a couple of inches off their paunches, and motion-picture directors taking four weeks off to get back into shape to start another picture. The lay-out was just what we needed: a good gym, an indoor and outdoor ring, a steam-bath, good rubbers and plenty of room for road work.

After everybody had unpacked, Danny called the group together on the porch of his cottage and laid down the law. He looked business-like and athletic in his gray flannel pants, old blue sweater, boxing shoes and baseball cap.

"From here on," he began, "we quit kidding around. I'm in charge as of now. You, Acosta, if there's anything he can't savvy, tell him in your own lingo. Molina, this is your schedule. Up at seven. Roadwork, six or eight miles, alternately running and walking as fast as you can take it without getting exhausted. Then a shower and a brisk rubdown. No monkey business on the road. I'll usually be along with you to show you how I want it. Breakfast at eight sharp, as many eggs as you want, but no pancakes or soft foods. That's out. After breakfast a long rest. You'll walk a mile or so before lunch. After a light lunch, you sleep for an hour and then begin to limber up. Shadow boxing and a couple of rounds of

153

sparring with George come next. Then a session on the light bag and another on the heavy bag, practicing the punches I'll show you. Then about fifteen minutes of rope-skipping and some calisthenics. Doc'll give you the ones I like best, exercises that'll loosen you up, get you to move around a little faster. No other kind of exercise is worth a damn. Then you'll get on the table for a thorough rubdown. You'll rest from three to five and then take a long walk. Supper will be at six. After supper you can take it easy for a couple of hours. Cards, anything you like. Then a mile walk and lights out at nine-thirty. No liquor. No eating between meals. No women. That's it. Any questions?"

Only Acosta spoke up. "Eight miles a day? I think this is too much for El Toro to run. Since he already is very strong."

"Look, Acosta," Danny cut in, pronouncing his name with an R on the end, "get this in your head once and for all. Strength has nothing whatever to do with it, at least the kind of strength Molina's got. It's speed, headwork, timing, even with the big fellows. Those big, bulging, weight-lifting muscles of his will just get in the way."

Acosta said nothing. The eager, glowing face with which he had first told me his story was glum and disappointed now. Only occasionally, as at the station when the cameras were trained on him, did he show any of his previous animation. The big dream of bringing Toro to America in triumph was rapidly losing its quality of personal achievement for him.

That afternoon they let Toro off easy with a brisk two-mile run. Danny asked me if I wanted to go along, but I told him I wasn't quite ready for suicide yet. Climbing on and off a bar stool was exercise enough for this athlete. Danny always accompanied his fighters on road work. It certainly was one for Ripley. How a guy of his age and his habits could pace a healthy young athlete for six miles was one of the mysteries. Either

Danny's guts were made of reinforced steel or an alcoholic diet is not as injurious as its detractors claim it to be. Except for a slight middle-age bulge at the waist, Danny's figure was still lithe and athletic. He ran easily, with a relaxed, springy motion, which was like the movement of a gazelle compared to Toro's heavy lumbering behind him. George followed them, jogging along in a way that made it look as if it were no effort at all.

When they came in, about fifteen minutes later, Danny and George were still running easily, but Toro was all in. He seemed to be favoring his right leg. So Doc put him right on the table and looked him over. "Here it is," he said, fingering Toro's enormous calf. "Just a little Charley. I can rub it out in a few minutes." His long, skillful fingers worked Toro's taut leg muscles. "Better take it easy on running him for a while," Doc said as he worked. "Y'see, these muscles of his are knotty from all that lifting. They go into a Charley easy. They don't slide over each other like you need 'em to in running and boxing."

"What's Nick Latka trying to do to me?" Danny said. "See how much I can take? All that weight and no legs."

"It is perhaps the change of climate," Acosta suggested. "El Toro is not use . . ."

"Shut up," Danny said.

He hadn't had a drink all day and his face looked drawn. I knew sooner or later Acosta was going to get on his nerves. Danny left Doc to finish rubbing out the charley-horse and went back to his cottage to smoke a cigarette. I followed him. He drew on his cigarette a couple of times and crushed it out impatiently. "Son of a sea-cook," he said. "All my life I wanted a good heavy-weight, and what do they send me? A big oaf with no legs."

That evening after supper I took a stroll with Toro and Acosta. We walked slowly along the edge of an orange grove. The valley heat still hung in the air. The large, rose-tinted moon was a fifth carbon of the close, hot sun that had beat down on us all day. I walked quietly half a pace to the rear of them, and after a while they began to talk to each other frankly, as if they had forgotten my presence, or perhaps that I could understand. In Spanish, I noticed, Toro wasn't nearly the halting, inarticulate ox he seemed in English. He was able to express himself clearly and with considerable feeling.

"You did not tell me the truth, Luis," Toro said. "You told me I could make much more money and not work so hard as I must in Santa Maria. But to train like this man wants of me is much harder than I have ever worked for my father. And I do not like it as well."

"But the work you do in Santa Maria you must do all your life, until you have perhaps sixty or seventy years," Acosta argued. "Here you must work very hard, it is true. But when you have boxed one or two years you will have enough money to live like a lord in Santa Maria the rest of your life."

"That I could be back in Santa Maria right now," Toro said. "Even without the money."

"You must not talk like that," Acosta scolded. "That is a very bad way to talk. After all I have done for you, to bring you to this country, to put you in the hands of such important managers. How many poor village boys would like to have your opportunity!"

"I would let them have my place, with much pleasure," Toro said.

"But you do not understand," Acosta said, a little impatiently. "None of them have your magnificent physique. This is what you were born for. It is your destiny."

When I got back to the cottage, George was sitting outside on the porch steps by himself, half singing, half mumbling a song that seemed to have no end.

Doc was inside, sitting at a little desk in the front room, his deformed body hunched intently over something he was writing.

156

"Catching up on your fan mail, Doc?"

Doc turned toward me, slung a thin, angular leg over the arm of his chair, and took a half-smoked cigar from his mouth. "Aw, I'm just making some notes."

"What kind of notes, Doc?"

"Pathological," Doc said, "I guess you call it."

"About punch drunks?" I said.

"That's right. Case histories of punchy fighters. There hasn't been much technical stuff written about it."

"How many really wind up punchy?"

"Well, maybe half the guys who stay in over ten years, but I'd only be guessing," Doc said. "You see, Eddie, the trouble is, nobody's made a scientific survey. Lots of boys are wandering around cutting up paper dolls and there isn't any kind of medical record. Every case I hear about, I write it down in my notebook. Maybe some day I'll do something with it."

"Why not try to put it in an article?" I said. "It'd make a damn interesting piece."

Doc rubbed his damp, high forehead reflectively. "Not without that M.D.," he said. "I know what doctors think of laymen who write books on medicine. If there's anything I don't want to be, it's one of those loud-mouthed quacks with a few fixed ideas. So I'll just stick to my goddam fight racket and let my brother write the books."

He took out a handkerchief, mopped the perspiration that seemed to be constantly on his face and turned back to his notes.

Danny was inside on the bed, studying *Racing Form* with a pencil in his hand and a half-empty bottle of Old Granddad on the table beside him.

"Help yourself, laddie," he said.

"No thanks, Danny," I said. "I'm in the desert for a week. I do this to myself once every year. It's like banging your head against a stone wall. Feels so good when it stops."

Danny reached for the bottle and raised it to his lips.

"I was on the wagon when I had Greenberg and Sencio. I stayed on it pretty good when I had Tomkins too, bless his black heart. But I'll be split down the middle if I'll come off the stuff for a big muscle-bound lummox of a weight-lifter."

He set the bottle down on the edge of the table, so that it threatened to fall at the slightest vibration. Danny absorbed his liquor so well that you had to watch for things like that to realize how far along he was. He returned to the *Form* studiously and encircled one of the names.

"Something good for tomorrow?"

"I'm just checking workouts and speed ratings," Danny said. "Then if they post one of the horses I've spotted, I bet him."

"Your system work?"

"There's only one system that works, laddie. To know who's gonna win."

"What do you play it for, Danny? What's in it for you?"

"Oh, I don't know. Same reason you put salt on your eggs, I guess. Spices things up a little bit." He reached for the bottle again. "A weight-lifter! At my age I get a weight-lifter!" His mouth went to the bottle with desperation.

Danny slept it off in the morning, something he never did when his mind was on his work, but Doc put Toro through his paces. Toro did everything he was told, but there was none of the zip and spring of a man whose body likes to move. His rope skipping was awkward and heavy-footed, with the rope constantly catching on his ungainly feet.

After lunch Danny gave Toro some exercises on the light bag, and then, with the heavy bag for a target, he began to give him pointers on the jab. "I claim a man can't even begin to call himself a professional boxer until he can jab," Danny said. "A good stiff jab throws your opponent off balance. When he's off balance he's a better target for your other punches. The jab isn't just waving your left hand in the other guy's face. You've got to step into your jabs, springing off your right toe and going forward on your left, like a fencing motion or a bayonet thrust. It's all the same idea, straight from the shoulder, with your body behind it always keeping 'em off balance. Like this."

Danny faced the bag, bouncing on the balls of his feet, and even when he wasn't actually moving his body undulated with a weaving, shifty motion, automatically prepared to slip inside a straight right or snap away from a left. His jabs bit sharply into the bag and he recoiled so rapidly into position again that it all became one motion. Then he called George over and demonstrated on him. George allowed the jabs to connect with his face, rolling with them slightly to absorb the shock, but at the same time letting himself be hit hard enough for Toro to be able to see the effect. Then, with George still the target, Danny told Toro to imitate him. Toro lurched forward, drawing his left fist back before pushing it out ineffectually toward George's jaw.

"Never draw back on a punch," Danny said. "That's what you call 'telegraphing.' And you lose part of your force."

Toro tried again. His enormous fist floated slowly into George's face. Danny shook his head dismally and led Toro back to the heavy bag. With his legs spread apart, Danny stood behind the bag, doing his best to transfuse a few drops of his ring wisdom into this dinosaur.

"Mr. Lewis," George said, "you gonna be careful who the big boy fights?"

"Oh, we'll be careful," I said.

"That's good," George said. "He's a pretty nice fella. I wouldn't want to see him get hurt too bad."

"He won't get hurt," I said.

I went over to Danny, who was demonstrating the left

jab in shadow boxing now. "Danny, I'm going into town," I said. "Anything I can do for you?"

Danny wiped his forehead and took a look at Toro. "Wait a minute," he said. "I'm going in with you." He called over to Doc, who was sitting on a bench, reading the papers. "Keep him working on the bag for a while. George can show him what I mean. Then move him around the ring for ten-fifteen minutes, no punches, just feeling things out with George. Then give him some good stiff exercises, as much as he can stand. Try to keep him up off his heels on the rope-skipping. I'll be back some time in the morning."

"Okay," Doc said. "Say, Danny, if you see one of them outa town newsstands, see if you can pick up a New York paper."

"The Giants are still hanging on," Danny said. "What more do you want to know?"

"A guy likes to keep in touch," Doc said.

"Learn to relax, Doc," I said. "This is a vacation spot. Make like you're on a vacation."

Doc had a way of smiling that always made me sad.

As we drove out of sight of the camp, Danny said, "Laddie, I just had to get out of there for a while. There's nothing drives me nuts like trying to teach a man with no ability. And with that other little guy babbling Spanish at my elbow all the time, I feel like I'm going off my noodle."

"Think you can get him to go through the motions of looking like a fighter?"

"Aw, I don't know. I guess I can teach him one or two little things. But I don't want to think about it till I get back there in the morning."

When we turned off Ventura Boulevard, where the unadorned, rural gas stations begin to give way to more elaborate lubratoria with an unmistakable Hollywood influence, Danny gave me the address of a barbershop on Cherokee Avenue.

160

"But you just had a haircut, Danny."

"This is the address of a fella who will take a bet for me," Danny said. "I guess I get clipped one way or another, laddie."

After I dropped Danny off, I went up to our rooms at the Biltmore and got to work. I was making out a list of people I had to call when Vince came out of the bathroom in his pajamas.

"Hi ya, lover?" he said.

"Hello."

Vince said, "Everything's all right with Starr. We're matched with Coombs the 26th of next month. That gives you plenty of time to goose the people, doesn't it, lover?"

"Jesus, six more weeks in this town!"

"What's the matter with this town, honey?" Vince said. "You should see the poontang down in this cocktail lounge every night. Like shooting fish in a barrel." He broke wind noisily. "Did you say something, dear?" He pulled the seat of his pajamas away from his beefy rump and disappeared into the bedroom again.

I settled down to the phone and the business of selling my product. I got Wicherley's Clothes for Men to outfit Toro from head to foot in return for the plugs I promised to give them. I arranged with a furniture store to build an extra-size bed for Toro which I planned to photograph as it was carried through the Biltmore lobby. I sold the Western editor of a national weekly supplement on the idea of a two-page spread, comparing Toro's physical measurements with those of Hercules, Atlas and the giants of antiquity. The angle was to reach out beyond the sports pages, beyond the fight fans to the great public of curiosity-seekers. For lunch I took Joe O'Sullivan to Lyman's, where, after the second highball (padded to four on the expense account), I confided the important news that we were considering either Buddy Stein or

Cowboy Coombs as the first West Coast opponent for Toro Molina.

Next morning the item headed his column as a scoop. Coombs wasn't as well known to West Coast fans as Stein, O'Sullivan wrote, but he was a strong, experienced heavyweight who had fought the best in the East. This no one could deny. The only detail O'Sullivan had omitted was that he had invariably been on the catching end of all these fights with the best in the East. He had had plenty of experience in the ring, all right, mostly discouraging.

Stein or Coombs, Coombs or Stein. The sports writers kicked that one around for a week or so. When we had pushed this as far as it would go, we got a nice fat two-column for the announcement that Toro Molina, the Giant of the Andes, undefeated champion of South America, would have as his first American opponent none other than Cowboy Coombs, that formidable campaigner who was such a favorite with the fans along the Atlantic Seaboard, a great crowd-pleaser who had been forced to come west because no ranking New York heavyweight would risk his reputation against him.

"Among his many fistic achievements," the article drooled, "Coombs can boast of fighting a draw with the great Gus Lennert." The Lennert fight had been a draw, but it was nine years ago, back in the days when Coombs at least had the vigor of youth, when he had caught Lennert on one of those off nights that every fighter has. But fortunately the people who read the stuff had neither record books nor long memories, and the guys who wrote the stuff liked the color of our Scotch and our chips. All except Al Leavitt, who had a crack in that column of his about how apt Molina's first name was, since it meant bull in English. "It is interesting to note," wrote Leavitt, "that throwing this kind of bull is not the same sport practiced so enthusiastically in Latin countries. Mr. Eddie Lewis, on tour with Bull—sorry, Toro Molina, is a skill-

162

ful exponent of the Northern variety." Well, the hell with Leavitt. He was only one voice in this wilderness. He was the sort of fellow who comes to your cocktail party, drinks up all your liquor and then goes away and writes as he pleases. No loyalty. No principles.

I devoted the rest of the day to making the people of California Molina-conscious. I dusted off some old gags, pinned Toro's name to them, and phoned them in to some of the boys who had come to our cocktail party. I picked out the most imposing photograph of Toro to use on the posters. I had mimeographed sheets made of Toro's life story, with a tabulation of his physical measurements from the size of his skull to the circumference of his little toe. I had a girl come in and start a scrapbook of all the Molina items from the newspapers I had begun saving the day we hit town. And the funny thing is, as I glanced through the first few pages of this book, with the big picture of Toro lifting Acosta off the train, and the Sunday feature on how Luis discovered Toro lifting barrels in Santa Maria, I had a real sense of achievement. Whether what I had done was true or not, or whether it would ever do anybody any good was no longer my concern. Filling up that scrapbook had become an end in itself, like stamp collecting. That's what made it so easy to do, what almost sucked me into believing that so good a job was good in itself.

10

When the sun began to sink down behind the squat, ugly architecture of downtown Los Angeles, I began to think of some way to spare myself another social session with Vince. I had sat out the previous evening with him in the Biltmore cocktail lounge, and though the hunting was as effortless as he had said, I wasn't ready for indiscriminate mating yet. Beth's bitter words were still in my head. Damn it, I was making a living. I wasn't robbing anybody; the lies I told were just ordinary American business lies like everybody else's lies. They didn't do too much harm. What did she want of me? What was she being so goddam righteous about? If there's anything I can't stand, it's a righteous woman. Of the hundreds and thousands of eligible and relatively willing females in the city of New York, why did I have to pick on a dame who wanted to elevate me? Because you wanted to elevate yourself, a small voice hiding in one of the creases of my mind answered. It wasn't just her body that made me go for that New England stray. I liked to think so because it gave me less to worry about. But the first time I talked to her, I had a hunch that she wanted to elevate me, make me amount to something. It put me on my guard right away. I remember thinking there was something physically exciting about a girl who could be that pleasant to look at and still make so much sense. But I wanted her on my terms.

The first time I talked to Beth, all those numbers in the little phone books turned into dogs. They were nice dogs, pretty dogs, from Pomeranians to Russian wolfhounds,

164

but I didn't want them any more. I wanted Beth in a way I had never wanted any woman before. I wanted to enter not only into her body but into her mind, and the satisfaction of one seemed to intensify the satisfaction of the other. Beth gave me a sense of where I was and where I stood in time, and if my job with Nick was like a jail, a comfortable, cushy jail, but still a place of confinement, Beth was my contact with the outside world, who brought some of that world to me each visiting day. It was her world and, out here, it seemed as if it ought to be mine. Beth was my safety valve. And now the valve was shut. I was left to sweat in my own steam.

Vince came out of the bedroom, still in his pajamas. He had slept until one o'clock and then had his breakfast sent up. Now that the match was set, there wasn't much for Vince to do until Miniff arrived and they got together to work out the fight. He had really caught the gravy train this time.

"You know I've been thinking . . ." he said.

"An obvious exaggeration," I said.

"All right, wise guy," he said. "But I didn't get where I am with my beautiful body."

"Where are you?" I said.

"In the Hotel Biltmore," he said. "Room eight-o-one and two. Where the hell are you?"

"In limbo," I said. "The Hotel Limbo. And I don't even know the number of the room."

"You're working too hard," Vince said.

"Well, between us I guess we do a day's work," I said.

"Don't worry about this party." Vince pointed to himself indignantly. "If I don't take care of my end, all them fancy words of yours add up to double-o." He took his pajama top off and bent his soft belly as he tried to touch his toes in a half-hearted gesture of calisthenics. "Jesus," he said, "I'm slipping. Can't even touch my toes any more." He straightened up slowly and put his hands lewdly under his breasts, which were heavy with fat.

"Stop staring at me, you naughty boy," he camped in a falsetto and laughed.

"Go get some clothes on, goddam it," I said. "This is an office. Anybody's liable to come in."

"I know what's the matter with you, lover. You wanna keep me all to yourself."

"That's where you're wrong," I said. "I want to keep you all to yourself."

"All to myself," Vince said. "My old man told me never to do that."

"Go get your clothes on," I said.

Vince hesitated and then decided to be friends. For the first time in his life he had a first-class ticket on a fast express and it might pay to get along with the other passengers. "Okay, chummo. I was only kiddin'."

Vince retired to the bathroom. I had to get away from him. I thought of Stempel. I hadn't bothered to get in touch with him yet because I didn't know where he was any more. He had come out for MGM; I remembered that. So I called there and the girl who said *"Metro-Goldwyn-Mayer"* had never heard of him, but she passed me on to the one who said "writers" who told me that Stempel hadn't worked there for several years. Then I thought I remembered having seen his name on a Warners' picture and I called there. Yes, Mr. Stempel had worked there, but not in the last six months. Why didn't I call the Screen Writers' Guild? The Guild secretary had a record of every writer employed in Hollywood. I could reach Stempel at National, she said. National, it didn't seem possible. The author of *The Locomotive Dream*, one of the bright young hopes of my generation, was employed by the studio that specialized in blood-and-thunder Westerns. For me it was almost like discovering that the writing credit on *The Lone Ranger* was Thomas Mann. But anyway I made the call. Yes, Mr. Stempel had been on the lot. "He was checked out this afternoon," I was told. No, the Studio was not allowed to give out any personal numbers.

By this time I had to see Stempel. I had to find out what had happened to Stempel. In desperation I picked up the phone book, on the improbable chance that he might be listed. And there it was, easy as falling off the wagon, David H. Stempel, 1439 Stone Canyon Rd. CRestview 6-1101. One minute later I was talking to Stempel himself, his voice sounding exactly as high and boyish and enthusiastic as when I had seen him last.

"For God's sake, Eddie Lewis! From what cloud bank have you descended? Hop in a cab and come on out here."

As I taxied up through the streets of Los Angeles, which resembled small Middle-Western cities laid down side by side for miles and miles, I thought of Dave Stempel, David Heming Stempel, and what a demigod he had seemed back in the days when he was first reading his work in progress to us. David Heming Stempel could not have been better cast for a young epic poet if he had been picked out of the actors' directory by an experienced casting director. He was a big man, well over six feet, with that rare combination of size and delicacy. His eyes were light blue, quick to smile and yet intense, and he had a long, slender profile.

After dropping out of school I didn't see Dave again until I ran into him several years later, in Tim's on Third Avenue. He was only a year or two out of college then and *The Locomotive Dream* had made him the most talked-of young poet in America. This had been the first volume of a trilogy he had planned on "Man's inexorable struggle to conquer the Machine," as the dust-jacket had put it, and the second volume, *The Seven-Jewel Heart*, had already been announced for "early publication." That night, when I asked him what was new with him, he threw back that magnificent head of his and said, "You know I've always been curious to see what a real mythical kingdom looks like, so I'm going out to Hollywood for a couple of months. See if I can't smuggle out a little of their mythical money. My projects have become an awful strain on those Guggenheims. So I thought it might be an amusing idea to let Metro-Goldwyn-Mayer provide me with a fellowship."

That had been fifteen years ago. For half that time at least, Stempel's publishers had continued to announce the "imminent publication" of *The Seven-Jewel Heart*. I know because I kept watching for it after having practically memorized *The Locomotive Dream*.

My cab turned in at a large medieval-looking stone house. A maid led me through the cold, high-ceilinged living room to a cosy paneled little bar which had nothing to do with the style of the house.

"Eddie Lewis," Stempel said, as if our meeting had a real significance. "My Lord, you've changed, Eddie."

My first impression of Dave was that he hadn't changed at all. The face was still handsomely boyish, the figure tall and slender. The checkered tweed jacket and the polka-dot bow-tie accentuated his youthfulness. It was only when I looked at him more closely, while he shook the cocktails, that I began to see the little alterations time had made. His blond hair was going prematurely gray and thin and something had gone out of his eyes. As a young man he had been full of a bubbling, imaginative gaiety, but it seemed to me as he talked that this had been replaced by a nervous animation. We were reminiscing over the first drink, when Dave's wife entered. I was ready to say hello again, for I had expected the highstrung little mental one with the boyish figure who had published a couple of thin books of verse herself and who had treated Dave with the respectful admiration one only accords to the dead. But this one was a very young woman with bangs, shoulder-length hair, exotic eyebrows, an abundance of Mexican handicraft silver jewelry, fleshy breasts with which she was obviously pleased and a manner that was more like a performance. She could have been a Hollywood stock-girl passing as an intellectual or an intellectual posing as a stock-girl.

168

"Miki, Eddie's come out here with that giant prize-fighter we read about," Dave said.

"I think that's fascinating," Miki said.

"Miki and I go to the fights every Friday night," Dave said. "I love the rhythm of a good fight. I've seen them when they're pure ballet."

"What kind of a character is this giant?" Miki said, stealing a quick, approving glance at herself in the bar mirror as she talked. "It must be madly fascinating to study a person like that."

"Madly," I said.

The maid came in, looked at Mrs. Stempel significantly and went out again without a word. "Duck," Mrs. Stempel said, "let's go in to dinner."

Duck and Mrs. Duck sat at either end of a long Spanish Colonial table in the large, formal dining room. After the avocado salad, the maid brought out a bottle of wine wrapped in a napkin and set it down in front of Dave with an air of formality. "Thank God I had the foresight to buy up all the *Graves* I could find," he said as he uncorked the bottle expertly.

He poured a little into a wine glass and asked the maid to bring it down to Mrs. Stempel. He looked down the table at her, waiting for the verdict as she tasted the wine carefully.

"How is it?" he said.

"Not bad," she decided. "Is this the Thirty-three?"

When he said it was, she nodded wisely. "I thought so. The Thirty-three has an extra little . . ." She paused as if reaching for exactly the right shade of meaning and I wondered if it would be nuance, or even *bonne bouche*, but she ended with "something."

"It's really the funniest thing," Dave said. "I've been studying wines for, well, twenty years and this little minx of mine whose favorite drink when I met her was a lemon coke can tell one wine from another as if she's been at it all her life."

"I've just got a natural taste for it," Miki admitted.

While Dave carved the meat, he said, "Oh, by the way, Miki, I talked to Mel Steiner today."

"Oh," Miki said, and stopped to wait for something that was obviously of great importance. "Well, what did he say?"

Dave turned to me and politely led me into the conversation. "You see, Eddie, there's a little credit dispute on my last picture. A couple of writers who polished my script are trying to ease me out of screen credit. The way we settle these things now is by a Guild Arbitration committee. Steiner's head of the committee."

"Well, what did he say?" Miki pressed him.

"He says the committee hasn't reached a final decision yet. Though it doesn't look like I'm going to get screenplay credit. But I may get an adaptation credit."

"That's simply filthy," Miki said, and then as a lady at a costume ball might do, she let her little pink mask of culture drop for a moment. "I think that stinks," she announced.

"All they did was take my lines and rewrite them," Dave said. "Making sure to take all the rhythm and the poetry out of them."

"Additional dialogue, that's what they should get," Miki said, "additional dialogue."

"You see, Eddie," Dave explained, "to get screenplay credit, you've got to prove that you wrote at least twenty-five percent of the shooting script. So these credit-hounds always try to revise your script at least eighty percent. Writers with the souls of bookkeepers."

The maid filled our glasses again.

"I suppose this is probably all Greek to you," Dave apologized, "but these credits are our bread and butter. I spent nine months at Goldwyn's last year on a script that got shelved, and had to take a salary cut at National. Now if I lose out on this credit, I'm in trouble." A frown creased his high forehead. "Dammit, Miki, how many times do you have to tell that stupid wench not to go to sleep in the kitchen after she's served the main course? You know how I hate to look at dirty dishes."

"I know, duck," Miki said. "She's a Jukes on both sides of her family. But it's so hard to get help to come all the way out here. They're so independent these days."

"What do they think this is, a free country?" I said, laughing to show I was making a little joke.

When the maid had removed the coffee cups sullenly and Dave was about to pour our second brandy, Miki said, very charmingly, "If your friend will excuse me, I'll leave you boys alone. You probably have a lot to talk about."

She went over and bit Dave playfully on the ear. "Good night, duck," she said. "Good night, Mr. Lewis. Do come again soon. It's been fascinating."

There was pride in Dave's washed-out blue eyes as her full, confident figure disappeared. "God, she's a great woman," he said. "Don't you think she's a great woman, Eddie?"

"Mm," I said.

"I can't take my eyes off her," he said. "It's been three years and I still can't take my eyes off her. She's given me something, Eddie, something I've been searching for all my life. Without Miki and Irving I would have been a schizo for sure."

"Who is Irving?"

"Irving Seidel, my analyst. He's a great man. He's treated practically everybody I know."

From one of the book-cases that completely covered the walls, Dave pulled out a volume and read a paragraph to me. It was a book by Seidel called, *I Vs. Me.* Dave's library contained practically all the English, Russian and French classics, several shelves on psychoanalysis and most of the outstanding poetry and fiction of the past twenty years. And Dave's mind seemed as curious and as hungry for new literary experiences as it had been

171

fifteen years before. He quoted enthusiastically from a new Yale poet whose work, he said, reminded him "of a Marxist Gerard Manly Hopkins." He described the subtle relationships in a first novel by a young Southern girl whose involuted style fascinated him. And then, pausing to inhale the fumes from his brandy glass, he began to recite a strange, haunting poem about two robots in a mechanized utopia who are equipped with human hearts and discover the experience of love. At first it seemed to lack rhythm and form, and the sound of it grated on me, but gradually it began to shape itself into a pattern and its melodies were as unmistakable and provocative as the distorted, dissonant themes of Schoenberg.

When Dave paused to refill our brandy glasses, I said, "Never heard that before. What is it?"

"The prologue to *The Seven-Jewel Heart*," Dave said.

"It's—" I was going to say "fascinating" and then I remembered Miki. "It's swell," I said. "Have you ever finished it?"

Dave's face was flushed and his eyes went in and out of focus. There had not been a great deal to drink but suddenly his powers of co-ordination seemed to switch off. "Almost finished," he mumbled. "Jus' one more canto. Thasall, jus' one more canto. 'Fi c'd jus' get this town off my back . . ." He shook his head slowly and began to recite again, unintelligibly.

"But why can't you get out?" I said. "What holds you?"

"All I need is jus' one good credit, an' some o' this gold. I need more gold, Eddie, and then I'll—go to Mexico, six months, maybe a year, rediscover my soul, Eddie."

"But Dave," I said, "I can't figure it. You've been making big dough for years. You must have enough to . . ."

"This isn't dough," Dave said. "Dough sticks to your palms. This is a handful of worms that slip through your fingers. Know what this house cost me, Eddie? Five hundred dollars a month, six thousand dollars a year for this unspeakable abortion. And then Louise, a thousand a month, my fine for committing premeditated matrimony. And then there's my daughter, Sandy, just starting at Wellesley, a lovely, intelligent girl whose mother refuses to let her contaminate herself by visiting her disreputable father but somehow brings herself to accept his disreputable lucre, a disreputable five thousand a year. And then there's Wilbur, who is forty-one years old and who has finally decided what he wants to be—the brother of a Hollywood writer. One useless brother, three thousand per annum. And don't let me forget my innocent-looking, white-haired mother-in-law with the cash register ringing in her brain, who stipulated a yearly retainer of five thousand dollars. These are the weeds, Eddie, that choke the life from the delicate, tender roots of the poetic impulse. The weeds, the weeeeeeeeds . . ." He drew it out into an eerie chant. "That feeds, and feeeeeeeeds . . . upon these poor creative seeds . . ."

I had to go. I had to be away from this. I needed a drink. No, I had a drink. That's what I always thought I needed when I needed something else. I needed air. I needed to get out.

"Dave," I said, "I gotta run. Gotta be up early in the morning. Lot to do."

He begged me to stay, implored me to stay with such repetitious insistence that I felt the great bird had some nightmare fear of being left alone in this little cage. When I kept saying, "Gotta go now, Dave, gotta go," he insisted on going along with me to help me find a cab. He staggered out into the night and walked me down to the boulevard. We waited under a lamppost on the corner, and as a cab pulled into the curb, Dave stood with his legs apart, swinging slowly back and forth, muttering, "Wanna hear my lates', my very lates' poem, jus' written today, written on National's precious time."

173

His laugh mounted maniacally. As my cab pulled away, I could see him out of the rear window, lurching out of the glare of the lamplight back into the shadows of darkest Beverly Hills.

"Where ya wanna go?" The heavy, exasperated face of the cab driver turned to me.

"Biltmore," I said.

"Can't make it da Chicago Biltmore?" he said with angry humor.

"What's the matter, you don't like this town?" I said.

"You c'n have this town and seven points. Gimme Chi. Hacking in Chi you c'n make yourself a buck. The customers wantcha to live back in Chi. They leave ya real good tips."

Furiously he shot the cab into high. I was sorry for him. I was sorry for everybody, when you got right down to it. I was sorry for David Heming Stempel. I was sorry for Eddie Lewis. I don't want to be a little sad at forty, and sadder at fifty and a tragic bum at sixty. What was it Beth said: Some day, two words for an epitaph. Who said that? Beth said that. Beth had the courage of her convictions. Why didn't I call Beth? Why didn't I marry Beth? Hello, darling, just wanted to call and let you know I'm getting out of this racket. That's right, not even going back to the training camp. Yeah, I finally did it, made up my mind, rediscovered my poet's soul, no— that's Stempel. Rediscovered something anyway. Coming back on the next train, darling, coming back to you, and by the way, Beth, will you marry me?

I tipped the cab driver from Chi a dollar to brighten his evening and hurried into the lobby to place my call. Person-to-person to Miss Beth Reynolds, R as in righteous, E as in elevate, Y as in yearning. I'm not drunk, my brain rejoiced. I'm not drunk this time. Just a little wine and some brandy, but I'm not doing this because I'm drunk. I'm doing it because I can't stand the failures any more, the fakes, the frauds. I'm doing it because I don't want to be another David Heming Stempel, a poor man's, less-talented David Heming Stempel. I don't want to wander around on my hands and knees searching every corner for my soul as if it were a lost collar button.

"Hello, hello . . . There's no answer?" It was three hours later in New York, which made it two o'clock in the morning there. She had to answer. Where could Beth be at 2 A.M. on a Sunday morning? "All right, then cancel the person-to-person. I'll talk to anybody at the hotel desk. Hello . . . Do you have any idea where I could reach Miss Reynolds? She's away, away for the week-end? . . . Oh . . . well, will you take a message? Just tell her that . . . Oh, never mind, never mind. I'll call again some time."

All the excitement was left behind me in the phone booth. There was a dull, twisting pain in my stomach. I never realized before that jealousy was something you could actually feel in your belly like a green and indigestible apple. Beth was my girl, and now that I wanted and needed her I couldn't even get her on the phone.

I wandered into the cocktail lounge. The Muzak was playing Guy Lombardo. A couple of drunk out-of-town business men who thought they had to be comic as well as spendthrift were pawing a couple of ladies who received their attention with bored, business-like acceptance. A woman in her thirties was sitting alone at a little table, drinking beer. She looked over in unenthusiastic flirtation as I stood at the entrance. Just another bar, another night, another meaningless woman. I turned and went upstairs.

There were empty whisky and soda bottles on the table in the sitting room, and a stale, sour smell in the air. I looked into the bedroom. All the windows were shut, and the shades drawn, and it was hot and close in there. Vince's clothes were scattered around the room, his shirt on the bathroom door-knob, his shorts on the floor, while piled rather neatly on one chair were the clothes of a woman. Her silk stockings were folded carefully over the foot of the bed.

Their inconsequential lust had spent itself and they were asleep now, with their heads close together on the pillow. How peaceful they looked together! In the morning they would rise as strangers, with not even a kiss or perhaps a kind word, but tonight they were enfolded together in serene sleep. What misfortune or perversity led this woman to wander so casually into the bed of Vince Vanneman? Vince groaned and rolled over, pulling most of the bedclothes with him. The woman, momentarily uncovered, moved toward him in her sleep, fitting herself against his fat back and rump. It was an instinctive, primeval action, the female seeking warmth and protection from the male, and there was something about its performance in this room under these conditions that bore me down into a bottomless depression.

I couldn't face the morning with this abandoned couple. So I phoned an all-night car-for-hire and drove out of the silent city into the dark, rolling countryside. I drove into Ojai just as dawn was filtering into the valley. Crickets were chirping and the birds were awakening. I tiptoed into the cottage and the room I shared with Doc. Doc was sleeping on his stomach, snoring rhythmically, the covers outlining his deformity. As I slipped into my bed wearily, I remembered it was a good thing I had come out here because I had some photographers due in the morning to cover Toro's training routine. As I sank into sleep, I was thinking of gags and catchy poses I could use for the lay-out. Just before I went off completely, I remembered somewhere earlier in the evening having told myself I was through with this racket. But it hadn't even entered my mind again as I drove up. Like a well-trained homing pigeon, I had headed straight for my Giant of the Andes. Well, I had made my bed, I guess, and here I was, lying in it.

11

I GOT a good idea," the photographer said. "Sit him down on the ground and photograph him with his feet close to the camera, so they'll look a mile high."

We sat him down.

"How about this?" I said. "Stand him up and shoot up at him—the skyscraper angle."

"That's a honey," the photographer said.

We stood him up.

"Now let's get a big close-up, one of those distortion jobs. Shove that big puss right into the lens."

We tilted his head. We posed him with wine barrels, hung him from the branch of a tree like Tarzan. We had him putting away six fried eggs, being massaged by two rubbers at one time. We photographed him with his enormous gloved fist in the foreground, sighting along his forty-inch reach. We caught him "in action" with George, "landing his famous *mazo* punch, which, our caption was going to inform the unsuspecting reader, Toro had developed back in his little Andean winery when he used to drive the bung into the barrel with a single blow of his heavy mallet.

The *mazo* was just a wild roundhouse right swing, which any third-rate professional could parry with his left, and counter with a right that would have caught Toro exposed and off balance. But fortunately for this racket, the fight fan who knows the finer points of the sport is a rare item. Most of them just come for the passive pleasure of seeing one guy beat the hell out of another guy, and if you give them something like a *mazo*

177

punch to chew on, they'll turn cheerfully to their neighbor and say, "Boy, here comes that old *mazo* again."

When we had enough pictures, Danny put Toro through a couple of rounds of shadow boxing. Shadow boxing, working through all the motions of offense and defense, against an imaginary opponent, can be beautiful to watch. With a fast, skillful boy who knows what he's doing, it becomes a kind of modern war dance. The fighter weaves and feints, shoots his punches sharply into the air, pivots and circles. But Toro just plodded dully around the ring, pawing the air.

"Faster, snap it up," Danny snarled.

Toro looked over with the white of his eyes showing in fear. He was afraid of Danny. He knew Danny had no use for him. He made an effort to move faster and sharpen up his punches, but it was just as Danny said: the big knotty muscles were in his way. He breathed hard with the effort of impressing Danny.

"Jesus H. Christ," Danny said.

"But this shadow boxing, it is not natural for him," Acosta hurried to explain. "This does not mean that when he is in the ring with . . ."

"Will you dry up and blow away?" Danny said. Acosta's eager face drew back into a subdued pout. Danny rang the bell impatiently. "All right, George," he called. "Let's go two three-minute rounds." As George shuffled into the ring, Danny said, "Keep him working, keep him busy, don't give him a chance to loaf."

George pushed one glove against the other casually. "You want me to do everything but hit him, that right, chief?"

"Tag him when you see an opening. That'll teach him to cover up. But don't lean on them," Danny said. Then his voice took on the tone of exasperation with which he always addressed Toro now. "Now keep working that left in his face like I told you. And when you see an opening for your right, don't forget to turn your left foot in a little bit and twist your body at the waist. Like this." He demonstrated on Toro. "Now, do you think you can remember that?"

"Okay, I think, yes," Toro said, looking to Acosta for encouragement.

Maybe Danny was too close to see it, but Toro was beginning to bear some resemblance to a fighter. At least he didn't have the stiff, flat-footed stance of an old bare-knuckle bruiser any more. He stepped out on his left foot to jab, still rather mechanically, but you could see he was beginning to get the idea. But the jabs didn't seem to jar George at all, and even when one of Toro's rights connected, George absorbed it effortlessly.

"Arms," Danny emphasized when the round ended, "you're still punching with your arms. How many times do I have to tell you it's body and shoulders and shifting that makes a puncher? Like this." He was a full foot shorter than Toro, but he set his feet, dropped his right shoulder and snapped a straight hard left that landed exactly where Danny meant it to, right under Toro's heart. Toro staggered back, injured and amazed. Knowing Danny, I realized that exasperation and impatience had driven him to throw a much harder punch than he intended.

Toro's large eyes looked hurt. He rubbed the red blotch that was spreading below his heart. "Come on, come on, that didn't hurt you," Danny said. "Now let's see another round. And punch this time."

In the next round Toro threw right hands as hard as he could and George caught some of them just to show Toro how it feels to land solidly, but there still wasn't anything behind them. Toro brought up another of his looping rights and George caught it on his arm, drawing Toro off balance and then moved his left in a straight line toward Toro's chin and Toro staggered back. Danny rang the bell in disgust.

"He can't beat an egg," Danny said.

"I'm worried about that button," Doc said. "That's the damnedest glass jaw I ever saw. Must have his nerves right on the surface there. A lot of these oversized guys have that trouble."

"Pardon me, if I may say one thing, please," Acosta began, "I think perhaps you make the mistake to change Toro's style. This big swing of his which you do not let him do, this is the punch that Lupe Morales . . ."

"Goddam it, you little Argentine windbag," Danny cut in, "if you butt in once more I'm going to bounce you right out on your can. Stop jabbering at me. And for Christ sake stop trying to sell me. You can't change this bum's style any more than you can change the hair-dress on Mike Jacobs' head. You can't change what you haven't got."

"From the first day you are not sympathetic to Toro and me," Acosta said. "You are jealous because all your life you have look for a great heavyweight and it is me, Luis Acosta, who has find him."

"Keep away from me," said Danny, who had a temper but did not like to fight. "Keep away from me. Eddie, get him away from me."

"I have to go into town right away," I said to Acosta. "Miniff and Coombs come in today. Want to ride in with me?"

"Yes, I will come," Acosta said. "I am tired of the insults. I am tired of being push around like a beggar. They do not appreciate me and my El Toro. Maybe they will think different when El Toro has knock out this man Coombs."

Acosta hadn't been told that Coombs was set to make like a swan. The fewer people who know these things, the less loose talk. Toro didn't know either. A fighter usually gives a more convincing performance when he thinks he's on the level.

As we were walking back to the cottage to pick up our things, Toro caught up with us. "Luis, do not leave me here alone," he said in Spanish. "If you leave, I wish to leave too."

"But you cannot leave. You must train for your fight."

"I have trained enough for many fights. I am tired of all this training. When we left Mendoza, did you not promise not to leave me?"

Acosta looked up at him and patted his arm. "Yes, that is what I promised in Mendoza," he said. He smiled sadly. "All right, I will stay."

Toro's big, simple face relaxed into a grateful smile. "And when we have made enough money we will go home together?"

"Yes, we will go home together."

"It is possible that we will go home together this year?"

"Maybe this year, maybe next year."

"Hey, Molina," Doc yelled over, "you know better than to stand around when you're sweating. Hurry up and take a shower. Then get dressed for road work."

As I was getting into the car, Danny leaned his elbow on the window and said, "Expect to be talking to Nick soon?"

"Probably tonight," I said. "I thought I'd call and let him know how things are going."

"I'd lay two to one he knows more about it than you do. He can outfox foxes. But listen, laddie, if you talk to him, tell him I want to lose this Acosta bird. I haven't punched anybody for serious since I quit the ring. If I see a fight coming in a saloon I run a mile. But something tells me if I don't get that little squirt out of here, I'll forget myself."

"But Toro's lost without him, Danny. He needs him for morale."

"If he could only wise up to what a bum he found," Danny said. "It's his walking around with his head in the clouds that drives me nuts. Keeps reminding me what a crook I am."

"You're not a crook," I said. "Whenever you get a free

181

choice, you level. Your real larceny guy is happier when he takes it off the bottom."

"I'll tell you how full of larceny I feel, laddie. This Sunday, I'm going to mass, right along with Molina. First time in over a year. I only go when I do something I don't like."

I didn't go down to the station to meet Harry Miniff and his formidable Eastern heavyweight because sometimes discretion is the better part of public relations. But there was quite a delegation on hand to greet the prominent Broadway sportsman, as Miniff was blithely identified that morning by one of the columnists I had drinking out of my hand. I would like to have seen it, though. Little Miniff, the hungriest of the hungry, as ignored and insulted a man as ever faced daily humiliation on Jacobs' Beach, being greeted by Nate Starr, the promoter, and Joe Bishop, the matchmaker, as if he had a stable full of champions; and old Cowboy Coombs, who always looked a little surprised to find himself still on his feet, being treated with the respect usually reserved for more vertical pugilists.

I had given Miniff the pitch by airmail, writing most of his dialogue and warning him urgently not to refer to Coombs as "my bum" in public, as he was inclined to do. "That is all right for those of us who know and love you, but I don't think it will contribute to the success of Toro's debut," I had written. To which Miniff had answered graciously, "Okay, I will give my impersonation of a guy what has all his bills paid and his IOU's called in. And I'll try not to call my bum a bum."

According to the evening paper, Miniff had played his part faithfully, if somewhat ungrammatically. There was a picture of Coombs' puffy, flattened face, captioned, "GIANT-KILLER?" and under it a brief interview with Coombs' mentor, in which he said, "This giant don't scare us. We don't fear nobody. We give up a big money match in the Garden to take this fight, that's how confident we are we can walk all over this Man Mountain. The bigger they are the harder they fall."

Late that afternoon Harry came up to the hotel. He had bought a new hat to celebrate his change of fortune, but the way he had already twisted it, with one side up and the other side down, it looked exactly like his old hat. To this day the top of Miniff's head and I are complete strangers. I am sure if you were to look in on Miniff taking a bath you would find him with his hat on. Miniff seemed as determined to go into his grave with his hat on as other adventurers were about their boots.

"Well, how was your trip, Harry?" I said.

"Terrible," Miniff moaned. "Why'd they haveta put this place so far from New York? My ulcers don't like to travel."

"This is the healthiest climate in the world," I said. "This'll make a man of you, Miniff. All this fresh air and sunshine."

"I get dizzy in the sun," Miniff complained.

"Wanna shot?" Vince said, pouring one for himself.

"Whatta you wanna do, kill me?" Miniff demanded. "The milk, I'm strictly on the milk."

"Tell Room Service to send up one Jersey," I told Vince. "We can keep it in the bathroom while Miniff's here. Anything to eat, Harry?"

"Gimme a sturgeon sandwich on rye," Miniff said.

"Sturgeon," I said. "Where the hell do you think you are, Lindy's? This is California."

"Don't they eat in California?" Miniff wanted to know.

"Only nutburgers and cheeseburgers," I said. "How about a nice fruit salad?"

"Fruit gives me hives," Miniff said. From his breast pocket, he took out three short, fat cigars, stuck one in his mouth and passed the others around.

"Ten-cent cigar," I said. "Don't let these write-ups go to your head, Harry."

"I like my old ones better," Miniff said, "but I gotta keep up a front."

"How's Cowboy?" I said. "He understands he's to tell everybody he's betting on himself to knock Toro out? I want to build this up so it sounds like he's fed up with giving a foreigner so much publicity and out to knock his head off."

"But don't get him so steamed up he can't go in two," Vince said. "Got that, I want him to go in two."

"Two!" Miniff said. He pushed his hat back with a quick motion of his hand. "That's too quick. The fans don't like it. They don't get their money's worth. I gotta better idea."

"Shove your ideas," Vince said.

"Gimme a chance," Miniff begged. "Whatsamatter, we ain't got free speech in this country no more?"

"What the hell office you running for you wanna make a speech?" Vince said. "Run as spittoon cleaner and ass wiper and maybe I'll vote for you."

"Aaaaaaaah," said Miniff in rebuttal. It was a gutter sound, a harsh, embittered protest against bigger men with better connections. "I gotta weenie for improving the take and you dial out on me."

"All right, let's have it," Vince said magnanimously. "Ten to one it stinks, but let's have it."

"My bum and your bum," Miniff began, "they fight even . . ."

"Take it away, it stinks," Vince cut in.

"Going into the seventh, eighth, ninth, it's still even," Miniff continued. "Then in the tenth, with thirty seconds t' go, your bum lands and my bum rolls over and plays dead. D'ya buy that?"

"You couldn't give it to me with Seabiscuit for a bonus," Vince said.

"But your bum comes in right under the wire," Miniff's voice rose and accelerated. "It makes more talk. The guy's a hero."

184

"Just because it's the Hollywood stadium, we don't haveta give 'em a movie," Vince said.

Miniff mopped his forehead with his short fingers in a nervous gesture. "But my way we get a rematch. Eddie writes it up how my bum is convinced he lose on a fluke and wants revenge. Then in the rematch my bum goes in two like you want. What's wrong with that, tell me what's wrong with that?"

"Don't be so shoving hungry," Vince said. "You get seven-fifty for the fight and an extra two-five-o for the act. What more d'ya want?"

"I want it twice," Miniff admitted. "Twice won't do you no harm and we c'n use the difference. We ain't had a fight since Worcester. And the bum has five kids to feed."

"Shove the kids," Vince said. "What does this look like, a relief office? Coombs goes in two. If it lasts too long they'll see what a dog we got. Ten rounds and the ref'll throw 'em out for not trying. Ain't that right, Eddie?"

"I'm afraid it is, Harry," I said. "The longer Toro's in there, the worse he's going to look. And Coombs can't go too many rounds without falling down from force of habit."

"Well, anyway I c'n pay up my back rent," said Miniff philosophically, chewing on his cigar as if it were nourishment.

A week before the fight, the press came up to have a look at our "human skyscraper," as some of the boys were calling him now. The camp was opened to the public too, and there were a couple of hundred sightseers every day, laying down their buck for a hinge at the freak. There were always a good many women in the crowd. There was something about his brute size that seemed to exert a Stone-age influence on the girls. I made a mental note of this for future reference. Atavism, I labeled it.

Everybody seemed impressed as Toro bent and

stretched that Brobidnagian torso. While he was shadow-boxing, I went into the dressing room to talk to George, who was lacing up his ring shoes for the last heavy workout he was going to have with Toro before the fight.

"The two-seventeen took my baby away," he was singing under his breath. "The two-nineteen will bring her back some day . . ."

"George, there's a lot of reporters out there today," I said.

"I understand, Mr. Lewis," he said. And he chuckled again in that way he had of making the whole deal seem ridiculous, profoundly ridiculous, foolish and pointless.

"Toro's supposed to be a hitter," I reminded him.

"Don't worry, Mr. Lewis," George said, "I'll make him look as good as I can." And the low-pitched, good-natured laughter rose from his belly again, untainted by meanness, a warm and compassionate but disconcerting laugh.

The sparring looked all right. George cuffed him around a little in the first round and tied him up in clinches that Toro was strong enough to break out of. In the next two rounds George mistimed his slips just enough for Toro to catch him with that looping right. George tossed his head, as if to shake off the effect of the punch and fell into a clinch. Just before the final bell, after being short with a right hook, George caught one high on the head and dropped to one knee. It really didn't look too bad. The only funny thing was that when George rose and touched gloves, Toro wanted to make sure George wasn't hurt before continuing.

"What the hell's going on?" Danny said when Toro hesitated.

"He does not have the wish to injure George seriously," Acosta explained.

"Now I've heard everything," Danny said. "Tell him to keep fighting, goddam it, until I hit the bell."

"Is the big joker kidding?" asked the young, jowly reporter who had met us at the train.

186

"No, he's just afraid of his own power," I ad-libbed. "You see, back in Buenos Aires one of the guys he kayoed spent ten weeks in a hospital and damn near died. Ever since then he's been afraid he might kill somebody." It sounded so good I thought I might as well blow it a little louder. "In fact, it might be a good idea if you sports writers reminded the referee as a public service that it's his responsibility to the citizens of California to stop his fights before Molina inflicts serious injury. We're out to win as impressively as possible, but we don't want to kill anybody."

"What's the name of this guy he almost killed?" the reporter wanted to know.

I called over to Toro, whose face Doc was wiping with a towel while Acosta was pulling off his gloves. "Toro," I said in Spanish, "what was the name of your first opponent before you came up here?"

"Eduardo Solano," Toro said.

"Got that?" I said, and I spelled it out for the reporter. The next morning he used that for his lead.

Al Leavitt was up there too. "Well, what do you think of him, Al?" I said.

He just shrugged. "I never go by training," he said. "I've seen beautiful gymnasium fighters look like palookas in the ring. And I've seen good fighters who always looked lousy in their workouts."

A wise apple. But he didn't bother me. You always have to figure on one of those. The rest of the press was fine. My book of clippings was getting fatter each edition. The training camp attendance had built nicely. Toro Molina, Inc., was already in the black. And Nate Starr told me the stadium had been sold out for a week. Five-dollar ringsides were being scalped for two and three times their official price. We were ready to move into town.

The first day back in L.A. I took Toro out to MGM for some publicity tie-ups. I had an old buddy out there, Teet Carle, opening doors for me. Toro was wearing the new gabardine Weatherill had cut for him and he looked like a million pesos. He took a child's delight in this sartorial splendor, with his new specially built two-tone shoes and his size 8½ straw hat that would have made Miniff a nice beach umbrella. The pictures we knocked off were right down the old Graflex groove. There must be something about the chemistry of a press agent and a still camera that makes it impossible for them to produce any other kinds of pictures except the ones I set up at Metro—Toro squaring off with Mickey Rooney standing on a box; Toro with a couple of pretty stock-girls in bathing suits feeling his muscles; Toro on the set with Clark Gable and Spencer Tracy showing off the size of his fist. "Two stars see fist that will make Coombs see more stars," I captioned that one.

The Main Street gym, where Toro and Coombs were to put in their final workouts, looks like a shabbier twin of Stillman's in New York. The street is gaudier than Eighth Avenue. It offers cheap burlesque houses and dime movies for adults only, dim and dingy bars with raucous juke-boxes and blousy B-girls, your fortune for a dime, your haircut for a quarter, whisky for fifteen cents, love for a dollar and a five-cent flop.

Outside the entrance to the gym was the usual sidewalk gathering: boxers, managers, old fighters, hangers-on. On the curb a huge, shabbily dressed, fight-scarred Negro swung good-naturedly at a much smaller Negro who had sneaked up to goose him. "Keep away from there, man," the big Negro cried, grinning with a mouthful of gold teeth. It was only then, as he raised his large, punished face, that I saw he was blind.

George went up to him and said, "Whatcha doin', Joe?"

The blind Negro cocked his head. "What you want, man?"

"Putcha hands up, brother," George said gaily, "and see if you can still lick Georgie Blount."

"Georgie!" the blind man said. "Where *you* been, gate? Gimme some skin, man."

They both laughed as they shook hands. George told him what he was doing out here and then Joe said, cheerfully, "Well, we gave 'em some fights, didn't we, man? We really did it, didn't we, George?"

"You're not kidding," said George. "I still got a dent where you hit me in the ribs."

"Man, oh, man," Joe chuckled. "Them was the days."

George looked at Joe and reached into his pocket. "Here's that sawbuck I owe you, boy. Remember that time in K.C.?"

"K.C.?" Joe said.

"Yeah," George said, and pushed it into his hand.

Joe's grin disappeared into that curiously dead expression of the blind. "Good luck, Georgie," he said. "See you around."

Going up the long, grimy stairway that seems to be the standard approach to every fight gym, George said to me, "That's Joe Wilson, Joe the Iceman, they used to call him. He col'cocked so many of 'em. I fought him four times. He sure could hit you a real good punch. Busted two of my ribs one night out at Vernon."

"How long you been fighting, George?" I asked.

George's eyes narrowed in a private smile. "Tell you the truth, Mr. Lewis, I lost track."

"How old are you, George?"

George shook his head mysteriously. "Man, if I ever told you, they'd take me off the payroll and send me straight to the old folks' home."

Upstairs were the same dirty gray walls, the same lack of ventilation and sanitation and the same milling activity of concentrated young men with narrow waists and glistening skins, bending, stretching, shadow boxing, sparring, punching the bags or listening earnestly to the instructions of men with fat bellies, boneless noses, dirty sweatshirts, brown hats pushed back on sweaty foreheads, the trainers, the managers, the experts. Only here on Main Street there were even more dark skins, not only black like those that had come to outnumber the whites in Stillman's, but the yellow and brown skins of the Filipinos and Mexicans who poured into the gym from the slums of L.A. For if racing is the sport of kings, boxing is the vocation of the slum-dwellers who must fight to exist. When were the sons of Erin monopolizing the titles and the glory: the Ryans, Sullivans, Donovans, Kilbanes and O'Briens? When waves of Irish immigration were breaking over America. Gradually, as the Irish settled down to being politicians, policemen, judges, the Shamrock had to make room for the Star of David, to the Leonards, Tendlers, and Blooms. And then came the Italians: Genaro, LaBarba, Indrissano, Canzoneri. Now the Negroes press forward, hungry for the money, prestige and opportunity denied them at almost every door. In California the Mexicans, fighting their way up out of their brown ghettos, dominate the light divisions: Ortiz, Chavez, Arizmendi and a seemingly endless row of little brown sluggers by the name of Garcia.

In the center ring, throwing punches at the air, ducking and weaving as he crowded an imaginary opponent to the ropes, was Arizmendi himself, who seemed to have inherited not only the strong, stoic face of an ancient Aztec, but the courage and endurance as well.

As Toro climbed through the ropes for a light workout with George, a short, plump, brown-skinned guy in a cheap but spotless white linen suit and white shoes came down to a corner of the ring, raised a megaphone to his lips and began to announce in a Spanish accent, made more inarticulate by too many blows on the head, "Eeentro-ducing, ot two hondreed ond seventy-wan pounds, the beegest heavyweight in the worl' . . ."

"Who is this clown?" I asked a second who was going to help Doc in the fight Friday night.

"Oh, that's Pancho, one of our characters," the second said. "He's a little punchy. Been around here for years. Thinks he's an announcer. Nobody pays him but he comes in the same time every day just like he had a job. For practice. The guys throw him a quarter once in a while. And the dope spends every nickel he has keeping himself in them white clothes. He once saw an announcer in a white suit and I guess it kind of stuck in his bean."

Coombs climbed into the adjoining ring. He was heavily built and seemed ready to wink at anybody who would smile at him. I watched Pancho raise the megaphone to his lips, throw his head back and close his eyes in ecstasy. "Een-tro-ducing ot two hondred and seex pounds thot great hovyweight from da yeast, Cowboy Coombs."

One of the regulars in the place, an unshaven, bald-headed second with a couple of swab sticks in his mouth, started toward Pancho, and the little Mexican began to back up, half-threatening, "Stay 'way from me, you barstid, stay 'way from me."

"What goes with him?" I asked the second.

"Aw, that's just a running rib," he said. "The fellas know what a nut he is about stayin' so clean. So some of 'em go over and rub their burnt matches down his suit or smudge his white shoes just to hear him holler."

Pancho kept backing and pleading as he worked his way crabwise until he reached the door and darted out. Some of the boys were amused. "Did you see that little greaser run?" Vince laughed.

The next day, the last training session before the fight, we found Pancho at his regular post, busy making those announcements to which no one paid any attention. I just thought Vince was going over to give him a quarter when he started toward him. I didn't realize anything was up until Pancho started backing away frantically just as he did the day before. The whole crowd of us, who had come in together, saw how Pancho retreated until he reached a high stool near the entrance. He drew his feet up, wrapped his arms around himself and pulled his head in like a turtle. "Stay 'way, you stay 'way," he was crying.

"Don't be afraid of me, *muchacha*," Vince laughed, and drew a long streaky line down the arm of Pancho's coat. Pancho stared sorrowfully at the smudge.

Toro was bewildered. "Why did he do that?" he asked in Spanish.

"A joke," I said. "*Un chisto.*"

"*No entiendo,*" Toro said. He did not understand. Vince's cruelty was too complex for him. He went over to Pancho, who was still sitting there brooding over the affront.

"Why did he do that to your fine white suit?" Toro said in Spanish.

Pancho answered in the bastardized Spanish of California Mexicans. What he called Vince has no satisfactory equivalent in English profanity.

Toro turned to Acosta and said in Spanish, indicating Vince with his head, "Tell him to give this man ten pesos."

"That is in American money two dollars," Acosta said. "You wish him to have two dollars?"

"I mean ten dollar," Toro corrected himself.

When Acosta relayed this to Vince, Vince kept his hands in his pockets and said, "How does this jerk rate a sawbuck?"

"You give," Toro said.

"Listen to him. Now he's a big shot," Vince said.

"Go on, you cheap skate, give 'im ten bucks," Danny said. It was the first thing he had said to Vince since we hit California.

"Aah, you guys make me sick," Vince said. But he produced.

When Pancho saw his money, he just shook his head. "Go 'way," he said. "You big barstid."

"What's the matter with you, you punchy?" Vince said.

For men in Pancho's condition, that's the chip on the

shoulder. "Who ponchy?" he demanded. "I not ponchy. I got job here. I announcer. Maybe you ponchy."

Vince laughed. Toro turned to Acosta again. "Give me ten dollar," he said. He handed the bill to Pancho solemnly. He could not explain what had happened, but some simple peasant intelligence seemed to make him understand that the carefully nourished dignity of Pancho Diaz had been outraged.

While Toro was having his workout I dropped down to Abe Attell's, the dark, narrow saloon and beanery that tunneled under the gym. You could go in there at ten A.M. for a beer and sit around until midnight, watching the old fights on a streaky movie screen. The pictures ran continually, pausing only long enough for one of the bartenders to change reels. A hoarse sound track of the noises fight fans make when things happen in the ring began to deafen you. Sometimes a young boxer or a sports writer would sit down to watch a fight, but most of the spectators, who must have seen these same films countless times, were jug-heads and shabby ex-fighters just hanging around, waiting for another break, another manager, a chance to pick up beer-money sparring with somebody's prospect or working as a second, or waiting to put the bite on an old pal or a newcomer on the way up with money in his pocket.

On the screen, Jack Dempsey, crazy with viciousness, fighting like a man who has tracked down a lifelong enemy, was swarming all over big, slow, flabby Jess Willard, smashing Jess down every time he got up and breaking his ribs, his nose and his heavy jaw. A seedy-looking wino sat down opposite me with his back to the screen and started muttering to himself. When my eyes shifted for a moment from the grainy violence of the screen, he tried to smile, but it was only the unhappy mechanical grimace of a man who is ready to offer a spurious, tenta-

tive friendship in return for a fifteen-cent glass of sauterne.

"I seen you somewhere before, ain't I?" he said for
openers.

"I've never been out here before," I said.

"Oh, I fought all over, K.C., Louisville, Camden, New
Jersey. Young Wolgast." He spoke the name proudly and
stopped to watch the effect.

The only Wolgasts in my book were Midget, the flyweight champion, and the great Ad, who knocked out
Battling Nelson in forty rounds and finally fought himself into amnesia. But Young Wolgast looked as if he
needed a little moral support, and it didn't cost anything
to open my mouth and say, "Oh."

"Mushy Callahan," he said. "You know, the great
Mushy, I shoulda knocked him out. I had him out on his
feet, see, but I didn't know how bad I hurt him and I
let him jazz me out of it. I got him laying right on the
ropes, all set up for the kayo and I don't go in." The
disappointment was still sharp in him, but he couldn't
stop himself from pressing down against the point of it
with perverse torment. "If I put Mushy away I can write
my own ticket. I'm the hottest thing in town, and like a
jerk I let him bluff me out of it. I don' know how bad
I got him hurt, see . . ."

Mushy Callahan won what they call the junior welterweight championship from Pinky Mitchell back in the
middle twenties. So the fight this Wolgast is worrying
about must have taken place ten, maybe fifteen years
ago. But time is all turned around in Wolgast's head. For
two or three seconds in his life he had a glimpse of glory,
and down through the shabby years of obscurity, those
precious drops of time have grown and grown until they
have blotted out the rest of his memory. "I rush him into
a corner and clip him with a right uppercut," he was
saying, his fist closing in reflex, "and then like a dope I

194

step back, I let him get away, he's out on his feet and I don' even know it."

His head hung down on his chest, heavy with wine and self-disgust. On the screen it was Dempsey and Carpentier now, the first million-dollar gate, curtain raiser on the Golden Age of boxing and gold-plated bunk and ballyhoo. A sharpshooter from Reno moved into New York with the big idea that a fight wasn't just a contest of skill and brawn; it was a dramatic spectacle, and he proceeded to stage it accordingly. So it was Carpentier, the war hero versus Dempsey, the slacker; the fearless French light-heavyweight against the 200-pound bully; the clean-cut, smooth-shaven, gentlemanly veteran, representing patriotism, sportsmanship and boxing skill, and the glowering slugger with a three-day's beard who had fought his way up from the hobo jungles. There were the 80,000 high-pressured fans screaming their lungs out for Carpentier because Tex Rickard and his press agents, taking advantage of their simple-minded morality, had been careful to present them a hero to cheer and a villain on whom to vent their volatile anger.

As I got up from my beer, leaving another sauterne for Young Wolgast, the almost-conqueror of Mushy Callahan, the screen had moved on to Philadelphia, with Dempsey and Tunney. Now it was Dempsey, the Horatio Alger boy, a colorful champion who was always in there giving his best, a friendly, quiet-spoken fellow outside the ring, but a furious competitor from bell to bell, facing the aloof, bookish, cautious, undramatic, methodically effective Tunney. That was the Rickard pitch on that one, and the villain of Boyle's Thirty Acres was transformed into the hero of the Philadelphia Sesquicentennial for whom 130,000 people were cheering themselves hoarse, taxing the worn-out sound equipment as I turned my back on this ancient history and came out into the light of the street.

Standing with the sidewalk fraternity outside the entrance to the gym was Harry Miniff. As soon as he saw me come out of Attell's, Miniff ran over and buttonholed me. "Jeez, I gotta see ya about somp'n, Eddie. Walk down the enda the block with me." When he made sure we were far enough away from the others, he began, trotting along to keep up with me and talking up into my face feverishly.

"Eddie," he says, "any time you want I should do something for you, you know me, kid, the shirt off my back."

"Keep your shirt on, Harry," I said. "What do you want?"

"Leave my bum stay in there for a while, maybe seven, eight rounds, how about it, Eddie, for a pal?"

"That's not my department, Harry. You'll have to speak to Mr. Vanneman who does the choreography."

"That Vanneman, if he had a peanut factory he wouldn't gimme the shells," Miniff said.

"Do you realize you are speaking of one of my business associates?" I said.

"Associate," Miniff said. "You call that crumb an associate. Listen, Eddie, for a pal, talk to Vince, get him to leave my bum go six rounds, five, I'll settle for five."

"But what's the difference whether he goes in two or five?" I wanted to know.

"Two, it makes him sound like a washed-up bum," Miniff explained. "Five, that's more of a respectable bum. Five, maybe I can make a few dollars selling the bum to the smaller clubs, Santa Monica, San Berdoo, you know, five, it gives me something to talk about: he was giving the guy a helluva fight for four rounds and the streffis and the strallis, but two . . ." he shook his head despondently, "two don't give me nothin' to work on. Me and my bum'll starve on two."

"Harry," I said, "relax. Leave it alone. Let him go in two. Maybe we'll do business again."

"Hey, I gotta idea," Miniff brightened. "I know a real

good bum in Frisco. Tony Colucci. I useta handle him oncet. Great big bastard, almost as big as your bum. You put me on the expense account and I'll hop up there and see if I c'n . . ."

"Quit racing your motor, Miniff," I said. "One bum, I mean one fight at a time. Damn it, now you got me doing it."

Little Harry Miniff, beetle-faced and weevil-legged, was holding on for dear life.

"Okedoke," Miniff said, "but I'm telling you, Eddie, this Colucci'll be sensational. . . ."

O n the day before the fight I went down to meet Nick, Ruby and the Killer, coming in on the Super Chief. We drove uptown to the Beverly Hills Hotel, where Nick had reserved a bungalow, and had lunch by the pool.

"I've been promising Ruby this trip to California for years, haven't I, baby?" he said. "Nick never failed you yet, did he, baby?"

"No, honey."

She had a new up hairdo, a little fancy for daytime; Ruby was one of those women who belong to the evening and never look quite wholesome by light of day.

"This is really our second honeymoon," Nick said expansively. "I always told you we'd have our second honeymoon in Sunny Cal, didn't I, Ruby?"

"I thought that's what we were doing in Miami last winter," Ruby said.

"Aah, that was nothing," Nick said. "That was just getting in practice for the second honeymoon." He bent over and kissed Ruby, a little roughly. She didn't draw away, but she no longer thought it was ladylike to be kissed in public.

"Killer," Nick said, "go back to the bungalow and get me some cigars."

The Killer, a short, trim figure in his fancy Hawaiian shorts, obeyed.

"You should have brought Toro over for lunch," Ruby said. "How does he look in his new clothes?"

"Haven't you been reading the papers?" I said.

"You've been doing good, Eddie, real good," Nick said.

"That Sunday supplement with the full-page picture of Toro opposite that Greek god, that was very okay. I knew what I was talking about, didn't I, kid? That guy is money in the bank."

The Killer was back with the cigars. They came in individual aluminum containers. Nick opened his with tender care. The Killer held the match for him. "New cigar," Nick said. "Made special for me in Havana. Dollar 'n a quarter a piece. Go ahead, Eddie, take all you want."

"Honey, don't you know it's not polite to tell people what everything costs?" Ruby said.

"Listen to her," Nick said, leaning back, crossing his legs and holding that big cigar like a scepter. "Did you ever see a kid from Tenth Avenue get so smart?"

"Nicholas," she said. She put her sun-glasses on in a gesture of annoyance and began reading the book she had brought with her. *Three Loves Hath Nancy*, it was called, and from the cover you could see that Nancy was a high-chested, red-headed wench who helped win our country's independence by diverting Cornwallis' attention from one kind of conquest to another.

Three cute-looking girls with slender, tanned young bodies in little dabs of bathing suits walked past us toward the pool and stretched out in the hot sun. "Oh, brother," the Killer observed, "how wudja like to take care of them?"

"How many times I have to tell you, don't talk dirty around Ruby?" Nick said.

"Aw, I'm sorry, Ruby," the Killer said.

"You never did know how to talk in front of a lady," Ruby said pleasantly.

The Killer took it smilingly.

"Nate Starr says he coulda filled the ball park for this fight. Even with Coombs," Nick said. "That shows you what publicity'll do, eh, kid?"

"I wonder what'll happen after they've seen him once," I said.

"They'll come again and like it," Nick promised.

"What if they get wise to us?" I said.

"Then I'll fire you," Nick said cheerfully.

The night of the fight we started off at Chasen's, the place the Hollywood biggies go when they want food, drink or to be seen. There were Nick and Ruby, the Killer and a little stock-girl with a cutie-pie face, the kind that always seems to be in stock. We got down to the stadium in time to see old George box the semi-final. He was fighting a chunky, battle-scarred club-fighter, Red Nagle, who came into the ring wearing a faded Golden Glove bathrobe, on the back of which the numerals *1931* could barely be made out. George climbed through the ropes, worked his feet in the rosin and sat down in his corner with a deliberate casualness, an old-timer getting ready to go to work, neither frisky nor afraid.

At the bell the white fighter came out of his corner with a rush that brought a shriek of excitement from the crowd. Red got plenty of work at the club because he scorned any pretense at self-defense and went in swinging. But George calmly side-stepped that first charge and put a sharp left to Red's eye. Red was the kind who takes two to land one, swinging all the time, and George was methodically riding with the punches or slipping inside, countering nicely. But from a distance it must have looked as if Red was murdering George, for the cheers of the gallery gods shook the place with every wild, futile swing. They were pleading with Red to put him out in a hurry.

In the seat next to me sat a broad, beefy-faced fellow with a high-blood-pressure complexion and a big mouth. "Come on, Red, send that boogie back to Central Avenue." He hunched forward in his seat, jerking his shoulders in time with Red's blows. Whenever Red landed, he'd let out an excited, deep-bellied laugh.

George fought in spurts, moving with bored relaxation, pacing himself carefully, never wasting a punch unless he saw an opening and winding up each round with a twenty- or thirty-second flurry to catch the referee's eye. In the fifth round George nailed his man with a right hand as he rushed in, and Red dropped to the canvas with blood dripping from his left eye. But he was up again without a count, brushing the blood away with his glove and rushing George fiercely into the ropes, where he whaled away at him with both hands, not doing much except wearing himself out, for George was catching them on the arms and the shoulders. But the fans loved it. They were on their feet, with their hands megaphoning their violent encouragement, "Attaboy. Get him! Knock him down! Murder that nigger!" A movie-comedian's girl in tan make-up, styled sun-glasses and a large black straw hat that tormented spectators for three rows behind her lifted her voice to a screech that pierced the general roar, "Kill him! Kill him, Red! Kill him!" And the man next to me added his gravel-voice, "In the breadbasket, Red. Those shines don't like it down there."

Working quietly in the clinches, and maneuvering his opponent around so he could look over his shoulder at the big clock that told him how many seconds were left in the round, George was giving that bad eye an unspectacular but thorough going-over. But the white boy kept boring in, forcing the fighting, weak on brains but strong on heart, the kind who have to show how brave they are by jumping up after every knockdown without bothering to take advantage of the count, the kind the fans go crazy about for a while and then don't recognize when they're buying peanuts or papers from them a year or so later outside the stadium.

When the bell ended the last round, Red kept on swinging until the referee grabbed him, but George dropped his hands automatically and shuffled back to his corner to sit down and wait for the decision. George had four of the six rounds on my card, but the referee called it a draw. With his eye a bloody smear, Red threw his arms around George in a broad gesture of sportsmanship and mitted the crowd happily. They gave him a big hand as he left the ring. Most of them thought he had won. There were scattered boos for George as he climbed out through the ropes.

"Nice work, George," I shouted over to him as he passed on his way up the aisle, and he turned for a moment to give me that easy smile. The boos and the cheers, the glory and the name-calling, it was all in a night's work to George. Five minutes from now he'd be in the showers humming one of those songs. An hour from now he'd be down on Central Avenue with his own people, eating fried chicken and chips and laughing softly about the fight, "If that white boy could fight like them people out there thought he could, I wouldn't be sitting here enjoying this bird." Something like that he'd be saying.

The lights were on all over the arena and everybody was standing up, waiting for the main-eventers. The loudmouth next to me pulled the seat of his pants where it had creased into his buttocks and said, "That jigaboo was lucky to get a draw."

Ruby waved across the ring to a platinum-haired star she had known back in the chorus. "Look at Jerry," she said to Nick, "doesn't she look marvelous? I hardly knew her with that new hair."

The air was foul with cigar and cigarette smoke. The ringside crowd were sleek, prosperous actors, directors, movie executives, theatrical agents, song-writers, politicians, insurance men, and their sleek, stylized women and the big-time lawyers who helped to reshuffle them from time to time. I noticed Dave Stempel and Miki, who were sitting near by with a young, tired-eyed heiress and her current Number One boy.

Cowboy Coombs came down the aisle, his broad, scuffed-up puss split with a silly grin of showmanship.

Miniff hurried along beside him with a half-smoked cigar clenched in his mouth. The Legion Band, which had been tearing itself apart with a ludicrous version of popular swing that never lost its military influence, stopped for a moment and took off on "The Hall of the Mountain King." That was the cue for Toro to make his entrance. Just one of the little gimmicks I thought up to help the show along. Toro was wearing a white-satin bathrobe with an Argentine flag on the shoulder, a symbol of a mountain peak on his back and the gold-lettered words: THE GIANT OF THE ANDES. Danny and Acosta were both wearing white T-shirts with the word MOLINA on their backs. The other two seconds, similarly attired, were both Acosta's size, selected for their diminutiveness to accentuate Toro's height. The staging looked even better than I had hoped. Towering more than a foot-and-a-half over the seconds who flanked him, with the enormous expanse of white satin emphasizing his superhuman size, he moved toward the ring like a strange throwback to the giants of prehistoric time. When he reached the apron of the ring he didn't climb through the ropes in the usual fashion; he stepped over the highest strand. It got the hand I figured on. But Toro forgot to wave, as we had told him to. This was his first appearance before an American crowd—a North American crowd, as he would say—and he looked nervous and bewildered. He knew he hadn't made a good showing with George or satisfied Danny, and he and Acosta had probably swallowed all that big talk we had planted about the formidability of Cowboy Coombs.

They killed the lights, we all bowed our heads and the band gave us The Star-Spangled Banner, with one of those dramatic baritones on the lyrics.

At the bell Coombs tore out of his corner as if he were going to make short work of Toro and fell ferociously into a clinch. They pushed and pulled and pawed their way through the round. All of Coombs' violence was in his face, which he worked pugnaciously, and in the aggressive way he breathed through his busted nose. Toro floundered around, trying an occasional jab and now and then throwing his wild right before his feet were set. The most energy expended in the round came from Acosta, who bent forward as if he were going to jump into the ring himself and kept up a running patter of semi-hysterical instruction, which was far more entertaining than the fight. As the round ended, he leaped into the ring, got in the way of Danny and Doc, put his mouth against Toro's ear and gesticulated excitedly. I could see Danny's face grow taut with irritation.

In the second round they wrestled each other for the first minute, and then Toro pushed his right glove toward Coombs' chest and Miniff's warrior sank slowly to the canvas and stretched out comfortably. At ten he made a half-hearted effort to rise and flopped down again. Toro looked surprised and dragged Coombs back to his corner. That was all in the act too, though Toro didn't know it. I just told him in case he won by a knockout, it was considered good sportsmanship up here to help the man back to his corner yourself.

There were scattered boos from the more observant, but the fans, collectively, seemed to be satisfied that they had seen a quick and decisive knockout. As I pushed my way up the aisle the cash customers were happily expressing their gullibility. "What a build!" "He's got King Kong beat!" "Ya couldn't hurt that guy with a sledge hammer!" "That last one musta hurt!"

But I heard someone behind me say, "How did you call it, Al?" and the answer snapped back, "They ought to give Coombs an Oscar for the Best Supporting Performance of the year."

I looked around and saw it was Al Leavitt, the wise guy from the *News*. I kept going as if I hadn't seen him. Why bother with him? He wasn't even syndicated.

In the corridor, outside the dressing room, a large

crowd of hero-worshippers, curiosity-seekers and band-wagon boys were gathering. Inside were the reporters, celebrities and the usual visiting firemen who always manage to find their way to a winner's dressing room after a fight.

As soon as he saw me, Acosta ran over and threw his arms around me. His eyes were wild and he looked as if he were on the stuff, but it was just the over-stimulation of personal triumph. "He win! He win!" he shouted. "My El Toro, is he not everything I say?" Then he ran back and kissed Toro who was lying on the rubbing table. Toro seemed pleased with himself too. "I hit and he go boom," he said several times.

Danny was standing off to one side, eyeing the scene coldly. "Come on, Doc, get him into a shower," he said irritably. "Whatta you want him to do, catch a cold?" His face was very white and his eyes had that washed-out look that always settled in them when he was drinking.

Acosta looked like a busy little tug-boat towing a great liner as he led Toro to the showers. "Please, out of the way, out of the way," he shouted importantly, pushing through the dressing-room crowd. At the entrance to the showers, Toro paused and turned to Doc. "This man I knock out, he is not hurt, no? He is okay?"

Doc assured him that Coombs was going to recover. Toro had dropped it in there as if it had been rehearsed. I noticed several of the reporters scribbling it down. "You see, he's scared to death he's going to kill some-body," I explained. "Ever since he almost knocked that guy off back in Argentina."

Al Leavitt was leaning against the door with an un-wholesome smile on his face. "As a fighter that Coombs does a beautiful one-and-a-half gaynor," he said.

"You wouldn't trust your own mother, would you?" I said.

"Not if she was in the fight game," Leavitt said.

"Come on out to Pat Drake's and cool off," I said.

"Pat's throwing a little party—just four or five hundred people—up at his joint in Bel Air."

Drake was an ex-chauffeur for Nick back in his boot days who wandered into Hollywood when things got hot in New York, started working extra and went to the top as a rival studio's answer to Bogart.

"Okay, I'll come," Leavitt said, "but I'll still tab it for an El Foldo."

Drake's party was complete with swimming pool, floodlights, buffet, butlers, bartenders, a seven-piece orchestra, celebrities and all the other necessary ingredients of a successful Hollywood party. As usual, Nick had known what he was doing to choose Hollywood for Toro's debut. The Hollywood crowd were sufficiently immersed in sentimentalism, hyperbole and hero-worship to go off the deep end for Toro Molina. Male stars whose faces were altars of a new idolatry crowded around to shake Toro's hand and glamour-coated actresses whose pin-ups have become a national fetish flocked around like autograph hunters. Dave Stempel rushed up to congratulate me. "Terrific, Eddie, really terrific!" he said. "Like nothing human. Hits like a sledge-hammer."

Toro looked astonished and ill-at-ease. A soulful-faced star who was known for her genteel, ladylike roles was smiling up at him over her drink. Ruby came up to me with a cocktail in her hand and said, "I'd better rescue him from that glamour-puss. I hear she's the biggest she-wolf in town. Toro would be just dumb enough to go for her."

A few minutes later Ruby was dancing with him. Nick was inside playing stud with Drake and some other boys. Quite a couple, she and Toro. He was wearing a sharp white Palm Beach, one of those new suits I angled for him. Ruby was wearing a black low-cut, semi-formal gown with a large, black onyx cross pointing down the valley between her full breasts. Around her head was a black velvet snood. Her dark eyes were half-closed and her body moved with self-confidence. She was not as symmetrical and fashionably underweight as some of the film stars who had made sex appeal their profession, but there was a mature female luxuriance to Ruby that promised more than the slenderized narrow-waisted figures of the professional body-beautifuls.

I found Danny at the bar, which had been set up under a bright awning near the pool. He was waiting for the bartender to refill his glass. His legs were spread apart to balance himself and he was staring out over the crowd with pale, tired eyes. "Hello, laddie," he said when he recognized me. "You having fun, laddie? I'm getting drunk, laddie. Any objections?"

"How do you think it looked, Danny?"

His face twisted to a bitter smile. "You know what I think, laddie, I think it looked putrid. I think he's the goddamest saddest excuse for a prize-fighter I ever saw. I think we're all going to wind up with the Commish taking our goddam licenses away."

"Don't forget Jimmy Quinn and the Commission are like this," I said. "With Jimmy on top. He helps pick 'em."

Danny lifted his next drink off the bar. "Happy days, laddie," he said.

Just then Luis Acosta came up to us, ready for more embracing and congratulations. "Is it not true now everything I have say?" He couldn't help laughing as he talked. "El Toro is *magnifico*, no? He give you a big surprise, hey?"

Danny turned away from him without saying anything. Acosta's ebullience was suddenly checked. "I do not understan', please," he protested to me. "Tonight we have the first victory. We celebrate. We are all on the way to a big success. I think perhaps it is time we all are become friends, no?"

Danny turned around and stared at him so long before he said anything that Acosta began to shift his eyes in embarrassment.

"Go away," Danny said.

Acosta looked frightened, blinked rapidly as if trying not to weep and walked stiffly away.

Danny's rare stands of hostility always left him with a sense of inner discomfort. "I'm sorry," he said, "I'm sorry, laddie, but that little cheerleader is on his way home. He's through tomorrow."

"Nick's going to let him go?"

Danny nodded. "Nick's gonna tell him in the morning. How d'ya say it in spic talk, *adios?* It's *adios* tomorrow for Señor Acosta. *Adios.*"

I watched Acosta puffing up with pride again as he rejoined the party. A famous director and his divorced wife who had starred in his last picture were inviting Acosta to sit down with them. Soon Acosta was doing the talking. The gestures were where I had come in. "And so now my great discovery, El Toro Magnifico, is on his way to the championship of the world," he was undoubtedly saying. He had hitched a ride on a flying carpet and now he was soaring up into the heavens, happily unaware that the carpet was being pulled out from under him.

I wandered over toward the pool. Several couples were in swimming. The Killer was poised on the high-board, showing off his chest development, proud of his muscular little body. Knifing into the water he stayed under a long time. The little mouse who was his for the evening screamed and he broke surface, laughing. She pretended to be insulted but he dove down again and in a moment she was laughing too. In the morning I would hear all about it.

On my way over toward the dancers I passed Toro and Ruby, sitting on a stone-bench in the garden. Toro was laughing at something Ruby was saying. It occurred to me that I had never seen him laugh before. "We're having a wonderful time," Ruby said. "I talk to him in English and he answers in Spanish. I've promised to start giving him English lessons."

"She teach me the English," Toro said cheerfully.

"Swell," I said. "Only don't forget Danny's lessons come first."

It was just a very light jab and it didn't seem to hurt her. "He learns very fast," she said. She smiled at him and he became flustered and ran his hand through his hair.

"Hey, Molina, I been looking all over for you," a voice called from across the garden. It was Doc. "I've had a cab standing by for half an hour to take you back to the hotel."

Toro looked at Ruby. "I no tired. I stay."

Doc shook his head. "Know what time it is, after one o'clock. The only fighter I ever saw who could stay up all night and win was Harry Greb. And you ain't Greb."

Toro pushed his big lips out in his child's pout. "But I ask Luis. Luis say I can stay."

"Sorry, brother, Luis has nothing to say about this. I'm the bugler in this outfit and I'm blowing taps."

"I'm leaving in a couple of minutes, Doc," Ruby said. "I'll drop him off if you like."

"It's all the way downtown, Mrs. Latka," Doc said. "I'll take him home with me." He started to pull Toro to his feet. "Let's go, Molina."

I sat on the bench with Ruby as the hunchback led his charge toward the house. She asked for a cigarette and as I leaned toward her to light it for her I was conscious of an evil covetousness in her eyes. And it wasn't for me.

"Nick still in the game?" I said.

"You know Nick. He'll stay there till he comes out a winner if it takes him till tomorrow afternoon."

Nick played everything for blood, a penny-a-point gin game as seriously as no-limit poker.

"I never knew a guy who hates to lose as bad as Nick does," Ruby said. "When a horse he likes runs out or something, for a week or so there's just no living with him."

"I'd hate to be around when he finds he's backed a wrong horse," I said.

13

Next morning, while Toro went to church with Ruby, I took Acosta up to see Nick. With nothing else to write about, the sports pages had given Toro a big play, with one write-up spotting Acosta's running patter of exhortation through the ropes. This public recognition fattened his pride. All the way out to Beverly Hills I had to listen to his vainglorious variations on an already too-familiar theme. "You see, Luis tol' the truth when he say El Toro will make us all very rich and famous," Acosta said as we walked along the row of palm trees to Nick's bungalow.

Nick was having breakfast with the Killer in the patio. He was sitting in his monogrammed bathrobe, smoking a cigar and reading the papers. Acosta gave him his cordial little bow and his most ingratiating smile and began to word one of those flattering greetings when Nick cut him off. Nick always took the quick way.

"Killer, did you find out when that boat leaves for Buenos Air-ees?" he said.

"Thursday midnight from Pedro," Killer said.

"That's the boat you go home on," Nick said.

Acosta looked at him unbelievingly. "Please? I do not understan' . . ."

Nick looked at me. "You wanna tell him in his own language?"

"No, no," Acosta said, desperate-eyed, "I understan' the English. It is just that I do not understan' . . ."

"Well, if you understand English, that's it," Nick said. "Thursday at midnight we put you on the boat."

"No, no, I will not go. You cannot do this. I belong with El Toro. I stay with him!" Acosta cried.

"Shhh," Nick quieted him with his hand. "This is a classy joint. The guy next door is a bigshot. What d'ya want him to think I am, a bum?"

"But El Toro and I, we come together, we stay together, or he goes back with me," Acosta insisted.

"That's not the way it's gonna be," Nick said quietly. "Jimmy Quinn and me, we own Molina. If you want to take your five percent back with you, that's your business. But ninety-five stays here with me."

"But he's mine. He belongs to me. You took him from me. You cannot push me out like this," Acosta screamed.

"We put you on the boat Thursday night," Nick said.

"But why you make me go?" Acosta demanded. "What I do, what I do wrong?"

"You're a pest," Nick said. "You're not satisfied to sit back and take your lousy five percent."

The blood of anger was rising into Acosta's face. "I stay here," he yelled, "I fight. I see a lawyer. I get El Toro back."

Nick calmly poured himself another cup of coffee. "No, you go Thursday. Your visa runs out next week. You can't get an extension on your work visa because we don't need you. My partner's already explained that to a friend of his who's got an in with the State Department. So we only got an extension for Molina. My bookkeeper'll mail you your five percent."

I was sitting off a little to one side, watching the conflict rise to its sorry climax as if it were a play I was seeing from a front-row seat. It would have been nice if my involvement in the action had been cut off cleanly at the fall of the third-act curtain. Nice, but unprofitable. No, I wasn't in the audience, I was on stage, no matter how close to the wings I tried to inch my chair.

"No visa," Acosta said, the fight gone out of him, pursing his small lips as if he were going to cry. "You fix it so I get no visa. You fix it so I must leave El Toro here." The little eyes were moist with frustration now. The jaunty arrogance, the elaborate self-importance had been torn away from him, leaving him as small and scrawny and absurdly pathetic as a defeathered bluejay.

"Now I'll tell you what I'm going to do for you," Nick said. "I'm going to give you a five-thousand-dollar advance against your percentage. You'll get that in cash on the boat Thursday if you tell Toro you want him to stay here with us and that we'll look after him. Have we got a deal?"

Acosta looked at him dully.

"Don't forget, if you don't tell Toro, he stays, and you go just the same," Nick said. "Only without the five G's."

"I understan'," Acosta said.

I couldn't look at his face. Somehow I had the crazy feeling my complicity would increase the more I looked at that face.

"Well, you want that dough?" Nick said. His voice was unemotional, business-like. "Is it a deal?"

Acosta nodded slowly, almost as if he had become disinterested. "All right, a deal," he said with the boredom of the defeated.

Nick indicated me with his cigar. "Eddie'll sit in with you when you tell Toro," he told Acosta. "Just so I'll know."

Acosta turned around to include me in his distrust of Nick. I could feel myself being dragged from the wings onto the middle of the stage. I looked down at my lap. I wanted to tell him I was sorry, that I wouldn't have done this, that I understood what identifying himself with Toro had meant to him. But what was the percentage? Was there any use dealing myself out of Nick's favor when I couldn't do anything for Acosta anyway?

Some day, if I played my cards right, things would be different. By then, maybe I'd have bought myself enough time off to finish my play. And if it clicked, Beth and I could . . . But meanwhile, here in the hot sun of the patio in Beverly Hills, things were happening the way Nick wanted them to happen and all I could do was vote *Ja*.

The way Acosta continued to sit there after Nick had said everything he had to say reminded me of a badly punished fighter who remains in his corner after the last round is over, waiting for enough strength to rise and climb out of the ring.

"All right," Nick said. "I guess that's it." He beckoned to the Killer. "Take Acosta back to the hotel and stay with him until Eddie comes down."

"But, Meester Latka, this is not right. El Toro . . ."

Nick nodded to the Killer. Menegheni took him by the arm and moved him toward the gate. All the formality was crushed out of Acosta now. There were no good-byes from Nick. The Killer opened the gate with his free arm and pushed Acosta through it.

Nick stretched luxuriously and lit a fresh cigar. He had forgotten all about Acosta. The moist eyes, the crushed look hadn't touched him. He tipped his chair back from the table and opened his robe to let the sun beat down on his chest. "This sun is for me," he said. "Take your clothes off and get comfortable, Eddie. I got some shorts you c'd wear."

"I'm afraid they wouldn't fit me any more," I said.

"I been noticing that," Nick said. "You oughta take care of yourself, kid. There's a swell Finnish bath up on Sunset Boulevard. All the stars take their hangovers there. Sweat all that poison outa your system."

A little while later we were alone together in the steam room, basking in the pleasant enervation of the moist, hot atmosphere. Nick picked up a limp sports section from the level below him and re-read the account of last night's fight. I had done a little business with the guy who had the by-line, and the story read the way we wanted it to read.

"Well, Eddie, we're on our way," Nick said. "The write-ups read good this morning. Real good. Let 'em say Toro's a stinking boxer, call him clumsy if they want to, long as they make the public think he really clouts those guys. That's what they come for, that, and to see some little guy cut him down." He stretched out on his back in an attitude of exaggerated well-being. "This is living, isn't it? California, loafing in the afternoons, money coming in. Latka doesn't throw you any bad ones, does he?"

This was the best job I ever had all right. More money, less to do, and the kick of putting something over. Even Acosta didn't have too much to complain about. Already he had cleared ten thousand, which added up to a lot of pesos for a two-bit circus manager on the village circuit.

"Did I tell you about that kid of mine?" Nick was saying. "He and his partner won the New England scholastic doubles championship. You should see the size-a the cup he got. Must be this big. And it says Nicholas Latka, Junior, right on it." His face softened with an expression of parental pride. "How d'ya like that, Nicholas Latka, Junior, right along with all them high-class handles?"

"Have you picked out a college for him yet, Nick?"

"I'm gonna try to get him into Yale. I've heard a lot about that Yale. It seems to be a real class joint."

The heavy-muscled Swedish masseur opened the door and stuck his head in. "Ready for your massage now, Mr. Latka." I lay there a few minutes longer letting the heat draw the poison through my pores. Later, when I came out into the air after the massage and the cold shower, I felt refreshed. But that feeling only lasted until I got back to the room in the Biltmore that Toro and Acosta shared.

Acosta was sitting at the window looking out. Toro was reading the funny papers, to which he had recently become addicted. The Killer was playing solitaire. He picked up the cards quickly when he saw me come in. "Boy, am I glad to see you! I had a matinee on this afternoon."

He ducked out. Acosta didn't look up from the window.

"Tell him yet?" I said.

He shook his head.

"You better tell him," I said.

He looked at me helplessly. Then he turned to Toro, his face dull with resignation. "El Toro," he said in Spanish, "this Thursday, I must go home."

"But how is that possible? I fight again next week," Toro said.

"You must stay here after I leave," Acosta said.

Toro's comic section slid to the floor. "Luis, what are you saying? Why should I stay without you?"

"Because . . . because it is better that way," Acosta said heavily.

"How—how can it be better?" Toro protested. "You promised we would always stay together. And now you would leave me here with these strangers?"

Acosta rubbed his small hand over his face. "I am sorry I cannot stay with you, Toro."

"You must stay," Toro said. "You must stay or I go too. I will not stay without you. I will not stay."

"El Toro, listen to me," Acosta said, speaking in a flat, measured voice. "You have to stay. It will still be good for you. You will come home as rich as I have always promised. I will come to meet you at the boat."

"Luis, do not leave me, please do not leave me," Toro suddenly begged. "I do not like these people. I am afraid of these people. If you go, I go too."

Acosta looked at me pleadingly. There was nothing left to do but tell him everything, his listless eyes seemed to say.

"El Toro, you cannot go with me. You cannot go because these men own you. They own you now."

Toro's big face studied Acosta, foolish with confusion. "They—own me?"

He had never been aware of the deals and percentage cuts by which Luis had sold part of his contract first to Vince and then to Nick and Quinn. Acosta had thought it would only bewilder him. Now he looked at Toro with the shame of betrayal and did not know what to say.

"How do they own me, Luis?" Toro asked again.

"I sold them your contract, El Toro."

"But why—why did you do that?"

"Because I did not have enough importance to get you up into the big money by myself," Acosta explained. "This way you will fight in the Madison Square Garden —maybe for the championship. This I did for you, El Toro."

Toro's lips puckered. His eyes betrayed a quick, instinctive fear and then narrowed with suspicion. "You sold me, Luis. Then you can buy me back again, please."

"No, that is impossible—impossible," Acosta said, his voice rising irritably. "You must stay here. You must."

Bewildered, Toro shook his massive head. "I thought you my friend, Luis."

"You'll be all right," I interposed. "We'll look after you."

Toro turned to look at me in surprise, as if he had forgotten that I was there. He looked at me for several seconds, without saying anything, until I began to feel embarrassed. He shook his head again, this time with a kind of pity. He said nothing more to either of us. Slowly he went to the window, where he stood, his huge back to us, and looked out at the downtown traffic.

That Thursday night Vince and the Killer came to take Acosta to the ship. Up to the last moment he had been begging me to get Nick to change his mind. He even offered to cut himself down to two and a half percent, if he were allowed to stay. My promises to talk things over with Nick kept him quietly hopeful until the end. What was the use of letting Acosta know there were never any appeals from Nick's decisions? His word was always good, for you or against you.

Neither Vince nor the Killer liked the idea of driving Acosta all the way out to San Pedro, and they treated him more like a man who was being deported for a crime than a man who had been systematically double-crossed. I found myself thinking of a dozen other places I'd rather have been when Acosta said good-bye to Toro. Acosta put his short arms as far around Toro's great waist as they would go.

"*Adios, El Toro mio,*" Luis said almost in a whisper.

Toro just turned away. I stood there trying to think of something to say. He muttered hoarsely, "I thought he was my friend."

"Come on," I said, "I'll take you to a movie."

Toro liked our movies. He was especially fond of music and seemed to enjoy most those big musical extravaganzas with a hundred girls dancing on a hundred pianos in which Hollywood excels.

The newsreel included a feature on Toro himself, training at Ojai, with the inevitable newsreel gags, showing him square off against a flyweight chinning himself on Toro's arm, and ending with his huge face grinning into the camera in a gargoyle full-head close-up. As we left the theatre a group of kids surrounded him and asked for his autograph. But neither the dancing girls nor the little taste of glory seemed to do anything for Toro's state of mind. He withdrew inside himself. On the way back to the hotel, when I tried to break through his silence by saying in Spanish, "Don't worry now. We're all going to be looking out for you," he answered me haltingly in English, as if he refused to share with me the intimacy of his own language. "I wish I go home," he said.

The next day we all took the train down to San Diego for the second fight on Toro's itinerary. Vince had lined up a colored heavyweight by the name of Dynamite Jones, a local pugilist of established mediocrity who had been winning in the border city. In return for five hundred dollars, Jones had agreed to leave in his dressing room what Dynamite he possessed and to accommodate us with a diveroo in the third.

Toro's training in the San Diego gym attracted capacity crowds to every session, even though he looked even more listless than he had at Ojai. Danny was so disgusted he devoted most of his time to the local bars and horse rooms, leaving Doc to continue Toro's education in the manly art. Doc did what he could. He had enough liking for Toro to want to teach him how to take care of himself in case he ever got in there with someone with the handcuffs off. But Toro lacked either the primitive drive of a rough-and-tumble killer or the systematized consecration of the athlete. He was lethargic and moody and dreaded the sweaty monotony of roadwork and the daily grind at the gym. He obeyed Doc's instructions with reluctant obedience. But except for learning to hold his left out in the more or less established way, and to move around with slow, graceless orthodoxy, there wasn't much improvement in his boxing ability. George obligingly permitted himself to be knocked over occasionally to keep alive the myth of Toro's punching powers, but our Man Mountain still hadn't learned to hit hard enough to bother a healthy featherweight.

I had the fight reporter of the only morning paper up to the room a couple of times and sized him up as a nice guy on the lazy side with about as much integrity as I had, who would just as soon shove my stuff in with his name on it as grind it out himself. So I sat up there at the Hotel Grant, making with the adjectives.

There wasn't a day when I didn't have a qualm or two for what I was doing. At the same time I had to admit that on the bottom level I was getting a real kick out of putting this big oaf across as the world's most dangerous heavyweight. The morning of the fight, for instance, when I read the copy in the first column of the sports section under Ace Mercer's by-line, it handed me a laugh, I suppose a laugh of superiority.

Fresh from his sensational two-round knockout victory over highly touted Cowboy Coombs, Man Mountain Molina, the Giant of the Andes, 275 pound human pile-driver, faces Dynamite Jones, the pride of San Diego, in ten rounds or less at the Waterfront Arena tonight.

Although outweighed by eighty-five pounds and standing only six-feet-one, just a little guy when you're looking down from Molina's stratospheric six-foot-seven, Jones and his manager "Whispering" Al Mathews have been going up and down cauliflower alley grabbing up all the short money they can find. "We ain't afraid of nobody," Whispering Al confided courageously to this writer after Dynamite's final workout yesterday.

Dynamite is well known to San Diego fans, who have yet to see the dusky battler down for the full count. He will be meeting a lethal puncher of superhuman strength in the Giant of the Andes who is already being spoken of as a championship contender . . .

Jones was a tall, rangy boy with more stuff than I would have expected from a second-rater out there in the sticks. He came out of his corner as if he really meant to make a fight out of it, with stiff jabs that made Toro look clumsy and flat-footed. Toro threw a wild right that almost knocked himself down as Jones ducked. The crowd laughed. Ten seconds before the end of the round, Jones feinted to the body, sucking Toro into dropping his hands, and crossed him with a straight right to the jaw. Toro's knees buckled, and if Doc and Danny hadn't jumped through the ropes at the bell, he might have gone down.

The crowd was on its feet, cheering Jones as the colored fighter danced confidently back to his corner. That was part of Toro's appeal of course. They came not only to see the brute flatten his opposition but also with the deeply rooted hope that just once, the little guy, the underdog, the dimly realized symbol of themselves would triumph over the Giant as David the eternal short-ender felled Goliath.

Toro staggered back to his corner in a daze. Doc had to use smelling salts to sharpen his dimming senses.

"What goes with this Jones?" I asked Vince.

"If the jig tries anything," Vince said, "he ends up in the bay."

"Maybe he just wants to make it look good for a round or two and doesn't know how little Toro can take."

"If that jigaboo tries to cross us, we got protection," Vince said. "I got my guy workin' his corner."

That was the first time I realized what a really thorough fellow Vince Vanneman was. It wouldn't win any merit badges for any of us, but if it hadn't been for his foresight things would have turned out even worse than they did.

Jones came out for the second round as if the understanding we thought we had was actually made between two other guys. He wouldn't stand still for Toro to connect with his ponderous rights. As he kept moving around Toro he was scoring with sharp punches that had the crowd on its feet, begging for a knockout, defying the slow-moving giant with blood-thirsty abuse, "Knock the big bum out! Send him back to Argentina! Attaboy, cut him down to your size!"

Fortunately, Jones was a punishing but not a finishing puncher or he would have written an untimely 30 to our whole campaign. But when the second round ended, Toro wandered back to his corner with blood dripping from his mouth and his eyes staring uselessly. Doc worked over him with his educated fingers, massaging the back of his neck, while a handler squeezed a spongeful of cold water over his head, and checked with vaseline the trickle of blood that ran from the corner of his mouth.

"It's the business all right," Vince said.

"Jesus," I said. "This is some tank artist, this Jones."

"My guy's talkin' to him," Vince said. "My guy's a real tough fella. He'll tell that nigger what'll be if he don't splash this round."

The representative of our interests Vince had placed in Jones' corner seemed to be doing plenty of talking. He was leaning through the ropes with his sweaty, larcenous face close to Jones' ear, pouring it to him. But when Jones came out for the third round he was still trying. He knocked Toro off balance with a smart left jab to the mouth and followed up with a straight right that sent Toro stumbling back against the ropes. Any moment I expected to see Toro start caving in, in sections, and my lousy five percent not worth one of Danny's torn-up bookie tabs. It made me realize for the first time how hungry I was for that dough, just as hungry as Nick, or Vince or Luis Acosta out there on the high seas on his way home to the smalltime. Just like Acosta I found myself up on my feet begging Toro to stay with him.

Jones was getting wild now, with the disobedient urge to knock Toro out. His left hand shot over Toro's shoulder and Toro brought up a looping right from the floor that caught Jones on the chin. It didn't hurt Jones so much as it caught him off balance, and Toro, trying clumsily to follow up his advantage, shoved Jones with both hands, and the colored fighter half-slipped, half-fell to the canvas. As long as he was down and the referee (with whom Vince had done a little business) began to count, Jones decided to rest on one knee until the count of six, for he was beginning to be arm-weary from throwing so many punches at his wide-open target.

But when he arose at six, a towel came fluttering up out of his corner. Vince's guy was working overtime to earn his fifty clams. Jones tried to kick the towel out of the ring and go on fighting, but the referee grabbed him and led him back to his corner. Then he came back and raised the hand of our bewildered superman. A terrible roar of protest rose from the crowd. In a second the air was full of flying cushions, programs and bottles. Some of the fans in their wrath started breaking up their seats and hurling the pieces into the ring. With police running interference we hustled Toro back to the dressing room. With a quick fifty to the sergeant, we got away in his police car.

"What happen?" Toro asked me in innocent confusion.

"Don't worry, you won the fight fair," I told him. "It's just that the people aren't satisfied until they see you kill somebody. So they didn't want the fight stopped so soon."

Toro smiled through his bloody lips. "One ponch and he goes boom," he said. "Just like first time."

For once in my life I had no desire to fraternize with reporters. So instead of going back to the hotel or catching a train, we went straight to a garage and hired a car. We drove up the coast until we thought we were safely out of range of the little stink-bomb we had exploded and stopped at a small auto-court, or Motel, as they like to call them in Cal. The guy Vince had working for us in the other corner was with us too. His name was Benny. He was one of those ex-lightweights who blow up into heavyweights as soon as they come off the training and get on the beer. As soon as Doc put Toro to bed after a warm bath and a light massage, so he'd rest easier, Benny gave us the lowdown on the little comedy (in the Greek sense) that had been going on in his corner. It was a hot night and he was on his third beer when he opened his sweat-stained shirt, revealing a fat, hairy chest on which were tattooed the words, "Pac. Coast lt-wt champ, 1923," and the exaggerated nude figure of a woman called Edna embracing an Adonis-like creature in boxing trunks, boxing gloves and a sailor hat captioned Battling Benny Mannix. The Battler managed to raise the group's morale somewhat by inhaling and exhaling his fatty diaphragm in such a way that the tattooed figures undulated together with impressive realism.

"This jig comes back after the first round cocky as hell, see," Benny began in an injured tone. " 'Christ, I didn' know that big fella was such a bum,' he says. 'An' I thought I was layin' down to save myself punishment.'

" 'Don't get no fancy ideas,' I tells him, 'or you'll get a helluva lot more punishment 'n you figured on.'

"But when the jig goes out for round two, he's still full of wrong ideas, see? 'This guy's got nothin',' he says, 'I c'n stiffen this guy. The hell with them five C's,' he says to Mathews. 'We c'n make more flattening this joker.'

"Well, I tries to tell him if he keeps up the wise talk he's sucking around for a hole in the head, but the jig don't scare so easy. He's got this giant-killin' on his mind. So when I'm massagin' him I try to squeeze his muscles so they'll go dead on him and when I wipe off his face I accidentally rub some alcohol in his eyes, so when we send him out for Three he's brushing his eyes and he ain't quite the weisenheimer he was when he came in from Two. But even then he's beatin' your guy real bad when he goes down from that slip. So I figures, what the hell, this jig is just wrong enough to get up off the floor and belt the big jerk out. So I sees my chance and throws in the towel."

Danny sucked out the last of a pint bottle of rye. "I don' like it," he said. "Twen'y years in the racket I never have a run-in with the Commish. All that's gotta happen now is I lose my license."

"Aah, shet up your bellyachin'," Vince said. "Always cryin' about your goddam license. Shove the commissions, both of 'em. Leave Jimmy and Nick take care of 'em."

"But damn it, if you're gonna set these fights up, why don't you do it right?" Danny demanded. "The woods are full of bums ready to fall down for a price. But you, the great fixer, gotta pick a guy who likes to win."

"Aah, go shove yourself, spithead," Vince said in rebuttal. "What am I, a mind reader for Chrisake? How the hell should I know what goes on in that dinge's double-crossin' brain?"

"If I lose my license, I'm dead," Danny said. "You, you can always go back to pimping."

"Why you son-of-a-bitch!" Profanity spewed from Vince's fleshy mouth as he lunged heavily toward Danny, starting a wild punch that Danny blocked neatly. Danny made no effort to retaliate as Benny, George, Doc and I grabbed parts of Vince's aroused anatomy and pulled him away.

"Never do that," Danny said quietly, his face strangely white, his thin lips drawn to an angry line.

"Yeah, well, no jerk is gonna call me them names like that," Vince blubbered.

"Whatta you wanna do, wake Molina?" Doc said. "Let the guy sleep. He needs his sleep."

"Aah, shove him too," Vince said. He settled back on the couch with a crumpled copy of *Crime* he had picked up on the train down to San Diego.

I went outside to smoke a cigarette in peace. Across the highway the surf pounded on the beach with relentless monotony. The sky was clear and moonlit. Looking up into it, the tension of the smoke-filled Motel room seemed as foolish and far away as an argument you had with your brother when you were eight. In a few minutes George Blount came out and joined me. "Man, oh, man!" he said and chuckled softly.

"One of these days Danny's going to clip him," I said.

"Mister McCuff's like me," George said. "Don' want to fight nobody 'cept for money."

"Why do you think it is, George?" I said. "Why is it most you guys don't go in for these grudge matches?"

"I don' know," George laughed. "Maybe you go roun' punchin' fellows and catchin' punches so long you just get it all outa your system. Maybe every man's got just so many punches in him and when you get rid of 'em all in the ring you just don't want to hit nobody no more."

I walked down the road a quarter of a mile or so with him, not saying much of anything but conscious as always of his deep serenity.

"Boy, we really stank up the joint tonight," I said.

"That fella oughta go home," George said. "That fella oughta go home before something bad happen."

That was easy to say, when all you were getting out of it were three squares and a little pocket-money. But Toro Molina had already turned them away in two cities. He was an oil well just beginning to come in and you don't turn off a profitable flow just because your hands are getting a little dirty, not where I come from.

As soon as we read the papers next morning we knew we had troubles. The State Boxing Commission had tied up the purses of both fighters, pending an investigation. The fight we had lined up for Oakland was postponed. Toro couldn't read the papers well enough to learn what had happened, so at least he was happy. Only he wanted to know where the money was that he had earned. Vince slipped him fifty dollars. He had never had a large American bill of his own and he seemed content with it. "Feefty bocks, hokay," he kept saying.

You could have chipped the air up for ice cubes when Nick came in.

"Well, gentlemen," he said, "this is great. This is just great. This is just what we needed, like a hole in the head."

Vince started to blubber and bluster through an explanation, but Nick's hard, sharp voice knifed through his defense.

"I'm not inarested," he said. "When I was a kid I learned one thing and I learned it good. Never do nothing halfass. Whatever it is, if you're gonna do it, do it. The kid who stole an apple off the pushcart and ran away, he's the dope the cop always caught. The guy who followed the old man home, bopped him in the hallway and took his whole goddam pushcart, he's the one who got away. That's been a principle with me ever since. Like this build-up we're giving Molina. You say you slipped the nigger two-fifty to lay down. (It had been five hundred when I heard it, but maybe Vince held out the other half.) Hell, make it worth his while. It's worth it to us. Don't be a piker. Think big. Give 'em a grand. Only give it to 'em after the fight. No dive, no dough. You got that? Now this time I let it go. Maybe this sun is making me soft in the head, but I let it go. Next time you fumble you're out on your ass."

"Yeah, but we gotta contract," Vince pouted.

"Sure we gotta contract," Nick agreed. "But give me trouble and see how quick I tear up the contract. I got Max Stauffer," he said, mentioning the Darrow of corruption. "You louse me up and rightaway Max has ten reasons why the contract's no good that'll stand up in court." He opened his closet drawer and paused discriminatingly over his impressive collection of hand-painted ties. "Now screw, both of you," he said. "Pat Drake is bringing a couple of big men over from the studio, and you guys don't look dressed good enough."

The investigation dragged on for a couple of weeks and I had a job on my hands trying to make it look as good as possible in the papers. One of the things working for us was the convincing way Toro reacted to the charges. "Me no fight feex," he insisted. "I no crook. I try hard."

Vince also expressed indignation that his professional integrity should be impugned. The whole thing wound up with the Commission exonerating Toro and his managers completely, but finding Benny Mannix guilty and suspending his license to second fighters in the State of California for twelve months. Benny had admitted throwing in the towel because he had placed a large bet on Toro, which he was afraid he might lose. This handful of verbal sand in the eyes of the Commission hiked our overhead up five hundred bucks, which was Benny's price for taking the rap. The Commission ruling was only binding so far as California was concerned, so Vince sent Benny on to Las Vegas, where we had a date with a full-blooded Indian Miniff had dug up for us by the name of Chief Thunderbird. Chief Thunderbird, Miniff was insisting with characteristic whimsicality, was the heavyweight champion of New Mexico.

Now that the Commission loosened the strings on the San Diego purse, Toro wanted his money. He wanted to send a chunk home to the family in Santa Maria. He wanted them to realize down there what a rich man he was becoming in North America. But Vince explained to him that there couldn't be any pay-off until Nick's bookkeeper Leo figured out Toro's net take after overhead and managerial cuts had been deducted. "Meanwhile here's another fifty," Vince said. "Any time you need money, just ask me."

Toro was very pleased. He had all the money he wanted. All he had to do was ask Vince. And as soon as his percentage was figured out, he would send enough to his father to begin building that home that was going to put the de Santos mansion to shame. Perhaps he would even go back for a vacation—I held out the hope that this was possible when he was well-enough established—and sanctify his relationship with the lovely Carmelita.

While we were waiting for the Commission to make up their minds about that San Diego business, I was walking down Spring Street with Toro one afternoon. Toro could never go by a music store without stopping to press his nose against the window and gaze wonderingly at the radios, phonographs and musical instruments. This time he said, "I come back pronto," and darted into a music store. In a few minutes he returned with a portable radio in his hand, loudly broadcasting a swing band. "Feefty dollar. I buy," Toro said happily. People kept turning around to stare at us, not only for Toro's size but for the volume of the unexpected music.

"Toro, turn that thing off," I said. "Nobody plays a radio in the street."

"I like carry music," Toro said.

Beth should see me now, I thought, playing nursemaid to an elephantine idiot. Everywhere we went, Toro carried that silly radio around, always turned on with the volume up. When we went to a restaurant he placed it tenderly on an empty chair and smiled at it lovingly as he ate while it filled the room with the nasal music of cowboy songs. "In Santa Maria no music in box," he said. "I bring back many to my village for give away."

I don't think Toro knew there was any way of changing those bills. You either had to buy something for fifty dollars, it seemed to him, or you might as well throw it way. He blew the second fifty all at once in the arcade of the hotel and hurried to show me his latest acquisition. It was a tiny gold key in a miniature heart-shaped gold lock.

"Who's this for?" I said.

"For Señora Latka," he said.

I looked at it more closely. On the back of the lock was engraved in small letters, "The key to my heart."

"You can't give her this," I said.

"Why not?" Toro wanted to know. "She nice lady. I like very much."

"Her husband likes her very much too," I said.

"I like her too," Toro protested. "She nice to me. Good lady. Go to church every Sunday."

Well, finally there was nothing to do about it but take him up to Beverly Hills, so he could present his little trinket to Ruby. Nick was out playing golf with Pat Drake, as it happened, and she was home alone. Although the sun was shining, we found her inside drinking her way through a batch of side-cars. "Why, Toro, that's sweet of you, that's awfully sweet of you," she said, and

228

she pinned the locket over her heart in a provocative gesture.

While I drank along with her for a little while, Toro just sat there silently staring at her in simple-minded shamelessness. She was a stunning woman, with the agelessness of the full-blown voluptuary. Though her behavior was above reproach and almost studiously lady-like, I wondered if it was the influence of the side-cars which made me sense that Toro's presence was stimulating her to a more animated charade than usual.

Just as we were leaving, Nick came in with Pat Drake and he seemed pleased to be able to show off his giant protégé to the film star. If he were at all disturbed by Toro's present to Ruby there was no hint of it in his reaction. "The guy shows pretty classy taste," he said good-naturedly, looking at the locket. He poked Toro playfully in the ribs. "All set for that guy in Oakland, Man Mountain?"

"I ponch. He go boom," Toro said.

14

IN OAKLAND we polished off in four a character called Oscar DeKalb and in Reno an alleged heavyweight by the name of Tuffy Parrish collapsed from a vicious slap on the chest, which added another five thousand to the take of the corporation. By the time we came into Las Vegas, "with the new scourge of the heavyweights, the Giant of the Andes, seeking his fifth straight knockout victory," the East was beginning to rise to the bait and AP wanted fifty words on the outcome of the Chief Thunderbird fight.

"Turn that goddam radio off," Danny said on our way up to the hotel. The more success we had the more irritable Danny seemed to be getting. Larceny just didn't come naturally to him the way it did to Vince. He fought it all the time.

Toro was still hanging on to his radio. Jazz, cowboy music, spirituals, Latin songs—he didn't seem to care what it was as long as it was something that came out of a box he could carry around.

As soon as we were settled, Doc and George took Toro out to stretch his legs. Danny ducked out to find a place to bet a couple of good things he thought he had at Belmont. Vince was on the phone trying to get hold of a broad he used to know in Las Vegas and I was in the bathtub reading the *New Yorker* when Miniff popped in.

By the time I finished the story and came out with a towel around my middle, they were already in an argument.

"But this Mex is no second-rate bum," Miniff was

230

insisting. "He's a first-rate bum. Why, he coulda been a contender if he was managed right."

"You mean back in the days of Corbett?" I said.

Miniff's ferret eyes turned on me reproachfully. "Aahh," he said in rebuttal. "He's oney twenty-eight year old. Whaddya thinka that?"

"I think in that case he must have fought his first professional fight when he was six," I said. "I looked him up in the record book."

"He's a real tough bum," Miniff said. "Six-four, weighs two-twenny-five. He's a man-mountain hisself. He'll look real good in there with your guy. Lettum go for seven, huh boys?"

"One round, pal, one round," Vince said.

"One round!" Miniff wailed. "Nail me to the cross, go ahead crucify me, one round! Seven rounds, it looks like your bum is knocking over real opposition. One round, it's a farce. That's what it is, a lousy farce."

"Keep your voice down," I said. "Do you want the whole town to know what round we got it greased for?"

"Seven rounds, I could maybe make myself some money with this Indian," Miniff whimpered. "Whatsamatter with you guys, you never wanna let me make no money?"

"For Chrisake you're gettin' a thousand from the club and another five from us for the act," Vince said. "Three months ago your ass was hanging out. What more d'ya want?"

"For goin' so quick I wanna grand," Miniff said. "One grand for the hoomiliation."

"Listen to him, he wants," Vince said to me with righteous derision. "A punched-up greaseball he picks up in a poolroom and alluva sudden he wants!" His mouth opened in a mocking laugh.

Miniff did want. He wanted desperately. He never seemed to be able to get out of the petty-cash department.

"I'll tell you what I'll do with you," Vince turned to

Miniff in sudden imitation of Nick. "I'll give you an extra two-fifty you c'n keep for yourself. Your bum don't have to know anything about it. That way you come out the same as when you split an extra five down the middle."

And that's the way they settled that, with Vince saving us two-bits (which he probably pocketed) by convincing Miniff to hold out on his fighter. The next afternoon I was in our room sipping a rye highball and bending over a hot typewriter whipping up some porridge about this fight's being for the Latin Heavyweight Championship of the World when Miniff came in crying the blues louder than ever. It was a hot fall day, but he still kept his hat on and the heat of the sun plus his own internal fires brought the shine of perspiration to his small, unhealthy face. All the way through the bedroom Miniff kept up his miserable soliloquy. "No wonder I got the bite in the belly. It's these bums, these stinking bums. Oh, Jesus, I wish I had as much money as I can't stand them bums."

"What's the matter, Harry?" I said. "Relax." I pointed to the bottle. "Help yourself."

"The amber?" He recoiled in horror. "I haven't got enough troubles! Why, my ulcer is havin' ulcers! You wanna know why, you take this bum of mine, this Chief Thunderbird he calls hisself."

Vince was still lying in bed, in his underwear, sleeping off a big night. He rolled over irritably. "Whatsmatter? Whatsmatter?" he said.

"My bum, he's off his nut," Miniff said. "He says he don' wanna quit to your bum. Alla sudden he talks like he ain't already been belted out thirty-eight times already."

"What's the matter, doesn't he think he's getting enough dough?" I said.

"It ain't the dough," Miniff said, and then he hesitated as if he were ashamed to say it. "He says it's his pride."

232

Vince sat up in bed, scratched his hairy chest and reached for a cigar. "Pride, for Christ sake! Whaddya mean, pride?"

"That's what he says, pride," Miniff shrugged. "He hasn't got to eat, he has to have pride yet. The whole trouble starts when he sees this Molina work out in the gym yesterday. 'Why, he's a bum like me,' he says right away. And then, you know these punchy guys, he begins to get sore about it. He's almost as big as your guy, so he gets to thinking how different things'd been if his managers had greased things for him the way you's doing with Molina. Gets to feelin' real sorry for hisself, see? An' on toppa that, some a his relatives off the reservation is comin' in to see the fight. He says he's ashamed for 'em to see a dog like Molina belt him out in one. He says for dough he don' want it, he says. He says he's still got his pride."

"Shove his pride," Vince said. "You think he's the only tanker in Las Vegas?"

"But the fight's the night after tomorrow," I said. "We got all this publicity working for us. There's seventy-five hundred already in the house. We're out of pocket if this sensitive fellow doesn't keep his word like a gentleman."

Miniff wiped his forehead nervously. "The aggravations I gotta put up with from these stumblebums."

"Maybe you could slip the guy a mickey," Vince suggested.

"Whatta you think I am, a crook?" Miniff demanded. "Eighteen years in the business, I never got mixed up in no rough stuff. No mickeys and no beatin' up guys. I got principles."

"You're breakin' my heart," Vince said. "You're breakin' my heart. Oney I'm gonna break your little neck if this creep-a yours gives us any trouble."

Miniff's hairy little hand shoved his hat back farther on his head and wiped his face in a convulsive gesture.

"I tell ya the guy won't budge." He turned to me as the more reasonable listener. "I'm talkin' to a wall. His brain is jammed like somebody dropped a rock in the machinery."

"Tell you what you do," I said. "Bring the fellow here after his workout this afternoon. Maybe we can get somewhere with him."

In a couple of hours Miniff was back with his problem child. He looked like a full-blooded Indian, all right, a tall, powerfully built man, with the long, impressive head of a Navajo warrior. In another time, you couldn't help thinking, he might have been a great tribal chieftain, but now he was just another scuffed-up pug, the nobility of his face hammered into a caricature of the eternal palooka, the high-bridged, Roman schnoz pushed into his face, ears on him that would look like cauliflowers even to a cauliflower and sunken eyes overhung with scar tissue. Only he had a way of fixing you with those eyes, sort of proud-like and melancholy that made you want to look away.

"What seems to be the matter, Chief?" I said.

"Molina don't knock me out," he said.

"Why, you good-for-nothing bum," Vince said. "What record are you protecting, for Christ's sweet sake? I suppose you never took a dive before. Why, you been in the tank so long you're starting to grow fins."

The Indian seemed numb to abuse. He didn't say anything.

"It's just business," I said. "There's no disgrace to it, Chief."

The Indian just sat there looking out at us from the depth of his battered dignity. Miniff screamed, Vince threatened and I reasoned, but he just shook his head. Miniff was right, it was just as if a rock had fallen into the mental machinery and the brain had jammed. He sat there immune to abuse, bribery and the danger of physical violence. Maybe it was only a dim protest against

234

a life of profitless punishment that made him slam his mind against us and refuse to submit to further humiliation at the hands of these white-faced jackals riding high on the towering shoulders of an over-sized, over-rated bum.

The morning of the fight the Indian was still holding out and all of us were jittery—all, that is, except Toro, who was really beginning to think that boxing came as naturally to him as Luis Acosta had once told him it did. I ponch and he go boom—that's the way it seemed to Toro as one opponent after another flopped down beneath his ludicrous onslaught.

As soon as Nick got in, we ran over to his suite to dump our troubles in his lap. The manicurist was just putting the finishing touches on his nails as we entered. Ruby met us at the door on her way downstairs to the beauty parlor, although she looked more as if she had just stepped out of one. The Killer was on the phone making a date for Nick with Joe Gideon, who ran the casino downstairs. Apparently the syndicate had an interest in the joint.

"So you two geniuses can't handle one dopey fighter," Nick said. "What would you do if I wasn't around? You know, that's why eventually we have to have all the money." He looked at his trim, polished fingernails. "Tell Miniff to send his boy to me."

We went over to the arena, where Toro and the Chief were weighing in. Vince whispered the word to Miniff, who passed it on to the Indian under his hand. At first, Miniff told us, Thunderbird didn't want any part of it. But Miniff impressed him with what a big man this Latka was and hinted that he might be interested in buying Thunderbird's contract and taking him East to fight in the Garden. Hope is the blind mother of stupidity, and the big jerk went for it.

I went back to the dressing room and sat with Toro while he put his clothes on after the weigh-in. He had hit the scales at 279, four pounds more than the last fight. Toro was putting on the gray, double-breasted plaid I had picked out for him in L.A. He looked at himself in the mirror and smiled at the well-groomed, well-tailored figure he presented.

"You look mighty sharp there, boy," I said.

"You take picture?" Toro said. "I send picture to Mama and Papa to show them I am dress up like a de Santos."

"Sure, we'll send all you want," I said.

"Señora Latka, she is also here?" Toro asked me as we left the dressing room.

"Yes, she's here with Nick," I said.

"I go see her now," Toro said.

"Take it easy. You'll see her when you see Nick."

"We go for walk. We talk."

"I noticed that," I said. "I suppose Nick's noticed it too. What do you find to talk about?"

"We talk . . . nice," Toro said.

"In Spanish," I said. "Tell me in Spanish."

"The Señora is very kind and sympathetic," Toro explained. "She is more like the ladies of Argentina. I like to go to church with her. And after church I tell her something about the life of my village. About my family. About the *Dia del Vino*, the first full moon of the harvest time, when the fountain in the village runs wine for all to drink and even the village beggars stagger like lords."

Maybe that was all it was, I thought. Ruby, in her instinctual way of reaching out to men, was more like the women of Toro's village. Perhaps Ruby was only supplying the personal touch which the rest of us were too lazy, too selfish or too busy to supply. But the fear—completely unjustified by anything I had seen and lurking only in the evil back-alleys of my mind—that her touch might become too personal prompted me to say, "Go a little slow with her, Toro. I've seen Nick when he's mad. I wouldn't want him mad at me."

236

"But there is nothing wrong in what we do," Toro said in Spanish. "She is a good woman. She goes to church. We do no one any harm."

We walked back to the hotel together. "This man I fight tonight—big fellow?" he said.

"Yes, he's big," I said, "but you ought to beat him, all right. Just keep throwing punches."

I wondered how Nick was making out with that Indian. The Indian wasn't much, easy to hit and as muscle-bound as Toro, but he was more of a fighting man, with better co-ordination, and I hated to think what he might do to Toro if he held out on his refusal to go in under wraps.

Ruby was still down in the beauty parlor, so Toro went up to his room to put away those three chops that would have to sustain him until fight time. I thought it would be interesting to see how Nick was jockeying the Indian, but when I put my head in the door Nick told me this was strictly between him and the boy and to go take a powder for myself. At the bar I met Miniff, who hadn't been allowed in either. "Jeez, I'm worried," he said with a sigh of venality. "You gotta admit it, my bums has always been reliable. When I say they go, that's when they go. If this jerk crosses me, it's terrible for my reppatation."

About half an hour later, the Indian came down. Miniff beckoned him to the privacy of the men's room off the bar.

"Well, what happened? Give," Miniff begged.

"He told me I shouldn't say nothing to nobody," the Indian said.

"But you're not gonna ootz us out of that extra dough? You and Nick got together?"

"He's a pretty smart fella," was all the Indian would say.

Half an hour from fight time I was still as much in the dark as the cash customers. When Benny Mannix came in from the Indian's dressing room to go through the motions of watching Doc bandage Toro's hands, I asked him if he knew what was going on.

Benny shook his head with irritable bewilderment. "It beats the hell outa me. Know what the guy does? He takes me aside 'n tells me to go out 'n get him a little piece a chicken wire. Chicken wire, the guy wants! So a couple minutes later when I run down the wire, he says, 'That's good. Now go get a pair of pliers and meet me in the can.' I think the guy's crossing over to the silly side a the street, so I try to con him out of it. 'Okay,' he says, 'okay, after the fight I'll just tell Nick you din wanna co-operate.' 'You mean this is Nick's idea?' I says. 'Who else aroun' here has any ideas?' this Thunderbird comes right back. So I shut my mouth before I catch any more flies and I meet him in the can with the pliers like he asks."

"Wait a minute, Benny," I said. "Let me smell your breath."

"I should drop dead this second if it ain't like I'm telling you," Benny says, offended that I should doubt his veracity. "So when we get into the crapper together he says, 'Now cut off a little piece.'

" 'How small?' I says.

" 'Small enough to fit 'n my mouth,' he says.

" 'What the hell?' I says.

" 'Now have you got a rubber on you?' he says.

" 'A rubber?' I says. 'Sure, but . . .'

" 'Okay, now slip the wire into the rubber,' he says. 'There, that's it. Now keep it in yer pocket, an' when you put the mouthpiece in my mouth make sure you got this underneath it so it'll lie flat against my gums.'

"Holy Jesus," I said.

"I seen 'em do a lot-a tricks but this is a new one on me," Benny said.

So that's the way it was when the fight began. The first time Toro held his left in the Indian's face, the chicken wire did its work and the blood began to trickle

out of one corner of his mouth. But it wasn't bothering
him yet. He fought back. He could punch a little with
his left hand and he let it go a couple of times, forcing
Toro back. The customers stood up and yelled. It looked
as if the Indian could take him. Again you could feel the
mass frenzy to see the giant punished and humiliated. Men
who were good to their mothers and loved their children
shouted encouragement for the Indian with passionate
hatred for the hulking, inept figure who retreated before
him. But every time Toro pushed his left glove into the
Indian's face, blood came forth to meet it. By the end of
the round he looked as if he had stopped an oncoming
truck with his face.

Miniff and Benny did what they could for the cuts
between rounds. The Indian came out of his corner with a
looping right hand that made Toro grunt, but in the
clinch that followed, Toro pawed at his opponent's face
and the Indian's mouth became a bloody mess. Toro's
gloves were sticky with it too and each time he brushed
the Indian's face they left an ugly red blot. The Indian
kept boring in, but the blood pouring out of his mouth
was beginning to bother him. Before the round was half
over his mouth and Toro's gloves were so soggy they made
a sickeningly squashy sound when they came together.

"Stop the fight, stop the fight," some of the ringsiders
were beginning to yell. Women hid their faces behind
their programs. The Indian sprang out of his corner
with show-off courage, but his face was a bloody mask.
He missed a wild swing which sprayed the white shirt of
the referee and some of the ringsiders beneath him. Toro
backed away and turned to the referee with a question in
his eyes. He had no stomach for this. The more tender-
hearted among the fans, and those who had wagered on an
early knockout were on their feet now, chanting "Stop it,
stop it!" The Indian, seeing the referee move toward him,
shook his head and charged in recklessly. But the referee
caught his arm and led him, apparently under protest,

back to his corner. It was all over. The Giant of the Andes had scored his sixth consecutive victory by a TKO.

Toro crossed himself as he did before and after every fight. Then he went across the ring to see if the Indian was all right. The Indian, his mouth still bleeding profusely, rose to embrace Toro. The crowd loved it, all their blood-thirst suddenly run to sentimentality. Toro got a fair hand when he left the ring. But everybody stood up and cheered or applauded the Indian as he climbed down through the ropes with his mouth wadded with blood-soaked cotton. The Indian smiled through his pain and mitted the crowd happily. The boys from the reservation, up in the bleachers, screamed his name exultantly and he responded with a wave that was full of pride.

Nick looked over at me and winked. "Good fight," he said. It had looked convincing, all right. I wondered what touch of sadism in Nick made him dream up a gimmick like that. Maybe it was just a hard, sound business idea. There was no blood-lust in Nick, just money-lust.

"That was too bloody," Ruby said. "I hate to see a fight like that."

"Aah, that was nothing," Nick said, pleased with Ruby's reaction. "Ruby misses all the knockouts," he said. "She's always hiding her eyes under her hand."

"I hate to see those boys get hurt," she said. "At least I'm glad it wasn't Toro."

I walked back to our dressing room. Toro was lying on the table getting a rub-down. Danny was slumped in a chair, staring at the floor. He had been drunk ever since we got to Las Vegas.

Vince fell into a burlesque pantomime of Danny's condition. In this act of condescension, performed for my benefit, there was more than a hint of comradeship between us. You and I are the guys who keep this show going, the grimace seemed to say. And I suddenly realized with a sickening shock that my old hostility to Vince, boldly unconcealed on the train going west, had been pushed further back in my mind and discreetly suspended as our common interest in the success of our venture inevitably drew us closer together.

"What you doing tonight, son?" Vince said. "How about me 'n you going out and getting into trouble?"

I was Vince's friend. It was a terrible thought. All my insults had bounced off him harmlessly. Their pointed vulgarity had only succeeded in making our relationship more intimate than it would have been if I had merely ignored him. Vince, suffering the unbearable loneliness of the gregarious heel, had taken me for a friend.

"Tell me where you're going to be so I'll be sure not to go there," I said.

"Catch me at the Krazy Kat around twelve," Vince said, just as if I had begged to accompany him. "That's where these divorce dames hang out. Let's have ourselves a little poon hunt."

That's the way nearly everyone talked along the streets I worked. That's the way I was beginning to sound myself. But somehow I heard Vince's words one by one in all their forlorn and godforsaken vulgarity, coming out of that fat white neck rising over the open yellow sports shirt. They were not familiarly meaningless phrases, but separate counts indicting me for my degradation. Instead of meeting the charge head-on, I sidestepped and walked over to the rubbing table and looked down at Toro. Doc was massaging a red splotch along his ribs where the Indian had let those right hands go.

"Nice fight, Toro," I said.

"Too much blood," Toro said. "No like bleed heem too much."

"He's worried about the other guy," Doc said. His damp, homely face creased into a cheerless smile.

"How about the Indian?" I asked Doc. "Think he's okay?"

"I guess he'll live," Doc said. "But I'll bet he'll be eating his dinner through a straw for the next couple of days. Those blood vessels in his gums are probably cut all to hell."

I went across the hall to have a look for myself. If the club doctor was going to send him to the hospital I ought to know it. The headlines even popped into my mind—a box on the sports page—MOLINA TKO VICTIM RUSHED TO HOSPITAL. For a second I was horrified to realize this was a day-dream, or rather a night-dream of vicious wishfulness.

Over in the other dressing room, the house doc was still working over the Indian. A small crowd of handlers and well-wishers were grouped around the table, their tense, silent faces turned toward the Indian's terrible mouth.

Miniff was standing at the sink, with his shirt off, washing his hands and face. For once he was without his hat and his small bald head looked naked and pathetic with nervous blue veins trellising across it. He was so short that he had to stand on tiptoes to look into the mirror.

"How's your boy?" I said.

"He ain't mine no more," Miniff said. "Soon as I pick up my check and pay him off, I kiss him off for good. I want no part of him."

"This is the first time I ever saw you throw away a dollar," I said.

Miniff picked up the short, straggle-ended cigar butt he had placed carefully on the edge of the sink, and shook his head. "I never want to go through nothing like this again. That bum like to drove me crazy. I don' want no part of him. That screwball almost gets me in wrong with a big man like Latka and then he lets 'em chop his puss up like a hamburger when he coulda stretched out on the canvas in round one, nice and comfortable, like he was home in bed. I'll never figure that one."

"He had to save his pride," I said.

"Pride!" Miniff seemed to chew the word and spit it out again. "Would you let your mouth get cut to ribbons when allatime you could let yerself down easy without even scraping an elbow?"

"I don't know," I said. "Maybe I wouldn't know."

"Pride, nuts," Miniff said.

The doc had decided to send the Indian to the hospital for a couple of days. Nothing serious, just superficial hemorrhages, but he didn't want to take any chances.

I rushed out to make sure there were a couple of photographers on hand to catch the Indian being loaded into the ambulance. That was the kind of publicity that falls into your lap. You can't buy it and you can't dream it up. A small crowd of busybodies pressed around him. A couple called out, "Attaboy, Chief!" The Indian waved feebly. He must have been pretty sick from swallowing all that blood. In his own stupid, and unnecessarily brutal, martyrdom, he had won his victory. To us it had been just another little skirmish in the long campaign, but the Indian had given his blood in a cause neither Nick nor Miniff nor Vince could ever understand.

15

I DIDN'T bother to go back to the dressing room. Danny had already drunk himself beyond companionship, and the realization that I had drifted into Vince's zone of intimacy had me back on my heels. I left the arena and started on a lonely prowl for a quiet place to buy myself a drink. But the first bar was too much of a crum-joint, the next too crowded, the third too desolate, and so it went until I found myself at the end of the short street that led right into the desert.

It was a mild night with millions of stars in the sky. The quiet took me away from the meaningless noise of many mouths, away from the bars and the jukes. I had to think. It was a long time since I had tried to think. In the fight game, I didn't think; I merely got bright ideas, hot flashes, used them, kept the wires burning. When I was a kid I used to raise turtles. I'd pick one out of its bowl and instantly it would draw in its head and feet and become a cold, dead lump. A moment before it had been a live, scurrying thing. I'd drop it down into another bowl and its head would pop out; its feet would shoot forth and it would be scrambling around again. It had no idea where the hell it was going, but moved with frantic, aimless haste, exactly as I had been dropped down and had kept going in the fight game. For some reason I couldn't understand, and only at odd, out-of-the-way moments protested against, automatically my brain would begin to spark, my legs would start working, and I'd be off on my feverish, pointless journey around and around my little bowl.

I put my hand to my mouth. I didn't know why for a moment, and then I remembered Chief Thunderbird. I had no chicken wire pressed up against my gums, but I was flicking myself with steel-tipped self-reproach in a last-minute effort to hang on to what was left of my pride. The events of the evening passed before me in all their tawdry melodrama. Nick, Vince, Danny, Doc, and Toro, that monstrous figure I had helped create. I had to get away from all of them; I had to rack up on this rat-race before the trap was sprung. How had Beth described my job? Interesting at thirty, a blind alley at forty, a last refuge for a bum at fifty.

Beth's words. Beth and her damned New England conscience following me all the way out here into the desert. How much had I ever wanted Beth? Were we ever "meant for each other," like lovers on the screen? Had I ever wanted to marry Beth? Were my occasional marital tendencies merely the automatic reflection of Beth's need for permanence? The tentative, the casual relationship was all against her upbringing. Back of all her dissatisfaction with me was her dread of uncertainty, aimlessness and impermanence. Far away from her in a world she could never make herself know, I was rootless and rotting.

I wanted to hear Beth's voice again. I think I even missed the brisk impatience with which she liked to dismiss me. I walked back along the neon-glowing street until I came to a little saloon called Jerry's Joynt. I kept on walking past the bar to the phone booth in the rear. I gave the operator Beth's number. The circuits were busy; it would be a few minutes, she said. I went back to the bar to wait. All the customers seemed either silently morose or garrulously unhappy.

A fellow in cowboy boots down the bar was telling the bartender about our fight. "Best goddam fight I ever saw," he was saying. "The goddam bloodiest fight I ever saw. Boy, you shoulda seen it, Mike."

Next to me a seedy little drunk was confiding his

domestic troubles to a half-listening truck driver with a union button on his cap.

I turned the volume way down on everybody and tried to listen to my own thoughts. What a setting for a play a place like this would make! Gorky's *Lower Depths* with an all-Las Vegas cast. Beth would approve of my thinking in terms of a play instead of a fight fix.

The phone was ringing. I rushed to answer it.

"Hello. On your call to New York City. The circuits are still busy. Do you wish me to call you again in twenty minutes?"

Another twenty minutes, another drink, another hard-luck story from the guy who didn't want to go home to his wife. I don't know why I drank. Drink makes some men talk honestly and well; it urges others to foolish lies. Drink slows my rhythm, depresses my nerves, releases fears that crawl inside me. I thought with envy of Toro sleeping up there at the hotel in serene ignorance, Man Mountain Molina, the Hyper-Pituitary of the Andes, who would remain asleep when he woke in the morning. As I thought of Toro I recalled, with that trick compartmentization of the free-associating mind, a reading assignment in Freshman English: John Milton's *Samson Agonistes*, the great giant in the hands of his enemies who had put out his eyes and exhibited him in chains for the amusement of the Philistine crowds.

But how could Samson's plight be compared to Toro's, with all those stumble-bums flopping on their flattened faces for him? What danger was he in? Danger? A red light flashed in my mind. I was seized by an inescapable foreboding, and yet, for the life of me, I could not imagine what could possibly happen to him. Was that red light really in my mind or was it just the flashing red tubing outside the window spelling out the words "Jerry's Joynt"?

The bell in the booth was ringing insistently. I lurched toward it and finally had the receiver off the hook. Yes, yes, this was Mr. Lewis. Could I have my party now?

With the door closed I could hardly breathe in the booth. The closeness made me dizzy, made the walls float around me, around and around in my head.

"Hello, *hello*, darling."

"Hello, Eddie. What's been happening to you?"

"I know, I know. I've been meaning to write you . . . But this has been such a rat-race . . . I started a long letter to you in L.A. . . ."

I didn't need television to see Beth shaking her head on the other end of the phone, half amused, half resigned.

"Eddie, sometimes I think you just want to be a character."

"How's everything been, Beth? You could have written me too, you know."

"Things have been awfully calm, Eddie. Nothing much has been happening. I've just been working and coming home early. Doing a lot of reading."

"You weren't home reading the Saturday I called you up at 2 A.M."

"Oh, I was probably away for the week-end. I've been going out to Martha's a lot."

Martha was a roommate of Beth's at Smith who had made quite a splash as a fashion designer. Martha had never been very subtle about what she thought of me. I knew it wasn't going to help my cause any to have Beth out at Martha's.

"Martha's finally decided to give up her job and get married. An awfully nice boy from Brookline. You wouldn't know him. She actually wants to settle down and raise a family."

"What the hell are we talking about Martha for? How about us, baby? All this time away from each other and we haven't even started talking about you and me."

"Is there anything new to say about us, Eddie?"

"Well, I've missed you like all hell. But you're right, I guess that isn't very new."

"I've missed you too, Eddie. I really have. I wish I

didn't, though. I feel it's kind of a weakness of mine . . . to want you any more."

"Now listen, Beth. Why make a problem out of it? We're in each other's hair for good. Why don't you relax and admit it?"

"You sound awfully sober. Are you sober tonight, Eddie?"

"More than sober, baby. I've been thinking. This fight we had tonight just about gave me a bellyful. I'm just about ready to tell Nick to find himself another boy."

"Just about ready, Eddie? Eddie, aren't you ever going to *be* ready?"

"Sure, sure. I'm ready, but you know how Nick is. You just don't go up to him and quit. You've got to ease yourself out."

"But you've been easing yourself out ever since I've known you."

"Just wait, Beth. I'll prove it to you. I ought to be back in a few months. Wait for me, Beth."

"Wait for Nick, you mean. Oh, Eddie, walk out on him. Please. It's easy, believe me."

"I will. I'm going to. But I've got to feel my way. You don't understand. I'll need every nickel I can get out of it. Then . . ."

"All right, Eddie. Get all the nickels you can. Keep on kidding yourself."

"For Christ's sake, Beth, what else can I do? Just wait and you'll see."

"I don't know what else you can do. I honestly don't. Let me know when you've had enough. Good-bye, Eddie."

She hung up while I was saying "Good-bye." I pulled the folding door of the booth open and stepped back into the hubbub of Jerry's Joynt. I moved over to the bar to have another drink. Maybe I shouldn't have called Beth. Maybe I should have gone straight to Nick to turn in my uniform, climb down off the gravy-train and head east. Maybe I should have talked only to myself and made up my mind, once for all, to do what I had to do. Well, after all, there were a few things still to be said to Nick, and this was the time to get them off my chest before making my getaway.

The party at Nick's suite looked like a Cecil De Mille production of how modern robber barons entertain themselves. Coming in cold out of the loneliness of my one-man jag I had an impression of big, prosperous thick-skinned mammals of the masculine variety laughing loudly from expansive bellies, of women who were Aphrodites of the make-up box, all eyebrow pencil, eyeshadow, lipstick, hair-dos and perfume that incited you to conventional passions. Floating toward me, cool and ladylike, was Ruby, wearing a black tulle evening gown and a Spanish comb in her hair, sensual in a removed and stately way. Ruby's eyes had a strange luster and she walked with a telltale but successful effort at steadiness.

"Well, it's about time you showed up, Eddie," she said, and she kissed me affectionately on the cheek. "Come on over and I'll pour you a drink."

Looking at Ruby and then hearing her talk never failed to surprise me. She was like a common show-girl who walks on stage into a high-born, glamorous part, but for whom the dramatist has neglected to write any lines.

"We were all hoping you'd bring Toro," Ruby said.

"Toro's a country boy," I said. "He needs his rest. This stuff won't do him any good, Ruby. He's confused enough as it is."

She looked up at me, but I wasn't sure whether she got it. That was another thing about Ruby. She could look at you steadily with those enlarged dark pupils in what would appear to be a reaction of profound intelligence, but it was only an elaborately convincing charade of intelligence.

"He's such a sweet boy," she said. "Takes his religion so seriously. I just love to go with him Sundays. Honestly we can all learn a lot from people with simple faith like that."

"Yeah," I said, reaching for my drink, "I guess we can. Where's Nick, Ruby? I've got something to tell him."

"Over there," she indicated with her head. "With that fat fella in the corner."

Nick had a glass in his hand too, but he must have been nursing it all evening. Nick was too smart and too organized; his pattern was woven too tightly for promiscuous drinking. Nick drank when he needed a drink to put someone at ease. Now in the small, sloppy, unraveling hours of the morning he managed to remain remarkably dapper, sober and wide-awake. His tailor-made, sharkskin suit fitted him almost too perfectly, and his lean, closely shaven dark face seemed even sharper than ever in contrast to the bleary, sagging countenances of his guests.

"Hello, Shakespeare," he said, glad to see me.

"Nick," I said, "I want to talk to you."

"So do I, kid," he said. "Let's go out on the balcony for a couple of minutes."

He stood on the balcony with his legs apart, blowing smoke into the night.

"I wish these jerks would start clearing out of here," he said.

He offered me a cigar, but I refused it. I had been smoking Nick's cigars for years and blowing smoke rings to spell Nick Latka or Toro Molina or whatever he had on his mind.

"Nick, I . . ." I tried to begin.

"I know what you're going to say," Nick interrupted. "And I'm ahead of you. You think you ought to have a raise. Well, you're not going to get a fight out of me. You've done a hell of a job, Eddie. You actually have the public believing this bum's a great fighter. I'm a bullish sort of a guy, but I didn't think the fans would buy him so fast. You been away from the East, so you don't know what's been happening. We're ready to get out of this chicken-feed circuit. Charley Spitz in Cleveland says he's got five thousand on the line for Toro to fight anybody—Joe Floppola. The customers just want to see him. In Chi, we can get a fifteen-thousand guarantee against forty percent of the gross for him to go with Red Donovan. Red's manager, Frank Conti, owes me a favor. Then with a win over Donovan, who's beaten some pretty fair boys, Uncle Mike will be ready to bring us into the Garden. Quinn was out to see Mike already and they talk about putting Toro in with Lennert two months after the Lennert-Stein fight Thursday night."

"But you own 'em both," I said. "Isn't it bad business to let one eliminate the other, when . . ."

"I'm still ahead of you," Nick said. "Don't forget I haven't got nothing to do with Toro yet, officially. I've still got Vince and Danny fronting for me. So after Toro gets a win over Lennert, Gus retires—which he wants to do anyway—and you announce that Quinn and me have bought up Toro's contract from Vince and Danny. Could anything be simpler?"

"But Gus has always been on the level," I said. "Gus never went into the bag for anybody in his life. What makes you think you could get Gus to . . ."

"I already been through all that with Gus just before I came out," Nick said. "Gus is thirty-three next month. He's been in the ring fifteen years. He's not thinking of his career any more. What he wants is a couple of real money fights, enough for him to take things easy the rest of his life, good investments, a couple of good annuities, so his kids will be all right. We got his financial set-up all figured out to his satisfaction and Mrs. Lennert's. You know, she's always been a little sore at me for talking him into coming back. She wanted to keep him in that hamburger stand of his, even if he was making peanuts. Well, we showed her how in two fights Gus can make himself around a hundred thousand dollars. With Stein in the ball park, Uncle Mike figures to gross around four hundred G's, with Gus getting twenty-five percent. That's a hundred divided between us and Jimmy. I decided on account of it's Gus, and he's racking up we'll leave him take two-thirds without deductions. That's around sixty-five thousand for openers. Then with Toro in the Garden we ought to do a hundred 'n fifty G's easy. On account of Toro's getting such a build-up from knocking over Lennert, I figure he ought to be satisfied with ten percent, which puts Lennert's cut at fifty-five thousand, leaving Gus around thirty-six G's."

A couple of times I tried to break in on this overwhelming flow of grosses and percentages with the beautiful speech I had worked out on my way over to Nick's after my talk with Beth. But this was like trying to fight an Armstrong—leaning on you, crowding you, never giving you a chance. It was no use. Nick's adding-machine mind kept right on computing each fight in dollars and cents.

"So sixty-five and thirty-six, Gus has got his hundred thousand fish. The win over Gus makes Toro a logical opponent for Buddy Stein and then we're really in the tall grass, with a million-dollar gate, if we play it smart. So, Eddie, I want you to know I realize what you mean to this deal. Of course, five percent of Toro's slice of a million bucks—if we make it—that isn't Chiclets. But meanwhile I'm putting you down for one-five-o per week, and we'll push it to two hundred right after the Lennert fight."

Six hundred a month, that was a respectable improvement over my old job on the *Trib*, and with Lennert and Stein coming up after Cleveland and Chicago, Toro could stand to gross around $250,000 for the year, which would mean a nice little $12,500 on top of my regular

7,500. $20,000! How many guys in America would throw up a job that averaged them four hundred bucks a week just because the job pinched their souls a little bit? Hell, even Beth could see the wisdom of that. And it wasn't as if I were mortgaging myself to Nick for life. Why, another couple of years of this, with maybe a hike to $25,000 the second year, and I'd have enough of those little green coupons to take things easy, get that play out and wrap it up, if I feel like it. And meanwhile, think of all the valuable material I was getting. Why, my plans weren't changed, my integrity was still intact, I was just racking up gradually instead of all at once, like Gus Lennert, who figured to take an awful beating from Stein for his sixty-five thousand, coast through the Toro fix for an easy thirty-six and then live out his days on a farm like a country squire. I was just thinking like a moon-struck freshman when I was out there on the edge of town deciding to blow Nick off.

This wasn't selling out. This was just playing it smart.

16

Wɪᴛʜ Dynamite Jones and Chief Thunderbird finally salted away in the record books as early knockout victims of Toro Molina, we thought we needed an easy one. So for Denver Toro's opponent was a "Negro protégé of Sam Langford's who has faced the best in his division." Of course, he turned out to be our own Georgie Blount.

But I had to start earning my dough again when a local reporter—another Al Leavitt—came up with the discovery of George's identity. That is what makes a press agent's ride so nerve-racking. Just when you think you're free-wheeling down a four-lane highway, some jerk tosses a handful of tacky truths in your path.

But a smart guy takes trouble in stride and puts it to work for him. So right away I gave out a story, capitalizing on the fact that George had been a sparring partner who had had a row with Toro when he claimed that Toro had knocked him out when they were only supposed to be having a light workout.

> "No ordinary spar-boy (I worked my plant into the leading Denver sports column), Blount has stood up to some of the outstanding heavyweights in the country, including Gus Lennert, who won a close, split decision over the Harlem Panther. So in an unprecedented act of insubordination for a sparring partner, George challenged the Giant of the Andes to go into a room with him, lock the doors and have at it in a regular old-fashioned knock-down dragout. The Molina board of strategy frowned on this impromptu (and unprofitable) rivalry, however, and

so tomorrow night Denver fight fans will be treated to the privilege of sitting in on the first grudge-match in the Argentine Behemoth's spectacular American career of seven straight knockouts over such formidable opposition as Cowboy Coombs, Dynamite Jones and Chief Thunderbird, undisputed champion of the Southwest until the Man Mountain stopped him in Las Vegas recently in three torrid rounds."

At the weigh-in, the day of the fight, George, doing his best to play his little part for the Latka Repertory Theatre, wouldn't shake hands with Toro.

We had told Toro that George had quit his job with us because he really thought he could beat him, but even so Toro could not comprehend George's discourtesy. "Why he no shake hands?" he asked. "George my friend, no?"

It takes real talent to lose as convincingly as George did that night. Nobody Toro had fought had shown him off to such good advantage. From the way Toro moved his shoulders and set his feet, George could tell just when Toro's punches were going to start. All he had to do was move in toward the blows instead of going away from them, as he would have ordinarily. The force of his body smashing against Toro's fist made a sound that could be heard all over the arena. Nobody hearing that impact could doubt Toro's prowess as a puncher. And when George fought back, he was careful to avoid that big glass jaw that was such an open and tempting target.

In the fourth round George exposed his belly to a particularly resounding wallop from Toro and permitted himself to be counted out. Magnanimously forgiving in victory, Toro insisted on helping George back to his corner, where, in a gesture right down the fans' cornball alley, he offered him his hand. There was something almost mystical about Toro's ability to perform just the right gesture without realizing how well it fitted into our act. It was an old plot, but the fans, going for the grudge match with their mass talent for self-hypnosis, bought the happy ending just as if it were Saturday night at the Double Feature.

Relieved to see that George had recovered so quickly, Toro waved to the cheering crowd and jumped down from the ring. George followed him, moving with his familiar, deliberate ease, an ambiguous smile on his massive face.

When we pulled out of Denver, George was left behind to make it look kosher. A couple of days later he caught up with us in K.C., where we were getting ready to knock off another tanker.

"George, how did Toro feel to you in that fight?" I asked.

George smiled with his mouth, but his eyes kept their seriousness. "He just can't bang," he said. "And when a heavyweight can be reached and he can't bang . . ." George shook his head. "You better watch the big fella, Eddie. Watch him close, man, before something real bad happens."

But the only thing that happened in K.C., in Cleveland where we filled the Municipal Stadium, and in Chicago where we did close to $80,000 with Red Donovan, was to add three more to our string of knockouts and sign the papers for the big fight with Lennert in the Garden.

Toro's cut for the eighteen minutes of alleged fighting must have been around $20,000. But all he had been seeing of it were the 50's and C-notes that Vince came up with whenever Toro put the zing on him. After the Chicago fight, though, Toro smelled money. "You give now, I send my papa for build big house," he told Vince. Vince reached into his pocket, pulled out a wad and peeled off five hundred-dollar bills. "Any time you need dough, just ask me," he said with unusual affability.

Next morning when Toro and I were walking down Michigan Boulevard, we passed the Lake Shore National Bank.

"*El banco grande!*" Toro said.

"One of the biggest," I said.

"I go in," Toro said.

"What are you going to do, put your five in the bank?"

"I come back pronto," Toro answered.

When he came out he had a fistful of Argentine bills. Over two thousand pesos. "Look how much money," he held it up to me happily: "This feel like real money."

The day we got to New York, Toro achieved immortality—at least for one week. He made the cover of *Life*. And if this wasn't honor enough, he was urged to come up on the floor and take a bow when Joe E. Lewis spotted him at a ringside table at the Copa with Vince and me. My job was a breeze now. I didn't have to scrounge any more. Reporters came looking for us. Even when Runyon devoted a full column to ridiculing the whole Man-Mountain build-up, ending by describing Toro as the Ghastly Gawk of the Andes, the undisputed Side-Show Champion of America, it didn't really put the whammy on us. In America a knock is just a plug that lets itself in the back door. Nick had guessed right, as usual. Toro's freakish size, plus the knockout record we were compiling for him, was tapping the public's incredible credulity.

Just before he was ready to leave for Pompton Lakes with Vince, Danny, Doc and George to start training for the Lennert fight, a white, special-body, Lincoln phaeton appeared at the hotel entrance. The afternoon before, when he was supposed to be resting, Toro had sneaked off and ordered this little number at a mere five G's. Apparently he wasn't such a meatball that he couldn't find a way to get around Vince's reluctance to declare a dividend. It wasn't in his nature to learn how to throw a left hook without telegraphing it, but it hadn't taken him long to find out how to join the great American fraternity whose password is "charge it."

When he heard what the grunt for this white job was, Vince wanted to send it right back to the floor. Toro pouted and protested, "My car, my car, I buy!"

"Let him have it," I told Vince. "Why get the guy sore over a lousy five thousand bucks when the real dough's starting to roll in? Leo can take it off the income tax, for transportation. And meanwhile a white Lincoln is publicity."

So Toro drove off to Pompton Lakes with his portable radio, his entourage, and Benny Mannix at the wheel of the Lincoln phaeton. As I stood on the curb in front of our hotel watching them lose themselves in the morning traffic, a phrase popped into my head, the last line of that Wolcott Gibbs' profile on Luce in Timestyle, "Where it will end, knows God!"

I had been back in town two days already without seeing Beth. Her excuses seemed to be on the level, and yet they were the sort she would have found some way to finesse in the days when we were clicking together.

With all that time behind us, I hadn't thought I could slip back so quickly into the old role of hopeful suitor. I even found myself sending her flowers all over again.

On the morning of the third day I called Beth and said, "Look, I'm going nuts. When am I going to see you?"

Something in my voice must have reached her, for she said, almost too calmly to please me, "How about right now? Come on over and have breakfast, if you like."

On my way over I picked up a box of candy. It was a silly thing to do. What seemed more sensible was to stop at a bar on Sixth Avenue for a courage-cup.

Beth opened the door and said, "Hi, Eddie," in her direct and friendly way. Her attitude seemed crisp rather than cool. But she had never been demonstrative until the moment of demonstration itself. Like most women, she had a way of setting her own emotional climate.

"Make yourself comfortable, Eddie. I've got to rush back and save my toast. I still burn it!"

She was wearing smartly tailored beige lounging pajamas that made her figure look stylishly, rather than merely, thin. I followed her through the book-lined room with the familiar modern furniture, past the combination radio-phonograph whose illuminated dial had been the only glow of light in the darkness of our first night. Alone with Beth again after all those uncertain months, I could feel growing in me the desire to break down her reserve, to force her back to the spontaneous response I had drawn from her before. But even surrounded by these erotic landmarks, the radio, the studio couch, the thick yellow rug, I had the strange sensation that I was feeling all this for the first time. I felt the same excitement, the same longing, the same curiosity about her as in the beginning.

She served breakfast on a little table by the window in the kitchenette, with eggs boiled just three minutes the way she knew I liked them, crisp bacon and the buttered toast that she always had to scrape. As we sat there together I wished more than ever before that this could be every day. Something—I still couldn't give it a name—had blocked my setting this up on a permanent basis when it was still in my hands. What had stopped me? At this moment marrying Beth seemed like the most natural thing in the world. I am going to count slowly up to ten and then I'm going to make the first sober proposal of my life, I thought.

"Well, how was your trip, Eddie? Was it fun, was it interesting?"

You mind-reading, subject-changing vixen, I thought, jabbing me off balance just when I'm getting set to throw my best Sunday punch.

"Oh, you know," I said. "Same old squirrel cage."

"But you love it," she said. "Why don't you admit it instead of acting as if you were too good for it, as if you were just slumming?"

"For Christ sake, Beth, let's not start that again."

"Okay, I'm just getting awfuly tired of all these people knocking what they're doing but keeping right at it year after year."

"This is a goddam serious way to begin a day."

"Don't you remember?" she said, smiling to take the curse off it, "I'm always more serious before I've had my first cup of coffee."

"I remember," I said.

She looked at me sympathetically. She had never looked at me that way before and I resented it. What if I just got up and grabbed her the way I used to do? Some atavistic conviction that male force could prevail where everything else had failed must have driven me on.

"Eddie, what are you doing?"

Almost from the moment it began, it ceased to be instinctive. It had already become a self-conscious effort, but somehow it couldn't be stopped. It seemed as if I had to bull it through, even though I already felt the terrible futility of this approach.

"Eddie! For God's sake!"

"Beth—darling—please . . ."

"Stop it, Eddie! Stop!"

She was pushing me away. The strength in her mind and in her body was holding me off. My own body felt heavy and slothful in defeat. I felt limp and spent, the body hunger gone as completely as if it had been appeased instead of rudely frustrated.

"The coffee," Beth said. "The coffee's boiling over."

She brought two cups back to the table. I felt her accidentally brushing against my shoulder as she set mine down and I edged away.

"This is the moment I hate," Beth said as she sat down. "The messy time."

I didn't say anything. I felt terribly angry with her. And yet I was conscious of being unreasonable. After all, she wasn't one of Shirley's girls.

It was typical of Beth to pitch the conversation to its true level, to say exactly what she meant about exactly what had happened.

"Eddie, I've had plenty of time to think it over. Nights when I missed you—I'm terribly used to you, in lots of ways—almost afraid to start over again with somebody else—and yet there were days when—I might as well tell you this, I've been straight with you on everything else—days when it was a relief to have you out of my life—It wasn't getting anywhere."

"When I called you from Las Vegas," I said, "I wanted to marry you. I've always wanted to marry you, Beth."

"Yes, I think you have, Eddie. But not ever enough to do it. I always had the feeling if it were going to happen I'd have to sit down, pick the day and make you go down for the license. Marriage is an old-fashioned thing, Eddie. I guess even a gal like me, who's been on her own for years, wants someone to come along and just carry her off."

The coffee had a sour taste. I always used to kid Beth about her coffee. "So this is the . . . blow-off?"

"Eddie, you know I—hate those words. Not the words themselves, but what they stand for. Why are you afraid of being soft—ashamed to show what you really feel for people—afraid to try anything better than you're doing—for fear you'll be a flop? The play, for instance . . ."

"I've been thinking about that play. I've got some of the scenes worked out in my head, I . . ."

"Eddie, I hate to say this—it probably sounds so smug —but you're never going to do that play. You've been telling me scenes from that play from the first night we met. You've been talking it right out of existence. You won't finish that play any more than you'll quit the fight business. You just haven't the courage to do it."

"Thanks," I said. "What is this, tell-off day?"

"I guess it did come out a lot clearer than I expected," Beth said, apologetically. "I've been mulling it over so long. But I wish we could have worked it out, Eddie. I wish we could have. You know that, don't you?"

"Sure," I said. "This is how the story ends, can't we be friends. It's been set to music."

I wanted to call the wisecrack back, wanted to show her I was bigger than that, wished I could think of something to say that would send me out of there a generous, understanding citizen. But I didn't seem to have it in me. I went out with the smallest, meanest, foul ball of a parting shot I could think of. "Well, I suppose Herbert Ageton is a better bet at that. After all, he's had a hit on Broadway."

"Oh, damn you, Eddie, damn you!" Beth cried out, and her eyes were suddenly full of angry tears. "You're such a heel! What makes you such a heel? Eddie, you of all people! You make me so God-damn mad sometimes."

I felt exhausted, I felt exhausted with the effort of having all these years tried to keep my marriage to Beth in suspension. I never wanted to let go of it and I never wanted to face the consequences of holding on. But finally, now, when I was forced to let go, where did that leave me? Maybe I was lucky to be rid of her, always harping at me, trying to reform me, make me quit the fight game. I wanted to get out of town. I didn't want to stay in the same town with her, even a real big town like N.Y. Real big. I knew better than to say "real big." I knew better than a lot of things. But it was easier. Danny and Vince and Doc and George, they all said "real big." Why should I be any different, why should I be any better, what was so special about me that I should look down on those guys? But I did look down on them, and why shouldn't I? I knew more, I understood more, I felt more. Who else in this crowd of bums, lushes and grifters worried about Toro, wondered what he was feeling, saw him in any real perspective? Who noticed when he was lonely, bothered to walk around town with him, tried to give him some guidance? And yet Beth called me a heel! She had the nerve to call me a heel!

I took a train out to the camp. I felt better as soon as I got off. I was back in my own world, or at least in a world I felt equal to.

Benny Mannix met me at the station. His venal, unattractive puss made me feel at home. "How's everything going, Benny?"

"T'ings ain't so bad, kid. We got a nice set-up here."

"How's Danny behaving himself?"

"Danny, he's kinda tapering off. Oney had a pint so far today."

"Sounds like he's almost on the wagon. And how's my boy getting along? Toro."

Benny shrugged. "Da bum tries, you gotta give 'im dat. He didn't look too bad wit' Chick Gussman dis afternoon. That's this new light-heavy we got in from Detroit who fights kinda on the style of Lennert."

It was just after dinner when I got there, and Danny was sitting out on the porch with Doc and some of the other sparring partners. Danny was reading the *Morning Telegraph*. He looked almost sober.

"Still trying to beat 'em, Danny?"

Danny grinned. "I gave that up a long time ago, laddie. I'm just along for the ride. But this Shasta Rose"—he tapped the racing form—"if she don't run away with the Maryland at Laurel tomorrow I'm gonna . . ."

"Turn in your chips and quit," I interrupted.

Danny shook his head and smiled. ". . . throw these lousy form sheets away and play my own hunches."

"He couldn't do any worse if he picked 'em blindfold," Doc said. "He's the bookie's friend, Danny is."

Everybody laughed at Danny. At a training camp it seems as if everybody is waiting to laugh at everybody else. There was a dice game starting in the parlor and Doc, Gussman and the other boys on the porch joined it.

"That Gussman, he knows how to handle himself for a kid," Danny said as the new light-heavy went in. "Kinda reminds me of Jimmy Slattery, when he was gettin' started, a regular Fancy Dan, not quite as fast as Jimmy maybe, but he's got natural ring sense. If I could take him in hand 'n teach him to sharpen up his punching a little . . .'"

Danny sighed and looked off into the gathering dusk. "Boy, to come into New York with a real fighter again, to walk down 49th Street and have all the guys come up and say, 'Saw your boy take that guy last night, Danny. You really got yourself something there . . .'"

"Why don't you sign this Gussman?" I said. "Why don't you bring him along?"

"What's the percentage, laddie?" Danny said, dead-voiced again. "If the guy's too brittle and he don't work out, I've wasted a lot of time. And if he looks good, Nick moves in and takes over, and pretty soon the kid has to throw one or he wins one he don't deserve. The hell with that. Nick's got me by the short hairs, laddie. Sure it's my own fault, but when did that ever make a guy like it any better?"

"Anyway," I said, "I'm glad to see you looking so sharp."

"Yeah," he said, "I'd like to win this one. I'd really like to beat that Lennert."

This had been Nick's idea, to bring Danny back to his job by not letting him know the Lennert thing was in the bag. Danny knew Lennert hadn't done any business before, so it wasn't too difficult to convince him. And since he had never learned as much about the fight business as he had about fighters, he bought the line that Nick didn't care who won this time because he owned them both. Danny was a sucker for most of the fighters he had handled, but Lennert was the exception. Lennert was a business man, not a miser exactly, just careful about his money. If some old pug came along whom Lennert had licked and put the arm on him for a sawbuck or two, Lennert had been known to stall on the ground that the guy was a boozer who would just drink the dough away. But Danny didn't care what the guy did with the dough, figuring it was only money and that was none of his business. That was the difference between them. When Lennert made his comeback, he figured he knew as much about conditioning and strategy as Danny and insisted on being his own boss. Pretty pig-headed, Lennert was. When he came back he made no bones about being in it purely for the high dollar and not to take any unnecessary chances. Once in a while, for instance, Danny would want Gus to go in and carry the fight to an opponent whom Gus would be content to stay away from and counterpunch, winning an easy decision on points without extending himself when he might have been able to do something more spectacular. That wasn't honest prizefighting, in Danny's book, but then, even though one would never know it from some of the things he had had to do, Danny had a sense of purity, of real nobility about the game that an ordinary pro like Lennert wouldn't understand. Lennert went in for boxing the way he ran his diner in Trenton, not robbing anybody, just cutting them as close as he could without stepping over the line.

"You don't really think Toro could take Lennert if they're both sent in to win?" I said.

"Don't be too sure, laddie," Danny said. "Let's not kid ourselves, Gus hasn't got much any more. That beating he took from Stein didn't do him any good."

"I never thought he could take that much any more," I said.

Lennert had looked like his old self against Stein until he began to run out of gas. From the seventh on, Stein had had him down in every round, but couldn't keep him there. The referee was just about ready to stop it when the fight ended. Lennert was still on his feet, but no longer able to defend himself. He had collapsed on his way to his dressing room.

"He showed a hell of a lot more guts than I thought he had," I said.

"That was business," Danny said. "He was figuring how much bigger the Molina fight would draw if Stein didn't knock him out. So he let Stein beat his brains in, to make an extra ten or fifteen G's. That's Gus. I know him. He don't care about being a hero. All he's worried about is how much dough he can lay aside to retire on."

"You think Stein really slowed him up?"

"I saw him the next day, when he came up to the office to pick up his money," Danny said. "I thought he was acting kind of funny, sort of slow-like, like something was hurting him in his head or something."

"I heard Stein hit him so hard Gus cracked his head on the floor," I said. "Gus is a pretty old man to take those pot-shots in the head the way Stein throws them."

"He's lucky Toro can't hit," Danny said. "I guess that's why he picked him for the bow-out. He figures Molina can't do any more 'n lean on him once in a while or maybe stamp on his toes with those size fifteens. But believe it or not, laddie, I think I got Toro working a little better. I been spending a lot of time with him this week. I got him throwing a pretty fair right uppercut, and he's getting so he don't just wave that left hand like it was a flag."

"Danny, you could teach a wooden Indian to box."

"Well, at least a wooden Indian wouldn't buckle every time you tap him on the jaw." Danny laughed. "I think I got a pretty good defense worked out for Toro's jaw this time. Only if he wants to look any good in there, he's gotta pay a little more attention to his training." Danny rubbed the back of his hand across his cheek nervously. "That's why I'm glad you came down, laddie."

"I'm just the word man," I said. "What have I got to do with it?"

"You can talk to him. Maybe in his own language he'll listen better."

"Sure I'll talk to him. What do you want me to talk to him about?"

"About Ruby. You better talk to him about Ruby."

"Ruby? What goes with Ruby?"

"I don't know," Danny said, "but I got ideas."

"You mean Ruby and Toro? No, Danny, I can't buy that. Why, Toro doesn't know enough . . ."

"How much do you have to know, laddie?"

"Jesus, are you sure, Danny? Toro is no intellectual giant, but I didn't think he'd be dumb enough to fool around with what belongs to Nick."

"Well, all I know is he's been driving over there in that goddam Lincoln of his every chance he gets. I been letting Benny take him out for rides. You know he's worse than a kid with a new toy with that thing. Well, Benny told me the big sap's been slipping him dough to drive over to Green Acres. And Toro goes inside and doesn't come out for an hour. Well, I don't know, maybe I got a dirty mind, but if Toro isn't getting in, Ruby's not the girl I've heard she is."

"Jesus!" I said. "I hope you're wrong. I'd hate to think what'd happen to Toro if Nick ever catches onto that one."

"It's a funny thing," Danny said. "You'd think a guy as smart as Nick would keep a little closer check on a broad like that."

"They all got their weak spots, the smartest of 'em," I said. "And, for Nick, I guess it's believing Ruby's a real high-class dame."

"Well, you better talk to him," Danny said. "Even if Nick doesn't catch, that kind of business won't do him any good in there with Lennert. And I want to beat Lennert. I just want to see if I can do it with this lunk."

Doc came out on the porch. When he smiled he did not stop looking sad, but merely superimposed the smile over the permanently tragic lines of his face. "How about a little two-handed pinochle, Danny?" he said. "You might as well lose it to me as to the books."

"Don't gimme that," Danny said. "I'm the champion pinochle player of Pompton Lakes."

"Since when could a Mick ever beat a Jew-boy at pinochle?" Doc said, and winked at me.

I sat on the porch alone for a while, half listening to the guys inside talking to their dice. I thought of Toro and George walking out there on the back road and wondered what they found to say to each other, Toro with his pidgin English and his child's mind and George making his own music deep in his throat. "There it is, boys, the hard way!" someone called out, with the gloating laughter of the triumphant. I was tempted to go in and fade that guy. He sounded like the kind of fellow who took so much pleasure in winning that he pressed himself too far.

But I supposed I should wait and talk to Toro. Goddamit, since when was I Toro's keeper? What business was it of mine whether he hung the old horns on Nick? That's just it; it was my business. It wasn't my inclination; it wasn't my personal interest; it was simply my job, my five percent interest to see that Toro stayed away from trouble.

"*¿Qué tal, qué tal, amigo? ¡Buenas noches!*"

Toro had loomed up on me, his gums showing in a clownish smile. I hadn't realized how glad he would be to see me. He seemed actually relieved to have me back. I hadn't thought anything about it, but this had been the first time we had been separated since Acosta left. Toro didn't speak enough English to have a real conversation with the others, and anyway those who bothered with him at all treated him with the belittling kindness one might bestow on a trained dog. We talked for a while about the little things, the quality of the food at the camp, the peace of the countryside after our hectic tour, how hard Danny and Doc were working him, the album of pictures of him in fighting poses I had promised to prepare for his family. In a little while Benny came out with the message, "Doc says it's time fuh yuh tuh hit da sack."

"I'll go up and sit with you while you're getting ready for bed," I said.

It was a large, sparsely furnished room with a comfortable-looking old-fashioned wrought-iron double bed. As soon as he came in Toro turned his radio on with the volume up. An elocutionist for the NAM was talking about the unique opportunities for self-made men who believed in the American Way. But Toro didn't seem to care what it was, as long as it was loud. I wandered over to his bureau. There was a pile of papers under his comb and brush. I picked them up and looked at them. They were quick pencil sketches that Toro had drawn, primitive in perspective but with surprising force and humor. The first was obviously Vince, all neck and fat in the face with little eyes and a large cruel mouth. The next one was Danny, with an exaggerated flattened nose and with X's for eyes. He was bent over a bar. The next was Nick, looking considerably more hard-boiled and sinister than I had thought him. It made me realize for the first time what Toro must have thought of him. Toro had always seemed perfectly docile in his presence, as if he had no feelings in the matter. But the sketches seemed to bespeak a resentment, even a kind of understanding of these men that Toro either had hidden or was unable to express. No matter how crude these sketches were, they showed a certain limited talent that no one would have expected from this lumbering giant. But the artistic quality of the next picture was considerably lower. It was a schoolboy's amateurish and sentimental attempt to draw a beautiful woman. The woman was obviously meant to be Ruby, though a younger, more slender, more ethereal and completely romanticized version of Ruby. The snood she wore around her head, instead of creating an effect of the exotic as Ruby actually intended it, gave her in Toro's picture a spiritual, almost Madonna quality. It was clearly a work of love, marred by the mawkishness that such works often have.

When Toro caught me looking at it, I thought he was going to be angry, but he was only embarrassed. There seemed to be no anger in Toro. All the violence in his nature had shot out into big bones, into girth and heft.

"You draw very nicely, Toro."

Toro shrugged.

"Where did you learn to draw so well?"

"In my school when I am a little boy. My teacher show me."

I held up the sketch of Vince. "This one very good," I said, finding myself mimicking Toro's basic English. Then I looked at the one that was supposed to be Ruby. "This not so good."

"So beautiful as the Señora I cannot make," Toro said.

"And if you know what's good for you, you won't try to make the Señora either," I said.

"*No me comprende,*" Toro said.

He wasn't just an overgrown lummox now; he was all the natives I had ever known who retreated into the convenient dodge of not understanding the language. "*No me comprende,*" they say, and they look at you with what is clearly designed to be their most stupid expression, though their eyes betray them with a faintly mocking defiance.

"You'll *comprende* all right if Nick catches you fooling around with his wife," I said.

A deep hurt came into Toro's eyes. "No fool around. The Señora my friend. She treat me very nice. She like talk with me. She no laugh at the bad English. With the Señora I am not, not . . . *solitario.*"

"Lonely," I said. "Why should you be? Who the hell is lonely when they're with the Señora?"

Toro's large, passive eyes brightened with resentment. "*No es verdad, no es verdad,*" he broke into Spanish. "No one else is with the Señora. The Señora herself has told that to me."

"Listen, you stupid bastard," I said, "I'm trying to help you, the way Luis would have tried to help you. Help you, help you! Understand?"

Toro's face became sullen and unfriendly. "Luis no help. Luis no friend. Luis leave me here alone. He sell me like a *novillo* to the butcher. Only the Señora, she treat me like a man." Only he used the word *hombre*, which has a special ring of pride in it.

"That's what I'm afraid of," I said. "That she'll treat you like too much of a man."

"The Señora my friend," Toro insisted. "The Señora and you and George my only friend."

And none of them can do you any good, I thought. Your only friend is the man who puts you back in the wine-barrel business in Santa Maria before it's too late.

17

THE next afternoon, while Toro was pawing his way through his workouts with George, Gussman and a couple of other obliging carcasses, I decided to run over to Green Acres and take a personal reading on Ruby. Driving up the long, winding approach to the house I passed the chauffeur, Jock Mahoney, in an old turtle-neck sweater and cap, looking as if he had just run right off a page of Frederick Lewis Allen's *Only Yesterday*. Jogging at his side was a tall young fellow in gym pants and a dirty sweat-shirt.

"What you doing, Jock, getting in shape for Delaney?"

Mahoney grinned good-naturedly. "Delaney wouldn't be so tough now. But, Jesus, fifteen years ago . . ." He shook his head and smiled at his memory of a bad thirty minutes. "I thought I was back in my old man's saloon, fighting three-four guys at once."

The young man doing roadwork with Jock had a fresh, neatly chiseled face that would have been handsome enough for Hollywood. But its symmetry was marred by an expression of disdainful self-confidence. "Eddie Lewis —meet the kid nephew, Jackie Ryan," Jock said.

"Come on, Jock, for Chris'sake, ya want me to catch cold?" Ryan demanded.

"Okay, okay. You jog on, I'll catch up to yuh," Jock said affably. He looked after him proudly. "He's gonna be the best fighter we ever had in the family. You shoulda seen him win the Golden Glove welterweight champeenship of Joisey. Nick's got him on the payroll. Just wants him tuh fill out 'n develop for a year. He's a comer, Mr.

Lewis. But, Jesus, he's a hot-headed young sonofabitch. Thinks he knows all the answers awready. He ain't a bad kid when you get to know him, a course. And a comin' champ if I ever seen one. If I c'n just keep him away from the broads. You know how them kids are when they're seventeen—too big for their britches."

I started to inch the car forward. "Well, take care, Jock. The kids okay?"

"They'll be beatin' up their old man any day," he called after me happily as I drove off. Ryan didn't acknowledge my wave as I passed.

I found Ruby out on the chaise-longue on the sun-porch, reading a book. She was wearing ornate lounging pajamas, and even though this was just a week-day in the country, her glossy black hair was elaborately dressed. A half-filled box of dates was on the near-by table.

"Hello, Eddie," she said. "Long time no see."

I looked around for a chair. She made room for me beside her.

"Good book, Ruby?"

She held it up. The title was *Maid-in-Waiting*; its wrapper displayed a dashing-looking fellow in a be-plumed hat looking roguishly over the shoulder of a young lady with impudent breasts. "I liked last month's selection better," Ruby said. "But it's in my favorite century. I'd've just loved to live in the seventeenth century. All those off-the-shoulder gowns. The women were so much more—distingay. I think the men were a lot more attractive too."

I wondered what Ruby would have been doing in the seventeenth century. Probably pretty much what she was doing now, only maybe as the mistress of a big madeira king or a power in the spice racket in the Indies. But actually, Ruby's was a seventeenth-century marriage. Or even a fourteenth. Boccaccio had followed her into more than one boudoir.

"Nick coming out tonight?"

"You know Nick. He usually calls half an hour before he's coming and expects me to have a big roast-beef dinner waiting for him."

"I guess Nick's a pretty demanding fella."

"Oh, Nick's okay. I haven't got any kick against Nick. I never have to *ask* him for things, like some of the girls I know. Nick's sweet in a lot of ways. But . . ."

"But?"

"What do I tell you all this for? You'll probably just repeat it to Nick."

"Now wait a minute, Ruby, I . . ."

"I don't know why you should be any different. Everybody else does. That little louse Killer, I'm afraid to open my mouth when he's around."

"You're not comparing me with the Killer, for Christ sake?"

"No, you're a gentleman, Eddie. At least if you have an affair, you don't go around telling everybody about it, play by play. That's what I like about this seventeenth century. Everybody had just as good a time, but they had some manners about it."

There was something about the way her full, red lips moved that was for adults only. Somehow, everything Ruby did became a sensual act. She looked at me with her enlarged pupils, possibly just a physical affliction, some sort of astigmatism commonly mistaken for passion. Again I had the feeling—just a vibration as they say in the mental-telepathy racket—that it could be managed. That it was there if I wanted it.

"You know, you stimulate me," she said. "Nick brings home nothing but ignoramuses. Me, I'm different. I like people I can learn something from."

"Just what do you figure you can learn from Toro, Ruby?"

The look in Ruby's eyes hardened. "Just what do you mean by a crack like that?"

I shrugged. "I don't know. If the shoe fits, I guess . . ."

274

"And I considered you a gentleman," she said. "I thought you were different. But he's got you stooling for him just like the rest of his mob."

"Now listen, Ruby, this is strictly between us. Nick doesn't even know I'm here."

"Not much! And I thought we were just having a nice little talk about books and stuff. And all the time you're just snooping around like a private dick."

"Nick will never know I was here," I insisted. "I just wanted to remind you, Ruby, Toro is just a big, awkward goof. I hate to see him stumble into something he can't handle."

"Maybe Nick won't know you're here," Ruby said. "But just the same you're doing Nick's work. You're seeing that nothing happens to Nick's property. Just like all the rest of his mob. Well, goddam all of you. That goes for Nick too. Leaves me out here all week, with no one to talk to but a punch-drunk chauffeur and a fairy butler."

"Ruby, I don't care what you do. That's your pleasure. I'm just trying to look after Toro."

"You can keep Toro," Ruby said. "Tell you the truth, I'm sick of Toro. I'll admit I was a little curious about him at first, but you have nothing to worry about any more. If you came here to tell me not to lead your little boy astray, you can go back to your office and grind sausage about how your great Man Mountain is going to wipe the floor with poor old Gus Lennert."

"When're you going to leave our fighters alone?"

"You will please get out of this house at once," Ruby said with imitation hauteur, and then something gave way in her mind and she began to scream, "Get out of here, you cheap louse, you cheap, little louse! Get out of here, you bastard!"

Ruby's shrill profanity followed me through the house as I hurried to the marble hallway. But the butler opened the door for me and bowed me out with a wise smile.

275

When I saw Nick a couple of days later in New York, having lunch at Dinty Moore's with Jimmy Quinn and the Killer, he was in high spirits. Off the advance sale it looked as if we were going to get our $150,000 house, just as he had figured. Even the Garden fans who suspected Toro's record was padded with tankers were curious to see how he'd shape up against a first-rater like Lennert.

As part of the build-up, I brought an ex-champ down to the camp to be photographed looking Toro over. Afterwards I'd write up a little statement we'd plant in the papers about how he had visited both camps and picked Toro to win by a knockout because of his superior punching power and the streffis and the strallis and the voraspan.

The joker on our junket was Kenny Waters, ex-heavyweight champion, but definitely a third-road-company champ, a clown who would have been back digging ditches if he hadn't come along just at the time when the line on the heavyweight chart had flattened out. The title had been awarded to him while reclining flat on his back, crying foul. A year later he had lost his crown to Lennert, on a night when Gus still retained some of the vigor of youth. This defeat, ignominious as it had been at the time, still entitled him to speak with authority—no matter how counterfeit—about any contest in which his conqueror was involved. For this ex-champion it was a chance to bask for one more precious moment in the warm sun of publicity. To see his name in print just once more with his four-star civilian rank *former-champion-of-the-world*, I'm sure he would have been glad to pay *us* for his services.

I was up in my room writing Kenny Waters' eye-witness comparison of Toro and Lennert when Benny came in to tell me that some gee from Argentina was here to see me.

"Damn it, I'm busy," I said. "I promised the *Journal* I'd have this crap in by four o'clock."

"Well, dis guy's a big dealer," Benny said. "He's got

a car, it looks like they put wheels on a speed-boat. He drove it alla way up from Argentina."

"Tell him I'll be there in a minute. Keep him happy till I come down."

I finished up Waters' piece in a hurry. This is great, I thought, a ghost-writer for a ghost, a stooge for a stooge. While I laughed at this idea, a thousand little gnats of conscience whined in my head.

Waiting for me in the sitting room was a tall, swarthy, smoothly groomed fellow with two neat little mousetails of a moustache, in his early thirties, and a squat, dark-complexioned, stolid-faced, middle-aged companion in a baggy brown suit.

"Allow me to introduce myself, Carlos de Santos," the younger man said, rising gracefully and speaking English with barely a trace of Spanish intonation.

"This is Fernando Jensen," de Santos said. "He is the sports editor of our famous newspaper, *El Pantero*. We have come to root for our countryman in the big fight."

"In our country, there is very great interest in this fight," Jensen began ponderously, drawing from his pocket a folded and finger-worn clipping from *El Pantero* to show me his feature article on Toro's career. "El Toro Brings New Glory to Argentina," it was headed. "I wish to send back a daily report on El Toro's condition and activities," he continued. "You see, our country is a very proud country. We have a Strength-and-Health program to build up the bodies of our young men. Before I left I have written an editorial in which I consider El Toro Molina as the symbol of Young Argentina."

"Fernando here is a very serious fellow," de Santos added jokingly. "You shouldn't pay too much attention to everything he says." His brown eyes seemed to be laughing. "Can we see El Toro now? I have a gold watch I want to present to him in behalf of his fellow Santa Marianos."

Toro was just drawing on his running togs when we came in. He looked surprised when de Santos embraced him so warmly. Even though the young *estanciero* was obviously accepting Toro as an equal now, Toro still treated him with the shy deference of an obedient *paisano*. While de Santos gave Toro the latest home-town news, with a breeziness that did not succeed in overcoming Toro's obvious unpreparedness at this sudden familiarity, I went out to round up the reporters and photographers. News had been pretty slow around the camp and this was just what we needed to cover up the general sluggishness of Toro's workout.

We even got the newsreels out that afternoon for de Santos' presentation of the gold watch. The fantastic strength of the Molina barrel-makers had long been a legend in Santa Maria, de Santos said, and now the entire village was praying and burning candles for El Toro to bring back the championship of the world. If El Toro defeated Lennert, the de Santoses were going to fill the village fountain with wine and declare a two-day holiday.

That had everything. It couldn't have had more schmalz if I had dreamed it up myself. And I noticed that young de Santos, for all his playboy chatter, had managed to work in his commercial for de Santos wines, which were just beginning to hit the North American market.

While the newsreel men wrapped up their cameras, and de Santos and Jensen were telling the reporters they had also brought with them fifty thousand dollars raised by a group of de Santos' wealthy friends to bet on Toro, Toro just stood there in a daze.

"Well, this must be a pleasant surprise," I said to Toro. "Now you'll have someone to talk to."

"He wishes me to call him by his nickname, 'Pepe'," Toro said unbelievingly. "Imagine me, an *aldeano*, addressing a *de Santos* as Pepe!"

He showed me the gold watch with its sentimentality engraved on the back. "To El Toro with pride and affection from the House of de Santos."

"And he asks me to call him Pepe," Toro repeated. "In

his whole life my father has spoken to Carlos de Santos only once. But you have heard his son with your own ears asking me to call him Pepe." It was more than he could comprehend. "I have much luck, Eddie. Just like Luis like me, and young Carlos de Santos asks me to call him promise. I have everything I want—money, honor, people Pepe." He pressed his lips together in a simple gesture of determination. "I must beat this Lennert. I must show my countrymen they have not come all this way for nothing."

"You'll beat Lennert," I said. "You're a cinch to beat Lennert."

"One ponch, I hope he go boom," he said.

The camp was too quiet for Pepe that evening. There was nothing doing but the regular nightly crap game. So he suggested that I take him and Fernando into town and show them the sights. The three of us squeezed into the Mercedes-Benz he had brought up from B.A. Pepe, it developed, was a dirt-racing driver as well as a polo player and pilot, and the way he pushed that M-B into the city seemed to combine all those accomplishments. It was not without a certain fear that I realized I was in the hands of a playboy. A playboy in my book is not the carefree, luxury-loving character that word usually calls to mind. It is someone trying to escape from the neurotic riptide of an over-abundance of money and an insufficiency of responsibility.

First we had to go up to the suite they were keeping in the Waldorf Towers so Pepe could change into more suitable clothes. He indicated an impressive display of bottles on the table. "I'll be out in a jiffy, old fellow. Help yourself." The Scotch was Cutty-Sark. There was also some champagne brandy, some Holland gin and a couple of bottles of Noilly-Prat.

Fernando was ready in a couple of minutes, but Pepe must have been in there at least half an hour. When he finally appeared, he looked like one of those ads the tailors always show you when you are selecting a style that never comes out looking on you as it did in the picture.

"Now where shall we go, boys?" Pepe said, with an empty, festive smile.

"Depends what you're looking for," I said. "Music, celebrities, girls?"

"Who's interested in music and celebrities, eh, Fernando?" Fernando smiled heavily. Pepe produced a gold cigarette case, filled with *Players*, and selected one gracefully. "Don't worry, my friend," he said to Fernando, winking at me happily, "I will swear to your wife you spent every night at the training camp."

Pepe tipped his way to ringside tables, ordered the waiters to keep the wine flowing and fell verbosely in love with each successive blonde who came on to dance, sing, or smile across her cigarette tray. It was apparent that he was to have a happy and costly Broadway debut. Early in the morning at the Copa, he was saying, "The one second from this end—who looks like a little golden kitten—do you suppose she would like to come up to the apartment for a nightcap?"

"Look, Pepe," I said—he had already offered me a large guest-house all to myself whenever I came down to Santa Maria—"that little tramp takes a hinge at your layout in the Towers, and you're in trouble."

"But she is so beautiful. For her I would not mind a little trouble . . ."

When the party broke up, the garbage collectors who herald the dawn in New York were banging and scraping the cans on the sidewalk as if in protest against the more fortunate citizenry with cleaner jobs at more convenient hours. On the corner of Eighth Avenue I bought the morning papers from an old woman with a shawl around her head. Automatically, I turned to the sports sections as I walked back to the hotel.

The *News* had given the de Santos story a nice play. "Argentine Scion Arrives to Cheer Former Employee,

Toro Molina. Brings $50,000 to Wager on Ex-Barrel-Maker of Famous De Santos Vineyard."

And further down, I read, "Toro Molina faces the acid test of his spectacular career this Friday night when the undefeated giant gets a chance to try his celebrated *mazo* punch on the formidable ex-champion, Gus Lennert."

I recognized my own words, words I had written so many times they began to assume the weight of truth. On the bottom of the same page was a large cigarette ad in which a recently crowned middleweight champion was advising his fans to smoke a well-known brand because it was the only cigarette that didn't affect his endurance. I thought of all the people involved in this pious lie: The fighter, the copy writer, the advertising and cigarette executives, the newspaper publishers and finally the great mass of readers themselves who acquiesce and make a lie, for all practical purposes, as easy to live by as truth.

How could I be blamed for pushing my product, the Giant of the Andes? Who was I to crusade for integrity? I was just trying to live in the world with a minimum amount of friction and pain. If this town was so stupidly credulous as to fill the Garden to see a harmless oaf maul a burned-out ex-champion, who was I to turn them away at the door? What if I did know better? What if I even saw the fight game for what it was, a genuinely manly art, dragged down through the sewers of human greed? What could I do about it?

But whom was I arguing with? Who said I had to do anything about it? I was looking up toward the sixth floor of Beth's apartment-hotel. What was I doing a dozen blocks away from my own joint off Times Square? Her light was on. At five o'clock in the morning, her light was on. Now I realized why my mind wasn't letting me rest. This wasn't a Hamlet soliloquy; it was my running argument with Beth. I peered through the locked glass doors into the hallway. The dreary shapeless figure of a middle-aged woman was scrubbing the floor. I had seen her there for years on my way to and from Beth's apartment.

I kept looking in at the scrub-woman while trying to make up my mind. How would Beth receive me? Would she see this as an act of determination daring enough to sweep away her resistance? Or would it seem to be just another alcoholic performance by a restless drunk who wandered through the gray canyons of the city's dawn in pursuit of a will o' the wisp—his decency?

Her window was a small rectangle casting its yellow shaft into the drab morning. There shines my conscience, I thought, one small compartment in this great edifice of darkness. And as I watched it, in a kind of hateful reverence, it suddenly went out. Down the empty street came a bony milk-horse calop-calopping wearily on the echoing pavement. His day had begun again. Back in harness with his blinders on. In that instant I remembered that I had to be out at the camp by nine o'clock to meet some out-of-town sports writers who were coming in to interview Toro.

18

I SHAVED, showered, tossed a couple of coffees down and called the Waldorf to see if the Argentine delegation was going out with me. Fernando answered the phone. Pepe had just gone to bed. He had left a call for four that afternoon. But Fernando wanted to go with me. He thought it would be a good idea if Toro, in his interview, said something about the growing importance of the national sports movement in Argentina. So for one hour on that bumpy local, with an off-key version of the Anvil Chorus pounding in my head, I had to hear about the growing enthusiasm for *Argentinidad*. Our Giant of the Andes was only supposed to be a national hero. But this self-appointed ambassador from south of the Amazon seemed determined to make him a hero of nationalism as well.

Toro was sitting on the porch listening to his radio and idly drawing faces in the margin of a newspaper. Training was over except for some light exercises in the afternoon and there wasn't much for him to do.

"Why you leave last night?" he said. "Lots of people come and ask questions. I do not know what to say."

I had never seen him in such a mood. The strain was beginning to tell. This was the first fight for which Danny and Doc had really put the pressure on, and the daily grind building up to the nervous tension of the tapering-off period had twisted even Toro's stolid intestines into the usual pre-fight knot.

Even with the reporters, to whom he usually showed

a peasant amiability, he was irritable and uncommunicative.

"It's a good sign," Doc observed. "He's in the best shape he's been so far. Down to two-sixty-eight. It's the first time he's had an edge. Danny has really been working the hell out of him. Trained him like he would for an old-time fight. Had him chopping wood, climbing trees and hopping fences besides his regular work."

"I'd like to see the big bum make a good showing," I said. "Those boys in the press row who can't be had will really be gunning for him."

"If you ask me, Danny's done miracles with him," Doc said. "At least this time he oughta look like a pro. He's finally got him punching a little bit and he's moving around a little better, getting off his heels."

After lunch Toro was supposed to lie down, but he told Doc he couldn't sleep. He was too nervous about the fight. He said he wanted to take a drive in his car. Danny, edgy with the terrible effort at sobriety he always made when he was taking his work seriously, jumped Toro irritably.

"Don't try to kid your Uncle Danny. I haven't let you out in three weeks, so now you want to run over and get Ruby to take care of you."

Toro's face tightened with anger. "You say that, I keel you, you son-of-beetch . . ."

"Tell you what I'll do," I stepped in. "Maybe the ride'll do Toro good. So I'll go along with him. Okay?"

They both agreed. Fernando was ready to come along, but for some reason Toro didn't want him. Even in Spanish he could never find the words to express his suspicion of his aggressively patriotic countryman. For Toro, phrases like "the power and glory of Argentina" had no meaning, no matter how many flowery adjectives were used to establish him as a symbol of *Argentinidad*. To him Argentina was the village of Santa Maria.

"Please," Toro said, when we were on the open road, "I go to see the Señora."

"Toro, I am your friend. What goes with you and the Señora?"

"I want to see her," Toro pouted. "I see her today."

"Maybe I can help you. But you've got to tell me more about it. I'll guard your secret like a confession. I promise."

"I have already confess to the sin of *adulterio*," Toro said. "But I cannot stop. I am in love with the Señora. I want the Señora for my wife. I want to bring her home to Santa Maria to live with me in the big house I build on the hill."

"But, Toro, *estás loco*," I said. "*Completamente loco.* Don't you realize she's married? Have you forgotten Nick, of all people?"

"It is not real marriage," Toro insisted. "She has tell me whole business. It is not real marriage before the Church. It is only civil marriage."

"But what makes you think the Señora wants to go with you? Has she told you? Has she promised you?"

"She says only maybe, it is possible," he admitted. "But she says she is in love with me, only with me. I will take her back to Santa Maria. And Mama will teach her how to cook the dishes I like. And we will be very rich with the money I make in the ring."

"That's great," I said. "That's the end of the movie, all right. Only you left out one little detail. Nick. What are you going to do about Nick?"

"The Señora is very intelligent. The Señora will find a way to tell him what has happen."

What could you do with a dope like that except clam up and enjoy the scenery?

Toro told Benny to drive to Green Acres. "Dat okay?" Benny asked me. Maybe it was just nasty curiosity on my part, masquerading as high purpose, but I let him go.

When no one answered the front door, we went around to the back and let ourselves in through the screen porch. There was no one in sight, so I followed Toro up the stairs. He seemed to know where he was going. At the end of the second-floor hall was Ruby's suite—she and Nick had separate apartments—an upstairs sitting room decorated completely in white. At the far end of the room, facing us, was a white piano. A man was sitting on the bench at the piano, but he wasn't playing. He had his back turned to it and his head was thrown back as if he were a mute going through the emotions of singing grand opera. We didn't see Ruby at all until we were half way into the room. From where we stood, her head had been hidden by the top of the piano.

When he noticed us, the man jumped up and I saw it was Jackie Ryan, Jock Mahoney's kid nephew. "Get outa here! Get the hell outa here," he was yelling. Ruby's voice, shriller than I had ever heard it, screamed. Even quicker than I could, Toro seemed to grasp what had been going on.

"*¡Puta!*" he shouted. "*¡Estás una puta, una puta!*"

He made a frenzied, awkward lunge for her, but Ryan who barely came to his shoulder, rushed forward and drove his fist into Toro's stomach. The punch caught Toro by surprise and sent him reeling backward. Then he lowered his head, amazingly like a fighting bull, and started to charge.

"Get out, get out," I ordered Ryan.

"Yes, for God's sake, all of you," Ruby screeched. "You too, Jackie."

"Okay, okay, I'm going," Ryan said and swaggered out with an air of casualness.

"Come on, Toro. We better go, too," I said. But he didn't hear me.

The first wave of Toro's fury was spent now. He turned to Ruby unbelievingly. *"Puta,"* he said. "Why you do this? Why you do this bad thing? And all the time you tell me Toro is the only one . . ."

"You lummox," Ruby shouted. "You filthy, sneaking lummox."

Her lips were unusually red in her pale, frightened

face. But as she stood there in her silk lounging pajamas, her superb, unimaginative self-control began flowing back into her.

"Why you do this bad thing to Toro?" he persisted. "Why? *¿Por qué?*"

"None of your business," Ruby said. "None of your goddam business. Just because I let you come up here a few times, you think you own me. All you men try to own me."

"But all the time we talk about Santa Maria. Maybe you go with me, you say."

Ruby looked at him without pity. "I had to tell you something, you baboon. Do you think I'd leave all this for a lousy little hole in Argentina? Spend my life with a dopey tenth-rate bum!"

Toro stared in bewilderment. "Toro no bum. Toro fighter. All the time win. Best fighter Nick has in whole life."

Ruby laughed. She had to get back at him. After what had happened she had to do something to put him in his place.

"Listen, you slob," she said slowly. "You couldn't beat Eddie here if it wasn't fixed. Every fight you had in this country was fixed. All those bums you're so proud of beating, they were paid to take a dive, every one of them."

"Dive?" Toro said, frowning. "I not understand. Explain me what you mean, dive?"

"You poor sap," Ruby said. "Those guys you beat were letting you win—didn't you know that?—letting you win."

Toro's large eyes half closed in pain. "No!" he roared. "No! No! I no believe. I no believe."

"Ask Eddie," Ruby said. "He ought to know."

Toro turned to me desperately. "*Dígame*, Eddie," he begged. "*La verdad. Solamente la verdad. Dígame.*"

Having to stand there and swing that body blow to

his simple pride suddenly seemed to compound my crime. But there was no room to weasel out. "It's true," I said. "Your fights were fixed. They were all fixed, Toro."

Toro ran his hand slowly over his face as if his head held a terrible aching. Looking at him, you had the crazy impression that the whole front of his face had been beaten in.

He turned and rushed out. Downstairs, he charged out through the screen door, ran around the house and started wildly down the street. I jumped into the car and told Benny to follow him. We let him go for almost four blocks. He was beginning to run out of gas. He lacked the athlete's co-ordination to run easily on his toes. Gradually he slowed down to an awkward workhorse trot. We parked the car about fifty yards ahead of him, and as he came abreast we tried to herd him into the back seat.

"Go 'way, go 'way, you make me look like fool," he shouted.

"G'wan, get in dere," Benny said. He pushed Toro toward the car. He had nothing but contempt for him. The exertion had sapped Toro's power to resist. Wearily he submitted and climbed into the back seat.

All the way out to the camp, Toro sat huddled in the corner, staring down at his massive hands.

"Listen, for Christ sake," I said. "We were only trying to help you. Trying to get you that dough you wanted."

There was no response from Toro, no indication that he had heard me.

This wasn't in the script. Toro wasn't supposed to have any sensibilities, any capacity for humiliation, for pride or indignation. He was merely the product: the soap, the coffee, the cigarette.

"Honest, Toro, we weren't trying to make a fool out of you. We just wanted to make sure you got the right start. It happens all the time."

288

But Toro wouldn't hear me. He just sat sullenly in the corner, his eyes turned inward in shame.

When we reached the camp, Danny and Doc were sitting out on the steps with George and some of the boys.

"Hello, big fella," George said. "Have a nice ride?"

Toro stood on the landing, dwarfing all of us. Looking up at this inept and angry giant, his inarticulate wrath was terrible to see.

"You think you make joke of Toro, huh?" he accused us all. "You make big fool of Toro?" He went on into the house.

"What's eating him?" Danny wanted to know.

"Ruby just gave it to him straight about how he beat all those fellas," I said.

"Serves him right for nosing around the Duchess," Doc said. "It serves him right."

"Maybe we shoulda told him," Danny reflected. "It stinks bad enough without smelling it up with more lies."

"Aah, you guys sound like a lot of old women," Vince said. "He'll be all right. I'll go in and slip him another five hundred. That's the best kind of medicine."

But a few minutes later, when Vince returned, his fat neck was reddened with anger. "He says he don't want the dough. The jerk. And six months ago his ass was hangin' out. How d'ya figure a slob like that?"

When it was time for supper Benny went up to call Toro, but he wouldn't come down. Then George took a crack at it because he was closer to Toro than the others, but he came back alone too. So I went up to see what I could do. Toro was standing in front of his window, staring out into the gathering darkness.

"Toro, you better eat something," I said.

"I stay here," Toro said.

"Come on, snap out of it. We've got a beautiful steak waiting. Just the way you like it."

Toro shook his head. "I no eat with you. You make joke of Toro."

Then he turned around and confronted me. "This fight with Lennert? This fix too?"

"No," I lied. "This one is on the level. So if you beat Lennert, you have nothing to be ashamed of."

I was sorry to have to keep on with it, but I was in so deep there was no way out of this circle of lies. We were in a tight spot. The mood he was in now, he was liable to do anything in that Lennert fight. If he thought the fight was in the bag, he might even spill it to the Commission and that would be the end of the Lennert and Stein gravy. We could even wind up before a Grand Jury. I wish I could have had a choice, but there I was. I had to make him believe this fight was on the level.

Toro drove his enormous right first into the open palm of his other hand. "I win this fight," he threatened. "I show you Toro no joke. You no have to fix for Toro. This time you no laugh behind me."

"Okay, okay," I said. "Now come on down and get yourself some steak."

19

HEAVYWEIGHT RIVALS IN CRUCIAL BATTLE TONIGHT—MAKE FIGHT PREDICTIONS

"Toro to Get Boxing Lesson And First Licking," says Ex-Champ

by
GUS LENNERT

I feel confident I will snap the Man Mountain's winning streak tonight. Although I have plenty of respect for his strength and punching ability, I expect to out-box and out-general him in our 15-round bout in the Garden. Giving away 75 pounds doesn't frighten me. He may be a giant, but giants have been licked before. Don't forget Goliath. The bigger they are, the harder they fall. I have never been in better shape and am betting on myself to dispose of this Argentine invader and go on to become the first ex-champion to regain his crown.

"I Will Knock Him Out in Five Rounds," says Argentine Giant

by
TORO MOLINA

When I was in Argentina I have heard already of Gus Lennert. He was Champion-of-the-World then. Even though he no longer holds the title, I realize he is still a great fighter and the most dangerous opponent I have faced. But I will be surprised if he is still there for the sixth round. My advantage in weight, age and strength should wear him down in the early rounds. After that I am counting on my *mazo* punch to put him away. I predict that this fight will be one more step up the ladder toward my goal of achieving what my idol, Luis Angel Firpo, came so close to doing—bringing the championship to Argentina.

I READ back over these brilliant pieces of creative writing I had just knocked out. Not bad, I thought. As convincing as this stuff ever is. Toro's essay was a re-write of one I had written a year earlier for a French middleweight, but who'd know the difference? Certainly not the suckers who read the stuff. The other one sounded more like Lennert than Lennert himself. Next thing I know he'll begin to think he's Tunney and want me to write his speeches on Shakespeare to give the boys at Harvard.

Next, I dreamt up a follow-up piece for Gus on "How I Got Licked," for the morning after the fight. Usually I had to knock out those first-person post-mortems in that high-tension interval between the end of the fight and the *Journal's* deadline. But this time I figured I might as well clean up all the literary labors at once. So I batted out something that began, "In my thirteen years in the ring, I have stayed with the best of them. So I can honestly say this Argentine Giant is the most powerful puncher I ever faced. I look for him to take the mighty Buddy Stein and go on to the championship."

Most of the time you just threw this stuff together, slapped the guy's name on it and shoved it in. But Gus was exasperatingly particular about the way his name was used. Wise to all the angles on how to gather unto himself that extra buck, Gus saw a profitable sideline for himself as a spot commentator on the big fights. He had even suggested that I might be able to work up a daily column for him. On the chance that there might be something in it for me, I had promised to take these by-line pieces out to him to check them over before I sent them through.

Gus lived in a modest white frame house in a middle-class section of West Trenton. His wife met me at the door in an apron. She was just getting the boys' lunch ready, she said. With the purse from the Stein fight and his savings, Gus must have had at least a hundred G's in cash and securities, but I don't think they had ever had a cook. Gus liked to make you think it was because he was so fond of the missus' cooking. But what he was really fond of was that lettuce in the cooler.

Gus was sitting in the breakfast nook in a worn, red bathrobe, an old pair of pants and bedroom slippers, with a lot of papers spread out in front of him. His hair, sharply receding from his forehead and showing signs of gray at the temples, was unkempt, as if he had just gotten out of bed. He hadn't bothered to shave, in the old fighters' tradition that the extra days' growth was an additional protection to his face. He looked much older than when I had last seen him at Green Acres. You would have put him down for closer to forty than thirty. The Stein beating seemed to have taken something out of him. I could count where the six stitches had been taken after Stein had split his right eye in the fourteenth round.

When I came in he frowned at me as if his head was hurting.

"Goddamit, you sure take your own sweet time getting out here," he greeted me.

"Sorry, Gus," I said. "I missed the ten-o'clock train. Hope it didn't inconvenience you."

"Well, we still got telephone service," he said. "Thank God I can still pay my phone bills. You could of called Emily. I got up at nine-thirty especially to be ready for you. What's a matter, too much celebrating last night?"

"Hell, no, I was in the sack before midnight. I wanted to be sure and be in shape for the fight tomorrow night."

I thought that might get a rise out of him, but he didn't even smile.

"I had a lousy night," he said. "Must a been three o'clock before I could get to sleep. Finished two whole murder mysteries. That's why I coulda used the extra hour this morning."

"I'm sorry," I apologized again. "I guess I should have called you, Gus."

"Well, that's the way it is," Gus said in a voice surly

with self-pity. "When you're on top the phone never stops ringing. But when you're on your way out, nobody gives a damn."

From the kitchen came a loud, boyish screech, and then a general hubbub. Gus jumped up, opened the door and shouted in, "For God's sake, Emily, how many times do I have to ask you to keep them quiet? I knew I shoulda gone to the hotel last night. Now are you gonna make 'em shut up or do I have to come in there and knock their heads together?"

He came back to the table, closed his eyes and pressed his fingers against the right side of his forehead.

"Feeling okay, Gus?"

"Just a lousy headache," he said. "Hell, no wonder, the racket those kids make around here."

He squeezed his eyes together and massaged the triangle between his eyebrows.

"Jesus, it looks like I have to do everything." He picked up some of the pages in front of him, on which there were long rows of figures. "I pay a business manager two hundred bucks a month to handle my investments and he can't even add right." He tapped the papers irritably. "Found two mistakes already. And these fifty G's I make tonight, he's trying to sell me on the idea of putting it in annuities. Annuities is a lot of bunk. I been figuring it up and it don't pay. I carry a hundred thousand straight insurance. That's the only kind to have. If I got fifty thousand to invest, I'd rather put it in something like Treasury Bonds."

He was starting to figure out how 2.9 percent of fifty thousand compared with setting up a trust fund. You could see he loved to write those big figures down and multiply them.

"Look, Gus," I said. "I've got a lot to do yet today. Want to take a gander at this stuff?"

He read it over as if he were Hemingway guarding his literary reputation, with his pencil poised critically over each word, occasionally shaking his head and rereading a sentence. "This line here," he quibbled, 'Don't forget Goliath.' That don't sound good. Maybe some people don't even know who Goliath is."

"Anybody who reads the *Journal* and doesn't know who Goliath is," I said, "deserves to read the *Journal*."

"If you wanna succeed in this writing business," Gus insisted, "you gotta write so everybody can understand you."

"But since you're comparing Goliath to Toro, it'll remind everybody who he is."

"Goddamit, why does everything have to be an argument," Gus said, his voice rising. "My name's going on this, so I guess I can have it the way I want it."

He took my copy and began correcting it, erasing several times. "There," he said, "that's a little more like it."

I looked at it and said nothing. What he had written was, "Don't forget how David overcame Goliath." He went through the rest of the copy, making his petty and niggling changes and handed it back without looking at me.

"There," he said. "Every goddam thing I've got to do myself."

I kept quiet. But I couldn't figure why he was under so much pressure for a fight he was going to throw.

He stood up, rubbed his head again, and walked me to the door. "How does the house look?"

"Even Jacobs can't kick. Nothing but some three-thirties left and they'll be gone by fight time. It's a hundred and fifty easy."

"If it wasn't for those goddam taxes I'd make myself some money," Gus said.

"I wish I were paying those taxes," I said. "Well, see you, Gus. Take it easy."

"I just hope it looks all right," Gus said. "That big clown better fight enough to make it look good. All I need now is for the Commish to smell a rat and tie up our purses."

"Stop worrying," I said. "It'll be all right. It's money in the bank. You haven't got a thing to worry about."

As the front door closed behind me, I could hear the Lennert kids cutting up in the kitchen again. "For God's sake, will you keep those damn kids quiet?" Gus shouted. "How many times do I have to tell ya? I got a headache!"

Toro had driven into town with Pepe and Fernando. He wanted no part of us. Fernando, moving in, took him up to the suite at the Waldorf. We didn't see him until the weigh-in at noon.

"Howya feeling?" I said.

Toro looked away. He wasn't talking to any of us.

"Don't forget now, a good lunch around three o'clock," Doc said. "But remember, no fats, no gravies and no lemon-meringue pie."

But Toro wouldn't acknowledge Doc either. Fernando rubbed Toro's back possessively as he stepped off the scales in his shorts. "We will take care of him," Fernando assured us.

Gus got on the scales wearing an old towel that had printed on it in faded letters, *Hotel Manx*.

"Well, anyway, Gus, after this fight you oughta be able to go out and buy yourself a towel of your own," Vince said as Gus stepped down.

Most of the boys laughed. But Gus was a humorless man at best and this afternoon he was not at his best.

"At least I don't do nothing worse than swipe hotel towels," he said. It was not so much what he said as the irritable way he said it that infected the atmosphere.

Toro was waiting to step onto the scales as Gus stepped off. This is a moment of importance in the drama of any fight. The reporters watch the faces of the principals to see if the underdog betrays any fear of the favorite, or for those displays of bravado that may be part of a preconceived plan of psychological warfare, or for a sign of some highly publicized hostility, or for that exchange of smiles and good wishes that never fails to delight the sentimentalists.

But between Toro and Gus nothing happened at all. Gus just stepped on and stepped off with the indifference of a man punching in for work in the morning. Not to greet Toro wasn't snubbing him any more than the man punching in shows any discourtesy by ignoring the fellow behind him. But as Gus walked away, Toro watched him from the scales. Reporters who had no way of knowing what had happened to Toro in the last forty-eight hours may have described his eyes as being full of hate. But Gus had no special significance for Toro as an individual. He had simply become the most immediate target for Toro's exploding resentment against a world which had tricked and belittled him.

An hour before the fight you could feel the tension growing in the Garden lobby: the late ticket seekers, the sharp-eyed scalpers, the busy little guys making last-minute book, eight-to-five on Toro, five-to-nine on Lennert, playing the percentages.

Around nine, Toro came down from the Waldorf with Pepe and Fernando. Danny wanted to throw them out. Strangers in a dressing room always made him even more nervous. But Toro was stubborn. "They are my friends," he insisted. "If they go, I go too."

Danny had never paid much attention to what Toro said before, but this time Danny sensed something in Toro that was not to be denied, something wild inside him that wanted violence.

Usually Toro had waited to go down to the ring with the patient amiability of a prize Guernsey standing by to make its appearance at the county fair. But this time he asked how much longer it would be every few minutes. And finally when Doc told him to start warming up with a little shadow-boxing, Toro lashed out at his imaginary opponent with a fury none of us had ever seen in him before.

Lennert was first to enter the ring. As he worked his feet slowly in the rosin box, he responded to the cheers of his supporters with a tight, cheerless smile. His face was ghastly white in the glare of the ring lights.

Toro's white satin bathrobe with the blue trim and the Argentine flag on back got a tremendous hand as he climbed through the ropes. He didn't jack-knife over the top rung as I had had him do for the previous fights. Something about that omission vaguely worried me. It was a trivial but significant protest against the kind of circus presentation we had set up for him. I didn't know what could happen, but I had the same sense of apprehension a playwright would feel if one of his actors began the play by speaking unfamiliar lines that were not in the script.

I kept my eyes on Toro while the announcer introduced the usual celebrities, followed by some future attractions—the "highly regarded lightweight from Greenwich Village who has emerged victorious in seventeen consecutive contests," the Bronx middleweight "who has recently established himself as a fistic sensation and who never fails to make a spectacular showing," and several other boys whom Harry Balough managed to describe with artless and incongruous pomposity. Toro sat on the edge of his stool, anxious to begin. Even when a great cheer went up from the crowd and Buddy Stein swung through the ropes and mitted the crowd in a broad, ham gesture, Toro paid no attention. Stein was dressed sharply in a loud-check sports suit that set off his wide shoulders and his trim waist. The body that tired sports writers were always comparing to Adonis' moved with jaunty arrogance. He trotted over to Lennert's corner and, instead of the conventional and perfunctory handshake, kissed him on the forehead. The crowd laughed and Stein laughed back. They loved each other. Then he skipped across the ring to shake hands with Toro. Toro just let him lift his glove. He still didn't seem to see him. He didn't see anybody but Lennert.

The ring was cleared now. The referee brought the fighters together for final instructions. Gus stood quietly with a towel draped over his head, looking bored as he listened to the routine warnings about foul punching and breaking clean he had heard hundreds of times before. Toro fixed his eyes on his opponent's feet, nodding sullenly as the referee went through his spiel.

Then they were back in their corners, with their bathrobes off, alone and stripped for action. Toro turned to his corner, in a gesture of genuflection and crossed himself solemnly. Lennert winked at a friend in the working press. The crowd was hushed with nervous excitement. The house lights went down and the white ring was sharply outlined in the darkness.

At the bell, Gus put out his gloves to touch Toro's in the meaningless gesture of sportsmanship, but Toro brushed him aside and drove him into the ropes. This aroused the fans' erratic sense of fair play and they booed. Gus looked surprised. Toro was leaning on Gus, flailing his arms with ineffectual fury. When the referee separated them, Gus danced up and down, flicking his left into Toro's face and preparing to counter with the clever defensive timing that everyone expected of him. But Toro rushed him into the ropes again, not hitting him cleanly, but roughing him up, punishing him with his great weight, clutching him with one arm and clubbing him about the head with the other.

That was the pattern of the first round. Lennert wasn't able to make Toro fight his fight. His movements were listless. He lacked the strength to stand off Toro's wild rushes.

Toro looked even more aggressive as he came out for the second round. Up from the floor he lifted a roundhouse uppercut, the kind Gus had easily blocked and countered a thousand times. But this time he seemed to make no effort to avoid it and it caught him on the side of the head.

He shouldn't let Toro hit him that easily, I thought. Nobody is going to believe that. But I had to admit Gus put on a very good show. He actually seemed hurt by the blow. At least he fell into a clinch as if to avoid further punishment. Toro kept on trying to hammer at him even in the clinch. He wasn't what we'd call an in-fighter, but he had enough strength to pull one of his arms free and club away at Gus' back and kidneys. Gus was talking to him in the clinches, mumbling something into his ear. I wondered what he could be saying. Perhaps, "Take it easy, boy. What you so steamed up about? You're gonna win." Whatever it was, Toro wasn't listening. In his clumsy, mauling way, he was taking the play away from Gus. As we had figured the fight, Gus would outbox Toro for the first two or three rounds and then ease himself out around the sixth, whenever he caught one that would look good enough for the K.O.

But Toro wasn't giving him a chance to show anything. He was fighting him as if possessed, as if he had to destroy Gus Lennert. Just before the round ended, Toro rushed Gus again, clubbing the smaller man viciously, and his gloved fist came down heavily on top of the ex-champion's head. It wasn't a punch known to boxing science, just the familiar downward clubbing motion that cops like to use. Gus sagged. Toro clubbed him fiercely again and Gus sank to his knees. The bell sounded. Gus didn't look badly hurt, but he didn't get up. He remained on one knee, frowning and staring thoughtfully at the canvas. His seconds had to half-carry, half-drag him back to his corner.

"He's a bum, he wants ta quit," someone yelled in back of me.

Smelling salts, massage at the back of the neck and a cold wet sponge squeezed over his head brought Gus around by the time the warning buzzer sounded for round three. He opened his eyes and then closed them again and shook his head slowly as if trying to clear it.

"He's faking," the guy said behind me. "Look at him, he wants ta quit."

Several other skeptics took up the cry.

At the bell, Toro ran across the ring. Gus tried to hold him off with a feeble jab, but Toro just pushed it aside and brought his fist down on Lennert's head again. Gus dropped his hands and turned to the referee. He was muttering something. Whatever it was, the referee didn't understand and motioned him to fight on. Toro clubbed him again. Gus stumbled back against the ropes and sat down on the middle strand with his head buried in his arms. There was a wild look in Toro's eyes. He was going to hit Gus again, but the referee slid between them. Gus continued to sit on the ropes, cowering behind his gloves. The way it looked to the fans, he hadn't really been badly hurt. It looked as if that guy behind me was right. It looked as if he were doing an el foldo, all right. I couldn't figure it. Gus had more sense than to quit without going down. Even if he wanted to go home early, he had enough ring savvy to give the crowd the kind of kayo they paid to see. But he just kept sitting there on the rope, with his head bowed in his arms as if he were praying. The referee looked at Gus curiously. Then he raised Toro's hand and waved him back to his corner. The crowd didn't like it. The guy behind me was yelling, "Fake!" The cry began to spread. Apparently just enough had leaked out about Toro's record to make some of the cash customers hyper-critical. Lennert's handlers jumped into the ring and led Gus back to his corner. He slumped down on his stool and his head fell forward on his chest. Part of the crowd had begun to file out, muttering their disappointment to each other. But thousands were still standing around, booing and crying, "Fake!"

"This act oughta bring vaudeville back," the comic

behind me shouted. People around him were still laughing when Gus suddenly pitched forward and slid off his stool. His head hit the canvas heavily and he lay still.

The powerful lights beating down on Gus' inert, expressionless face gave it a ghostly hue. A couple of news cameramen shoved their cameras at him through the ropes and flashed their pictures. The crowd wasn't booing any more. Around the ring curiosity seekers were pressing forward for a closer look.

The house doctor, portly, genial, inefficient Dr. Grandini, bustled into the ring. The handlers grouped themselves anxiously around the doc. This sort of thing didn't happen very often and they were frightened.

The guy behind me who first started yelling "Fake!" was pushing past me to get a better view of Gus. "He's hurt bad," he was telling a companion. "I knew there was something funny the way he sat down on those ropes."

"He just can't take it any more," his companion declared.

"I seen him put up some great battles here in the Garden," someone said.

"Well, he sure stunk up the joint tonight," said a gambler who had bet Lennert to stay the limit.

Barney Winch, and one of his lieutenants, Frankie Fante, came along.

"Hi, there, Eddie," Barney grinned behind his fat cigar. "How's my boy?"

"Looks like something's wrong with Gus," I said.

"Come on, Barney," Fante said. "We c'n see it at the Trans-Lux. We gotta meet those fellas outside."

"Have a big night?" I asked Barney.

"Not bad," Barney said.

Not bad, for Barney, meant twelve, fifteen thousand, maybe twenty.

They were carrying Gus out now. They carried him up the long aisle to the dressing rooms, with his white face staring sightlessly at the fans who had been abusing him with their cynical cat-calls a few minutes before.

In our dressing room, Pepe was inviting everybody to be his guest at El Morocco. Vince had managed to place the fifty grand for him and Pepe wanted us all to help him start spending it. But Toro was more excited than anybody else. He grabbed me when I came in and shouted, "Toro no joke. Toro real fighter. You see tonight, huh?"

"Everyone in Argentina will be talking about you tonight," Fernando said, coming in from somewhere. "This is a great victory for *Argentinidad*, for the pride of Argentina."

For the pride of Toro Molina, I thought. That's all that was at stake, and that's enough.

Doc came in from the hall. Nobody had missed him in the excitement. His hunchback and his damp, pale face framed in the doorway, he looked like a herald of doom. His nasal voice knifed through the celebration din.

"Gus is still out," he said. "He's going to the hospital."

20

We all drove over to St. Clare's Hospital in Pepe's car. I wished it had been just a cab, for somehow it seemed profane to use a jazzed-up Mercedes-Benz when you were going over to visit a guy in critical condition. Nobody said anything. Even Pepe knew enough to be quiet.

In the waiting room Doc talked to one of the nurses. The patient was still in a coma, she said. Lennert's doctor had called in a brain specialist. It was a hemorrhage of the brain; that's all she could tell him.

Doc came back and gave us the news. "Is that . . .? Is that . . .?" everybody wanted to know. Doc didn't know either. "I heard of cases recovering," he said. "Like when a scab forms on the brain. The patient lives, only he's got paralysis agitans; what we mean when we call a guy punchy."

Some people feel better when they keep talking. That's the way Doc was. Danny just sat in a corner biting his lip and fingering his hat. Toro held his crucifix in his hands. His eyes were half-closed and his face was a mask. His lips moved slowly. He was saying his beads.

"I didn't think Toro could hit him hard enough for this," I said to Doc.

"Chances are, Toro had nothing to do with it," Doc answered. "Gus probably came out of the Stein fight with those hemorrhages, see. Multiple hemorrhages. They can be awful small, no bigger than a pinpoint. But it just takes a little tap to start them. Or even getting a little too excited would be enough to do it."

"Gus was talking about a headache when I saw him the other day," I said.

"That sounds like it," Doc said. "That could be it."

"Jesus," I said.

"I heard of guys recovering," Doc said.

A little while later Mrs. Lennert and her two eldest sons came out of the elevator. They went right by us, down the corridor to Lennert's room. Toro looked up as they passed and then hung his head again. With his grave bent head, his sad brown eyes and the beads clutched desperately in his enormous hand, he looked like a battered monolith.

About two o'clock in the morning they wheeled Gus down the hall to the elevator. Mrs. Lennert was crying. Doc went over and asked one of the internes what the score was. He came back worried. "They're going to try to relieve the pressure," he said.

"What do you mean, try?" I said.

"Well, these brain things are tricky," he said. "You see, they've got to try to drain off the excess cerebrospinal fluid . . ."

"Goddam it, quit trying to show off your medical knowledge and tell me so I can understand," I said.

"Okay, okay," Doc said, "I thought you wanted me to tell you."

He was always sensitive on this point, but I couldn't help it. Danny came over and said, "What're the odds on this thing upstairs, Doc?"

"I wouldn't want to say," Doc told him.

Danny went back to his corner, sat down and started leafing through a *National Geographic* he didn't seem to be looking at.

At three o'clock Pepe and Fernando got tired and decided to go back to the Waldorf. They wanted to take Toro with them, but he just shook his head and bent over his beads. A little later Nick and the Killer came in. Nick was wearing a double-breasted blue pin-stripe and a somber tie. He must have dressed for the occasion. He looked very serious and yet I had the feeling his attitude was as carefully put on as his clothes. The expression on the Killer's face was a carbon of Nick's, only not quite as convincing. Nick walked over to the window where I was looking out over the monotonous rooftops.

"Do the best you can with the stories in the morning papers," he said.

"Jesus," I said, "how can you worry about the angles with Gus up there with a tube in his head?"

"I feel bad too," Nick said. "But someone's gotta keep his head. This could look very lousy for us. If the papers play up the angle that Gus was all through after the Stein fight . . . You know what I mean."

"Sure I know what you mean. Try to make 'em think Gus was a suitable opponent and not a beat-up old man with his brains full of blood."

"Take it easy," Nick said.

I could feel the pressure lifting when I blew off at Nick. After all, if anything happened, that's where the blame lay. It was Nick's baby. All I did was make the public buy it. If it hadn't been Eddie Lewis, Nick could have had ten other guys.

The hours ticked by. Nick paced restlessly, the Killer moving with him, slightly behind him, like a well-trained dog. A reporter from the *News* came up. Nick gave him what he wanted. "Gus has got off the floor plenty of times before," I heard him say. "But I'll be in his corner right to the end."

He didn't say anything about being in Toro's corner too. That wasn't public knowledge yet. I was all set to break the news of Nick's purchase of Toro's contract after Gus announced his retirement. If Gus kicked off, I found myself thinking, we'd better hold up the contract story until people began to forget a little bit.

Jesus, Gus was still on the table with the surgeons trying to get his brains back together, and here I was, burying the guy. Not only burying him, but beginning to work out a way to cover Nick. What do you call that, reflex action, psychological conditioning, or just plain depravity? Writing Gus off and realizing I was already working out the best way to sell his death to the public, it didn't come as quite so much of a shock when Doc came in and told us.

"I've lost not only one of the best fighters I ever had but one of the best friends I ever had," Nick was telling the reporters. "As Lennert's manager, I want to say that I don't blame Molina. He fought clean. It was just one of those things."

He isn't mourning, he's working, I thought. He isn't saying farewell to Gus. He's too busy protecting himself in the clinches. The credo of Henry Street, the *Weltanschauung* of the guys on the corner.

But why wasn't I speaking up to tell them this wasn't one of those things, that this was murder, that Gus Lennert had been sacrificed to human greed, his own included? No, I kept my mouth shut. Protecting myself in the clinches, too. An accessory before the fact. As the reporters turned from him, Nick looked over at me in what was almost a wink, a conspiratorial sign. After all, we were both in the same stable.

A photographer from the *Mirror* moved in and flashed a picture of Toro. Simultaneously it flashed in my mind that the picture wouldn't do us any harm; it caught Toro in an effective pose of repentance, saying his beads.

I had to lead Toro out. He was in a trance. Lennert's death wasn't filtered for him, as it was for us, through protective screens of sophistication and rationalization. Toro took it head on. He had killed a man. He wandered in fear and shock as the victim of an auto accident sleepwalks away from the wreck.

Mrs. Lennert came out while we waited on the curb for a cab. Nick was sending her home in his car. Toro went over to her. "I sad. All my life, sad. All the money I make tonight I give you. Every cent I give. I no want the money."

"Get away from me, you murderer, you," Mrs. Lennert said. She wasn't crying. "The fight was fixed and you still had to kill him. You had to show everybody how tough you are. The fight was fixed so poor Gus could get home early because he was sick, and you, you couldn't even wait. You had to kill him. You filthy, dirty murderer."

Then she began to cry. It was an ugly, retching cry, because there was still so much anger in it. Her sons helped her into Nick's car. As they drove off, Toro stood there, staring after them with his mouth hanging loose. He bowed his head and began to mutter, "Jesus Christo ... Jesus Christo ... Jesus Christo ..." We had to push him into the cab.

No one said anything for several blocks. Finally Danny broke the silence with something unexpected. "You know, when a guy goes, you feel like you owe it to him to say something real nice. But Gus, Gus was never much of a fella in my book. Only now I kinda wish he was. Because in a way, you don't feel quite as bad about losing a pal as losing a guy you never got around to liking."

"I liked Gus, *olav hasholem*," Doc said. "He sure was one hundred percent with his wife and kids."

"You and that Jew-heart of yours," Danny said. "You like everybody."

We pulled up in front of St. Malachy's, the little church that's squeezed in among the bars and cheap hotels of Forty-ninth Street. The garbage men were dragging the big cans along the pavement to their big churning truck. A drunk still living in the night before staggered past and wandered off toward wherever he was going. A hooker whose face wasn't meant to be seen in the daylight passed us slowly on the way home to catch up on her sleep.

I have never been much for churches, but I felt easier when we got the sexton to let us inside. The quiet and the candlelight created a better atmosphere for thoughts about the dead. Toro and Danny lit candles to the Virgin

308

Mother. Then Toro went into the sacristy to find the priest.

"I oughta confess too," Danny said to me. "If I hadn't had a grudge against the guy, I never would have whipped Toro into the shape he was in. I came up to the fight with hate in my heart, laddie. Maybe that's what did it, God help me!"

But Danny didn't confess, unless you would call me his confessor. He went over to another altar, stuffed a pocketful of bills into the offering box, and knelt in prayer.

Doc was sitting in one of the rear pews with his head bent. I went over and sat next to him while we waited for Toro to finish. "I had a strong hunch Gus had the canaries in his head after Stein," Doc said. "I knew something was wrong with him. I coulda said."

Sure you coulda said, I thought. Danny coulda said. I coulda said. Poor old Gus, counting his annuities, coulda said. We were all as guilty as Cain. All but Toro, in there in his spiritual sweat-box, carrying our burden. Yes, if the Father were really hep, Toro would be learning that he was just an innocent bystander, just the boy who happened to be around when the mob decided to cash in on a run-down ex-champion whose name still retained some of its marquee magic.

Toro returned from the confession booth, lit another candle to the Virgin Mary and dropped on his knees in front of the shrine. He stayed that way for several minutes. When we came out onto the street again, a cold gray light was settling over the city. A few early-risers were going to work with sleep-heavy but freshly shaved faces.

"I'm going home and crack my best bottle of Irish," Danny said. Home was a room-and-bath he kept in a shabby hotel off Broadway.

"I better call my mother," Doc said. "She worries about me."

When we dropped Danny off, we bought the morning papers from a listless middle-aged newsboy. Gus and Toro had the headlines. On the front of the *News* were big pictures of Gus lying on the canvas, Gus on a stretcher being carried to the ambulance, and Toro with his head bent, saying his beads. I turned to the story on Page Three. The Boxing Commission would investigate the death, but as far as the Chairman could see, "It seems to be a tragic accident for which nobody is to blame."

Well, maybe so. And maybe Jimmy Quinn had gotten to the good Commissioner. Maybe the Commissioner didn't actually have his hand out. Maybe he just wasn't very bright.

The story went on to say that Toro would be arraigned on the usual manslaughter charge. I hustled Toro down to the headquarters of our city's finest. Toro was frightened when they brought him before the police judge. He didn't understand what I meant when I told him all this was mere technicality.

The bail was nominal, just a G to save the face of the Department with those tax-payers who think prize-fighting is organized mayhem and should be run out of bounds. But Toro had the peasant's fear of officialdom. If it were necessary to pay out all this money, he reasoned, the Government must consider him a criminal.

I took him up to the suite in the Waldorf Towers, thinking Pepe and Fernando might be able to cheer him up, but he just sat there in a daze. Pepe talked about Santa Maria and the great three-day celebration they would have when Toro made his triumphant return.

"But I kill a man," Toro said, "I kill him."

"My friend," Fernando said smoothly, "there are some things worse than death. There is weakness and cowardice. That this poor fellow should die is most unfortunate, of course. But think what you are doing for our country! Every youth from Jujuy to Tierra del Fuego will want to be big and strong and victorious like the great El Toro Molina."

Toro's enormous, vulnerable chin lay on his chest. "But I kill this man. I do not even talk with him before, and I kill him."

"Maybe you should come back to Santa Maria before you fight again," Pepe suggested. "You can be my house guest."

"But I kill this man," Toro said. "For no reason, I kill him."

"Pepe is right," Fernando said. "After a few months' rest, you can have a tune-up fight in Buenos Aires. Perhaps we can bring down a Yankee, some second-rater . . ."

It made him smile to think of this public demonstration of Argentine supremacy. But Toro wasn't with him. Toro shook his head slowly. "I go home now. I fight no more. That I do not injure any other man."

Personally, I think I would have given up my cut in the Stein fight to see him go home. But Nick had him signed for the Stein fight in the ball park. And Nick was a stickler for contracts, when they worked his way.

The next day we all attended the funeral over in Trenton. Nick took care of all the expenses, and he really did it right. Everybody agreed that, as funerals go, it was just about tops. Nick was one of the pall-bearers, along with five ex-champions. Nick's floral wreath was in the form of a huge squared ring of white carnations with red carnations spelling out the words, "God Bless You, Gus." At the grave, the minister told us what a great man Gus had been, a man who never abused his strength, a home-loving, God-fearing, clean-living champion whose life should be a model to young America. After Gus was laid to rest, everybody stood around telling one another what a great guy he had been. Even people who had been up and down Jacobs' Beach for years, putting the knock on him were slobbering about what a pal they had lost.

As I came out of the cemetery with Toro, I saw Nick

helping Ruby into their limousine. He was wearing a black homburg and looked distinguished, if you didn't see him too close. She was very attractive in black with a black chiffon snood. If she noticed Toro, she gave no indication. The Killer drew a fur car robe over them. I looked in at her as the car drove away. Her face was somber, to befit the occasion.

Pepe and Fernando took Toro back to the hotel with them. He didn't seem to be coming out of it. I went down the street to a beer joint I had made a mental note of as we approached the cemetery. Some of the trade from the funeral had had the same idea. Danny was in the corner with a very full load. He hadn't changed his clothes since we dropped him off at the hotel the morning before, and the front of his suit was spotted because his hand had not been steady enough. His face looked bloodless; the light blue irises of his eyes were so washed out that they blended into the whites. The Irish gift for parlaying a deep sense of guilt into a marathon drunk had possession of Danny. "Never liked the bastard," he was saying to whoever would listen. "Never liked the bastard. So what? Drink to 'im anyway. Whatsamatter, anything wrong with that? Maybe you think I got no right to drink to 'im, huh, Mister? Well, le's drink to 'im anyway, even if he was a selfish, tightwad bastard."

An Irishman at a funeral who can't love the guy they're burying is in a terrible way. Especially when he figures he's been credited with an assist in putting the deceased where he is.

I didn't want to go from bar to bar with Danny and maybe run into fight reporters who would be trying to pump me on the Lennert business. So I went back to my room. I tried *War and Peace*, but I had forgotten who Marya Dmitrevna was again, and I didn't have enough patience to go back and find out. I tossed that aside and started reading "The Rich Boy" by Fitzgerald, but it was too probing for the way I felt. I wondered what Beth was

312

doing. I could imagine what she thought now that this had happened. But dammit, people are getting themselves killed all the time.

What was I thinking? I was just tired from the strain of the last few days. I closed the door to the bathroom. I raised the shades to let more light into the room. I wished I could call Beth. I didn't have Beth to call any more. I should have married Beth. I shouldn't have kept this lousy job so long. I should have written my play. Well, maybe it still wasn't too late.

I didn't want to stay in my room alone any longer. I walked over to Fifty-second Street, where the music was hard and loud and restless to the breaking point, a musical score to accompany the doubts and frustrations and villainies of Eddie Lewis, I thought.

Next morning I went up to the office to pick up my weekly retainer. Nick was talking to Kewpie Harris, who had Buddy Stein. Nick was wearing a soft-brown English tweed with a black armband. After Kewpie left, Nick went to his mirror and inspected himself carefully. Then he turned to me.

"Do you see a blackhead here?" He pointed to a spot near his mouth. It was there all right, but what did he think I should do, squeeze it out for him? He must have thought so, for he said, "Don't bother with it, Eddie. Oscar down in the barber shop has a way of taking 'em out without leaving a mark." He went back to his desk and swung his feet onto it.

"I just been trying to talk Kewpie into cutting it thirty-thirty when we go against Stein," Nick said. "He wants it thirty-three and a half—twenty-six and a half. He says Stein's beaten better fellas. I have to give him that, but not even Stein and the champ 'd draw like Stein and Molina. I figure with any kind of breaks we ought to do a million four, maybe a million six if we get really lucky. That means a nice half a million for us to kick around."

"In other words about three hundred thousand for Toro himself," I said.

"Or in other words at least twenty-five thousand for you personally," Nick answered.

"There's a slight hitch," I said. "Toro wants out. He told me he doesn't want to fight any more. He wants to go home."

"Who cares what Toro wants? He's got a contract with me. And I've got a contract with Mike and Kewpie for the ball park June nineteenth. Toro's gonna be there if we have to carry him into the ring."

"Maybe you better talk to him," I said.

"I got more important things to do," Nick said. "Ruby and I are going to Palm Beach for six weeks. I haven't been spending enough time with her lately. A wife like I got, you just can't treat her like any dumb broad. She says we gotta have companionship." He looked proudly at the picture on his desk, a photograph taken many years earlier. "Jesus, it used to be all a wife needed to keep her happy was a new fur coat every year and a rub-of-the-brush once in a while. Now she's gotta have companionship." He tried to pass it off as a joke, but his respect for Ruby was too deep. "She even wants me to read her goddam books."

He went to the door and called out, "Hey, Killer, tell Oscar I'll be down in ten minutes." He went to the humidor and gave me one of his cigars. I tore the band off it and was going to throw it away when he said, "Read it, read it." It said, "Made exclusively for Nick Latka by Rodriguez, Havana."

He took his double-breasted herring-bone overcoat off a hanger and gave it to me to hold for him. "Oh, by the way," he said as he slipped his arms through, "break the news of my buying the Molina contract from Vanneman a couple of weeks after I'm gone. I don't have to tell you how to handle it. You know. Everything in good taste. Class, Eddie."

He put his hand on my arm confidentially. "You know, Eddie, it may sound cokey, but we could go as high as two million with this fight. God knows I never wished Gus any hard luck, but . . . well, this thing that happened isn't doing us any harm. Some of these columnist boy-scouts who've been wondering out loud about Toro's opposition. Well, you can't make it look any squarer than killing a guy, can you?"

"No, that should quiet any suspicions," I said.

"Nobody would ever believe a guy checked out while trying to take a dive," Nick said. "So we'll have that going for us."

"Yes, that's a break," I said.

"And it makes your job a helluva lot easier, selling that *mazo* punch. You know how the public is, they'll all be there to see if maybe he can kill another guy."

"Yes, it's great," I said. "Lennert sure did us a favor. We had no more use for him anyway. He might as well be pushing up daisies."

But Nick wouldn't even permit me the luxury of anger. "I know how you feel, kid," he said. "I guess you think I'm doing handsprings because Gus went out when it could do us the most good. Hell, I always took care of Gus. I threw him everything I could. But I figure, when a thing happens, it happens. We still gotta live. That's my psychology."

21

Next morning we broke the story of the Stein-Molina fight. It broke big all right. Nick hadn't overestimated the value of the Lennert tragedy. Every heavyweight fight is a simulated death-struggle. Those fans who rise up in primeval blood-lust and beg their favorite to "Killim! Killim!" may be more in earnest than they know. Death in the ring is not an everyday occurrence, not every month or even every year. But it always adds a titillating sense of danger and drama to all the matches that follow. For the sadism and cruelty of the Roman circus audience still peers out through eyes of the modern fight crowd. There is not only the conscious wish to see one man smash another into insensibility, but the subconscious, retrogressive urge to witness violent tragedy, even while the rational mind of the spectator turns away from excessive brutality.

These psychological factors, combined with Stein's authentic viciousness and Toro's bogus savagery, made their coming bout another Battle of the Century. Even the sports writers, who were calling Toro the "Man Monstrous" and "El Ponderoso," had to admit that the Stein fight would be worth seeing as Toro's first real test. And the hacks, who are always along for the ride, were pulling out all the stops, conjuring up the Dempsey-Firpo thriller and passing on to their readers our pitch about Toro's ambition to avenge the defeat of the Wild Bull of the Pampas.

When the phone rang, I was lying in bed, wondering

how Nick figured to do business with Kewpie Harris and Stein. It was Fernando. I must come right over. Toro had just seen the papers. He was very angry. He said he was not going to fight Stein. He was not going to fight anybody. He was going home.

I threw my clothes on, grabbed a cab and hurried over to see Toro. I wasn't as convincing as I should have been because I didn't entirely blame him. But I tried to show him how there was no way out of the Stein fight. Nick and the Garden had his name on the dotted. The Stein clause had been written into the Lennert contract. If he took a run-out powder now, Toro would end up in the river, wrong side up. And since he had come this far, it didn't seem sensible to pass up the six-figure dough finally coming his way.

But all Toro said when I wound up my oratory was, "No. I go home."

Pepe and Fernando tried to reason with him too, but he just sat there, shaking his huge, solemn head, saying over and over again with maddeningly childish monotony, "No. I go home."

I told Pepe to take him out to a midnight movie, or a call house or whatever else he could think of—anything to get Toro out of himself. But there seemed to be no temptations left for Toro any more. All he wanted was to be away from us, to be home and at peace again. If it had been up to me, I think I would have let him go. But I knew, for his own good, he had to stay. He didn't know Nick and the boys as well as I did, friendly fellas until you crossed them.

Toro, unconvinced, finally went to bed and I returned to the hotel. It was a little before three when Fernando called me again. Toro had disappeared. He must have sneaked out into the corridor while they thought he was sleeping. He had left with a suitcase and his portable radio, which would seem as if he was leaving for good.

I tracked Nick down at the Bolero, an East-Side night

317

club the syndicate owned. He was surprisingly calm. I had forgotten that essentially he was a man of action. He rose to occasions like this. "No, don't call the police," he said, answering my question. "It would look too lousy. Might hurt the gate. We'll find him ourselves. I'll send some of the boys out. He's too well known to get very far."

Nick's boys checked all the outlets of the city, the stations, airports and bus terminals, to see if Toro had bought a ticket. Fernando remembered that Toro had made some kind of a threat to go back to Argentina alone if he had to. So Benny, Jock Mahoney, Vince, the Killer and I drove to the waterfront in the white Lincoln. We cruised past the docks of all the lines that had ships going to South America. We asked the watchmen if they had seen him. One of them told us that the American Fruit Company had a freighter leaving in the morning for Buenos Aires—at Pier Six. We rushed down. We stopped at the entrance to the pier, and all of us got out and looked around. There was only a quarter moon and the waterfront was draped in a gray-black fog. The lights on the freighter looked yellow and blurred.

Suddenly Benny called out, "Hey, I think I see the bastard." He sprinted toward the huge sliding door that blocked the entrance to the pier. We followed him. It was Toro, all right. He must have been waiting for the gate to open in the early morning. He started running when he saw us. I joined the chase with the others. I was part of the pack running the quarry down. Toro's movements were as ponderous outside the ring as in. Jock and the Killer caught up with him quickly, grabbed at him and slowed him down. Benny, Vince and I ran up and surrounded him. Toro tried to break out of the circle, but Benny held him from behind, and Jock and Vince closed in from the sides. Toro shook them off, and for a moment he was free, but he had only taken a few steps when they were on him again. He cursed us in Spanish and kept shouting, *"Ya me voy. Ya me voy,"* I'm going. The Killer reached up and drove his small fist into Toro's face. Toro roared and wrenched his shoulders back and forth to break our grips but we held on and began to drag him toward the car. He struggled furiously against being pushed back into his Lincoln. In the darkness our milling figures, above which he towered, must have looked like ancient hunters grappling with some prehistoric beast. Suddenly the greast beast went limp, and we half-pushed, half-lifted him into the car. Benny slipped his blackjack back into his pocket. "The son-of-a-bitch won't lam no more tuh-night," he said.

Next morning I talked things over with Nick. He was leaving for Florida that afternoon. "Tell you what you do," he said. "Take the big dope and the two grease-balls and go out and have some fun. The Killer will get you all the gash you want. Do anything as long as you don't let that big bum knock up a high-school girl or get him-self a dose. When he's had his fun, take him out to the country and start training. Maybe that's what he needs to get over this Lennert business." He gave me a thick roll of bills. "That oughta cover it. Entertainment. I'll get Leo to take it off the income tax."

Pepe liked the idea and there was nothing Fernando wouldn't do for his country. So we started that afternoon. Pepe broke out a case of champagne and the Killer sent up six girls, including a couple of spares, in case some of them went flat, he said. What we started that afternoon may have lasted a week or maybe it went for three, I never knew for sure. I think I remember Pepe betting Toro a hundred dollars he couldn't drink a bottle of champagne without stopping and Toro falling asleep on the floor and Pepe having one of the girls wake him up in a way that made us laugh. I think I remember all of us breaking in on Fernando and catching him in his BVD's, the old-fashioned kind, shoes, socks and garters, looking like the straight man in a pornographic movie.

It seems to me there was a showgirl of Amazonian proportions sent up expressly for Toro, and I think we all watched and cheered them on. There was a night in Philadelphia, or maybe it was Boston, for I guess we were moving around, when we all seemed to be in a large bed together. I think it must have been in a house because I vaguely remember a mirror on the ceiling. There was a girl named Mercedes who came from Juarez and claimed to be one of Pancho Villa's numerous daughters, who taught us, among other things, the Mexican anthem, and there seemed to be an endless switching of partners and good-natured comparing of notes. There were girls who were spiritlessly accommodating and there were girls who were impersonally tempestuous. There were girls who would submit to the most extreme indignities but would not allow their ears to be assaulted with profanity. There were girls who did not hesitate to assume conventional postures but primly drew the line at variations. And there were girls who indulged in entertainments that are not to be described. For some reason I remember a girl named Olive who talked a lot about her little son, Oliver, and who, at the moment when it could be least appreciated, suddenly burst into tears. I remember a pretty little Irish girl who wouldn't go into the bedroom with Toro because he frightened her. And there was a prematurely gray woman of obvious breeding whom we picked up in the hotel lounge falling down drunk and who confided to me that she had had a secret yen for Toro from the first time she read about him. There was the morning I came downstairs for breakfast and found it was dark outside and already time for cocktails. I went back to our rooms and there was Toro, nude, asleep on a bed. Fernando was snoring in the other bed. He looked very ugly with his bloated face and his squat, hairy body in his underwear. But Toro, even in that disheveled hotel room, among the stale glasses and the mashed cigarette butts, didn't belong in the backwash of a debauch. He was too big for the room, too big for the bed, stretched prone like a tremendously larger-than-life statue that had somehow come loose from its base and toppled over. I wondered if I should wake Toro, so he could eat something. Fernando could lie there until he rotted, for all I cared. I wondered where Pepe was. I was pretty wide awake for so early in the morning. Or was it evening? Awake. A wake. A wake for Gus Lennert. We are really having us a wake, Gus. I'm awake, a wake, a wake for Gus Lennert. The Mexican Indians bury their dead and get drunk in the cemetery and sing songs and tell bawdy stories and have themselves a time. And who is to say there's a better way? But that is a pure wake, like the drunken wake of the Irish, and this is a lewd wake, a wake for the depraved and degraded, a wake to call forth devils and summon witches, a stewed crude nude lewd debauch of a wake, to copulate ourselves into such deadening stupor that we no longer see the self-accusing fingers of guilt pointing at our eyes.

Toro was lying on the bed in his immense nakedness. It was evening instead of morning and I was wondering if I should rouse him. He was sleeping heavily. As I watched, he rolled over on his side. "*Ya me voy, Papá. Ya me voy,*" he was muttering. Let him sleep, I thought, let him sleep, let him think he's home.

When I came out of it, I didn't know where I was. The inside of my mouth felt like lumpy cotton and a maddening tom-tom was beating in my head. "Take this," Doc said. "It'll settle your stomach." It wasn't my stomach coming up; it was remorse. I could feel it heaving up from my belly, that terrible, dragging, end-it-all sense of remorse. The restless succession of women, no more remembered than chain-smoked cigarettes, Fernando with his garters, the daily seduction of Toro Molina, the whole empty, frenetic saturnalia closed in and threatened to crush me.

A picture on the bureau came slowly into focus. It

was staring at me, a nice, cool face, staring at me. My picture of Beth. I was in my own room. "Where is everybody?" I said.

"You saw Pepe off at the boat last night," Doc said. "He's coming back with a crowd in time for the Stein fight. Fernando has gone out to Pompton Lakes with Molina. We'll just sweat him out the next couple of weeks."

"How about Danny?"

"Danny's down there too. But I don't think we better count on Danny too much. Danny's been on the flit so long he's sweating alcohol."

Doc put his hand on my forehead and then he felt my pulse. His hands were amazingly alive, damp and nervous, and yet strangely reassuring.

"Thanks, Doc."

But I guess I didn't have to thank him. Doc liked to play doctor.

I didn't bother going out to the camp very often. Nothing much was happening there. When you visit a camp you can tell right away what the morale is, whether the place is taut and business-like, or loused up with lushes and gamblers, whether it's dully methodical, slothful and lackadaisical or keyed-up and confident. The atmosphere around Toro was listless. Usually it's either the purpose of the manager or the energy of the fighter that sparks a camp. But this time Danny was squandering his time and his money in the grog shops and the horse rooms, and Toro walked through his workouts like a somnambulist.

When he talked about Toro, George shook his bronze-molded head. "I'm worried about him," he told me. "He fights like a zombie. He just ain't there at all. That's no way to get ready for Stein. The big fella's gotta be *up* to stay in there with Stein."

I went out again for the last workout before they came into town and I could see why George was worried. This kid, Gussman, giving away around eighty pounds, had to pull up so he wouldn't knock Toro's head off right in front of the reporters. Toro was hog-fat in the belly because Fernando had more or less taken over the camp by default, and let the big slob put away too much fattening food.

The day before the fight there wasn't a hotel room to be had in New York. Fans had driven in from all over the country. A delegation from Stein's home town came in on a special train, with everybody from the Mayor to the favorite madam, and took over a midtown hotel. *Variety's* list of "In's" was almost twice as long as on an ordinary Wednesday. Pepe and his Argentine delegation of assorted millionaires, politicos and playboys staged a big luncheon at the Ritz. The Argentine Consul General welcomed his countrymen, and Fernando spoke for the Argentine Athletic Association. The Giant of the Andes was rising in the fistic firmament, he said, just as Argentina herself, the land of giants, was rising in the Pan-American firmament. They must have applauded that one for two full minutes. Throughout all the speeches, Toro's name was waved like a flag, the blue-and-white of our contentious neighbor to the south. Then Toro was called on to say a few words. His face was stolid. There was no belligerence in him, nationalistic or otherwise. "I do my best," he said. "Then I go home."

All the Broadway restaurants were full of guys talking fight, laying or taking the nine to five on Stein. There must have been an easy million ready to change hands by six o'clock.

By seven there was already a tremendous crowd milling around the ball park. There was the last-minute scramble for tickets, the scalping, the squatters' rush for the unreserved section, the gamblers working the suckers right up to the opening gong. Walking up and down in front of one of the entrances was a blind man with a tin cup and a sandwich sign over his shoulders. "Kid Fargo," it said, "Former Heavyweight Contender. Used to Spar with Jack Dempsey."

The smart money was going on Stein because it had to ride with him until he was licked. There hadn't been a puncher like him since Dempsey. But there was plenty of Molina money, from people impressed by mere size, ballyhoo and the manslaughter of Gus Lennert.

Lumbering into the ring were the first of the brace of muscular mediocrities Uncle Mike always foisted on his public when he knew the main attraction was so good he didn't have to bolster it with expensive preliminaries. The Stadium was a sell-out, all the way up to the gallery gods on the top tier who paid five dollars for the privilege of being able to say that they had attended a ring classic. And even above them were the thousands of curious bargain hunters who paid top-story dwellers a dollar to watch the spectacle from the windows or rooftops. And beyond them were the millions of radio listeners in swank metropolitan apartments, lower middle-class homes, slums, small-town houses and farms from coast to coast.

The ringside—or what Uncle Mike cagily called ringside—fanned out for three hundred rows, a true cross-section of the prosperous, including the Governor, the Mayor, the Chief of Police, Broadway headliners, Hollywood stars, and all the representatives of the best legal and illegal rackets, the Wall Street boys, industrial tycoons, the socialites, insurance men, advertising executives, judges, prominent lawyers, big-time gamblers and the top mobsters who never get their name in the papers. Nobody who was anybody was missing a chance to be seen at ringside.

The crowd was laughing at the antics of two barrel-chested incompetents who were waltzing through the curtain-raiser. "Turn out the lights, they wanna be alone," a big voice bellowed from the mezzanine. It still got laughs. Someone ought to write new material for the fight fans. The same old saws to express the old derision, the displeasure with bloodless, painless, actionless battle. "Can I have the next dance?" . . . "What we got, da Ballet Russe?" . . . "Are you bums brother-in-laws?" . . . "Careful, you goils might hoit each other!" But the protests were still relaxed and good-natured. The crowd was working up to its excitement slowly. The catcalls were still without real contempt. The most high-tensioned of all American sports crowds hadn't roused itself yet. It was still behaving as if this were merely a sport.

I went back to the dressing room to see Toro. Fernando and George were helping him get ready. Danny was there too. He was mumbling. He was trying to tell Toro something. But Fernando pushed him away. Toro removed his clothes slowly, as if reluctant to change into a fighter again. He didn't say anything to me when I came in. He wasn't saying anything to anybody.

"I think he's full of geezer tonight," Doc whispered to me. "He's had the trots all day."

"Maybe he's just scared this'll be another Lennert," I said.

"I just hope it isn't the other way," Doc said.

Pepe came in with some of his Argentine pals. They all made a fuss over Toro, gave him the big embrace, told him how much money they had going on him and went out to enjoy the semi-final. They were full of ready laughter and carefree rooting-section enthusiasm. Toro didn't say anything to them. It was just as George said: he wasn't really there at all.

Nick came in with the Killer and Barney Winch. All three were wearing tailored camel-hair topcoats. Toro was sitting on the table in his bathrobe. Doc was rubbing his back.

Nick set himself in front of Toro. "Listen, you bum," he said in a hard, quiet voice. "I just wanted to let you know something. My wife's told me all about you."

Toro looked up slowly, waiting for the blow like a slaughter-house steer.

"She told me you came over to the house one day and tried to get fresh with her. I ought to kick your head in, you double-crossing crud, you. But I don't have to take the trouble. This fight tonight is the first one you ever fought for me on the dead square. So I don't have to mess up my manicure on you. I can just sit out there in the front row and have the pleasure of seeing Stein beat your goddam brains out. I hope he kills you."

He slapped Toro once sharply across the face. Toro just stared at him. For several minutes after they went out, Toro continued to stare stupidly into space. Chick Gussman, who was fighting the six-round special, came in after a win by TKO in three, exhilarated by his showing. He tapped Toro playfully and said, "Looks like a big night for the Latka stable, kid." But Toro didn't even see him. The semi-final was over in a hurry, and it was Toro's turn to go down. For the first time since I could remember Danny wasn't in shape to work the corner, so Vince took over with Doc and George, who was holding the bottles.

"Well, good luck, Toro." I tried to put something into it, but my voice sounded flat and hollow. My hand was extended and Toro took it in a soft handshake. That was when I noticed he was trembling.

Buddy Stein entered the ring first. The crowd roared and screamed its approval as he danced around in a blue silk bathrobe with a white bath towel draped over his head. He reached down over the ropes with his taped hands and shook hands with lots of people, Jack Dempsey, Bing Crosby, Sherman Billingsley . . . A beautiful blonde in the third row pursed her lips as if she were kissing him, and he winked. There were more women than usual tonight. Both fighters were good draws with women. Stein was dark, curly-haired, unusually handsome for a fighter. He had one of those broad-shouldered, narrow-hipped builds, tapering down to surprisingly graceful legs. He was a vain bully boy with the personality of a show-off and the stage presence of the matinee idol accustomed to adoration. He had often been complimented on his smile—the Stein grin, it was called sometimes—though actually it was the nasty smile of a man who had found a way of channeling his natural cruelty into a profitable career.

In spite of the hamming and clowning with the crowd, Stein was a serious practitioner of assault and battery, trained to a sharp fighting edge. He pranced around the ring with an ominous, pent-up vigor, warming up with short, shadow-boxing hooks that shot viciously into the air.

The reception for Toro was friendly but reserved, and there were a few scattered boos from skeptics and from old Lennert fans who clung to the primitive notion that the ex-champion's death was in some way due to an excess of brutality on Toro's part. Actually, as Doc and George pulled off his flashy bathrobe, I was reminded once more of the enormity of the joke nature had played on this giant. His colossal shoulders, bulging muscles and record chest expansion would seem too great an advantage against even the most formidable opponent, and yet his menacing physique contained a gentle, placid disposition with less fighting instinct than the average ten-year-old boy, and considerably less aptitude.

The huge flood-light system over the stadium dimmed out and the ring became an intense white square cameoed in the vast darkness. The announcer requested one minute of silence for "Old Gus, a real champion who went down fighting, with the Great Referee counting over him the Fatal Ten."

The stadium went black as the impatient fans stood up in a touching demonstration of bogus bereavement, while the bell tolled ten with sound-effect impressiveness.

As the lights over the ring came on again, and the

announcer had finally introduced all the famous fighters and identified the contestants with needlessly elaborate formality, the mass tension surged, and a barbaric roar rose from 80,000 throats. The referee gave them final instructions and sent them back to their corners to await the opening bell. As their handlers drew their robes from their shoulders at last, the contrast in their sizes brought an excited gasp from the crowd. Toro, almost six feet eight, weighing nearly two hundred and eighty pounds, looking a little fleshy around the waist, crossed himself and waited for the bell in a kind of docile bewilderment. Stein, an even six feet, with a hard, lithe, rippling body, weighing one-ninety-six, shuffled his feet back and forth with restless impatience and worked his shoulders from side to side as if he were already in there flailing away at his mammoth adversary.

"Kill 'im, Buddy," the blonde in the third row begged in a shrill, unpleasant voice.

The bell brought Stein streaking across the ring to face Toro moving slowly out of his corner. Toro held his left out in the mechanical defense Danny had taught him. Stein felt him out carefully, showing considerable respect for Toro's advantages in weight and reach. He flicked stinging jabs into Toro's face, feinted with his right and held his famous left as if he were going to let it go, but he wasn't taking any chances yet. Toro was boxing rigidly, pushing his long left toward Stein's head and keeping the smaller man at a distance. Toro had finally learned the rudiments of boxing, but his execution was clumsy and had no zing. His footwork was slow but correct, and once he followed up a left jab with a right cross that managed to reach Stein's ribs. Stein smiled and snapped Toro's head back with a sharp jab. Stein's jab looked harder than Toro's best punches. Buddy pressed his lips together and a sneer came over his face as he shot another jab in. The pain aroused Toro slightly and he tried a one-two with elementary timing.

The left reached Stein's face, but the right, the *two*, lobbed harmlessly into the air as Stein slipped it neatly and drew Toro into a clinch. Nothing much seemed to be happening in the clinch, but when the referee came between them Toro's eye was reddened and blinking. It looked like a thumb job. Stein had been around; he was very cute. As they separated, Stein held out his gloves in a broad gesture of sportsmanship. Toro, momentarily blinded, failed to reciprocate and touch gloves. The crowd booed his ungentlemanly conduct. In tonight's drama they had cast him for the villain.

Some of the bleacherites began to clap their hands rhythmically to show their impatience. "Quit stalling," they yelled. Stein, with the sensitivity of the vain, moved in to satisfy them. He started a right to Toro's body, and when he saw the big arms go down, he suddenly pivoted and let the left hand go for the first time. It caught Toro hard on the side of the jaw. Toro sagged. I was sitting close enough to see how his eyes turned in. Stein danced back to his corner at the bell, hamming it up a little with his chest out. Toro walked back to his stool slowly and sat down like a man with a bellyful of beer.

Stein was waiting for him as soon as he got up again. He was speeding up his tempo now. Toro tried to box him again, but Stein feinted, exactly as he had done before, sucked Toro out of position and crashed his left into Toro's reddened eye. A lump was swelling over it with abnormal rapidity. At that moment I wanted to be away from this, away from what could only be the relentless tormenting of a helpless freak. But something gripped me with terrible fascination, just as did all 80,000 of us, waiting in a kind of death-watch for what already seemed inevitable.

It had ceased to be a contest; it was a bull-fight, a thrilling demonstration of man's superiority over the beast, the giant, the great shapeless fear. The voices of the onlookers were growing tight with excitement. "Work on that eye!" "Get that eye!" "Close that right eye for him!"

Stein obliged. Measuring Toro coolly, he smashed the swollen eye. Toro's heavy lips parted in pain, revealing the ugly orange mouthpiece. Staring balefully at his attacker with his one good eye he had suddenly become a grotesque and incredible throwback to Cyclops. Stein was working him over with methodical viciousness now. The short, savage blows pounded Toro with sickening monotony. When the bell ended his punishment for sixty seconds, Toro hesitated foolishly for a moment, trying to decide in which direction his corner lay. The referee guided him back to his stool.

Doc's fingers digging into Toro's limp neck, the water George poured over Toro's head and the smelling salts Vince held to his nose gave the giant a semblance of recuperation with which to face the next round. But Stein was stabbing him with animal fury now. His lips were drawn tight over his mouthpiece and his eyes had a homicidal intensity. You could almost feel the pressure of the accumulating cruelty of the crowd closing in on the ring. "Get him! Get him!" "Knock him out!" "Kill 'im!" the cries mounted in hysteria. The lump over Toro's right eye had risen to the size of an egg. Stein drove Toro back with another straight left that was beginning to split Toro's mouth. Then, with all his might, he jabbed at the lump, smashing it as if it really were an egg, but an egg full of blood. Instantly the right side of Toro's face was a crimson splotch.

"That's the way, Buddy. Kill 'im!" the blonde in the third row screamed.

I looked over at Nick, who was sitting with Ruby in the front row, directly across the ring from me. He was just sitting there, pulling calmly on a long cigar and watching the proceedings with a kind of bored attentiveness I had seen on his face hundreds of times at the training camps. Ruby was wearing a spectacular black

330

felt hat with a band of spangles around the crown, framing a powder-white face with fierce dark eyes and a deep red mouth. From where I sat, she seemed to be enjoying herself.

Another savage shriek was torn from the throat of the crowd and people all around me jumped up to see Stein catch Toro in a corner, where he rained rights and lefts at his head until Toro began sliding down the ringpost to squat ludicrously on the floor. Some people laughed. The referee pointed Stein to a neutral corner, where he bounced crazily, waiting to get at Toro again. "Stay down, Toro, stay down," I shouted. But for some inexplicable reason of that dogged, semi-conscious brain, Toro pulled himself up and tottered heavily toward Stein. The bell postponed the slaughter for another minute.

In his corner, Toro lay back against the ropes drooling blood from his torn mouth and gasping for breath, exhausted from the terrible punishment he was absorbing. His one half-open eye closed in an agony of weariness. Doc's fingers did their best. With all their strength they pressed together the lips of the cut over the right eye to try to stem the bleeding. Then Doc patted collodion over the wound and it seemed momentarily to congeal. Meanwhile George tried to rub some life into the huge, musclebound, all-but-useless legs, and Vince shouted profane instructions into his swollen ears.

After all this preparation, Stein tore across the ring at the bell and knocked Toro down again with the first punch. All of Doc's work had come undone and the cut above the eye dripped blood into the dirty canvas. There was no point, no honor in continuing this demonstration of a big man's hopeless inability to compete in coordinated viciousness with a smaller man of proved superiority. When Toro got up again I don't think he even intended to try. His face was a gory mess and he stumbled forward to receive more blows, a broken and battered hull of a man foundering on a sea of pain, relentlessly buffeted by the angry waves of blows, and borne up only by some unknown fund of pointless endurance.

The crowd was screaming for a knockout now, begging for it, pleading for it, a wild-eyed cheering section of bettors who were riding on a Stein knockout, of fans inspired with an angry sense of misplaced justice who resented Toro for his fraud-fattened record and mistook this beating for the revenge of integrity, and finally the vast audience of the frustrated and the brow-beaten who could not help taking a deep vicarious pleasure in being in on the final transformation of an overpowering giant into a pitiful wreck of human flesh.

Somehow Toro weathered that round, dragged himself back for first aid and staggered out glassy-eyed to offer himself up to Stein once more. Why didn't they stop it? Why didn't Doc stop it? Doc must have been under orders from Nick to let it run. What about the referee? Well, for one thing they don't like to stop a heavyweight fight too soon because the big boys are supposed to be able to take it. And then I remembered another thing. Vince had said something about laying eight G's to five that Toro would still be there for the eighth. Vince and the referee, Marty Small, had done business before. Marty didn't have to do anything crooked, just let Toro keep going as long as he could. Vince would take care of the rest.

For three more minutes, with the roar of the crowd pitched to a manic fury, Stein cut the crippled giant down. Toro tumbled over and writhed to a kneeling position and when he rose with his knees shaking, Stein knocked him down again. He rolled over onto his knees with his battered head pressed against the canvas. Then with a perverse and useless courage, he struggled to his feet again. With one hand on the ropes, he kept himself from falling. His other arm hung limply at his side. Blood poured from both eyes, and a new stream of blood gushed from his mouth. Swaying back and forth, in blind and helpless bewilderment, he waited for the little man to attack him again. Stein leaped in with a powerful right to the body that made Toro bend over. Then he straightened him up with a paralyzing left to the jaw. Toro toppled over. He fell so awkwardly that his ankle twisted under him. With horrible concentration, he lifted himself to his knees. He crawled forward on his knees, slipping in his own blood, like a dying beast. His mouth was open and the lower part of his jaw hung hideously loose. "Jaw's busted," I heard someone say. The big orange mouthpiece flopped out of his mouth and rolled a few feet ahead of him. For some reason he did not understand, he crawled painfully toward it and tried to stuff it back into his mouth in a slow-motion gesture of futility. He was still fumbling with his mouthpiece when the referee finished his count and raised Stein's hand. Buddy danced around happily, mitting his gloves over his head to acknowledge the ovation of the crowd. Toro was still trying to stuff the mouthpiece back into his mouth when Vince, Doc and George dragged him back to his corner.

22

Satisfied and quiet now, the crowd was filtering slowly toward the exits. Going up the aisle I met Nick and Ruby, the Killer with one of his girls, Mr. and Mrs. Quinn and Barney Winch.

"Did you ever see a worse bum?" Nick said.

"We should swap him to Harry Miniff for an old jock strap," Quinn laughed.

"Nice talk in front of the girls," Nick said, taking Ruby's arm.

"But there goes your meal ticket," I said.

Nick drew me closer. "Don't worry, kid. I made a deal with Kewpie Harris. We've got a piece of Stein."

"Come on over to the Bolero, Eddie boy," Quinn said. "Just ask for my table."

"I don't feel like it tonight," I said.

"I can get you fixed up with something nice in the show," the Killer said.

"I'm not in the mood tonight," I said.

I went back to the dressing room. Toro was sitting on the rubbing table with a bloody towel over his head. Doc was still trying to check the flow of blood from his nose and mouth. Toro's smashed and swollen face hung limply on his chest. He was trembling. The reporters pressed around him, oblivious of his condition in their eagerness to round out their stories.

"When was the first time he hurt you, Toro?"

Toro muttered through his torn mouth. "Jesus Christo . . ."

"What punch was it that gave you the most trouble?"

"Jesus Christo . . ." Toro said.

"Like to have a return match?"

"Jesus Christo . . ."

"Where the hell is Grandini?" Doc said. "George, go down the hall and see if you can find Dr. Grandini. He better have a look at this jaw."

Toro's head shook slightly from side to side like a man with palsy. The lumpy, sliced flesh over his eyes was turning purple and the broken jaw hung open.

"Lie down," Doc said. "Better lie down."

Toro just sat there in blind agony, shaking his head slowly. "Jesus Christo . . ." he whispered.

They took him up to Roosevelt Hospital, and set his jaw for him. I went over to see him in the morning. His upper and lower jaws had been wired together; his cuts had been stitched; he was taking liquids through a glass straw. The lumpy discolored bruises on his face made him look more like a huge gargoyle than ever.

There was something he was trying to say to me. He tried to mutter through his wired teeth and his swollen, lacerated lips, but no sound came. Finally I caught some of the words forced from his throat. "I go home now. My money . . . money . . ."

"I'll get it for you," I said.

On the way out I passed Vince in the hall.

"Well, this is the last place I ever expected to see you," I told him.

"Aah, what's-a-matter with you, you think you're the only white man in the outfit? You think you got an exclusive on seeing the guy?"

"What's your angle, Vince? Don't tell me you're just coming in to cheer him up. That's not my Vince."

"I just thought maybe I could help the guy," Vince said.

"I didn't know you knew that word," I said.

"There's a lotta things you don't know, chum," Vince said and went in.

Well, it was a funny racket, I thought. I've seen boys beat each other so that neither would ever be as good again and then throw their arms around each other in an embrace of genuine affection. I've seen a father sit tight-lipped in a corner and let his son bleed like a pig for ten rounds and then, when it was all over, take his boy's disfigured face in his hands and burst out crying. They were unpredictable, the toughest of them, whimsically and inconsistently tender. Maybe that was Vince. Maybe somewhere in that fat, coarse face, in that fat, lewd brain, was a hidden core of humanity I had missed, or that had never been tapped before.

I went up to the office to see about the money for Toro. Nick was home sleeping off a late night, the Killer said. "That's where I shoulda stayed," he complained. "Christ what a night! Didja ever have a Chinese acrobatic dancer, Eddie? I thought I seen everything, but . . ."

"Killer," I said, "how can I get Toro's dough for him?"

The Killer looked disappointed. "Talk to Leo," he said. "He's in this morning."

I went down the hall to see Nick's bookkeeper. He was working over a ledger. He looked small, pale and devoted, the way bookkeepers are supposed to look, except for his eyes, which were put there to warn you.

"Busy, Leo?"

"Well, I'm breaking down the take on the fight," he said.

"What was the exact gross?"

"One million, three hundred and fifty-six thousand, eight hundred ninety-three and fifty cents."

"I promised Toro I'd pick up his money for him," I said.

"I'll have to look it up in the file," Leo said.

He thumbed through his file professionally, LATKA, LEWIS, MANN, MOLINA . . . "Here it is." He licked his forefinger and removed several sheets from the file. He studied them carefully.

"There's a small balance," he said.

"A small balance? Are you kidding?"

"It's all down here in black and white," Leo said.

I reached for the sheets and stared at the rows of figures, all neatly typed and itemized. My eye ran down a column of astronomical figures. There was $10,450 for training expenses, $14,075 for living expenses and $17,225 for publicity and entertainment. There were items, all beautifully padded, for equipment, sparring partners, transportation, personal amusement, phone calls, telegrams and good old miscellaneous. There was a little matter of $63,500 in cash, alleged to have been advanced to Toro by Vanneman. And, finally, there were the managerial commissions, the Federal and State taxes and "personal gratuities for favors rendered." By the time all this had been duly subtracted from purses which totaled almost a million dollars, there was a small balance, all right. Exactly forty-nine dollars and seven cents.

"Wait a minute," I said. "This is highway robbery. Vince never advanced Toro any sixty-three thousand. You must mean six thousand."

"That's the way I got it from Vince," Leo said. "He gave me all the tabs."

"So Toro winds up with forty-nine dollars and seven cents," I said. "What are you guys so generous for? What do you leave him the five sawbucks for?"

"You can add it up yourself if you want to," Leo said.

"I know you can add, Leo. I've seen you add for Nick before. I've seen you subtract too."

"Everything is in order," Leo said. "I can show these books to anybody."

"Sure," I said. "You've got those numbers trained, Leo. You got those numbers jumping through hoops for you."

"If you have any beefs, talk to the boss," Leo said. "But you can't find no bugs in my books. I'll show my books to anybody, any time."

I jumped into a cab and hurried over to Nick's apartment on East Fifty-third. It was around noon. Nick was having his breakfast, alone in the dining room in a silk midnight-blue bathrobe with a large N. L. embroidered over the breast pocket in Spencerian script.

"Nick," I began, "I've just been talking to Leo."

"Yeah?" He was crumbling his toast carefully into his soft-boiled eggs. "Did you get yours all right, kid? You should be in for around seventeen G's."

"But, Nick. What about Toro? All Toro's got is forty-nine bucks. A broken jaw and forty-nine lousy bucks."

"What's it got to do with you, Eddie?"

"What's it got to do with me, I . . ." What *did* it have to do with me? Where were the words to bridge the unbridgeable? To reconcile the unreconcilable?

"You just can't do that to a guy, Nick. You just can't let him get beat to death and then leave him with a hole in his pocket."

"Listen, Eddie, the slob got paid off. You can see it on the books."

"I know," I said. "I just saw the books. I know Leo and his books."

"Then it's just tough titty, isn't it?" Nick said.

"Jesus, Nick, after all, the poor son-of-a-bitch is human. He's . . ."

"It's just tough," Nick said.

"For Christ's sake, Nick. For the sake of Jesus Christ, you can't do this."

"Go back to bed, Eddie," Nick said, reaching calmly for his coffee. And the terrible thing about it was the way he said it. I knew he still liked me. I knew, God forgive me, he thought I had class. He was always going to count me in. "Go back to bed and sleep it off. You're spoiling my breakfast."

I went back to the hospital to see Toro. "You mustn't stay very long," the nurse said, outside his room.

"How is he getting along?"

"He's under sedation. Still suffering from shock. His left side is partially paralyzed, but the doctor is confident it's only temporary."

Toro was lying on his back, staring up at the ceiling. His face was a mass of blue and purple blotches. He turned his head slowly when he heard me enter.

"*¿Mi dinero?* My money . . . my money?"

I shook my head. I didn't know what to say.

His eyes searched me frantically. "*¿Mi dinero . . . dinero?*"

I don't know why I should have been the one to tell him. But I figured I was the only one who would take the trouble to break it to him easy.

"Toro, I . . . I don't know how to tell you this, but . . . it's gone. Toro, it's all gone. *Se fue.*"

"*¿Se fue?*" Toro muttered through his wired teeth. "No. *No es posible. ¿Se fue?*"

"*Lo siento,*" I said. "Toro, *lo siento.*" That's what the Spanish say for "I'm sorry," but it means literally, "I feel it," and that was the way I meant it.

A wrenching groan came up out of Toro's throat. He stared at me unbelievingly for what seemed at least a full minute. Then he turned slowly away from me and stared into the wall. Suddenly his great shoulders began to heave and he was shaken by dry, guttural sobs. It was a terrible thing to see a man of such size crying so desperately.

Finally I said, "Toro, I'm terribly sorry. I wish there was something I could do." Then I thought of my own seventeen thousand. "Say, I've got an idea! I can let you have five thousand dollars." I was going to say "ten," but some little bookkeeper in my brain cut it in half for me. "At least that would get you home."

"But it . . . is all my money . . . all . . . all . . . I make it all . . ."

"Sure, sure," I agreed, "but what can you do? They've

339

got you coming and going. Be smart and take the five, Toro."

He turned from the wall and glared at me.

"*Vaya*," Toro whispered hoarsely. "Go. All of you . . . Go away from me."

All of you. What did Toro mean, *all of you?* He must have me mixed up with the others. I was Toro's friend, the only one who cared, the only one who sympathized. And yet, he had said *all.* He had said *all of you.*

"But, Toro, I'm your friend, I want to help you, I . . ."

"Go," Toro whispered. "Go . . . go . . . go . . ."

As I walked slowly down the corridor, Vince appeared. He was wearing a big wrap-around camel's hair overcoat.

"Hello, lover," he said.

"Vince," I said. "I can't believe it. Don't tell me you're coming to look in on Toro again."

"Sure," he said. "He's my boy now. I gotta see how quick I can spring him. We got big plans together."

"You mean, you and Toro?"

"Yeah. I just bought his contract back from Nick this morning. Just because he loused himself up in town doesn't mean there isn't plenty of scratch to be picked up in the sticks."

"But he's through, Vince. He's all washed up."

"For the Garden, sure. But I figure we can still pick up a nice piece of change going back over the same territory, in reverse. This time the home-town fans'll put their bucks down to see the local boy beat hell outa the Giant. We got a name that's still a draw and we don't even have to bother to rig anything. I already got him booked with Dynamite Jones for the Bull Ring at Tiajuana. We'll let the people guess maybe last time it was a tankeroo and this time Jones is going in without the handcuffs. I bet we do twenty thousand."

"Vince, you're crazy! What makes you think Toro wants to go on fighting, after last night?"

"You're not thinking so good today, lover. He's got to fight. He's broke."

340

I thought of Speedy Sencio. I thought of all the broken and burned-out fighters the Vince Vannemans of the world were forever patching up and shoving back into the ring. But I was too disgusted to think of anything to say.

"You know, I'd like to cut you in, kid," Vince was saying. "After all, me and you're good pals. But, well, to level with you, Eddie, you been on the flit too much this last trip. I haven't got the dough to throw around like Nick. I just don't think you're worth it any more. But if I change my mind, I'll let you know." He reached out and pinched my cheek. "No hard feelings, though, huh, lover?"

He sauntered down the hall toward Toro's room. I stood there helplessly. I wasn't good enough for Vince.

There was only one more little thing I could do for Toro, I thought. Pepe and Fernando could take him home with them. Pepe would provide for him. I ducked into a phone booth in the hospital drug store and called the Waldorf Towers. The hotel operator transferred me to Information. The De Santos party checked out at noon, I was told. Their forwarding address was the Hotel Nacional in Havana.

I wandered back to my room. Something led me to the closet. I opened my trunk. The bottom drawer was full of old stuff, articles, press clippings, letters—I couldn't even remember why I had kept them—and down in the middle of all this mess, there it was, *And Still Champion* by Edwin Dexter Lewis, three names, to give it class.

The pages were yellowing. But that didn't matter. I could get them re-typed. As I looked at the title page I had a dream's-eye view of the Theatre Guild poster in front of the theatre. I started to read the first act. I tried to make myself believe in it. But what was the use? How long could I go on kidding myself? The dialogue was forced. The characters were props. The bones of the plot stuck out all over. And this was the blank-check to fame I had been holding out for myself all these years. The Pulitzer Prize number! All I had written was the first act of a bad play. Just twenty-three pages of a play that was going back into the bottom drawer of my trunk, where it belonged.

I pushed the trunk back into the closet again. It felt frighteningly insecure to be without my play. What was I now? Just what Beth said I was, just another guy working for Nick.

It was early in the morning when I found my way to Shirley's. Lucille was cleaning the bar room and Shirley was playing solitaire.

"Eddie," she said. "You look like hell. You look like the kid's last fight. What in God's name is the matter with you?"

"The worst of them all," I said. "The biggest heel of them all. The only one who knew right from wrong and kept his goddam mouth shut. The only one who knew the score, knew what was going on and still kept his hands in his pocket. The worst, the worst, Shirley, the worst of all."

Shirley came over and looked up into my face.

"Come on," she said. "Forget it. It's time for bed."

When I awakened, the room was dark, the shades were drawn and I didn't know whether it was day or night. All I knew was that there was a woman in bed with me, and for a moment I thought it was Beth. I fumbled for a match to light a cigarette, and when I lit it I realized with a shock that I was in the room into which Sailor Beaumont and other beaten fighters had crawled in search of solace and relief from pain.

Shirley? What was I doing with Shirley? Shirley never went to bed with me. Shirley only took to bed her badly beaten fighters. Just a succession of substitutes for the Sailor. Everybody knew that.

I know the goddam trouble with me, I thought.

Enough brains to see it and not enough guts to stand up to it. Thousands of us, millions of us, corrupted, rootless, career-ridden, good hearts and yellow bellies, living out our lives for the easy buck, the soft berth, indulging ourselves in the illusion that we can deal in filth without becoming the thing we touch. No wonder Beth wouldn't have me. A heel, she called me, a heel, the biggest heel of all.

"I know the goddam trouble with me," I suddenly said aloud.

"Eddie, honey, what's the matter with you? Stop fighting yourself. Whatever it is, don't worry about it," Shirley said quietly.

Her bare arm went around my neck and her generous breasts pressed against me soothingly.

"Go to sleep now. You'll feel better when you get up."

But even as I floated off into warm, cowardly sleep, I realized why it was that she had taken me into her bed at last.

Budd Schulberg has written some of the most powerful and popular novels of the twentieth century, including, besides *The Harder They Fall*, *What Makes Sammy Run?* and *The Disenchanted*, and the screenplays for *On the Waterfront* and *A Face in the Crowd*. Born in New York City, the son of Hollywood film pioneer B. P. Schulberg, he was educated at Los Angeles High School, Deerfield Academy, and Dartmouth College. After a brief stint as a screenwriter in Hollywood, he served in the navy during World War II and was in charge of photographic evidence for the Nuremberg Trials. Through the years he has written widely on boxing, including a collection of his most memorable pieces, *Sparring with Hemingway*. He has received the A. J. Liebling Award from the Boxing Writers Association and is the only nonfighter to receive the Living Legend of Boxing Award from the World Boxing Association.

ELEPHANT PAPERBACKS

ELEPHANT PAPERBACKS

Theatre and Drama
Robert Brustein, *Dumbocracy in America,* EL421
Robert Brustein, *Reimagining American Theatre,* EL410
Robert Brustein, *The Theatre of Revolt,* EL407
Irina and Igor Levin, *Working on the Play and the Role,* EL411
Plays for Performance:
    Aristophanes, *Lysistrata,* EL405
    Pierre Augustin de Beaumarchais, *The Marriage of Figaro,* EL418
    Anton Chekhov, *The Cherry Orchard,* EL420
    Anton Chekhov, *The Seagull,* EL407
    Euripides, *The Bacchae,* EL419
    Euripides, *Iphigenia in Aulis,* EL423
    Euripides, *Iphigenia Among the Taurians,* EL424
    Georges Feydeau, *Paradise Hotel,* EL403
    Henrik Ibsen, *Ghosts,* EL401
    Henrik Ibsen, *Hedda Gabler,* EL413
    Henrik Ibsen, *The Master Builder,* EL417
    Henrik Ibsen, *When We Dead Awaken,* EL408
    Heinrich von Kleist, *The Prince of Homburg,* EL402
    Christopher Marlowe, *Doctor Faustus,* EL404
    The Mysteries: Creation, EL412
    The Mysteries: The Passion, EL414
    Sophocles, *Electra,* EL415
    August Strindberg, *The Father,* EL406
    August Strindberg, *Miss Julie,* EL422

European and World History
Mark Frankland, *The Patriots' Revolution,* EL201
Lloyd C. Gardner, *Spheres of Influence,* EL131
Gertrude Himmelfarb, *Darwin and the Darwinian Revolution,* EL207
Gertrude Himmelfarb, *Victorian Minds,* EL205
Thomas A. Idinopulos, *Jerusalem,* EL204
Ronnie S. Landau, *The Nazi Holocaust,* EL203
Clive Ponting, *1940: Myth and Reality,* EL202
Scott Shane, *Dismantling Utopia,* EL206

ELEPHANT PAPERBACKS

65997606R00203

Made in the USA
Middletown, DE
06 March 2018